HELL'S GATE

TERROR

AT

BOBBY MACKEY'S MUSIC WORLD
(America's Most Documented Haunting)

By

DOUGLAS HENSLEY

Saint Matthew Chapter 12 verse 43 - 45

"When the unclean spirit is gone out of a man, he walketh through dry places, seeking rest and findeth none. Then he saith, "I will return into my house from whence I came out;" and when he is come, he findeth him empty, swept and garnished. Then goeth he, and taketh with him seven spirits more wicked than himself and they enter and dwell there; and the last state of that man is worse than the first."

CONTENTS

INTRODUCTION

What you are about to read is one of the most bizarre and unusual chapters in the history of America. Dozens of people have come forward to tell of their experiences inside the old building at 44 Licking Pike; twenty- nine were willing to sign sworn affidavits. The witnesses tell of several earth bound spirits and a series of violent, demonic attacks. Each incident actually happened, and, though fictionalized for the purpose of telling, the story is based on these true experiences. After five years of research, investigation and interviews, the story is written exactly as told by the victims.

For forty - one years, during the 1800's, the building was a slaughterhouse. The spilled blood from the slaughterhouse, and the proximity of the north flowing Licking River, attracted satanic worshippers who used the site for sacrificial grounds.

After the slaughterhouse, the building was, briefly, a bowling alley. During the 1930's and 1940's it was a successful gambling casino known as the Primrose. The owner was forced out by the mob. Later named the Latin Quarter, it was again a popular nightspot, but the owners were repeatedly arrested on gambling charges during the 1950's. The building was more recently known as the Hard Rock Café, and was closed in January 1978 on request of the Police Chief due to fatal shootings on the premises.

Bobby and Janet Mackey were brought into this story in the spring of 1978 when they purchased the building with the intent to renovate it and turn it into Kentucky's version of "Gilly's." Carl Lawson was their first employee.

Some may not be willing to accept the concept of demons and spirits of the dead wandering amongst us. Some may not like to accept the idea that others are telling the truth when speaking of their encounters with the restless dead.

The phenomena within and about Bobby Mackey's Music World have yet to be satisfactorily defined by any explanation other than: "It's haunted."

PART ONE

HELL'S GATE

Chapter One

According to Janet Mackey, she felt something evil about the building the very first time she stepped foot inside the place. After several hours of discussing that day with her this is how she remembers it happening:

* * * * *

Gray dust poured through the open window of the brown Datsun 240 Z as Bobby Mackey drove the car around the back of the mammoth structure that had captivated his heart only a couple of hours earlier. Bobby looked at her while braking to a stop, crunching gravel beneath the tires. It was obvious to Janet that he already had his mind set to buy the building even though, from the outside, it did not look very much like a wise investment. The white, shingled siding of the first floor stretched out for a great distance and had suffered many long years of abuse from the hammering wind and rains. There were more places than one could count where weather had ripped and stolen away a shingle here and another there. Over top of the main floor was a second level that sat squarely on top of the first. It occupied but a small space. It appeared that it had been added on to so it could be used as an upstairs office or flat. It was constructed of gray, vertical clapboard with three square windows set at even intervals, windows that had seen and held captive the secrets and memories of the past long forgotten by mortals. It was apparent to Janet that this building was once a magnificent place where the elite had gathered on a daily basis, but now all that remained was the shell of its former self.

"Bobby, I don't know!" Janet said apprehensively as she reached over and squeezed her husband's right hand. "With the baby coming and all, do you think we ought to stick our necks out this far?"

Janet Mackey, a diminutive brunette, stood about five feet tall. She was in her fourth month of pregnancy with their second child.

"You'll love it!" he said as his sparkling, deep blue eyes scanned the outside of the building. "Come on. Let's get out and take a look around."

Bobby Mackey stood six feet tall with curly brown hair. He had moved to the Northern Kentucky area several years earlier and had become a household name as a country singer. His plans had been to move to Nashville, Tennessee to become a recording star. Until now, he had no desire of owning a nightclub. For some strange reason, though, this building had captured his heart. He had inspected the abandoned casino prior to bringing Janet to see it, and, when he did, he found himself experiencing some sort of dejavu. He had never stepped foot inside this place until that moment, but he seemed to know the layout of each room before entering it. He could not quite put his finger on it, but the structure seemed like home, some long, forgotten memory of the past.

* * *

Janet saw Bobby for the first time when he was singing at a Christian church revival in Lewis County, Kentucky. She found herself falling in puppy love with the bright young lad that same night. They were both thirteen years old. She did not see him again, that is, until several years later when her sister, Joyce Clark, married Bobby's brother, Charles. From that day on, Janet and Bobby were sweethearts.

Janet grew up in Lewis County near Vanceburg, Kentucky. She had six brothers and two sisters, and, like Bobby's family, they were all fine, country people. She loved listening to Bobby's white - haired mother, Doris as she told stories about Bobby's childhood. Doris had told her of Bobby's umbilical cord rupturing at the age of only one day old, after the county doctor had delivered him at home. Janet found it interesting that Bobby had been named Randy at birth, but, after he was rushed to the doctor's home, where the physician miraculously stopped the bleeding, his mother changed his name to Robert Randall Mackey and called him Bobby. To this day, she does not know why she changed her mind and his name. The inside of his baby book still reads "Randy's Baby Book."

Bobby had an uncanny ability when it came to music. His mother said he could sing songs long before he could talk. At the age of four, he won first prize in a talent contest at Trinity Grade School, receiving five dollars as his reward. He even got the chance to sing for the film crew of the pilot for ROUTE 66 when the Mackey's General Store was picked as an on- site filming location. One of Janet's favorite tales was about Bobby when he was a small child working in the family's general store. Doris told how the customers often came into the store and gave Bobby a nickel for the jukebox so they could hear him sing along with the Hank Williams songs.

* * *

As they climbed from the car, Janet glimpsed something moving at the top of a long set of concrete steps that led to the first floor of the building.

"Bobby, did you see that?" She asked hesitantly. "That metal door just opened all by itself!"

"Oh, Baloney!" Bobby laughed. "Somebody's either in there or the door was left ajar. Come on! Let's go up and look inside."

Somewhat skeptical, Janet followed her husband up the concrete stairs to the open doorway. Reaching the landing, Bobby gave her a boyish grin, then took her by the hand and led her across the threshold.

Once inside the darkened nightclub, Janet felt a slow, uneasy trepidation creep over her...a fear that she could not explain, but, nevertheless, a very real and disturbing fear.

"Is anyone here?" Bobby called out as they walked across the hardwood floor of the main ballroom toward the stage. His question was met only with dead silence.

"If no one's in here, who opened that door?" Janet asked as she paused barely long enough to take a deep breath. "It didn't just open by itself."

"Maybe it was the resident ghost!" Bobby laughed, "I sure hope it likes country music!"

A frown of half- fear and half- concern etched Janet's face as her deep- brown eyes bore into her husband's back just as he stepped up on the stage.

"Take a look around, "Bobby said as he reached the center of the fifty- five- foot wooden platform. "I've got a feeling you're going to be seeing a lot of this place."

Wading through a sea of wooden tables and chairs that were covered with dust, Janet uneasily moved to the back of the cavernous, dark- paneled room. The open, black- padded bar, lined with dusty stools, stretched out beside her. She focused her attention on a huge, pitted mirror that hung on the south wall of the room when suddenly she heard Bobby call out to someone.

"Hey, lady, wait a minute!" he yelled from the stage, shattering the silence. "Hey, lady! Wait!"

Janet turned and hurried toward Bobby, demanding to know whom he was talking to.

"No one!" he answered her in a confused tone, while running his left had through his curly brown hair. "It was just my imagination."

"What are you talking about?" She became slightly panicky as her fear returned, but now more intense...more threatening.

"I was up here on the stage, imagining the room filled with people dancing and singing, you know, and I thought I saw a woman in a white gown with long, light- brown hair, walking across the room near the front of the bar."

Uneasiness gnawed at Janet's heart. "Where did she go?"

"She disappeared in the dark by the door we came in, but it was nothing, Janet. I just let my imagination run away with me. That's all!"

"Nothing, huh?"

Walking down from the stage, Bobby took her by the hand to take her on a grand tour of the building. They made their way past the forty-foot bar to the main entrance and walked down a long, white, mirrored hallway to the front door. Having given a quick look through the glass door panes at the highway, they turned around, moved back up the hall, and pushed through the swinging, paneled doors that divided the entrance and the main bar area.

Ambling by the bar, they spied two open arched doorways to their right. Janet's eyes fixed upon the small, white sign over the portals. It read, "Fiesta Room." They stepped into the fifteen by twenty foot cubicle where Bobby spied another door to his right, near the back wall. He walked over and wiped his finger across the cob-webbed door, gently pushing it open. Glancing inside the long, narrow alcove, Bobby thought it must have been used as a storage room for liquor, since it was filled with empty whiskey bottles.

The room was about five feet wide and twelve feet long with old, weathered, brown boards on the north wall, indicating that at one time or another this room was added on from the outside. The other walls were made of old, gray; clapboard and were in poor condition. While Bobby stared into the cubicle, Janet glanced around the empty room at the pitted mirrors that lined the old brown- paneled walls. Her faint image in the glass glared back at her, giving off an eerie effect, as if it were someone else staring deep into her eyes, searching her very soul from the other side of the looking glass.

As Janet stood there, hypnotized by her own image, Bobby walked up behind her and took her by the hand, telling her to come with him. There was a lot more to see. They continued their tour of the quiet building, and as they did, the pipes creaked while the old hardwood floors squeaked and popped.

Just the building settling, Janet tried to convince herself as they moved down a wide hallway that was lined with beige leather. The couple stepped from the passageway into the infamous Casino Room, which was used for all types of gambling back in the 1930's and 1940's. The room was once filled with roulette wheels, dice tables, and other gambling paraphernalia. It was huge and cast its own eeriness in the darkened shadows. The ten-foot ceilings appeared to tower over the faded, rose pattern- filled carpet. The walls were lined waist high with the same beige leather that covered the hallway leading back to the Fiesta Room. Dirty white plasterboard stretched upward covering the rest of the walls.

Bobby's eyes fixed upon a small opening with green painted, steel bars some five feet to his right. He made his way toward the window, as Janet stood motionless staring at the wooden tables that were stacked in bunches: the square ones on the left side and the round ones on the right. A large pile of wooden chairs were stacked four high in the far right- hand corner.

Bobby peered through the bar covered opening and knew instantly that this was the cashier's window when the place was a gambling casino. Inside the room sat the biggest, round safe the man had ever seen. It was apparent to Bobby that the room had been built around the safe. There was no way anyone could have ever squeezed it in there. Bobby thought it strange, that he hadn't noticed this room earlier, when the real estate agent had taken him through the building. It was almost as if it had not been there. Maybe he simply overlooked it. But still he had to ask himself, how? He shrugged his shoulders and dismissed the thought, telling himself it was a mere oversight as he turned back toward his wife.

"Hey, Janet," Bobby exclaimed, "I forgot to tell you about the kitchen when we were in the main ballroom. It's back by that old mirror you were looking at. There's a full basement with dressing rooms and all kinds of storage rooms, and another room filled with old pots, pans and dishes. Someone's old, stripped, sports car is down there, too. That's not all! There's an office upstairs that could be made into an apartment or whatever we want to do with it. I'd show you everything, but I can't remember where all of the light switches are."

"That's okay." Janet sighed. "Can we go now?"

The couple headed back the way they came, and, as they moved into the ballroom, Bobby jumped up on the stage and began singing into the ballroom, "Together Again." A cold surge of fear shot through Janet, like ice water rushing through her veins, as she stood there on the hardwood dance floor staring up at her husband who seemed to be in some sort of trance.

As Bobby continued singing the song, his voice sounded more and more distant, and the unexplainable fear Janet was feeling became even more prevalent, crowding the room with an overbearing sense of evil. Her skin felt instantly clammy, and a nauseating hot sensation flooded her body, giving her the feeling that something inside these walls would surely choke the life from her if she didn't get out. The air inside the room was still and close and smelled too much like a crypt: a tomb, waiting to swallow her very soul at any hint of animosity. She slowly scanned the area with her eyes and felt something watching her from somewhere in the shadowy recesses of the room. She felt as if a thousand, tiny, dark evil eyes were staring at her from somewhere in the darkened shadows of the room.

"Bobby, let's go!" Her words finally came after she swallowed the lump of fear that had knotted up and stuck tightly in her throat. "Let's go. It's getting late. Did you forget we have to work tonight?"

"Okay," Bobby answered in a disappointed tone.

As they walked through the room a light suddenly flickered on, then off. Janet wheeled around on the balls of her feet and gave a blistering look toward the eerie bar area.

"Probably a bad light switch. Come on. You wanted to go." Bobby reached down and took his wife by the hand, once again.

When they reached the open doorway and stepped across the threshold, Janet gave one long stare back into the quiet building and noticed that the setting sun was shining a beam of light through the open door into the building. The glow blazed like a million burning embers, igniting the air and changing it into a thousand particles of luminous, yellow dust. It was as if the sun had painted some mystical road leading back inside the place. The glow engulfed the doorway and the inside of the ballroom with its own passionate tints. Janet felt safe now that she was back outside. But as she looked deeper into the overwhelming fiery tones that were lengthening in front of her, she felt another sudden jolt of fright when she saw a pair of red, unearthly eyes staring back at her. She blinked her eyes for one quick second, then quickly looked again, and was surprised to find the murderous orbs gone, vanished in thin air as if they were nothing but two specks of dust blown away by a fierce wind.

"Let's go," Bobby interrupted his wife's thoughts as he reached out in front of her and closed the door gently, until he heard the click of the lock securing itself.

Bobby descended the stairs with his wife right behind him. As they neared the bottom of the concrete steps, Janet looked back over her shoulder. She knew her fear of this place was not simply her imagination. This building consisted of more than wood, nails and bricks. Either it was a living thing, some evil being straight out of the bowels of Hell, or it was home for some diabolical entity far more dangerous than the woman could ever comprehend.

The Mackey's climbed into their car and headed for home, and as Bobby steered the Datsun down Route 9 Janet could not shake the horror that had invaded her mind. She silently wondered why Bobby couldn't feel the loathsome force that lurked inside those walls. She only hoped that he would change his mind about purchasing the place. She knew nothing she could say or do would change his decision about that house of evil if he decided to buy it. Bobby was an excellent husband, father and provider, but, when it came to making decisions, he was the boss. Besides, she doubted that she could ever convince him not to buy the place by arguing that it was inhabited by some unseen presence, a creature that rises up and takes on its hideous form when darkness falls.

Chapter Two

I spent many days and nights interviewing Carl Lawson concerning the haunting at the nightclub. This is his recollection of the first time he met the Mackey's.

* * * * *

A blistering afternoon sun baked the black shingles on the roof of Bobby Mackey's new nightclub as Bobby and Janet feverishly worked cleaning up the inside of the musty old building. Bobby sang "Together Again" silently to himself, remembering the first day he had seen the old casino and how, only a few weeks later, he had purchased the former "Latin Quarter" as a place where he could showcase his talents as a country music singer and musician. He decided to call the place Bobby Mackey's Music World. As he stood near the bar in his Levis and white sport shirt, smiling robustly, he looked like a man who had found his grail.

Janet, clad in pink maternity shorts and a matching top, was busy wiping dust and cobwebs from the tables in the main ballroom when, looking up, she was startled by the dark figure of a man framed by the shadows of the light of the open doorway. "Bobby," she called to her husband who had seen the man at approximately the same time she did.

"Can I help you?" Bobby asked as he moved toward the stranger. "I'm the new owner here."

"Hi! My name's Carl, Carl Lawson that is." The five- foot, six-inch stranger stepped out of the shadows and into the light. He was wearing faded Levis, a black T- shirt and dirty, white sneakers. He appeared to be about twenty years of age. His dark brown hair was combed back on his head, and he had a somewhat scraggly beard and coffee brown eyes.

Extending his right hand toward Bobby's, he continued. "I used to work here. I heard the place had been purchased so I thought I'd stop by and see what's going on." A broad grin crossed his bespectacled face as he and Bobby shook hands.

Bobby introduced himself and Janet to Carl, and then listened politely as the young man continued talking.

"If there's anything you need to know about this place, I'm the man to ask. I know where everything is. You know...like the fuse boxes, light switches, and anything else in here. In fact, I worked here for the past two owners. I've seen it all! I saw a man get shot to death in here. Hell! This place has got a history behind it that no one would believe!"

When Carl mentioned seeing a man killed in the nightclub, Janet felt as if she would jump out of her skin, but she kept quiet. Maybe that was the reason she had an eerie feeling about the building.

"By the way!" Carl said, interrupting her thoughts. "If you need a worker, I'm available. I can start anytime. Looks like you could use some help getting this place cleaned up."

Nothing else needed to be said. The Mackeys needed all the help they could get cleaning the giant building. There was more than enough work for ten men in the place. After a lengthy conversation Bobby told the young man to grab a broom and get to work. He advised him there was a lot of painting that desperately needed to be done and there was a mountain of garbage and debris that needed hauled out of the building.

"You're on the payroll as of right now!" Bobby exclaimed with a smile. "I'm going to leave you here with Janet. I've got some stuff upstairs that I need to take care of, so I'll see you later. Janet can show you what needs to be done. If you need anything just yell out or come upstairs"

For some unexplainable reason, Bobby took an instant liking to Carl and felt the man was trustworthy. He handed him the dust cloth that he had been using to wipe down some tables then disappeared from sight.

Carl turned to Janet with a wary, almost haunting expression on his face. "Don't worry about the ghosts in here!" he softly exclaimed. "They're my friends!"

A cold shiver passed through the woman's entirety as Carl's words faded into nothingness. She paused for a moment, as if hesitant about giving a reply. She flashed back to that first day inside this old Casino, and as she stood there staring at the young man, that same haunting fear returned, gnawing at her heart.

Before she could reply, a loud thud echoed from the Casino Room, stretching out through the rest of the first floor like a fading shot bouncing off a canyon wall.

"What was that?" she almost screamed as she reached out and grabbed Carl's arm, digging her fingernails into the meaty part of his flesh.

"I don't know," he whispered as he gazed down at her hand tenaciously gripping his arm. "Come on. Let's go see."

Releasing her grip on him, she cautiously followed him into the Casino Room where Carl spied a huge picture of a pink Flamingo on the floor next to the wall.

"That's what it was," he said as he walked over and picked it up by the frame. "Everything's okay! This old bird ain't gonna cause nobody any harm."

Grinning sheepishly, embarrassed by her own seemingly silly fears, Janet watched quietly as Carl rehung the picture over the discolored spot on the paneling where it had obviously hung for many years.

"I always did like this picture," he said to Janet, then looked up toward the ceiling and quietly, hauntingly whispered, "I'm back, and I'm here to stay this time. I won't leave again. I promise!"

Puzzled, and now even more frightened, Janet looked at Carl, then up at the ceiling, but didn't say anything. Just something else for me to worry about, she thought. He's talking to ghosts in here! That's great!

Carl turned his attention back to Janet, a smile forming on his face. "Let's go back to the ballroom and finish up," he said. "We won't have any more frights today."

The rest of the afternoon went by smoothly just as Carl had predicted, and, although Janet was still slightly fearful, the young employee seemed to alleviate some of her worry.

The setting sun cast long shadows across the room as Bobby and Janet started out the door to go home. "Hold on just a minute!" Janet told Bobby as she pulled Carl to one side.

"I've got some questions about this place," she whispered to the young handyman. "I want to talk to you tomorrow about it."

Turning toward her husband, Janet informed Bobby she was ready to leave. As they passed through the double glass paned doors leading out of the main barroom, Carl followed closely behind them down the long mirrored hallway that led outside to the front entrance. Once out on the sidewalk Bobby tossed Carl a set of keys. "Here! This is an extra set. Lock the place up. We'll see you in the morning."

As Bobby and Janet climbed into their car and drove away, Carl peered back inside the front glass-paned doors, his eyes searching the shadows of the mirrored hallway. "Good night!" he whispered aloud to no one in particular. Then, without another word, he slipped the key into the lock and gave it a twist until he heard the click of the dead bolt. He turned and headed for his house that was only a few doors away. Another day had come to and end.

* * *

Carl was quiet, gentle and soft-spoken, but surrounded by an air of cool mystique. His only vices, as far as anyone could tell, were cigarettes and a few shots of Jack Daniels.

Later that night, after having just taken a couple sips of "Jack Daniels," Carl climbed into the warmth of his bed around eleven o' clock and fell into a deep, restless, sleep. Not long after midnight, he jolted upright in the twin-sized bed, jerking back his white comforter, as his eyes popped open like a window shade that had suddenly let go. His body jerked as sweat poured from his brow, his heart pounding as if it would explode, and he nearly screamed out, but stopped himself so not to wake his mother and father in the other room.

Carl was raised a devout Catholic and never paid too much attention to nightmares. He was sure God would protect him from any harm, but the drama that had just besieged him was the most real...the most horrifying nightmare he had ever experienced. Assuring himself that he was awake now, he laid back down and pulled his body into a fetal position, lying on his left side, staring out the bedroom window at the hazy fog that had surrounded the white frame home. The rose, flowered wallpaper in his room appeared to dance amongst the shadows on the walls as the fog continued moving in. The fog always came at night, rising up from the Licking River and engulfing the house like some dark, wet, evil cloud, swallowing its victims, spitting them out in the morning, only to return to devour them inside its eerie mist once again.

It was half-past one before Carl closed his eyes and tried to forget about that stupid dream, but, when he did, the image of his nightmare came rushing back into his mind. He could envision the deep red blood trickling down the side of his neck as a huge bat sucked the life from his helpless body, which lay sprawled on the Casino Room floor.

"Just a bad dream! Ain't no bat gonna get me," he whispered as the fog descended upon the house like a giant weight and he finally fell back asleep.

Chapter Three

Tears welled up in Janet's eyes when she spoke of the first time she was attacked inside the nightclub. That day still haunts her. It is a day that will walk in the shadows of her memory forever. She recalled it as happening like this:

* * * * *

A bright yellow sun peered over the hillside, turning the dew-laden grass into a shimmering sea of emerald jewels, as Carl sat on the concrete wall adjacent to Bobby Mackey's Music World. He was huddled in a dark blue windbreaker in an attempt to fight off the morning chill. He fidgeted with his lighter, and then nervously puffed on the Marlboro between his lips as he tried to make some sense of the frightening nocturnal images that haunted him. The nightmare had seemed so real—too damn real! --And he shuddered uncontrollably at the thought of needle-like fangs sinking deep into his jugular. "Forget it, Carl," he told himself, as he tried to shake the morbid thought from his mind. The only diversion from the haunting thought was the occasional honking of horns as friends and neighbors passed by on the road that ran in front of the nightclub.

He took one last puff off of the cigarette and threw it to the asphalt just as Bobby's brown sports car came to a stop three feet away. Reassuring himself, once again, that it was only a bad dream and nothing more, he forced a weak smile as Bobby and Janet emerged from the vehicle.

"Good morning, Bobby....Janet," he greeted them while at the same time trying futilely to suppress a cough that rose up from nowhere.

They returned the greeting in what seemed like choreographed unison. Then, Bobby, obviously anxious to get inside the gargantuan building, told Janet and Carl that he was going upstairs to finish yesterday's work and that they should continue on from where they left off. Once inside, Bobby hurried up the stairs with child-like glee. Carl and Janet, puzzled but unquestioning, smiled at each other, shrugged their shoulders, and turned to begin the day's chores.

Unable to do any really heavy work because of her pregnancy, Janet decided to sweep the hardwood floor in the main ballroom. With broom in hand, she strolled toward the back of the cavernous chamber and flipped on the circuit breaker, flooding the room with a strange, shadowy incandescent light. Then she walked over and opened the two exit doors on each end of the west wall.

Standing on the balcony, outside of the ballroom, she stared at the railroad tracks, and took in a deep breath of cool, morning air. She looked down the concrete steps and remembered back to the very first day she climbed these stairs and stepped inside this place. After several seconds, she reluctantly returned her attention to the ballroom and stepped back inside to begin the task before her.

In the meantime, Carl was preparing to paint the Casino Room. Passing the doorway to the ballroom several times, he could see Janet as puffy little clouds of dust encircled the broom that she moved back and forth. He wondered how long it would be before she would decide to corner him, wanting to know what terrible secrets this place held.

Dismissing the thought, he spent the next few minutes wrestling a large aluminum ladder into the Casino Room. After surveying the huge chamber, he knew it would take all day to complete the job, so Carl headed to the storage room for the tools he would need.

Janet didn't know if it was actually starting to get hot inside the building or if her pregnancy was just making her feel that way. She wiped the perspiration from her brow and decided this was the perfect time to take a break. Laying the broom on the stage, she walked from the ballroom and went into the Casino Room to find Carl. It was time to get some answers.

She scanned the room, but Carl wasn't anywhere to be found. She stood quietly, listening, but didn't hear him either. Where can he be, she wondered as she turned to go back to the ballroom. As she walked toward the doorway, something made her stop dead in her tracks, her arms hung rigid as her eyes swept the darkened shadows of the Casino Room. As she stood there, motionless, a cold, soul-piercing chill passed through her body, causing her to shudder uncontrollably as the hairs on the back of her neck bristled.

Chill bumps stood at attention on Janet's arms as sweat poured down her face. Her lips began to quiver, and she had to pee. A whisper, inaudible, but nonetheless a whisper, gnawed on her ears. She fought back the tears that were rising behind her eyes like water against a weak dam.

*****

Pulling a brush and some scrapers from a box in the storage room, Carl froze. Something inside him screamed, shaking his mind into awareness. Then he smelled it...unmistakable...unrelenting.

The ladder against the Casino Room wall began shaking, vibrating, clamoring. "Carl! ...Bobby!" Janet's brain shrieked, but the words would not come. Her body trembled with seismic convulsions, and this time the whisper was loud and clear. "Get out!" it ordered again, the words ringing out in the room like two pieces of sandpaper being rubbed together.

****

Carl sprang to his feet, knocking over boxes, diving for the door. The perfume! The roses! It was happening again, dammit! Oh, God, he thought frantically, please don't let it hurt Bobby or Janet!

Get out, hell! Janet thought as the hunger to leave gnawed at her heart. She wanted to get out, to run and never look back, but the muscles in her legs were like water soaked sponges, and her feet became lead anchors. It was coming for her...closer...closer! Her stomach ached...the baby! No, God, she thought as everything became quiet, silent inside her. No! Please, God! Don't let it hurt my baby!

The glass doors exploded open and Carl flew down the corridor toward the Casino Room, muscles tense as his feet pounded the floor, rage over riding caution.

She couldn't even throw out her arms to try to protect herself as she stood frozen, watching the top of the ladder race toward her body.

Carl could see the ladder moving towards Janet, walking in a robotic stride, as if it had come to life bent on killing the woman. It was just inches from Janet, and suddenly everything seemed to happen in slow motion, like watching an old black and white horror movie, detached and fading.

Janet closed her eyes tightly, waiting for her impending doom when Carl's hands grabbed her shoulders from behind and jerked her to the right of the now falling ladder.

Dust flew through the room as the ladder powerfully slammed into the threadbare, floral-patterned carpet with a deafening clatter. The aluminum twisted and contorted as the rungs quivered and shook, creating and eerie, melodious harmony.

Neither Carl nor Janet uttered a word as the unearthly rhythms faded into the walls around them like the wind whispering through the trees. Janet began to sob, more out of relief than fear. Her face betrayed her tension. She felt she had just cheated death.

Carl took her left arm and gently walked her over to a nearby table. He pulled out a chair and dusted it off, motioning with his eyes for her to sit down.

"Are you okay?" His voice choked with sincerity and concern. "Should I go get Bobby?"

"No! Stay here! I'm okay," she whispered, as her eyes shifted back and forth, searching the room, waiting for some other hellish nightmare to appear.

"It's over for now," he spoke softly, trying to set her mind at ease. "Nothing else bad is going to happen to you."

She could sense in his voice that what he meant was nothing else bad would happen today, but she knew that tomorrow was less than twenty-four hours away.

"Carl, you said yesterday that this place was haunted. I want to know what's going on here. I have to know...now! Please!" Her voice was insistent...demanding...and he knew there was no way out of this. He had to tell her what he knew...all that he knew.

Chapter Four

After being attacked, Janet insisted on knowing what terrible secrets Carl knew about the place. According to their statements, this is what was said.

* * * * *

Carl sat across the table looking at Janet wondering what her reaction would be when he shared the secrets of this building with her. Her experience with the ladder had been traumatic, and he did not want to upset her even more, but he knew full well that she would not be easily fooled. He pulled a cigarette from his pocket and shakily attempted to light it with a pack of sweat soaked matches. After several failed tries, he tossed the unlit Marlboro to the floor. He hoped his anxiety didn't show, but, by the look on Janet's face, he knew there was no chance of hiding it.

"I'm going to tell you a story you probably won't believe, but I swear it's true". He looked nervously around the room.

Janet pulled her chair closer to the table and propped her elbows down on it. "Well? Come one!"

"Years ago this place was a gambling casino called "The Latin Quarter." All the gangsters came here during Prohibition. Rumors have it that a lot of murders happened inside here back in those days, and it's probably true. The mob kept a lot of things hidden, you know."

"What does that have to do with us?"

"Maybe nothing, but I've seen a lot of strange things happen in here. I've never told anyone what I'm going to tell you, but, after what happened today, I think maybe you ought to know". He sucked in a deep breath and continued.

"A few years ago, I was here alone cleaning the club. It was raining hard, and all of the doors were locked, so I didn't expect any visitors. Anyway, I'm busy doing my job when all of a sudden, I look up and there's this lady standing there. Scared the you-know-what outta me! After I got my breath back, I asked her what she was doing here. She just kinda giggled like a little school girl and said she was waiting for Robert Randall to come back for her."

"My God! That's Bobby's name. What did she look like, Carl? Even though Janet did not want to hear the answer, she felt a compelling need to know. A lump formed in her throat and she suddenly felt queasy as she listened to his description of the girl. She remembered back to her and Bobby's first visit together at this old place. But most of all, she thought of the girl that Bobby said he didn't see! Carl noticed the sudden apprehension that came over her.

"Is something wrong?" he asked, genuinely concerned.

"No," she lied, "it's nothing. Go ahead." She forced an artificial smile toward the handyman.

"Okay. As I was saying before, she said she was waiting for this guy, Robert, to come back for her. Then she got weird. She told me that Robert was her fiancé, and her Father didn't like him, so he killed him. She told me that she couldn't live without the guy, so she committed suicide right here!"

Janet sat up straight in her chair and stared into Carl's eyes as he continued his bizarre story.

"I figured she was some crazy woman who'd escaped from the nut-house. I told her she had to get out, but she just smiled and said she would never leave until her Robert returned for her. She said when he did come back, all hell would break loose, and when it did, she'd need my help. Then she just stood there with an innocent look on her face, which, buy the way, I noticed was almost as white as snow. She was really pale!"

"What did you do then?"

"I walked over to the bar and picked up the phone. I was going to call the police to come get her, but when I turned around, she was gone...vanished! I looked everywhere in this place that night, but there wasn't any sign of her. All of the doors were locked. There wasn't any way she could have walked out of here without leaving a door open".

"So has she ever been back?" Janet asked, already knowing the answer, but not really wanting to hear it.

"Yeah, I've seen her from time to time, but she always disappears before I can catch up with her. I figure she'll talk to me when she's ready." Carl looked up for a moment and stared toward the old flamingo picture on the wall. He felt a chill creep up his spine like tiny, tingling needles. There seemed to be a sparkling gleam in the pink bird's eye as if it were looking back at him, reading his thoughts. "You think I'm nuts, don't you!" Carl asked almost as an after thought.

"No, Carl. I don't," Janet replied, surprising him. "I've never seen a ghost, but I do believe something is in here with us, something not of this world."

Carl sat motionless looking straight ahead at Janet. He was grateful that he had found a friend that he could confide in without being ridiculed.

"Oh, one more thing!" Carl pressed on. "Once when I was drunk, I'm sure I heard her say 'Beware of the evil that hides inside.' Then, as if she was talking to someone else, she said, 'don't harm this man. He's the keeper of the beasts and the children.' I know it sounds weird, and I know I was drunk, but I'm sure I heard it. I've never understood what that meant, but I felt she was trying to give me some sort of message."

Carl sighed and looked over his shoulder at the fallen ladder, then wearily continued. "That's her name, by the way. Johana. Anyway, I smelled roses when I was in the storage room. That's why I came looking for you. I knew something was wrong. The smell of roses in here is some kind of warning for me that something is wrong."

"Thank God, you did!" Janet sighed, "But why would Johana want to hurt me? I haven't done anything...at least, I don't think I have."

"It isn't Johana. She's good, but whatever evil thing is in here, it's directing its forces against you. Try not to worry, though. I'm gonna stick close by. I'll get it figured out sooner or later, and then maybe we can do something about it."

"Believe me," she exclaimed. "You and Bobby will be in my sight at all times, at least within shouting distance! If anything else does happen I want to be able to yell for help next time."

"Let's hope there's not a next time! By the way, please don't tell anyone about this conversation, especially Bobby. He'd only think I was some sort of mental case and fire me and I really need this job."

"I won't." Janet promised then rose from the chair. "Speaking of the devil, I wonder what Bobby's doing upstairs?"

"Don't know. Let's go see."

Carl stood up and as he and Janet turned to leave the Casino Room, they heard it. It was a frantic scratching sound, with a terrible suddenness, coming from the floor beneath their feet. The noise grew louder, determined, as if demanding to be heard. Then it stopped as suddenly as it began.

"What was that?" She whispered with wide-eyed anticipation as she looked around the room.

"I don't know, but I used to hear it from time to time. It's like something's trying to lure me down into the basement. As much as I hate to admit it, I'm scared to go into some of the rooms down there, especially the China Room."

"The China Room? What's that?" She asked as the scratching sound drifted away.

"It's just a big room lined wall to wall with shelves where the old owners stored dishes and other cooking utensils, but there's something about it that makes my skin crawl. I don't know what, but I don't like it. Thank God the scratching stopped."

"Why do you keep coming back here Carl? If Bobby hadn't bought this place, I'd leave and never return again."

"I don't know. It's like something keeps drawing me back, and no matter how hard I fight it or how much I want to stay away, I can't. Whatever's here draws me back for some strange reason. It's like when that guy was killed here a while back, I swore I wouldn't never set foot in here again, but here I am!"

"What guy? What are you talking about?"

"There used to be all kinds of fights and stuff here, you know, stabbings, shootings. Anyway, the security guard ended up having to shoot a man one night, and he died. I smelled the perfume that night, too. It was really strong. I knew something terrible was about to happen!"

Carl looked away from Janet and she could tell by his expression that the memory of that night still disturbed him deeply.

"It's okay, Carl," she softly exclaimed as she placed a consoling hand on his shoulder. "Enough of this depressing talk! Let's go find Bobby."

****

Bobby was in the office on the second floor rummaging through stacks of cardboard boxes. He didn't even look up when Janet and Carl walked in.

"What're you doing, honey?" Janet asked, trying to conceal the fear that still lingered inside her. She had not discussed her thoughts about this place with Bobby because he didn't believe in ghosts, but, after her near escape with death, she knew the time was at hand.

"Just going through some old papers. What was all the noise about?" He still didn't look away from the yellowed sheets in his hand.

Janet and Carl looked at each other and simultaneously answered, "The ladder fell."

"Well, try to be more careful," Bobby remarked. "I don't need anybody getting hurt!"

Janet motioned with her eyes for Carl to leave the room. She didn't want to get him in the middle of a family argument.

"I'm going back downstairs and get to work," the handyman said as he turned and walked out of the room.

Once Carl was gone, Janet told Bobby the place was haunted and some unseen force had just attacked her. She tried to convince him not to open the nightclub for business, but he would not hear of it. She told him of her fears and suspicions and demanded he sell the place.

A loud argument ensued, so loud that the couple could be heard shouting at each other from down in the barroom. Carl was glad Janet had not involved him. Bobby would have fired him for sure.

Chapter Five

Carl stated after confiding in Janet he had been punished by some unseen force. This is how he remembers it:

* * * * *

Carl returned to the Casino Room and picked up the ladder, placing it against the wall. As he climbed to the top of the rungs, a feeling of dread enveloped his mind, and then it came back to him...the dream! It was haunting him again, and no matter what he did, he could not shake it. His dream had been like a river, with hundreds of tributaries of gripping fear flowing through his entire being.

He retrieved a putty knife from his hip pocket and began scraping the peeling paint from the wall, but he found it difficult to concentrate on the job. Images from the night before flashed through his mind like a kaleidoscope slide show. Suddenly, something icy cold passed by him, something unseen, but very real and very terrifying.

A stack of tables near the east wall suddenly fell over and crashed to the floor. Carl turned and looked down from the ladder, fixing his eyes upon a bright, yellow light near the fallen tables. The orb was about three feet in diameter and pulsated with its own eccentric energy. It seemed to have congealed from the air itself, taking on a vaporous form.

As he stood perched on the rungs of the aluminum ladder, the light twisted and turned and gave off a low hum. Then, without warning, it skipped across the floor like a rock bouncing across water and disappeared into the north wall of the room. Somewhat frightened and confused, he shifted his weight uneasily on the ladder, when something else flew past his face.

"No way!" He fought to keep his footing. "This can't be happening!"

The bat soared past his face again, and he aimlessly swatted at it hoping to knock it out of the air, but missed. Carl watched helplessly as the creature dipped and dived, slicing the air left, then right, seemingly mocking the man on the precarious perch. His eyes remained fixed on the bat until suddenly it rocketed through the door and out of the room.

"Okay, Carl. Keep it together!" he told himself. "It's just a coincidence. It can't have anything to do with the dream!" But, from somewhere deep within the reaches of his soul, he knew it was not over.

An eternity passed as his eyes scanned the shadows of the room, and he could feel the morose hostility of some presence building around him. It was the kind of evil that grinds the bones of even the bravest men and makes them weak and vulnerable, and it made him want to scream.

As he searched the room with a blank animal stare, the ladder began to jerk and shake violently. Carl grasped the rungs with white knuckles. He looked down to find the bottom of the ladder embraced by the same pulsating light...twisting, turning and...humming!

"Leave me alone!" he cried out, and instantly the light vanished like someone had flipped a switch. The ladder settled down against the wall, motionless, while Carl's heart jack hammered at full speed. What next, he wondered as he turned, facing out from the ladder only to hear the sound he dreaded more than anything.

The flapping of leathery wings was punctuated by high-pitched screeches as hundreds of flying rodents hurled through the doorway into the Casino Room. The fear hung over Carl's eyes like icicles as the bats zigzagged around the room, darting back and forth as if bouncing off invisible walls. The nightmare had come to life, only a thousand times worse than he could have ever imagined.

He bellowed out obscenities as hundreds of the creatures flew straight into his chest, like kamikaze fighter planes, attaching themselves to his black T-shirt. Their razor-sharp teeth gleamed in the strobe effect created by the horde of black vermin casting on-off shadows as they soared past the light. Ribbons of pain assaulted Carl's body as needle-like claws penetrated the fabric of his shirt. Two bats were climbing toward his neck. Coming closer. Closer.

Fear stricken, he leaped from the ladder, grabbing each of the filthy bats in his fists, bashing them into the floor as he landed hard, face down. He slung the bloody masses through the air and scrambled beneath a nearby table, trying to find refuge from his attackers.

Suddenly a loud, almost deafening heartbeat filled the room, and the leather that lined the lower part of the walls pushed in and out with the daunting tempo. The bats immediately zoomed out of the Casino Room, like a squadron of Hueys, as if the compelling Ka-thump Ka-thump was a command from some unseen general for them to retreat, even though they were winning the battle.

Carl remained hidden under the table, alone and afraid, as the heartbeat faded then ceased. He searched the confines of the room with his eyes, and, as he did, from somewhere behind him, a rumbling-whistling sound pierced the stillness, and a frigid, bawling wind with incredible velocity blew past him into the barroom, knocking over stools one after another like dominoes until the forceful breeze died.

Again it was quiet, but not the "what's going to happen next?" kind of quiet. It was the normal, everything's "all right" hush, and Carl knew that the show of force was over...for now.

"What the hell's going on?" he groaned as he crawled from beneath the table and pulled himself up into a chair, his face pale and his nose bleeding from when he had crashed his face into the floor. Still trembling, he wiped his nose across his sleeve and noticed that his shirt was torn. He wanted to run upstairs and tell Bobby and Janet what had just happened, but after over hearing their argument earlier, he thought better of it. His news would probably send Janet over the edge, and, even if it didn't, Bobby would think he was crazy and fire him for sure.

Question, one after another, besieged his jaded mind as he sat there quietly trying to sort things out. Why was this assault directed against him? Johana had always protected him. Why would she let this happen now? Why was the evil trying to hurt Janet? Could Johana be after Janet's Robert? After all, Bobby's full name is Robert Randall. Maybe he was Johana's lover returned from the grave. He found that thought staggering, but yet, maybe he had just put his finger on it.

Since nothing else happened, he rose from the chair, weary and frustrated. He was determined not to be run off by whatever was harassing him and Janet. He moved back to the wall and ascended the ladder to complete the chore he had begun. He needed answers, and Johana was the only one who could provide them, but wish as he may, he knew she would not appear to him until she was ready. He only hoped it would be soon.

The hours passed slowly as Carl labored to prepare the Casino Room for a fresh coat of paint. Bobby and Janet stayed upstairs the rest of the day going through old records of the Latin Quarter. They finally came down around five o' clock, at which time the threesome said their good-byes, with the Mackeys going to their home and Carl to his. What new horror would tomorrow bring with it? Carl wondered as he lit a Marlboro and strolled toward his house.

Chapter Six

When Janet spoke of being attacked for the second time inside the nightclub, she continuously rubbed the goose bumps that kept rising on her arms. As she told of this ordeal, her voice began to tremble and it became progressively more difficult for her to relate this next incident as she went on. This is what she said happened.

* * * * *

A smudge of sun dappled the cloud cover as Carl entered the nightclub the following morning. Bobby and Janet were already inside, and, to Carl's surprise they had with them a young sandy-haired girl in a pink slack outfit.

"Good morning," Carl said with a smile as he approached the trio, standing in the main ballroom.

"How's it going?" Bobby asked as he put his left hand on the girl's shoulder. "This is our daughter, Anita Dawn."

"Hello, I'm Carl. Glad to meet you."

Anita was an eleven-year-old perfect child, who seemed more mature than most kids her age. Both Bobby and Janet agreed that she was different from other children. She was extremely polite to everyone she met. She possessed a special quality about her that people could not quite put their fingers on. Her features were wonderfully sculpted like her mother's. Her face was peachy soft, and her cheekbones accentuated her country brown eyes.

As Bobby turned and walked up the steps and onto the stage, Carl asked Anita how she liked the place.

"She doesn't!" Janet answered for her. "She says it's spooky."

"It is, Mom!" the girl spoke up.

"I swear!" Bobby laughed as he shook his head. "Like mother like daughter! I'm telling all of you...there's no such thing as ghosts! It seems eerie in here because it's so big...that's all."

Bobby stood center stage and looked out across the ballroom. He placed his right hand in his blue jeans pocket and undid the top button of his red sport shirt with his other hand.

"It's a little stuffy in here," he commented with a smile as he looked around the room, imagining the place crowded with customers.

"Yeah, it is," Carl replied as Janet and Anita walked away moving toward the main bar area.

"We're going to put a popcorn machine right here," Janet told Anita as she raised her hand and pointed to the middle of the bar where a large, white beam extended from the black counter top to the ceiling. "And..."

"Mommy" Anita interrupted, "do you smell roses?"

"What!" Janet asked with a terrible suddenness as she flashed her eyes down at her daughter.

"It smells like roses on a grave," the child continued with a timid voice. "I don't like it here...I want to go home."

The girl's words sent a confusing rush of anticipation and dread through Janet. The fear was like the quick, hot touch of the devil shooting through her body. She backed up a hasty half-step, then prowled the area with her eyes.

"Let's go! You don't have to stay here." Janet exclaimed as she reached over with her right hand and took Anita by the left arm. I wish I didn't, she thought to herself as she walked her daughter back to the stage where Carl was sitting on the edge of the platform talking to Bobby.

"Bobby!" Janet said with a bite in her voice. "Anita's afraid in here, and I want one of us to take her home...NOW!"

"I don't believe this!" Bobby growled. He gave a sharp look at his wife, and then glanced down at Anita, who was looking up at him with something very fragile in her eyes.

"You are scared...aren't you?" Bobby's tone now more consoling than frustrated. "It's okay, honey. If you're afraid, I'll take you home, but I promise there's nothing bad in here."

Bobby stepped down from the stage, and took Anita by the hand. He looked deep into his daughter's eyes with a warm smile and assured her everything was okay.

"I've got to go look at carpet samples," He said as he looked at Janet. "I'll take her home first. I'll be gone a couple of hours. Will that be okay?"

"That's fine. Carl and I'll keep busy cleaning until you get back."

"See you later, Carl," is all Bobby said.

Carl nodded as Bobby turned and walked out of the room with Anita beside him.

Janet didn't say anything for about a minute, but once she was sure Bobby and Anita had left the building she turned to Carl with large timid eyes.

"Anita smelled roses...over by the bar! I didn't smell anything...did you?"

"No...nothing." Carl answered with a blank stare.

"God, what's going on?" Janet shook her head in frustration.

"I don't know, Janet. This is really getting to you, isn't it?"

"You're darn right! We've got to figure out what to do about this or I'm not coming back in here and neither is Anita. Bobby can just run the business without me...and I mean it! We've been arguing over this place like cats and dogs."

"Yeah, I over heard you when you were up in the office." He looked around the place. "Oh, well, everything seems okay for now. Do you feel like working or are you too upset?"

"I'm all right, Carl. I just want things to settle down. I wish Bobby could realize something's not normal here. No one could ever convince him this place is haunted. He talked to Norman and Jean Stamper, the people who got him to look at this building, and they assured him the place was not haunted, so he said he didn't want to hear anymore about it. He also talked to Beaulah Ewing about it. She was the woman who showed him through here before he brought me to see it. She's never seen anything unusual either. Bobby insists this is all my imagination. "Janet paused for a minute, fighting back tears. She felt like crying...screaming, but most of all, she wanted to beat the hell out of whatever was tormenting her.

"Let's go work in the kitchen," she finally said, after taking a deep breath. "I want to get it cleaned up so we can start using it."

"Sure," Carl agreed. "That's as good a place as any."

They moved through the ballroom and made their way to the kitchen, entering it through a swinging café door.

"This is a monumental mess!" Janet complained aloud. "It'll take three or four hours to clean this up, and that doesn't include painting it."

"Yeah, it's pretty bad," Carl laughed, "but we'll get it done!"

Pitted, oriental woks and cooking utensils hung from nails on the dirty, yellow walls. Grease stains covered the cabinet over top of the cast iron gas stove. Stacks of dirty, oriental plates, saucers and cups, lined the two white, wooden shelves that ran the length of the room over top of the stainless steel sink. Spider webs decorated each and ever corner of the kitchen, and the scent of mold and mildew engulfed the room.

As they surveyed the work ahead of them, a sudden, terrifying moan rose up from the basement directly under their feet. The beckoning wail echoed through an old laundry chute, making its way into the kitchen. Then myriad of sounds came spiraling up around the terrified man and woman electrifying the nerves in their heads. Voices, murmurs, and loud whispers filtered through the wooden floorboards and rose up, surrounding them as they both stood in awe. It was as if the voices were prodding and daring Carl and Janet to come and look for them.

Then laughter, like something right out of Hell, rang out in all directions from the basement. Great waves of shrieks and moans ripped through the entire building like thunder. It was as if the structure itself had come to life, joining in the diabolical clamor as though wedded to the haunting sound.

"Leave us alone!" Janet screamed, her body shaking violently, her nerves plucked out of tune.

For some strange reason, as quickly as it had begun, everything stopped, and there was nothing but a dome of silence, and eerier calm hanging in the room.

Janet turned to Carl, her eyes revealing terror like someone who had just come face to face with the grim reaper. "I can't take anymore of this," she stammered. "What are we going to do?"

"I don't know," Carl sighed. "Whatever it was...it's gone now. We can't let it scare us into leaving, though. That's what it's trying to do. I'm going to find a way to stop this, somehow, but I just need a little time."

As Carl tried to convince Janet that everything was okay for now, the sound of doors slamming rang out from the basement. It was as if someone was running from room to room, opening each and every door and banging it into its frame with an unnatural force.

"That's it!" Carl growled, baring his teeth, his brown eyes expressing more challenge than curiosity. "There's somebody down there, and I'm going to find them!"

Before Janet could utter a single word the banging instantly ceased and everything became quiet...calm, at least for now.

"It's stopped," she said, expelling a sigh of relief. "You don't have to go in the basement now."

"Yes, I do! I want to see who or what is down there. Do you want to go with me?"

"No," she gasped. "I 'm not going down there and I wish you wouldn't, either!"

"I have to. I'll be fine." He hoped he was right. "I want you to stay right here until I get back. If anything happens...anything at all, you get out of the building and wait for me outside by the front door."

"I will." She nodded her head in agreement, but was scared stiff at the thought of being left alone.

Carl turned on the balls of his dirty white sneakers and walked over by the sink where a two-foot piece of lead pipe lay on the floor. He picked it up, gripping it like a club.

"I'll be back," he said to Janet as he disappeared through the café door, marching like a soldier in his blue jeans and dark blue T-shirt, heading for a confrontation with the unknown.

Everything's okay, Janet tried to tell herself. Got to get busy working. That'll keep my mind off of this until Carl gets back.

She slowly moved over to the sink and twisted the rusty faucet. A brown liquid spurted from the tap for several long seconds before the water finally turned clear. She reached down and grabbed a small, brown plastic bucket, placing it in the sink under the tap. As she stood there, waiting patiently for the container to fill a black gooey substance suddenly began filling rapidly with the tar-like, plasmatic fluid and the room became engulfed with a sickening ammoniac smell of sweat and piss. The water pipes began gurgling, and a loud, banging noise coming from nowhere, yet everywhere, filled the room. Horrified, Janet started to turn and run, but before she could move a muscle, some veiled force pressed against her, wrapping its invisible arms around the woman's waist.

"Oh, God! Help me! Carl...CARL!"

The unseen entity squeezed tighter against the pregnant woman's abdomen as if it was trying to kill her unborn child. The force swept down on Janet and violently shook her to the left, then right, tearing at her brain. The room began to spin and everything became a blur as the entity started choking her with yet, another set of unseen hands.

Janet kicked, screamed out for help and fought wildly, trying to free herself from this blood chilling demon as it lifted her feet off the floor and began trying to shove her head first into the sink full of goo. The instinct to protect her baby turned into a bubbling violence as she struggled against the maddening inability to break free. The rage in her became a living thing. Her face became red and blotchy with anger as she fought back with all her might. The light in the room began flickering off, then on, repeatedly, at ascending speed.

"Janet!" Carl's voice stretched out from some other part of the building. "Hold on! I'm coming!"

Carl had heard her screams for help just as he had stepped into the main basement. He raced back up the stairs, heading for the kitchen to rescue the woman from whatever force had appeared this time. As his words soared into the room, the unseen entity let loose of its grip on Janet and sucked back into the walls. She crashed to the floor on her hands and knees. The light stopped flickering, and everything instantly became quiet again, as if nothing had ever happened. Carl spilled through the doorway holding the pipe over his head like a sword. He looked in all directions for anyone...or anything, but he found that he and Janet were all alone in the room.

Janet stood to her feet and dusted off her red maternity suit as she gave a blank stare at Carl, who was standing guard over her. Before either of them could utter a sound a loud, nerve-racking, pounding noise filled the structure from all sides and the voices...the horrifying, demonic laughter returned. The pots and pans that hung on the walls began shaking, and one by one, they sailed through the air past Carl and Janet, striking the café door and adjoining wall.

"Let's get out of here!" Janet screamed in hysteria as both she and Carl raced for the front doors. They fled from the building pushing their way through the front entrance, as once again everything became...calm. Carl followed Janet over to the concrete wall near the front door and wearily sat down beside her without speaking. He pulled out a cigarette and cupped his hands igniting it with his lighter. After taking a long draw, he turned toward Janet, who was now near the verge of insanity.

"Whatever's in there...it's after you," he said, speaking slowly, feeling his way. "I want you to stay away from here for awhile. I told you I'd find a way to beat this thing, but I can't do it with you here!"

Janet nodded in agreement without speaking. She was lost in her own thoughts and fears, but just then a horn honked causing her to return to the real world. It was Bobby, pulling up to the front of the building in his Datsun sports car.

Before he could get out of the auto, Janet moved quickly to the car and climbed in on the passenger side without saying a word. Bobby noticed the strange look on her face.

"What's wrong? Are you okay?"

"I don't feel good...that's all!" She replied without looking at her husband. "I need to go home."

"Sure! You look like you could use some rest." Bobby looked at Carl, who had just leaned down into the passenger window next to Janet.

"You'll have to take care of things here," he said to Carl. "I'm getting her home. I'll give you a call later."

"No problem!" Carl answered without really hearing what Bobby had said.

Carl stepped away from the car. Bobby drove away with his wife, who was still staring straight ahead as though she was in some sort of trance.

"Tell me what's wrong," Bobby insisted as he sped down Route Nine towards home.

"I just don't feel good," she whispered. "How come you're back so soon? I thought you said you'd be gone a couple of hours."

"I changed my mind. I took Anita home and asked Mom to watch her. I thought I'd stop back at the club and see if you wanted to go with me to look at the carpet."

"Bobby's mother, Doris, was staying with the couple, helping Janet around the house and watching Anita while Bobby and Janet labored at the nightclub preparing for opening night.

"No. Not today," she answered. "All I want to do is go home."

"I understand. This pregnancy's really hard on you, isn't it?"

"It's not the baby!" she snapped. "It's that building…I'm telling you…it's haunted!"

As the car continued down the highway, Bobby wondered what was happening to his wife. He had never seen her act this way. He gave no reply to her last statement. He was not about to get into another argument with Janet over a ghost. Besides, if there were such things as spooks and spirits inside the nightclub, why hadn't they bothered him? He steered the car toward home in silence.

Chapter Seven

It was difficult for Carl to remember this incident, but after thinking back on what he and Janet had endured, he finally recalled what happened next. This is what he said.

* * * * *

Three days passed without any diabolical display of force inside the building. Janet followed Carl's advice and had stayed away from the nightclub. Bobby met Carl around ten in the morning on the fourth day and assigned the handyman the job of cleaning the open bar.

He wanted the black leather washed and rubbed down with a wax compound. After giving Carl explicit instructions, Bobby said he was going to Cincinnati to look at some things for the nightclub. He told him he would not be back today, but he would meet him early the next morning. He bid Carl good-bye and left the building.

Carl had done such an excellent job for the Mackeys over the last few days that Bobby had more or less placed him in charge of the cleaning and cosmetic repairs that still needed done. He had swept all of the floors, carried out tons of trash, cleaned and stacked all of the tables and chairs, and had placed them in neat rows inside the Casino and main ballroom. Carl went to the kitchen and filled a bucket full of warm, soapy water, returning with the pail in one hand and a large, green sponge in the other. He moved all of the stools out into the middle of the black, tile floor in front of the bar and began washing down the leather when something suddenly caught his attention.

"Damn!" he growled, as he stood erect and stared through the room. The scent of roses quickly wafted through the air as a growing uneasiness, spiced with a touch of irritation, began welling up inside him.

"What in the Hell do you want?" he challenged.

A voice came from the ballroom, floating through the open bar like a thin whisper touching Carl's ears as he stood there, gazing into empty space.

"Get out!" The words glided through the air, more as a warning than a threat.

But before Carl could turn and run, a score of drinking glasses that were on top of the bar began flying through the air, smashing against the outside wall of the Fiesta Room. The bar stools began dancing and toppling over one by one to the floor as a foul, rancid stench filled the room. Then the sound of bowling balls rolling across the floor and smashing into wooden pins rang out from the ballroom, followed by maniacal laughter.

"Come on out and face me!" Carl demanded in a loud, almost hysterical voice. "What's the matter, you afraid?"

As his words died away, a pair of unseen hands suddenly grabbed the handyman by the back of the neck and flung him like a rag doll through the air. His body crashed into the wall near the hall doors and fell to the black tile like a sack of rocks. As he lay against the wall, Carl looked up and saw the unmoving figure standing there. It was a man looking back at him, but not a man made of flesh and bones. It was an apparition, the ghost of a man, but still Carl could see his face. The specter had short brown hair, parted on the side and cold piercing eyes. A hangman's noose was wrapped around his neck, the rope dangling down by his side.

Carl felt this demon man meant to kill him so he sprang to his feet and raced down the hall exploding through the front entrance as the laughter faded into the walls, swallowed up by the building itself.

Standing outside, Carl looked up at the overhead office window and saw a set of red, glowing, unearthly eyes staring down at him.

Then he saw the face, the same face that had confronted him only seconds ago.

"I'll be back! You son-of-a-bitch!" Carl screamed at the specter. "You're not running me off. It's you that's leaving here! I'm going to get Holy Water! Do you hear me?"

Carl jammed his hand into his pocket and jerked out the door key, slipping it into the hole and twisting the lock. He stepped away from the door and glared up at the window only to find the menacing spirit gone.

Carl cursed under his breath and turned from the building, walking to the gravel parking lot where he climbed into his blue 1974 Oldsmobile Cutlass. He gave a cold stare back at the building, then turned on the ignition switch and drove out of the lot spinning gravel under the tires as he went.

As he drove south on Route Nine the gas pedal suddenly slammed to the floorboard, sticking there. The car began picking up speed, swerving left and right toward on-coming traffic. Telephone poles looked like a black picket fence as Carl jammed his foot up and down on the pedal, trying to free it. Then, some invisible force grabbed the wheel directing the car into the path of a semi truck that was rapidly approaching Carl, head on.

"God, help me!" he cried out as he fought wildly, trying to regain control of the wheel.

As the car grew closer to the truck, the driver leaned on the horn, blowing it and waving his left hand wildly out the window. The Oldsmobile suddenly filled with the smell of roses, and, for no apparent reason, Carl suddenly regained control of the wheel just as the gas pedal sprang free of the floorboard. Carl quickly maneuvered the car out of the semi's path by driving to the left of the truck on the wrong side of the road. He brought the car to a screeching halt as it slid into a ditch, blowing out the left front tire and sinking to the frame in the mud. Visibly shaken, Carl gripped the steering wheel with both hands and leaned forward, almost resting his head on it. He asked himself it this was a warning from some demonic force from Hell? He wondered if he was being punished from trying to help Janet. He wasn't sure, but he knew that his doom was surely at hand until the car suddenly filled with the rose aroma. It had to be Johana who saved his life. But if that were the case, who was causing the havoc on him and Janet? And who was the ghost man with the rope hanging from his neck?

Finally regaining his composure Carl climbed from the car and groaned when he saw the blown tire. Since he did not have a jack, he began walking up Route Nine toward home to get one from his father's car.

"I'm going back in that building with Holy Water and bless everything in that place!" he grumbled as he strolled up the road. "I'm getting rid of whatever's in there... tonight!"

Chapter Eight

There were many obstructions that prevented the opening of the nightclub. One incident was a tragic fire that destroyed the entire south wing of the building. After reading the fire chief's report and interviewing Carl and the Mackeys, this is my interpretation as to what happened.

* * * * *

After returning to the car and changing the flat tire, Carl drove home where he spent the rest of the afternoon planning his attack on the entity, or entities, that dwelled inside the nightclub. Even though he was sure the ghostly figure that had confronted him earlier would be waiting, Carl was determined to try and run him and any other evil spirit out of there.

Carl had checked out some books on demonology at the local library and was sitting on the side of his twin-sized bed reading when the fire scanner on his wooden nightstand gave off a series of loud tones. He cocked an eye up and stared at the scanner as the dispatcher's voice came crackling through the speaker. It was about seven-thirty in the evening.

"Attention all Wilder Volunteer Fire Fighters!" the man's voice announced the message. "Report to the Wilder Fire House immediately. There's a confirmed fire at 44 Licking Pike!"

"Sweet, Lord!" Carl jumped to his feet and dropped the book on the bed. "That's the nightclub!"

Carl, who was a volunteer firefighter, ran to his closet, jerked open the door, and reached inside for his fire-fighting equipment. He grabbed up his yellow helmet, coat and boots, slipping into the clothing as fast as he could. In only seconds, he dashed through the house and exploded out the front door, racing on foot toward the nightclub. He made his way down the street with expressway speed, his back ramrod straight, his arms pounding like crazy. Coming closer to the nightclub Carl's eyes focused on the blazing building some two hundred yards away. An endless cloud of black, billowing smoke rose up from the roof, and flames danced and licked at the entire south wing of the building as Carl pushed his way through the crowd of onlookers who had parked their cars along the roadside to watch the fire.

Just as Carl reached the front entrance the sound of wailing sirens stretched out from all directions toward the nightclub. In only minutes, the fire trucks and life squads arrived, with men running in all directions. Some of them rolled out hoses, attaching them to hydrants, while others raised ladders and climbed to the top of the burning roof. The firemen, including Carl, worked feverishly trying to save the main building. In less than thirty minutes, the Wilder Fire Department had done its job. The firemen had saved the entire nightclub except the south wing, which had already been consumed when they had arrived. Some of the local residents had called their fire department "foundation savers," but after these same people had watched the volunteers risk life and limb to save an empty building, somehow that opinion changed.

Sometime later, as Carl assisted some of the other firemen roll up a hose; he spied Bobby simply standing there watching on from inside the crowd. He let loose of the hose and ambled over to Bobby with a grim look on his soot-covered face.

"I didn't know you were a volunteer firefighter," Bobby greeted him.

"Guess I didn't think to mention it," Carl told him as he lit a cigarette and took a long draw as if he was sucking in oxygen. "It's not as bad as it looks!"

"Seems like to me, you would've had enough smoke!" Bobby commented. "Those cigarettes aren't any good for you!"

"Ah yeah. I suppose you're right." Carl smiled as he took another suck on the tobacco stick, and then threw the cigarette to the ground.

Bobby's reply was not what Carl had expected. He figured his boss would be pretty upset and even try to blame him for the fire, accusing him of dropping a lit cigarette on the floor, or something like that. But Bobby bore burdens well. He had a strong and unyielding trust in God and always told himself there was a reason for everything good or bad that happens to people. If something good came his way, he called it a blessing, but, if some disaster, like this fire, fell down on him, he considered it to be a test of faith.

"How bad is the damage?" Bobby asked as he looked past Carl toward the damaged part of the building.

"The fire Chief says the south wing has to be torn down. That's where the fire started. All the rest of the place needs is aired out and the soot and smoke washed off everything."

"Well, it isn't so bad after all." Bobby commented. "We weren't going to use that part of the place for anything but storage anyway.

There wasn't anything in there but sleeping rooms where the maids lived when the place was a casino. We'll just do what we have to in order to get the nightclub open for business. I'll call some contractors and find someone to come and take care of the damage. I'm not going to be put out of business that easy!"

Carl simply shook his head at Bobby's determination. He couldn't believe the man possessed such a positive attitude about everything, even when being dealt a crummy hand of bad luck. Had it been Carl who owned the place, the fire would have been the last straw. Opening night at Bobby Mackey's Music World would have never occurred.

"Can we go inside and look around?" Bobby asked.

"I'm not sure," Carl replied. "We've got fans going inside the place to blow out the smoke, but, if you want, I'll go ask the Fire Chief."

"Do that!" Bobby insisted. "I want to take a quick look around before I head home to make those phone calls. It'd be a good idea if I know exactly what has to be done before I contact a contractor to come and tear down the south wing and fix anything else that might have gotten damaged."

Carl did as Bobby requested. He shouldered his way through the crowd and talked to the Chief, who was near the south side of the building. In a matter of minutes, Carl returned to give Bobby the good news. "The Chief said we can go in, but we're not to touch anything. He says he doesn't want anyone getting hurt."

"Don't worry about that." Bobby grinned. "I don't want us getting hurt, either."

The two men made their way past the onslaught of people who were still watching the firemen load their equipment. Carl entered the building first, with Bobby right behind him. They walked up the mirrored hallway, and pushed through the swinging doors, stepping into the main barroom. Since the electricity had been turned off, due to the fire, Carl pulled a flashlight out of his coat pocket and directed the beam through the dark barroom and across the black padded bar into the main ballroom.

"It doesn't look too bad in here," Bobby said as he fought back the tears caused by the lingering smoke. "Nothing appears to be damaged. Let's go check the Casino Room."

Carl led the way into the Casino Room where they inspected the cubicle for any damage. Bobby was elated to find that all the room needed was a good bath. He figured washing the soot off of the walls and floor would only take a few days. Satisfied that this room was intact, the two men made their way into the old cashier's office, the Fiesta Room, the restrooms and then back into the main ballroom. It was the same everywhere. The fire had not damaged any part of the main building. Nothing a good washing down wouldn't take care of. Bobby was relieved.

"I've seen enough," he told Carl. "It's not that bad, after all. I'm going to get going so I can make those calls and get somebody down here to take care of the damage. I want to get this place open for business before anything else happens."

"What about the upstairs office," Carl asked. "Shouldn't we go up there and take a look around?"

"Why don't you do that? I doubt there's anything wrong up there other than a bunch of smoke and soot on everything. Besides, I need to get home anyway. Janet's probably worried sick wondering if the place was burned to the ground."

Carl did not say anything, but he figured it would be just the opposite. Janet would have probably jumped up and down for joy if the place had been destroyed. If she was worried sick, it was because she was afraid the fire department would save the building.

"Do you want me to lead you outside?"

"No, that's okay. I can see good enough to make it. You go on upstairs and check out the office and I'll give you a call tonight. By the way, what started the fire"?

"The chief has no idea. He said it doesn't look like faulty wiring, but it doesn't look like arson, either. He told me to tell you that he's going to leave some men here to guard the place tonight, until the state fire investigator arrives to check the place out. The chief did say he doesn't know what to make of it. Strange, huh?"

"Yeah, it is," Bobby remarked, and then chuckled. "Maybe the ghost that Janet keeps telling me about started the fire. Why don't you tell the chief that!"

Before Carl could respond, Bobby turned around and walked through the semi-darkness of the room heading for the front door. Carl shuddered at the thought of going upstairs by himself. It was there that he last saw the mysterious stranger with the rope around his neck. He only hoped the bastard was gone, returned to Hell where he belonged.

Trying desperately to swallow his fear, Carl moved into the Fiesta Room and opened the door on the north wall, gazing up the dark stairs that led to the office. He wanted to turn around and get out of the place, but something inside him made him climb the steps one at a time until he reached the top landing.

He cautiously stepped across the threshold into the smoke filled office and instantly wondered why no one had bothered to place a fan up here. He beamed his flashlight through the fog-like lingering smoke and was relieved when he did not see his ghostly friend anywhere in sight. Satisfied that everything was okay, Carl turned to leave, but, before he made it out, the door slammed shut just as an evil snicker filled the room, bouncing off the walls all around him.

"Where's your Holy Water?" The raspy voice mocked him from somewhere inside the darkness. It was not just a raspy voice. The words sounded as if someone who had undergone a tracheotomy and was speaking through a voice box had spoken them. Carl instantly knew whom to expect when he turned around.

"Who are you?" He forced out the words as he stood there, motionless, staring at the door, with his back to the entity.

"The name's Alonzo," the scratchy voice answered him. "Did you really think I'd let you run me off? There's a lot more of us here than you think. You better stay out of our business or you'll die and you won't die game."

"What's that mean?"

"You'll find out if you keep interfering."

"I can't help you if you don't let me know what you want," Carl said. "You set the fire, didn't you?"

"That's right!" The disembodied spirit laughed.

"I'm not afraid of you!" Carl lied.

"Yes, you are!"

"No, I'm not!" Carl screamed as he spun around and shined his light through the room, trying desperately to see the menacing specter, but to no avail.

Once again, he found himself alone inside the room, but still he felt as if the apparition was watching him. Hell! There was no doubt about it! Not only was he being watched by unseen eyes, he could actually feel the presence of the entity coming toward him, drawing closer.

Carl moved backwards, toward the door, still watching straight ahead. He slipped his left had behind his back, feeling for the knob, gripping it tightly, and was surprised when the door easily opened.

He took a slow, half step forward then whirled around and jerked open the door, racing down the stairs as if his very life depended on it. He never looked back until he exploded through the front doors of the nightclub and found himself safely outside.

"People are watching!" Carl told himself as he knelt down on the sidewalk and gasped for air. "Get it together!"

As he tried to gather his strength and senses, he looked around at the crowd of people staring at him and silently wondered what they would say if he tried to tell them some evil being had just confronted him inside this place that he now considered to be "Hell's Gate." He knew better than to say anything, especially to the Fire Chief. If he did try to tell him some demon from Hell set the fire, he would be kicked off of the fire department and most likely find himself locked away in some rubber room inside an insane asylum.

Carl finally regained his composure and helped the other firemen finish loading the equipment back onto the trucks. Once the task was complete, and the emergency vehicles left the site, Carl walked toward home with his head hung low. He was exhausted, but not from fighting the fire. He never wanted to step foot back inside that evil place again, but he knew down deep in the reaches of his soul that he had to. If he turned tail and ran away like some sniffling coward he would never forgive himself if anything happened to Bobby or Janet. For some reason, he felt as if he been chosen to combat this evil force, and combat it, he would.

Chapter Nine

While conducting the interviews with Carl, he spoke of dreams, nightmares that seized his mind like some sort of warning. The bat was the first "warning", and it was only the beginning.

* * * * *

Days turned into weeks as Carl labored inside the nightclub cleaning down the soot covered walls and fixtures. Since the fire, there had not been one single show of force by the evil spirits that had wreaked havoc on him and Janet, and it made Carl wonder if some how it was over.

But what about the voice he heard upstairs in the office? Was that just his imagination? He wasn't sure, but, as the days went by and nothing happened, he felt more at ease inside the place.

Bobby had hired a local contractor to tear down the south wing of the building, and, with the job completed, opening day was drawing near for "Bobby Mackey's Music World."

After a particularly hard day of work, Carl curled up under his comforter and fell into a deep sleep. At one-thirteen in the morning on August 23, he jerked up in the bed and threw back the comforter. He slid his feet over the side and stared at the wall with a vacant look etched on his face. He felt a painful loneliness sitting beside him in the darkened room as he tried to digest what had just happened. He had just awakened from another nightmare, only much worse than the one about the bats. A clammy, cold sweat covered his face as he dwelled on the dream. Spiders! Hundreds of them—not hundreds— thousands of the hairy insects were crawling all over his body inside the barroom as he lay on the floor near the entrance to the Fiesta Room.

"It's just another bad dream!" he tried to tell himself. "Just a dumb nightmare!"

He crawled back under the covers and tried desperately to fall asleep, but to no avail. He lay awake for hours thinking about the days to come and wondering if the nightmare could be a premonition, another warning, just like the dream he had about the bats. He prayed he was wrong.

Unable to rest, he finally climbed out of the bed around eight o' clock and got dressed. He slipped into a pair of dirty sneakers, ragged Levis, and a white T-shirt, then walked outside and climbed into his car, driving to a nearby restaurant. After consuming a pot of coffee, and almost convincing himself that the dream was nothing but a dream, Carl paid his bill and headed for the nightclub, ready to begin another day of work.

Chapter Ten

It took two months to piece together the next turn of events that sent the pregnant Janet to the hospital. After extensive questioning of both Janet and Carl, we pieced the bits of information together like parts of an elaborate puzzle. This is what happened next.

* * * * *

Carl was surprised to see Bobby's Datsun parked in front of the building as he arrived.

"What's he doing here so early?" he asked himself as he climbed out of the Oldsmobile.

Carl walked to the front of the building and reached for the door handle to go on inside, but hesitated when the dream about the spiders came flashing back in his mind.

"It was just a bad dream!" he said as he shook his head, almost laughing aloud. He jerked open the door and strolled up the hall dismissing the nightmare as just that...a nightmare. Nothing had happened for such a long time; it had to be over! At least, that was what he kept telling himself.

He pushed through the double doors at the end of the mirrored hallway and was taken by surprise when he saw Janet sitting at the bar on a stool next to Bobby.

Janet had followed Carl's advice and had completely distanced herself from the premises since being attacked inside the kitchen.

"How's it going?" Bobby asked with a smile. "Look who I brought with me."

"Hi, Janet," Carl said cheerfully. "Long time, no see!"

"It's been awhile, hasn't it?"

"Listen, Carl," Bobby exclaimed. "We've been waiting for you to arrive. I didn't want to leave Janet in here by herself. I have to go to town on some business, and she decided she wanted to work upstairs in the office today. I want you to keep an eye on her until I get back." Bobby tucked his white sport shirt neatly inside his jeans.

"I won't be gone long," he reassured.

Bobby gave them both a warm smile and headed for the door to take care of some matters concerning the opening of the nightclub. Once he disappeared through the swinging doors and left the building, Janet turned to Carl with an inquisitive look.

"Has anything happened while I've been gone?"

"No. Nothing." Carl shook his head. "It's strange, huh?"

"Maybe not."

"Have you looked around yet?" Janet asked excitedly.

"No, why?"

"Just go look," she grinned. Janet climbed down from the black padded stool and followed Carl around the north end of the bar into the ballroom.

"That looks great!"

Bobby and Janet had brought a large stack of new, bright, red tablecloths, a box of small, round ashtrays, and some plants to the nightclub that morning. The tables were placed in neat rows throughout the room, and each had been covered with a tablecloth.

The plants, which Janet had bought from the back of a man's truck, were placed aesthetically around the rooms.

"There's not much left to do before we open," she said. "It's almost time."

"I know," he grinned. "I need to go down in the basement and get some lights. Bobby told me he wanted new ones in every socket. He got a case of 200-watt bulbs last week. That'll sure brighten this place up."

"That should make a big difference." She agreed.

"Will you be okay up here until I get back? I won't be gone long."

"Go ahead, I'm fine. I think I'll go on upstairs and get started. I'll yell if I need you."

"You sure?" he asked again.

"I'm sure." She smiled as she turned and headed toward the Fiesta Room that led to the upstairs office.

Satisfied that Janet was safe, Carl disappeared behind the stage and made his way down the gray, paint peeled wooden stairwell leading to the main basement.

Janet moved up the yellow stairway and walked into the office. The dark paneled room was about twenty feet long and sixteen feet wide. A small black, padded bar sat in the far left-hand corner of the cubicle. A wood grain desk and a black, leather office chair sat against the right wall. A stack of boxes that contained invoices and papers from the Latin Quarter blocked a small closet door to her left. Bobby had placed them there after going through some of the papers from the past. He planned on looking at each one of the invoices sooner or later. Bobby was intrigued with the history of this mammoth structure and wanted to know everything about it.

Janet moved across the red, wall-to-wall carpet and pulled the chair away from the desk. Picking up a dusting rag that was lying on the top of it, she began wiping down the surface when suddenly she became aware of a presence in the room. She slowly turned and searched the area with her eyes, but found no one there. Despite it being 80 degrees outside, the room became extremely cold. The memory of her last encounter inside the building spooked her, but, still, she convinced herself there was nothing to worry about.

Janet turned back to the desk and resumed wiping it down when she felt the dark presence again...only this time, closer! Her nostrils filled with the scent of roses, but the sweet aroma then turned to a sickening stench just as some invisible being suddenly pressed against her back, wrapping its arms around her waist.

"Let me go!" she shrieked. "Oh, God!...Not again!"

****

Carl started to pick up the case of light bulbs to carry them upstairs when the stairwell door slammed shut behind him. He wheeled around on the balls of his feet, dropping the cardboard box to the dirt floor as he stared at the door, waiting for someone to come crashing through it at any second now.

As he stood there, waiting, he caught a glimpse of something moving out of the corner of his eye. He turned to his left and stared up the massive open corridor. The chamber was lined with huge wooden beams that rose up from the dirt floor to the overhead rafters. The girders gave extra support for the first floor of the building.

"Who's there?" he called out, not really wanting to know.

Nothing.

"Is someone there?" he asked again, his voice now nothing but a thin whisper.

Nothing.

He looked straight ahead at the gray wall, gazing into the row of open doors that lined the panel. Each door led to a single, small cubicle that was once used as dressing rooms when the place was The Latin Quarter. Carl turned around and twisted the knob, but it would not budge.

"Damn!" he growled. "Come on! Open up!"

Before his words faded away the sound of a loud, powerful heartbeat began filling the confines of the basement. The Ka Thump – Ka Thump became so intense that he shoved the palms of his hands against his ears in an attempt to block out the intimidating sounds.

"My God!" he stammered as his eyes searched left and right, looking for the entity that he felt certain would show itself. "Janet's upstairs alone! I've got to get to her before it's too late!"

** * *

Janet twisted and turned, fighting to free herself from the entity that held her tightly as the room became icy cold.

"Somebody, help me!" She squeezed out the words as she fought back with all her strength. The office door, leading out to the stairwell, began slamming back and forth against its frame when suddenly the entity let loose of its grip on the expectant woman. Without hesitation, Janet ran for the stairs and started down when something pushed her. She screamed and fell forward, toppling down each step, but avoiding serious injury by grabbing the handrail as she tumbled to the bottom. Horrified, she dropped to both knees and stared up at the top landing just as a demonic whisper descended the stairs.

"Get out!" the bodiless voice commanded.

* * *

Carl frantically kicked his right foot into the stairwell door, trying to escape from the basement as the area filled with that haunting aroma that had assaulted him so many times before.

"Okay!" he shrieked. "You want a war...you've got it!" He spun around with both fist clenched at his sides, his eyes blazing with a blood chilling anger as they probed the chamber.

The basement turned instantly hot, and a loud zooming noise came from one of the far rooms down the corridor as Carl stared into the air, his eyes now like invisible daggers.

"No way" he shrieked when he saw a large swarm of yellow jackets circling in the air less than fifty feet away.

The insects dipped, turned, swirled, and rose up in the air like a miniature tornado as Carl watched on in awe. Then came the attack!

The yellow jackets massed together as one then darted through the basement in lunatic flight like a black and yellow missile soaring through the sky. Carl dashed for a nearby dressing room with the insects soaring straight for him. He leaped across the threshold, slamming the door shut just as the swarm reached it. The outside of the wooden door hummed and pulsated from the insects that blanketed it. They were trying desperately to find a way in so they could plunge their tiny daggers into Carl's flesh.

"Dammit!" he groaned as he leaned his back hard against the door and took a long, deep breath of air.

Safe from his attackers, Carl stepped away from the door and gazed through the pitch black of the ten by twelve room. Unable to see anything, he pulled his Zippo lighter out of his right pants pocket and thumbed the striker wheel. The tiny flame did not give off much light, but the full length mirrors that lined the dirty, white walls reflected the image of the flame through the room making it possible for him to see.

Dressing tables ran the length of the walls on three sides, directly under the pitted mirrors, and the room was filled with broken bar stools and wooden chairs.

As Carl continued searching the room with his eyes, he saw something to his left on the mirror. NO! Not on the mirror, but inside it! He strained his eyes at the image and saw that it was two, tiny, red dots...glowing in the dark...and they were growing and growing, glowing with an evil that could only have come from the bowels of Hell!

Carl could not believe it, but he saw a human face appear in the mirror surrounding the two burning embers that were supposed to be eyes. In a matter of seconds he found himself staring at some sort of blotchy, red head, flayed of its skin. He gawked at the demonic thing, and, as he did, a skeletal arm suddenly reached out toward him from inside the mirror and pointed a bony, elongated finger directly at his face.

"Leave here or DIE!" the creature commanded.

"Who are you?" Carl choked the words out. "Why are you here?"

"I have many names! Some call me 'The Ancient One.' Others call me the Morning Star!'" the creature responded in a low, threatening, raspy growl. "You are trespassing on my sanctified ground. The ground of my children who have followed and served me well! If you meddle any longer, you shall die a thousand deaths. It is I who command you to leave!"

Before Carl could respond, the demonic thing inside the mirror broke out into horrific laughter, and as it did, its face inside the looking glass began to glow red then white, becoming a mass of melting, oozing tissue, falling off in chunks from the mirror and striking the top of wooden dressing table with a series of wet smacks. The mirror immediately glowed to a bright, blinding surge of evil energy then suddenly went dim, and then dark, leaving Carl swallowed up in a drowning sea of fear and confusion.

"Ouch!" he groaned as the lighter became too hot from the flame and burned his thumb. He dropped the Zippo to the floor and turned around inside the blackness of the room, feeling his way back to the door. He placed his right ear against the wood partition and listened carefully for the zooming insects, but all he heard was the jack hammering of his own heart. He swallowed his fear and opened the door just a crack, peering out the opening with his right eye.

"They're gone!" he whispered out in disbelief. He jerked open the door and dashed across the room toward the closed stairwell. He reached the door and gripped the knob with both hands and to his astonishment it opened easily. He looked back over his left shoulder for a split second then raced up the stairs to find Janet.

As he ran from behind the stage, his feet pounding against the floor, the new jukebox that had been delivered earlier that same day came on by itself playing "The Anniversary Waltz." Carl didn't stop. He leaped off the platform and headed for the upstairs office as fast as his legs would carry him.

As he rounded the end of the open bar, he saw Janet sitting on a stool gripping her stomach with both hands. He slid to a stop and paused for a brief moment, sucking in a quick breath of air, then slowly walked to the center of the bar where the horror-stricken woman sat all alone.

"Are you okay?" he asked as he studied her flushed face.

"For now," her voice was flat and quiet. "It isn't over, Carl."

"I know," he apologized. "I shouldn't have left you alone."

Janet slowly spun around on the stool and faced Carl, who was standing three feet away.

"That thing grabbed me in the office just like it did in the kitchen!" she said through trembling lips. "It pushed me down the stairs! If I hadn't..." she paused and took a deep breath then stared at Carl with a blank look. "If I hadn't grabbed the handrail my baby and I could have been killed!"

"That's it!" Carl screamed furiously. He could not stand it any longer. If he held it in for one more second, he would have blown out his teeth. He spun around in the room and screamed out curses and threats at the evil that lurked inside the building until he became exhausted, but finally controlling his rage he turned to Janet.

"Let's get out of here until Bobby gets back." He sounded defeated.

He walked over and extended his right arm to the woman helping her off the stool just as the jukebox came to life again, playing the "Anniversary Waltz."

Janet jerked and wheeled around, staring across the bar into the main ballroom.

"Who is playing that song, Carl?" Her voice was trembling.

"I don't know," he whispered.

"Stay here! I'm going to check this out! " Carl said.

"No way!" she argued as she continued holding her stomach. "I'm going with you."

Carl slowly walked around the side of the bar with Janet beside him, and, when they stepped into the main ballroom, the music instantly stopped and everything became still, leaving a heart wrenching eeriness hanging in the air.

"Let's go!" Janet insisted. "I've had enough!"

"Yeah! Okay."

They walked out of the ballroom and disappeared down the mirrored hallway stepping out into the welcomed sunlight. Carl locked the front door and followed Janet over to the concrete wall where they both sat down awaiting Bobby's return.

"I've got to convince Bobby this place is haunted. I've tried to talk to him about this several times, but he just won't listen to me."

"What does he say?" Carl asked while cupping his hands and lighting a cigarette.

"He said If people hear we've got a haunted nightclub, we won't have any business.'"

"He's got a point there!" Carl replied. "But, still. If he doesn't do something about this, and somebody gets hurt in there, he'll be responsible! What if this story does ever leak out and somebody says they were injured in here by some demon? Bobby better hope no smart-ass lawyer ever get me on the witness stand because I won't lie for him or nobody!"

"I never thought of that." Janet sighed gustily. "What if those spirits could possess someone? Could you imagine some poor man or woman being taken over by a spirit when they leave here? The ghosts, or whatever they are, could cause them to have a wreck, and the police would simply think that they'd had too much to drink. You're right. We could be held responsible, but right now I've got to worry about me. My stomach's beginning to feel funny."

"Does it hurt bad?"

"It's just cramps," she said while gritting her teeth. "I could just imagine this..."

"What?" Carl interrupted her.

"I'll go to the doctor and tell him I want to be checked out because a ghost pushed me down the stairs. They'd have me locked up in some nut house somewhere."

"Janet!" Carl said seriously, changing the tone of the conversation. "That evil in there was waiting for you to come back. It hasn't bothered me since the fire, and it's never harmed Bobby. You have to stay away from here until I get this place blessed by a priest or something."

"You don't have to worry about that. I'm not going to take a chance on losing my baby. One way or another I'm gong to make Bobby listen to me tonight."

As her words drifted into the warmth of the August air, Bobby pulled up in front of the building, and, just like before, she climbed into the car and demanded to be taken home, telling him of her assault by the unseen attacker.

Chapter Eleven

I spent several hours with Bobby and then with Carl, piecing together what happened when Bobby rushed Janet to the hospital the following morning due to her injury. Both men agree this is what happened.

* * * * *

A dazzling, white blur of morning sun rose peacefully over the countryside, shining its beam through the bedroom window as Janet sat up and slid her legs over the side of the bed.

"Bobby, wake up!" she insisted as she rocked back and forth, holding her hands against her abdomen. "Come on! Something's wrong with the baby!"

Bobby pressed the knuckles of his hands into his eyes, rubbing the few pieces of sleep away, then sat up beside his wife. "What's wrong?" He took a deep breath of morning air and gave a hard stretch with his hands extended over his head.

"It's the baby!" The pain could be heard in her voice. "I think I need to go to the hospital. I'm having cramps like I'm trying to go into labor."

"Get ready!" Bobby demanded as he jumped from the bed and quickly slipped into his blue jeans and white sport shirt.

Janet hurriedly put on a blue maternity top with matching pants and combed her hair while Bobby woke his mother, asking her to keep an eye on Anita while they were gone. In a matter of minutes they were speeding north on US 27 toward Bethesda Hospital on Oak Street in Cincinnati, Ohio.

In less than an hour, Bobby had Janet in the emergency room. She was diagnosed as having premature labor pains. It was August 24, and the due date was not until November 30.

Bobby sat in the small, white waiting room that was crowded with red armchairs and a matching leather couch. He thought about Janet's conversation with him while they drove home from the nightclub the day before. She had tried desperately to convince him that some force had pushed her down the stairs and that he had to believe her when she said the building was haunted.

He could not understand his wife's obsession with the idea that some demonic force was inside the nightclub. But how was he going to convince her otherwise was beyond him? He had not been attacked by anything, and nothing unusual had happened to him, except when he thought he had seen a young girl in the ballroom the day he first took Janet to see the place. He assured himself that seeing that woman was just his imagination. He had to prove to Janet that the place wasn't haunted.

As he sat there waiting for word of his wife's condition, he decided to call Carl. He wanted to find out what he knew about all of this nonsense. Janet had told him if he did not believe her that he should ask Carl. Bobby stood up from the chair and made his way down the hallway to the phone booth where he dialed the nightclub. There was no answer. Bobby decided to try and reach him at home. He slipped the change into the money slot and dialed Carl's house, hoping like heck he would be there.

Carl was lying on his bed, looking up at the ceiling thinking of a way to exorcise the evil force from the nightclub when the phone began to ring.

"Hello, Carl here," he announced.

"Carl, this is Bobby. I'm at Bethesda Hospital with Janet. The doctor said she's trying to go into premature labor, and I need to ask you something. Do you know anything about a ghost or some demon inside the nightclub?"

"Ah,..." Carl stammered, not knowing if he should answer Bobby's question.

"Come on, Carl," Bobby insisted, "Janet swears something pushed her down the stairs when she was up in the office yesterday."

"Well, Bobby," Carl finally gave in, "there is something in there. Janet's been attacked more than once, and so have I."

Bobby could not believe what he was hearing. It was just too absurd...too ridiculous!

"Damn, Carl," he said with an irritated tone of voice. "There's no such thing as ghosts! I want you to quit talking to Janet about this, and, if she thinks she sees or hears anything in there again, I want you to convince her it's her imagination. If you continue agreeing with her about something evil being in there, I'll never convince her otherwise".

"But, Bobby!" Carl argued, "there is something in there...I've tried to keep her from coming back to the club until I figured out a way to run the thing off!"

"So you've talked to her about this more than once, huh?"

"Yes, sure I have. She told me she was going to find a way to convince you, but evidently, she hasn't."

"You've got that right!" Bobby's voice became tight with annoyance. "No one is going to convince me that there's some kind of evil spirit inside my nightclub. I hate to say this, but, if you don't do as I ask and help me convince her that nothing's in there, I'm going to have to make a change and find someone else to work for me. I don't want to do that, Carl. You're a good worker, and I want to keep you, but this nonsense about a ghost has to stop."

"Okay, I guess you're right." Carl sighed. "I won't mention it again, but what do I do if she does?"

"First of all," Bobby remarked, "you tell her it's just her imagination like I said, and then you come and tell me what she said to you. I'm going to put a stop to this before it goes any further. If I have to, I'll spend a couple of nights in there by myself to prove to you and everyone else that there's no ghost in the place. Nothing has ever bothered me when I was inside the building, and don't you think it's a little strange that you and Janet are the only ones getting attacked and no one else is seeing or hearing anything in there?"

"What about Anita?" Carl asked. "Remember when she got frightened and wanted to leave?"

"Sure I do!" Bobby scowled. "But she probably overheard me and Janet talking about all of this and let her imagination run away with her. Little kids get scared easy!"

"Yeah. I guess you're right," Carl lied.

"Good, that's what I wanted to hear!" Bobby exclaimed. "I'm probably going to be tied up here for awhile. I'll call you later and let you know what's going on as soon as I know something."

"Okay," Carl said, "if you need anything at all, just let me know."

After Bobby hung up the phone, Carl spoke to the empty room, "No ghosts, huh? I might have promised not to talk to Janet about it anymore, but that doesn't mean I can't do something about it!"

He lay on his bed and pulled a bag off the nightstand, inspecting each item inside it. He had gone to an occult bookstore to find books on witchcraft and demonology, and he had made copies of an exorcism spell he found inside one of the texts. He had also removed his mother's wooden crucifix from the living room wall and placed it in the bag. Inside the cross was a small vial of Holy Water that Carl intended to use to run off the evil spirits inside the nightclub.

Stuffing the items gently back inside the brown paper bag, Carl stood to his feet and took one more drag off of his cigarette, then crushed the butt into the round glass ash tray on the night stand.

"It's now or never!" he said as he took a deep breath. "I'm going down there and run that thing off."

The young handyman strolled through the house, out the front door, and headed down Licking Pike on foot toward the nightclub. He did not know if his plan would work or not, but he was sure going to give it his best shot. Someone had to do something to get rid of whatever was in there, and he felt as if he was that someone!

Chapter Twelve

What happened next was very difficult for Carl to discuss. Tears frequently threatened to flow during the interview process. This is the way Carl remembers it happening.

* * * * *

The sun stood proud in the white and blue sky as the heat radiated from the black roof of Bobby Mackey's Music World. Carl stood at the front door in his faded Wranglers and white T-shirt, staring up at the overhead office window. Everything outside seemed unspoiled, pristine and ever sunny. He could not see anyone or anything in the upstairs window; yet, he felt something watching him from the other side of the glass pane. He felt threatened by the strangeness of the building, but nothing was going to stop him from going inside and exorcising the evil spirit out of there, if he could.

With slight, watchful hesitation, he slipped the key into the hole and turned the lock while peering through the panes of door glass, expecting anything to happen at anytime. He cautiously stepped inside the mirrored hallway and listened for the slightest sound of movement, but there was only a roar of silence as he squinted his eyes, adjusting them to the semi-darkness of the hallway.

He pushed through the swinging double doors at the end of the hall and flashed his eyes left and right, probing every inch of the bar area as if he was a lion stalking his prey, waiting for just the right moment to make his move.

Nothing.

It can't be this easy, he thought. It knows I'm here so why isn't it showing itself? He slowly moved across the black tile floor to the middle of the bar, placing his brown paper bag of sanctimonious goodies on top of it. The items inside clunked resoundingly as the bag made contact with the black counter top. As he stood there staring across the open bar into the ballroom, a wave of grayness passed over him, a kind of dark premonition of things to come, and he sensed a supercharged tension in the air, as if at any second all hell was gong to break loose.

Still standing at the bar and staring toward the far wall, he squinted his right eye and caught a glimpse of something moving toward him. He turned around with his fists clenched by his side, but was completely taken by surprise when he found himself staring at a beautiful young woman some ten feet away.

The girl had short blonde hair and a full figure. She was of medium height and had an aura of untouchable glory about her. She was clad in a full-length, white gown that had a neatly tied ribbon at the neck.

"My name is Pearl," she said softly, her words floating through the air like a feather. "I need you help."

"What kind of help?" Carl questioned her as he readied himself for some kind of trick.

Before the woman could answer him, Carl heard the low whisper of laughter come from behind the bar. As he quickly turned around to see whom the snicker was coming from, he felt an instant sensation of excruciating pain as the ghost-man, Alonzo, plowed him in the side of the jaw with his fist. Carl rocked back on his feet and as he did he felt another blow to his ribs, this time from another attacker.

He fell to the floor, doubled up in pain, and out of his right eye, saw the figure of the woman named Pearl quickly fleeing from the room. When he looked harder at the woman, he felt another terrifying surge of fear, like an electric current shooting through his body, when he saw that the woman was without a head. Then came another blow to the side of his face, this time by a foot. Carl rolled over on his back, gasping for air and saw both of his attackers now.

Standing over him was the ghost of the man called Alonzo. Next to him stood another spirit with an evil, sinister look about him. He stood about five-foot-nine and had a short blonde hair. His eyes were a cold gray, with one of them almost blue in color. He, too, like Alonzo, had a hangman's noose around his neck.

"I warned you!" Alonzo laughed as he raised his foot and kicked Carl in the face again.

"Let's cut off the bastard's head like we did to that bitch!" the other ghost-man scoffed.

"I didn't cut off her head!" Alonzo argued with his ghostly partner. "You did!"

"You got hung for it, didn't you?" the other one sneered.

Carl lay there on the floor, writhing in pain, trying desperately to figure out what was happening, but, as he did, the ghost of Alonzo went insane with rage when the other wraith made mention of Alonzo being found guilty of some crime. Alonzo screamed out in anger and began kicking Carl in the ribs and face, while the other spirit laughed manically, until Carl fell unconscious.

Some time later, without any concept of time, Carl awoke on the bar room floor, his body bruised and battered from the vicious attack. He climbed to his feet, groaning out in pain. As he straightened, he jumped back in fear when he saw another ghost standing behind the bar in a white, long sleeve shirt and a green bartender's vest. The man was big boned with a fair complexion. He had an unlit cigar hanging out of the side of his mouth.

"What's your pleasure, son?" the man asked him in a friendly tone.

"I'm not your son!" Carl threw the words across the bar at him. "If you're trying to run me off like your friends just tried to do, you can forget it! You're the one's who are leaving here! Not me!"

"First of all," the man stated. "They're not my friends. And, furthermore, I'm here to help you run them off. The name's Buck. Buck Brady. I owned this place years ago. Go down to the China Room and break though the floor. There's an evil well hidden under it. It's a gateway to and from Hell! It must he sealed to trap the evil spirits in Hades where they belong."

"What in the world are you talking about?" Carl demanded to know.

"Many violent deaths have occurred here, but that's not the main concern. That well was used for satanic worship years ago and…"

The bartender's words were interrupted by a series of gunshots that rang out from the Casino Room, and suddenly, every light in the building began to flicker off then on. Carl wheeled around and gazed through the barroom for one quick second, then quickly turned back toward Buck, only to find him gone.

"Damn." He groaned when he found himself standing there all alone. For some strange reason, he almost wanted to trust the man who identified himself as Buck. He didn't seem like the other spirits who had appeared. He seemed kind, concerned, but, more than that, he seemed like a friend.

"Where are you, Buck?" Carl whispered and waited for a response that never came.

After several long anxious moments, he figured Buck had disappeared for a reason. He decided to check out the Casino Room, and, and with all due caution, he moved through the Fiesta Room, down the hall and stepped into the once great, once marvelous, gambling hall.

To the eye, the room appeared to be empty, but Carl knew that did not mean some entity was not there. The acid taste of gunpowder lingered in the air and something told Carl to turn around and leave the room before the show of force began. He was not going to be lured into another one of those bastards' traps.

He turned around and made his way back to the bar, where he reached for the bag of Holy Water and other items. As he did, a series of sudden, loud popping sounds rang out in the room, coming from somewhere near the swinging doors that led out into the mirrored hallway.

Carl laid the bag back down on top of the bar and followed the popping sounds. To his surprise, he found the strange noise to be coming from a large cactus inside the barroom next to the swinging doors. Confused, he knelt down and turned the black pot that housed the cactus. The popping noise grew louder and more intense.

As he continued inspecting the plant, the cactus suddenly, violently, split open, and hundreds of baby spider sprang out of the opening onto Carl's clothing and skin.

Carl shrieked out as he jumped to his feet, smacking his clothes and screaming in hysteria. This was just like his last nightmare. And these were not ordinary spiders. They were hairy, venomous, little tarantulas crawling all over him, ready to sink their tiny jaws into his flesh and steal away his very life.

On the verge of insanity, Carl bolted through the barroom, across the ballroom floor, and exploded out the back door, racing down the stairs toward the waiting ground below. He fled across the railroad tracks that ran adjacent to the building and raced through the wooded thicket like a frightened deer. Heading for the Licking River, he hoped if he submerged himself under water the insects would leap from his body and swim for their lives. He had to hurry before one of them reached his neck or face. With his allergic reaction to bug bites, it could possibly take just one to kill him.

At a dead run, Carl reached the river, leaping off of the bank, head first, and diving under the muddy surface, praying that he was right. He stayed submerged as long as he could, holding his breath until he thought his lungs would explode. Finally, he came up and quickly ran his hands over his head, face, and neck, feeling for any sign of the spiders. He took a deep breath and submerged again, this time swimming to the shoreline. He crawled up onto the muddy riverbank and quickly disrobed, checking each piece of clothing for any signs of the tarantulas. His theory had been correct. The spiders were gone, probably drowned in the water, and, as far as Carl was concerned, that was what they deserved.

The spiders crawling on the man had pushed him over the edge. He was going back in there and do what Buck had told him to do. He was going to bust up the floor in the China Room and learn what terrible secret lay hidden there.

Chapter Thirteen

This chapter continues the story of what Carl endured that morning. He remembered this chain of events with total recall and as he conveyed what happened next, his voice tightened and it became obvious that it took all of his strength to continue telling this bizarre story.

* * * * *

After slipping back into his wet clothes, and in a fit of rage, Carl marched up the hillside and through the woods, heading back inside the bar. It was he who was ready for war now. He'd had enough. Once back inside the barroom, he looked warily toward the cactus. It was totally intact, as though the spiders had never existed. Now even more disgusted, he retrieved his bag of items, walked back into the main ballroom, crossed the dance floor and disappeared behind the stage. Opening the door that led down into the basement, he descended the stairs with slow, careful steps until he reached the lower chamber. Even though he could not see anyone, he felt as if he was being watched. In a matter of minutes he found himself filling the threshold of the China Room. He swallowed hard, then stepped inside and carefully searched the cubicle with his watchful eyes.

To his right were yellow stained walls lined with gray, wooden shelving. Stacks of dirty plates, cups and saucers sat on the shelves. To his left was a rusty, steel door that was completely covered in white, woven spider thread. From the looks of things, the door had been shut for years. Straight ahead was a set of wooden stairs that led up to the rafters and stopped.

"That's weird!" Carl told himself as he wondered why someone would build a set of stairs that led absolutely nowhere. He had noticed the stairs before, but never gave it any thought until now.

As he stood there, staring through the room, he spied a pickaxe lying near the stairs, just in front of him. He crossed the room, bent over and picked it up. With a smirk on his face, he raised the tool over his head and struck the floor with all his might, the sharp tine of the axe piercing the old floor like a bullet penetrating someone's flesh. He struck the floor several more times, and, each time, the flooring gave way to his hammering blows until he had made a hole big enough to crawl into.

Carl knew Bobby would have had a cow if he knew he was down there tearing up the floor, but at the time he really did not care. He was determined to unravel the mystery behind this madness and put a stop to it, once and for all.

He knelt down, and then lay on his belly next to the hole. He pulled out a penlight from his shirt pocket and directed the beam under the flooring as he stuck his head inside the darkness, smelling the cold, moist musty air to the crawl space. As he looked in all directions he felt a surge of excitement when he saw what appeared to be a hidden well. It was about ten feet in front of him. The hole looked as if it had either caved in, or someone had filled it over. That did not matter to Carl at the time. Buck told him his answer was there, so he kept searching the darkness until he saw what appeared to be a ledger of some sort. He stretched his arm as far as he could, fumbling with the book until he had it within his grasp. He pulled it out of the hole, and sat up on the floor, inspecting his find.

"It's part of someone's diary." He muttered the words aloud as he wiped the dirt from the old, yellow pages and tried to read the words written down.

"My name is Johana," the diary read, "and I beg you to help me. I'm a prisoner in Hell. Search the spot light room."

There were only three of what appeared to be many pages of this ledger, and Carl had just read the only thing written inside it. Finding this part of Johana's diary made no sense to him. He could not figure out how his finding this little tid-bit of information was going to help him solve anything, but maybe the answer was upstairs in the spotlight room. That was where he would head next. Besides, Johana had always been a friend, and, if she needed his help, he was going to do whatever he had to in order to give her peace.

As Carl climbed to his feet, a creeping, rotten stench, coming from nowhere, yet everywhere, quickly filled the room causing him to become instantly nauseous. He coughed and gagged until he threw up.

Dropping the book back through the hole, he raced from the China Room and escaped through the back door near the railroad tracks, where he fell to his knees, still debilitated by the vicious odor. He knew some evil presence had sent that stench into the room for a reason. It wanted him out. Trying to regain his composure, he sat on the ground wondering if he should go back inside. His face and arms were covered with red splotches and he felt as if something was underneath the first layer of his skin, crawling and moving inside his body. He gritted his teeth and stood to his feet staring at the open door wondering what new horrors would await him once he stepped back into what he considered to be Hell's Gate.

Swallowing his fear, Carl slowly moved through the doorway and stepped into the basement. He cautiously moved through the lonely chamber, his eyes probing every inch of the quiet corridor until he stepped into the China Room. He crossed the floor and knelt down next to the hole to retrieve the diary, but to his surprise the ledger was gone. He jerked out his penlight and shined it into the hole looking in all directions under the floor, but to no avail. Some unseen force had stolen the text, but it did not matter, he had already read what Johana had written. Standing up, he shook his head in awe, turned and walked out of the room.

Making his way through the basement and up the stairs, he soon found himself inside the back stage area looking up at the trap door that led into the attic. The back stage room was about twenty feet long by ten feet wide and the walls were painted black. Anchored to the middle of the north wall sat the steel ladder that led up to the attic. A rusty lock hung from the hinge of the trap door, preventing entry into the area. Carl looked around the room for something to break the lock, and, to his amazement, he saw a hammer lying on a cardboard box in the corner of the room. It was almost as if someone was helping him, and if that was the case; it had to be Buck or Johana.
Fear of the unknown began knotting up inside Carl as his courage dwindled, but he was compelled to complete his task. He walked over, picked up the hammer, and then moved back to the

ladder. He mounted the rungs and climbed to the top, striking the lock over and over until it finally gave way to his hammering blows, swinging out of the hasp and falling to the floor with a loud clunk.

"Here goes nothing," he muttered. He stuffed the handle of the hammer into his hip pocket then pushed upon the door. The rusty hinges squeaked through the room as if announcing his arrival.

He cautiously raised his head past the cobwebs into the opening, and then climbed through the square hole, disappearing into the pitch black of the attic. He pulled his penlight out of his shirt pocket and pushed the switch, aiming the tiny beam in front of him. Except for the artificial illumination in his hand, the light was gone. Everything seemed lifeless. It was as if he had stepped into another world...another time. The large, lonely chamber smelled of stale, humid, wet rot, and it was oppressively hot from the sun baking against the black roof.

The area was huge. Except for the insulation tucked neatly between each wooden joist, there was nothing but empty space. The overhead rafters lined the attic above his head disappearing into the floor on both sides.

He waited for what seemed an eternity for something to appear, but there was nothing—no evil spirits, no entity, nothing at all. He inspected every inch in all directions, spying a small doorway some twenty feet or so at the end of a two foot wide catwalk in front of him.

Easing his way across the small passageway, he knelt down and looked through the doorway into the cubicle. Reaching for the rungs, he climbed through the opening and descended inside. Noticing a spotlight mounted on a tripod and a small window, he squatted down and found himself looking out at the deserted stage and dance floor below. He had found the spotlight room. Carl wondered to himself why he had never came up here before but he quickly dismissed that thought. He searched the small alcove, directing his beam of light at some old boxes in the left corner. He Sat down near one of the boxes and began sorting through old menus, invoices and other old papers. A rush of excitement over took him when he found the remaining part of the diary in the bottom of the box. Even the air seemed to hold its breath.

"This is it," he whispered in excitement. He quickly thumbed through the dusty pages that had yellowed with age until he came to the first entry.

"Today is Tuesday," Carl read aloud. "My father and I have had another argument. He told me to stay away from Robert. He said this would be his final warning. I don't know what I'm going to do. He said he would kill him. I would rather be dead than be without Robert.

Carl felt he had violated Johana by reading her personal diary, but he had to continue. After all, he was elated to find he was not crazy. This spirit, Johana, was indeed a true being, someone of the past, not a figment of his imagination. Carl began wiping beads of sweat from his forehead as he sat in the hot, humid shadows of the small room reading Johana's notes.

"It's after seven in the evening and I'm sick to my stomach," the diary continued. "I've been vomiting everyday for at least a week. I know what's wrong with me. I'm pregnant with Robert's child. If my father finds out, he'll kill me. Robert and I are going to sneak off together, soon. We're going to Chicago where Robert has a friend who is a talent agent. He is going to get Robert a job singing in an all night Cabaret and help him pursue his singing career. We are going to get a small flat, and Robert is going to sing six nights a week. I don't want to keep dancing as a chorus girl. I need to find an easier job. Being pregnant, I won't take any chances."

Carl's light flickered as the old batteries began to weaken, but he squinted and read on: "We have to be careful not to let my father know where we're going. He would hunt us down and kill both of us. He's insane. My father would do anything to keep me from Robert. He said that Robert Randall was a no count bum. He always calls him by his full name. I call him by the pet name I gave him, Robbie. He laughs at me when I do this. We love each other so much."

Turning to the next page, Carl wondered if he would find anything of value. The sweat continued beading on his flushed face and dripped to the floor as he read on.

"It's Friday now. Robbie and I are going to sneak off after he sings his last song tonight. I have everything packed for our trip. I can't wait to get out of here. I want to get as far away from my father as possible. I can't believe the day has finally come for me to escape his cruelty."

Pausing momentarily, Carl looked around the room. He felt something watching him, waiting, but nothing was there—at least nothing he could see. Turning to the next page, he continued reading and realized something bad must have happened to Johana. Her neat handwriting had turned to scribble, and old watermarks filled the page as though her tears had fallen onto the paper and smeared her writing before the ink could dry. Repeating the barely legible words aloud, Carl continued:

"I went to Robbie's dressing room and knocked over and over. No one answered, so I turned the doorknob and walked inside. He wasn't there. The blue shirt he had been wearing was on the floor, ripped all the way up the back. It was covered with blood. I know my father has killed Robbie. He'll rot in Hell for doing this."

Once again, Carl shook his light as the batteries continued to weaken and the beam flickered bright, then dim. Continuing on, the diary read:

"I don't know what to do. We were getting out of here. I'll never leave now. I'll kill my father and myself. I don't have a life without Robbie. This child inside me has no future without her daddy. I know it's a girl. I'm going to kill my father. He's a rotten, paid killer. He and Red have shot three or four men that I know of. They killed Tony in here two weeks ago over a lousy gambling debt."

Realizing he had proof of actual murders inside these walls, Carl became really involved, turning quickly to the next page.

"They took Tony's body down to the basement and carried him through the tunnel to the river. They don't think I know about the tunnel. They use it to bring illegal moonshine into this place. They think everyone is stupid. They get their bootleg whiskey sent here by boat up the Licking River. I can't believe they haven't been caught, all the times they have docked the boat and carried off stuff through the tunnel. Well, I'll see they get caught now. I'm going to write a letter to the government and tell them about the secret tunnel these fine upstanding men use at night. I'm going to tell them about the dead men they hauled to the middle of the Ohio River and dumped over board. I think they have buried some bodies in the basement. They filled in an old cistern with concrete instead of just covering it over. I wish Buck was still here. He was a kind man. My father had Red ran him off. They forced him to sell this place to their boss. They would have killed him if he had continued refusing their demands."

"It's the bartender!" Carl told himself. "His name was Buck!" Curiosity mounted into a compelling need to know as he continued reading.

"If I knew where Buck was I would tell him everything I know about my father and his friends. I heard Buck tell my father he would return here someday and get revenge. Buck swore this place would never thrive as a gambling casino again. If there is justice, he'll return, and I sure hope he does. I'm going to take poison and leave this life, after I poison my father. If there is life after death, I'll walk this place until my Robert returns for me."

Turning the page, Carl was astonished to find only blank paper.

"No way!" he groaned. "This can't be all! Johana must have written more than this!"

Quickly thumbing through the empty pages, Carl discovered more notes near the end of the book and continued reading Johana's last written words.

"It's Sunday now. I don't have much time to write this down. I did it. I poisoned my father. I sat at the kitchen table and watched him pour three cups of coffee. He drank every drop. He always drinks four or five cups in the morning. I drank a cup with him. We are both doomed. The poison is working on me. I can barely see to write this down.

"My eyes are blurred. I waited until he fell to the floor. I told him I poisoned him and he was going to rot in Hell. He laughed and told me he had sold his soul to the Devil and he would be here forever. He said he would control me in death, as he has in life. He told me the well was used as a gateway to and from Hell. I didn't understand what he was talking about. He said the well was the tunnel. He told me they found a sealed up well in the basement and climbed to the bottom of it. It was used to drain animal's blood into the river when the place was a slaughterhouse years ago. He and his friends dug from the bottom of the well toward the River, reopening the tunnel. He laughed at me and said he would return from Hell. He said he would keep Robert from me for all eternity. He said the Devil appeared to him in the well and he sold his soul for immortality. He will use the well to come back here. He told me his friends would cover up our deaths just like they've done before. No one will know we ever existed. He told me the well and the Licking River was used for satanic ceremonies because it flows north just like the Nile River. That's not the worst of it! As my father lay on the floor dying, this spirit came out of him and identified himself as Alonzo Walling. He mocked me, saying it was he who entered my father's body and took control of him, making my father kill Robbie. The spirit laughed and told me he and his friend were hung for killing and beheading a girl named Pearl. The spirit of Alonzo said he would make all pregnant women, who entered this place, pay with their lives. He said it was his pal, Scott, who actually killed the girl, but he, too, was hung for the crime, and because of that, all pregnant women would suffer his wrath. He said Pearl's head was buried deep down in the well and that it was a blood sacrifice to Lucifer."

Carl stopped for a brief moment, thinking about what he had just read. Now, he knew who Buck, Alonzo, Pearl, and the other guy were. Everything was coming together like pieces of a puzzle.

Carl sighed, then continued reading:

"I'm going down to the basement and pray over the tunnel in hopes that I can block the evil from coming here again. To whoever finds this book, please find a way to seal the well and keep my father and his friends in Hell. You are my only hope. If my prayers don't work, I'll be his prisoner forever and many more people will suffer their evil wrath. I'll never be with Robert again if you ignore this. My father should be dead by now. My body is trembling from the poison. My mouth is so dry. I don't have much time left. It's funny, I thought I felt my baby move."

Suddenly, Carl stopped reading again. He thought he heard footsteps under the light room. Peering out through the opening, he looked down at the stage and dance floor, but saw no one. He felt an overpowering eeriness swelling deep inside his body. It was as if he knew something was watching him, waiting...waiting to strike out at just the right moment. Although frightened, he continued reading the diary.

"It's raining outside. I can hear raindrops beating against the roof. I'm going to the basement and do what I can to stop my father and his evil. I'm taking the cover of this book and a few pages with me. If you have found this part of my diary, look in the basement for the other half. I'll try to write down what happens, if I can. I'm looking at the words I just wrote on the wall. Please, Robert, come back for me. The words make me want to cry. I have to go now or I won't have the strength to walk to the basement. I can't wait any longer. Please help me. I need your help. My love is powerful. I'll find a way to come back and be with Robbie if you, whoever you are, will only help me. Please...I beg you...help me. If I fail, you must seal the well."

That was it. Carl read every word that Johana had written down. He wiped a single tear from his left eye as he thought of the terrible agony the poor woman had endured.

Suddenly he recalled something Johana had written concerning words on the wall. He searched the panels with his failing penlight and found the faded poem over top of the spotlight window. Grief overtook him as he recited the pale words left on the wall by Johana:

> My love is as deep as the sea
> that flows forever.
> You ask me when would it end,
> I tell you never
>
> My love is as bright as the
> sun that shines forever.
> You ask me when will it end,
> I tell you never.
>
> But I will be waiting here
> with my heart in my hand.
>
> My love, I love you so much.
> You ask me when will it end,

I tell you never.

My love is till you die.
My heart cries out from Hell.
I will be waiting here.

As Carl finished reading the mournful words on the wall, the room became calm...quiet as a bottomless tomb. He stood motionless, trembling in the sudden wave of deafening silence that surrounded him.

All at once a startling, screeching noise from the attic caused Carl to beam his flickering light in front of his sweaty face. He slowly opened the spotlight room door and some them waiting for him. Screaming out in a leap of staggering fear, he found himself gazing directly at a colony of bats hanging from the overhead rafters in the attic outside the spotlight room.

"Where in the hell did they come from?" he groaned.

The filthy creatures of the night began flapping their wings, causing a harmonic sound as if they had come together in some sort of hellish, musical covenant. The terrifying concerto caused Carl to wonder if the bats were actually playing some sort of evil song for Satan himself. Just then the spotlight room became intensely cold and papers in the boxes began flying and twirling around the room as if they had been seized up by a miniature tornado.

He quickly climbed out of the room and cautiously moved back across the catwalk toward the trap door. He knew in only second, these winged creatures would drop from the beams to take flight, attacking him the very moment they stopped in their horrible, wing flapping music.

He slowly moved halfway across the catwalk, when once again, silence fell over the attic. He dropped through the square opening feet first, grabbing the top of the ladder with his left hand as his feet smacked against the rungs beneath him. Sticking the diary in his mouth, he gripped the ladder with both hands, scurrying downward, while hearing the flapping of the wings once again.

The bats had taken flight, and he knew they would be soaring through the trap door above his head in a matter of seconds. Just as his feet touched the floor the colony of bats rocketed through the opening about his head. Terrified, he ran from the stage, fleeing for his life. The sound of teeth gnashing and wings flapping echoed through the quiet building as he ran for cover. The bats grew closer, and those god-awful gasping sounds returned from inside the walls as he fled like a scared rabbit, the hammer falling out of his pocket and smashing onto the floor.

Hideous laughter came from the Casino Room as he frantically pushed his way through a restroom door near the bar, closing it behind him. He listened quietly as the bats smashed against the door that stood between him and death. The filthy things, one by one, attached their bodies to the portal and began grinding their razor sharp teeth in the tan upholstery that covered the door.

Carl gripped the swinging door with all his strength, holding the bats outside of the restroom until he could figure a way out of this situation. As he stood there, holding onto the handle of the door, the toilet suddenly flushed, causing him to jerk his head around toward the stalls.

"Who's there?" he demanded to know, his voice loud and strained. "I know someone's there! Come on out! What's the matter?...You afraid to show yourself?"

He knew better than to walk away from the door to check the stall. He was not about to take a chance on his grubby, little friends getting at him. He was in a serious predicament and he knew it. Then, from out of nowhere, a thick, black billowing smoke appeared, quickly filling the room. He slid to the floor with his back to the door as the shadow of a man appeared inside the dense smoke.

"Who are you?" Carl cried out. "Is it you, Buck? Help me!"

Through the smoke came laughter, then a diabolical whisper, "No, it's not Buck. He can't help you! No one can help you now!"

"Who are you, ... you son-of-a-bitch? Tell me!"

"The name's Red!" the man answered in a gravely, hellish tone.

Before the man's words could fade away the sound of a dog barking came from outside the door, and instantly, the threatening stranger stopped dead in this tracks.

"Stay out of this, Buck!" Red screamed. "You and the dog will pay if you don't!"

Looking away from Red for a split second, Carl cried out, his voice almost pleading. "Buck! Help me! I'm in here!"

"No one can help you! And I mean no one!" The ghostly enemy moved through the smoke toward Carl just as flames shot up from the wooden floor. Carl knew there was no escape this time. The bats were outside the door, and the room was becoming engulfed in fire. Just as things seemed to be going from bad to worse, the door suddenly pushed open, sliding the doomed young man across the floor toward the flames and this new entity that had been ready to snatch up Carl's very soul.

Turning toward the door, trembling, Carl readied himself to meet his fate, but, to his surprise, the ghostly figure known to him as Buck, stepped into the restroom. A large black Chow, with red, glowing eyes stood beside him. Buck faced the man called Red, his eyes boring straight ahead at the sinister apparition before him.

"I beat you once!" Buck said with vengeance. "And I'll do it again!" Buck looked down and smiled at Carl, who was still sitting on the floor. He placed an object in the young man's hand, the ordered him to leave the building. Carl quickly peered through the doorway and found that the bats had vanished. Then the big dog clenched its teeth gently on Carl's wrist, tugging at him in an attempt to lead him from the restroom. Up and on his feet, Carl raced across the barroom floor, through the swinging doors and down the hallway exploding out of the front entrance of the building. Once safely outside, he peered through the glass door panes and saw the black dog standing at the other end of the mirrored hall. The animal had made sure Carl escaped. The dog turned and disappeared out of sight, back toward the restroom, as Carl stood there, motionless, lost in a horrifying fairy tale come true.

Chapter Fourteen

It took Carl several days to remember in detail what happened next, but after going over it time and time again, he swears this is what happened.

* * * * *

"Dammit!" Carl shrieked out as he clenched both hands around the vase that Buck had given him and realized that he had left the diary inside the restroom. A look of disbelief, rage and frustration etched his face, since he had left the only evidence of Johana's existence behind to burn in the fury of the flames.

He took a deep breath then stared down at the vase. It was black, with a devil's face on it. It had two piercing, emerald eyes. He had no idea what to do with it, but he figured it had to serve some purpose.

As he stared deeply into the two, almost hypnotic orbs embedded in the vase, the front doors suddenly burst open, causing him to look up and squint his eyes toward the open hallway.

"It's that dog," he told himself as he watched the animal come down the hall toward the entrance.

The black canine stopped in the doorway and motioned with its head for the man to follow it.

Carl stepped through the entranceway and hated himself for even thinking about going back in the building, but he could not stop himself. He took slow, careful steps up the hallway and gently pushed through the double swinging doors, moving into the main barroom.

Maybe Buck needs me, he thought quietly as he inched himself toward the restroom. What if something had happened to his ghostly friend? After all, he had run away, leaving Buck to face that evil being by himself.

He stopped at the end of the bar just as a murmuring cloud appeared in front of him, congealing from the stale air itself. A glowing pulse, deep and forceful like a heartbeat, came from the globular haze dominating his vision.

The vapor rotated slowly, hesitantly, as Carl's eyes remained fixed on it. Suddenly, this unexplainable form of energy shot through the room over his head and disappeared into the men's restroom. He followed the cloud without hesitation, and, for some strange reason, he was not afraid anymore. A deep, genuine sense of relief came over him as he stepped through the door and saw the ghostly figure of Buck standing in the middle of the room. The flames were gone but the smell of smoke filled the room almost choking Carl.

Trying not to breathe the lingering smoke Carl told himself what was taking place was real—all too real! He could not blame these sights on some hallucinogenic chemicals. Recent events had troubled him, and he had tried to tell himself it was the Jack Daniels, but not this time. Coming to grips with reality, he realized he really was looking at a ghost. He looked down at the vase in his hand and then back at Buck.

"What's going on in here?" he asked apprehensively as he approached the specter. "I can't take much more of this!"

"Carl, Johana's a prisoner in Hell!" Buck answered. "The well in the basement holds her captive. Alonzo, Scott, and Johana's father are going to lure Robbie, who you know as Bobby, down to the basement. If he goes into the China Room, he'll be killed—his life destroyed once again. They don't just want Janet and her baby. They want Bobby, too!"

"What can I do? I'm just an ordinary guy," Carl asked in a thick, clotty voice. "You need an exorcist!"

"You have to seal the well and see that if remains sealed. Otherwise, the evil will lure some unsuspecting soul down there to release it once again."

"Is Bobby Mackey, Johana's lover returned from the grave?" Carl asked.

"Yes."

"What happened to Johana's diary?" Carl needed answers.

"It's gone, consumed by the fires of Hell."

"Was what I read all true?"

"Yes. This place was a slaughterhouse years ago. It was chosen as Satan's unholy ground because of the blood that was spilled here. It drained down into the well, and a secret cult of devil Worshipers conjured up Satan from that bloody hole. People were murdered, and parts of their bodies were thrown down there as a blood sacrifice to the Devil. In 1896 a girl named Pearl Bryan was murdered and beheaded by her boyfriend, Scott Jackson, and another man, Alonzo Walling, because she was pregnant. They killed her in Ft. Thomas, but disposed of her head in the well. Both men were hung for their deed. Neither of them would tell the whereabouts of her head because the world would have learned that they were Devil Worshipers. Had they told, the well would have been sealed, and Satan would have taken revenge on them. Scott and Alonzo's evil spirits walk this place, as well as Pearl. Pearl will never have peace until that well is prayed over and sealed. Once this is done, we'll be able to lead you to the woman's head in time. If you get that far, you'll have to see that her skull is buried with her body. We'll worry about that later."

"Will Bobby ever get to be with Johana if I seal the well?" Carl wanted to know. "Will Johana try to harm Janet and her baby if she is set free? What about Bobby and Janet's daughter, Anita? Will she be safe if I do this?"

"Johana would never do anything to harm Bobby or his family," Buck replied. "It's Johana's father, Alonzo and Scott who tried to kill Janet. They're the evil ones. Alonzo Walling made a threat just before he and Scott Jackson were hung for Pearl's murder. He said he'd come back to haunt the area and he kept his word. The well is like a magnet for evil spirits. They are drawn here to worship Satan and do his bidding. Johana's love is eternal. She only wants to be next to him. She may try to enter Janet's body from time to time only to be with Bobby for a little while. This will only happen if Janet allows it. I think she would if you tell her everything. Yes, Bobby will see her in time, but only after he fulfills his dream. Someday she'll appear to him while he's singing before a crowd, and he'll remember the love they shared years ago. But this won't happen until the time is right. When it is... you'll know it. Just remember what I've said— when the time is right, you'll tell this story to a man of our choosing, and he'll tell the world. The man will be Gemini. He will come from the dark side, but he will have crossed over to the light by then. We'll guide him to you if you defeat the unholy one."

As Buck finished speaking, the black dog appeared behind Carl showing its teeth and growling profoundly, warning Buck of some impending danger. Buck stared toward the main barroom for a brief second, then turned back toward Carl.

"They're going to kill Bobby and Janet's baby!" Buck exclaimed, with alarm in his voice. "You have to hurry if we're going to save that child. Take that vase and go home. Call every clairvoyant you can find. Tell them everything that's happened in here, but don't tell them about the vase. Wait for one of them to tell you that you need it to seal the well. You'll know what to do then. Follow their instructions, and you can defeat this evil. Go! Get out of here, now! They haven't stopped me from telling you this story because they're after the baby's soul! I should have known something was wrong when they didn't interfere. "Evil took this place from me and I'm back for my revenge. I told them I'd return someday and I have! I'll never allow an evil man to stay under this roof as long as I remain. Go! You have to get going now or that baby's doomed!"

Buck and his dog vanished from sight. Carl ran for the front door, still clutching the vase tightly as though his life depended on it. He had no idea what was going on at the hospital. He simply knew he had to do as Buck said. If this ghostly man was right, Janet's baby was in grave danger, and, even though Carl was not a rough, tough redneck who was beyond fear, he knew he had to save the Mackey child. He did not know exactly what to do, but he hoped he would find out by following Buck's instructions.

Chapter Fifteen

After talking with Carl about what happened next, he said that he could not remember the exact details, but to the best of his recollection, this is what happened.

* * * * *

Face sweaty and lungs gasping, Carl raced through the front door of his home and began fumbling for the phone book. His heart pounded like the beat of a bass drum. He placed his hand on his chest and took a slow, deep breath while quickly thumbing through the yellow pages, looking for someone who could help him drive the evil out of the nightclub.

He did not know how to spell "clairvoyant," but he got lucky and found the listing anyway. He hurriedly called three people, telling them of his unbelievable tale, but none of them could help him. One suggested he call a priest, and another told him to seek medical attention as he was mentally ill. The third told him to try calling a woman who lived along the river. She gave him the telephone number.

He thanked her and hung up. He dialed the phone number she had given him and hoped the person who would answer this call would have the answers he so desperately needed.

"Come on, lady! Answer the phone," he grumbled to himself. "Seven rings!...eight...Damn! Please be home!"

Expelling a sigh of frustration, he continued counting the rings. "Twelve, thirteen, fourteen. That's it! I give up," he growled disgustedly when all at once a voice came through the receiver.

"Hello." A woman's voice came through the line.
"Please listen to me!" Carl almost screamed through the phone. "Whatever you do, don't hang up!...I'm not a nut! I've got to find someone who can help me before it's too late! I...

"Slow down," she interrupted. "I'm not going to hang up. I can't help you unless you slow down and start from the beginning."

Listening to her crackling voice, he pictured her as an old, wrinkled lady, probably ninety or more, with white hair. She admonished him to remain silent until she finished speaking and began reciting words in a language that he could not understand. When she finished uttering the estrange words, she turned her attention back to him and spoke in English.

"Okay. It's your turn! They can't stop you from talking to me now."

Carl tried to tell her his story, but, as he did, loud hissing sounds, mixed with static came through the phone line, irritating his ear. "Do you hear that?" he asked. "Do you hear those sounds?"

"Don't worry about it," she replied. "I told you they can't stop you from speaking to me."

"Who can't?" Carl wanted to know, but deep down inside him he already knew that answer.

"You know who I'm talking about," the woman stated quite frankly. "Now tell me what it is you need of me."

In a matter of minutes, he had told her almost everything that had happened. As he finished speaking, she told him to find a vase, but not just and ordinary vase, she said it had to have the Devil's face on it.

Tears welled up in Carl's eyes when she spoke of the Devil's vase. This was indeed the person Buck had talked about. He knew he had found help at last.

"Bring me the vase, and I'll help you," she said. "You don't have much time. That evil in there has grown for many years. It has developed like a baby in its mother's womb, and now it's ready to be born. It's able to leave the building now. That's why some force took control of your car, almost killing you. It will not be contained much longer. The dark side will lure your friend there tonight. He'll be killed this very evening if that force isn't stopped. You must find the vase."

"I've got the vase!" Carl interrupted in a shout, his voice like that of someone who had jumped out in the street and roared for a taxi. "Buck, the ghost, gave it to me. Can I come over to your house right now?"

No!" You'll never find the place," she replied. "Meet me on the river bank where the two rivers meet at midnight. Bring a bottle of Holy Water and the vase. I'll be waiting for you."

Just then the phone went dead, causing Carl to cry out, "No! Don't hang up! What two rivers? Damn! She hung up!"

He quickly dialed the woman's phone number again, but to his surprise he got a recording.

"I'm sorry. The number you have dialed is not in service at this time."

A sudden, almost instant state of fear and confusion took control of Carl's thoughts as he stared helplessly at the black telephone. He felt everything go silent inside him. He was like a helpless child who had stumbled onto something that he could not understand.

Chapter Sixteen

Once again, Carl had difficulty remembering every detail as to what happened next, but after talking about this next turn of events, this is how I interpret what happened.

* * * * *

Carl checked his wristwatch periodically while contemplating his next move. He thought of the woman who would meet him on the riverbank this same evening. Her voice had been soft and confident; she seemed calm and unafraid, but that was on the phone. He hoped she was the right person to help him.

He had to assume the woman meant for him to meet her at the mouth of the Licking River where it fed into the Ohio. At least that was where he would go in search of her and the answers he needed. Several hours passed before he walked from his white frame house and climbed into his car, placing the vase beside him in the front seat.

Driving south on Route 9 to St.John's church, he fumbled under the seat with his right hand, steering the car with the other. He pulled empty candy wrappers, potato chip bags, and soft drink cans from under the seat, finally dragging out a small, empty pint bottle and bringing it up to his face.

"This'll have to do," he exclaimed. "I'll put the Holy Water in this. It's all I've got."

He pulled his car into the parking lot of the desolate, gray stone Catholic Church and stared into the semi-darkness, saying a silent prayer before leaving the safety of his car. He got out of the automobile and walked over to the concrete steps that led up to the double oak doors. He gripped the black handrail and paused briefly, looking up at the cloudless night sky. He noticed the full moon lit his way as though God had shined a guiding light for him. Dismissing the thought, he walked up the steps and went inside the church. He crossed himself and moved to the white, porcelain stand that was filled with Holy Water. He submerged the bottle and waited patiently as bubbles rose to the surface. Once the container was filled, he pulled it out of the liquid and screwed the lid back on. Checking his watch and almost deploring it, he knew it was time to meet the Gypsy woman along the rivers' edge. He knelt down and said the Catholic act of contrition, then stood to his feet and headed back outside to his car.

Driving north on Route 9, he passed by the club on his way to the river, and tried to assure himself that everything would be okay, but deep inside, he felt a sickening terror of what might happen when he re-entered the nightclub.

Thoughts of some demon swallowing his soul flashed in and out of his mind as he turned the wheel of his automobile, bringing it to a stop on a small dead end street that ran parallel with the Ohio River. Stepping from the car, he paused briefly, looking at the weeds and thicket, and listened to the splashing of waves against the riverbank some seventy feet away.

Before him in the dark shadows of the night loomed a small grove of trees, the moonlight filtering through the branches and casting long, eerie shadows onto the ground. He felt the threatening hostility of evil surrounding him once again and felt as if he was being watched by a thousand tiny, unseen eyes. He slowly entered the thicket, moving toward the river, and felt the night fall down upon him. It seemed that everything in the brush came alive, yet nothing lived, not even him.

Reaching a clearing, Carl stepped onto the top of a rock pile that towered some ten feet above the wet riverbank. As he edged his way across the slippery, moss-covered rocks, his right foot slipped into a hole, causing him to lose his balance. Pin wheeling his arms, he fell forward and rolled down the hillside to the muddy trail below. As his body came to rest along the riverbank, he grabbed his right ankle with both hands, screaming out in pain.

"I've broke my damn foot!" he groaned. "What in the hell's next?"

He sat up along the river's edge and untied his dirty, white gym shoe, inspecting the damage to his swollen ankle. The water splashed against him as he sat gripping his leg with both hands. The pain was instant and excruciating, causing him to become nauseous.

Suddenly, a dark shadow towered over Carl's body, causing him to forget the pain for one split second. Quickly turning and looking over his left shoulder, he looked up and saw a heavy set, white-haired gypsy woman, probably in her eighties standing behind him. She was exactly as he had imagined her to be. The woman knelt down beside him and spoke in a soft whisper.

"You must be Carl. I saw you fall. Let me check your leg."
He sat quietly staring at the woman as she carefully estimated the damage to his ankle. She moved her hands slowly up and down his leg.

"It's not broke," she said with a soft, warm voice. "It's a bad sprain, but you have to ignore it. You've got a long night ahead of you. Here, let me help you up."

The woman extended her hand and helped Carl to his feet, and surprisingly, his nausea seemed to fade away. Favoring his injury, he hobbled to a nearby tree and leaned against the trunk while the woman pulled some wild plants from the moist soil. She walked over to him and knelt down, rubbing the green leaves on his leg and ankle. For some strange reason, this seemed to relieve the pain, sending a tepid, soothing sensation throughout the extremity and allowing him to stand evenly on both feet.

In a matter of seconds the pale expression faded from his face and the pain greatly diminished. He reached into his back pocket and grabbed the bottle filled with the Holy Water and found it still intact. His fall had not shattered it, but all at once, he let out a desperate cry.

"Where's the vase? I dropped the vase! I had it with me when I fell." His voice began to break. "I've done it now! If anything happens to Bobby and his family, it'll be my fault!"

"It's okay! I've got it!" she exclaimed. "I saw it fly into the water when you fell over the rocks."

She placed her right hand into her red, nylon jacket and pulled the vase out, giving it to Carl. "It's time to get started. There's no time to lose." She sounded ominous. "Listen, and remember everything I say."

Staring directly into Carl's eyes, the old Gypsy began her instructions to this man who would soon face evil in its worst form. "You must pour the Holy Water into this vase and say the Lord's Prayer while you stand over the well."

She paused briefly, then pulled a small envelope from her pocket and gave it to Carl. "After you complete the prayer, pour this packet of powder into the vase," she continued. "Once you've done this, pour the contents of the vase over the well, allowing it to fall into the opening. At that moment, rebuke the devil by repeating these words, 'I rebuke you, Satan, and seal you in Hell for all Eternity.' Remember those words," she emphasized. "It must be said exactly as I have stated. Once you've done this, it'll be over. Don't be fooled, my darling man. From the very moment you enter the building, your life will be in grave danger. The evil will come at you in every way imaginable. Once you walk inside, there'll be no turning back. The dark side will try every evil trick, even beyond your wildest dreams. I can't tell you what they'll do, but I can safely say they'll do anything within their power to stop you. If you lose your faith for one moment, Satan himself will devour your soul. Expect the worst from this enemy. They know you're coming. There isn't anything else for me to say, except I'll be praying for you. One other thing, if you succeed, pray for the soul of Pearl so her spirit may rest in peace. There are many unrested, earthbound spirits in that well, including a girl named Nellie. Pearl's head must be found, but that will only happen after you seal the well and bind the evil where it belongs. It's time for you to get going. The evil one is luring your friend to that place even as I speak."

As the woman's words faded away she turned and quickly walked into the shadows of the night, disappearing from Carl's sight. At first, he thought she had merely gone to get something, but then it hit him. She was not coming back.

"Wait! How did you know about Pearl?" Carl yelled out as he limped up the riverbank looking for the Gypsy woman, who had vanished as quickly as she had appeared. "I didn't tell you about her. Wait! Don't go yet! What about your phone? It was disconnected after I talked to you? Who's Nellie?"

Carl searched the darkness with his eyes, waiting for a response that never came. She was gone, leaving him to sort out his thoughts and prepare for the most terrifying experience of his life. He turned and clawed his way up the moonlit riverbank and headed for his encounter with evil. He had no idea what was waiting for him inside Bobby Mackey's Music World, but one thing was certain: he was determined to stop this "thing" from destroying his friends.

Chapter Seventeen

After talking with Carl many times about what happened next, I found it incredible that his thoughts were more on Bobby than on what might be waiting for him to arrive at the nightclub. This is what he remembered.

* * * * *

Reaching his car, Carl climbed inside and started the engine. He looked into the rear view mirror and screamed in sheer terror when he saw the faint image of a decayed corpse with a rope around its neck sitting in the seat grinning at him.

He screamed again, spinning his head around at the same time, and was relieved when all he saw was empty space. "Oh, God!" he moaned as he jerked the gearshift into reverse and backed the car up the road. He knew the apparition was a warning, but his decision had already been made. He was going to that building to defeat the evil.

Carl drove toward the nightclub. His palms felt clammy against the steering wheel. Fear of the unknown knotted and writhed in his stomach. His thoughts were of Bobby and of all the things that had happened to this warm-hearted man since he had taken ownership of the club. It seemed strange to Carl that the two previous owners had experienced their own problems, but none so bizarre as these.

Thinking back, he remembered being with Bobby on one particular occasion when a dirty wino approached them asking for some money to get a meal in his stomach. He remembered Bobby reaching into his pocket and handing the vagrant a five-dollar bill. Carl found this to be very surprising.

"Why in the world did you give that bum any money?" Carl had asked. "Especially five dollars! He'll just go get a bottle of cheap wine!"

Bobby's reply was that of a tender, caring man. "It doesn't matter what he does with the money, Carl. It's the idea that a man asked for help and we didn't turn our backs on him. My father taught me to extend my hand to anyone who needs help. My dad fed many a railroad hobo when they passed by his store in Concord. What you do for another person will always be given back to you."

This was the first time Bobby had shown his tender heartedness to the handyman. Carl had previously thought of him as "all business" until that day.

As Carl continued driving toward the nightclub, he thought about the stress that Bobby had endured due to the fire and other problems hampering the opening of the business. One particular incident stuck in his mind. One night, Bobby was driving to a nightclub between Hamilton and Franklin, Ohio, where he was hired to sing that evening, when chest pains became so severe that he pulled into a gas station where an Emergency Medical Vehicle was being serviced. He had the paramedics examine him as he sat on the rear bumper of the ambulance. Fortunately, it was not a heart problem, just too much stress.

Because of all the things that had gone wrong, from the very first week Bobby took possession of the building, he certainly did not need to hear about demons and devil spirits haunting his place. Since Bobby did not believe in ghosts, it was probably better that he did not know what was about to take place.

As Carl's thoughts drifted away, the car turned the last curve leading to the nightclub, the headlights shining directly at the massive building. He brought the car to a halt in front of the main entrance and looked up through the front windshield. He could have sworn that he saw two red eyes staring back at him, as if they were daring the man to come inside.

Stepping from the auto, Carl paused and listened as the sound of crickets filled the still night air, and a bullfrog croaked in the woods near the river. The familiar lightning bugs flickered their tiny lights off and on, and hordes of flying insects resumed their nightly ritual of bombarding each other under the lights, as an occasional bat dove into the dogfight in search of its dinner. The dark and lonely place that he had named 'Hell's Gate' seemed perfectly normal.

Chapter Eighteen

When speaking with Carl about what occurred next, he had no difficulty in remembering what happened. He did not have to think very hard to recall that night. It was apparent that what had taken place would always be easily retrievable from somewhere in the back of his mind.

* * * * *

The door squeaked a menacing hello, as Carl pulled it open and stepped through. He placed his hands against his pockets, feeling the bottle in one and the vase in the other. They were both intact, and he intended to keep them that way. He took a long hard swallow, then disappeared up the dark mirrored hallway leading to the main barroom.

He cautiously ambled up to the bar, stopping at the end closest to the door. Jesus! I've got to get out of here, he thought as he suddenly became aware of some giant, unseen force coming toward him. He turned and started to run down the hallway in an attempt to leave the building, but, before he reached the threshold, invisible hands slammed against his chest, blocking his escape from the bedeviled prison. Remembering the Gypsy woman's warning, Carl forced a sheepish smile in an attempt to hide his fear from this unperceivable foe. He slowly backed toward the barroom, tying to swallow the hard lump of fear stuck tightly in his throat, until he finally found himself once again in the confines of the unlit barroom.

He backed up against the end of the bar and felt a sense of aloneness overwhelming him for a brief moment, but, as he stood there staring straight ahead, the hall doors abruptly swung open, then slammed shut.

"Here we go again," he told himself as the glass-paneled doors began swinging violently to and fro. His instincts told him to run for all he was worth, but he knew the evil inside the building was not going to let him get away this time.

Carl turned and headed into the ballroom, but, just as he stepped inside the chamber, some massive force wrapped its invisible arms around him, jerking him up and off the floor.

He began fighting, wildly swinging at the air as the entity squeezed him tighter, then lifted him higher into the air. He kicked, screamed, and flung his arms furiously, fighting back with all his might.

"The Holy Water!" he suddenly remembered as the demon violently swung his dangling body back and forth, as if he was nothing but a mere puppet suspended by a strong wire. He quickly slipped his hand into his pocket and brought out the bottle, unscrewing the lid as fast as he could. He raised the container out in front of his face, and then splashed some of the liquid over his head, the Holy Water dousing the beast. The creature gave out a blood-curdling howl, the high-pitched shriek echoing throughout the entire building as it released its grip.

Carl fell to his feet and quickly spun around facing the menacing monster before him. There it was, right before his bulging eyes. The creature stood seven feet tall. It had the body of a man, but two protruding female breasts hung down from its chest. The body was covered with thick, white, coarse, animal-like hair. Its head appeared to be half goat, half man. The beast stood there, staring at Carl, baring its yellow-stained, canine teeth, its gums exposing the fangs to the roots. Carl raised the bottle of Holy Water high over his head, and, with one quick motion, he splashed more of the liquid onto the beast. As the Holy Water made contact with the monster's face, the behemoth let out another horrifying, breath-taking howl. Its flesh began falling from its head in wet, oozing chunks, hair and all.

The monster continued growling and crying out in undeniable agony. Hunks of meat continued falling to the floor with a series of wet smacks as the creature raised a bony, skeletal finger, pointing it at Carl and slowly backed away from the man.

"You'll die!" it snarled in a terrifying, low, raspy whisper as it sucked itself into a large mirror that hung on the south wall of the ballroom. At that instant, Carl felt more frightened and alone than he had ever been in his entire life.

Once the demon was gone, Carl turned and searched the floor for the lid to seal the remaining Holy Water in the bottle. Spying the cap, he quickly bent down, grabbed it and screwed it back on.

He stood there completely silent, staring into the empty room, his heart pounding. His eyes were wide and bulging, his throat thick and dry. It was impossible to swallow the fear that was spreading in him like a raging fire in a dry pine tree forest. His heart still slamming back and forth like a pendulum against the inside wall of his chest, he timidly approached the front entrance, taking slow, careful steps.

As he neared the front door, another sound assaulted his ears, a thunderous earthquake of crashing tables falling, left and right, like a giant plow digging furrows in an open field, followed by the metallic slam-bang of bar stools smashing against the hard, black linoleum floor.

Carl whirled around, his eyes methodically searching the darkness, and he realized something huge, deadly, and imperceptible, without form or feature, was surging its way toward him.

Sweat beaded up on Carl's brow, his thoughts racing like an out-of-control locomotive. His heart was beating wildly against his ribs, pounding the blood through the tips of his fingers and toes.

Regaining his senses, he bolted for the entrance, slamming hard against the front doors, but they did not budge. It was as if they had been welded shut. Carl's chest tightened like a vise, and he sucked in huge gulps of air trying desperately to retrieve the breath that the barricade had savagely knocked out of him.

Carl turned and raced back up the hall in a state of frenzy, rushing into the Fiesta Room opposite the bar. He crossed the room and disappeared through the hall door that led to the Casino Room.

Once inside the hallway, he closed the door and locked the sliding dead bolt firmly into the slot. An incessant pounding, like that of a heartbeat, grew loud and forceful as he stood in the darkened alcove. It sounded like a giant slamming his feet against the ground in a fit of rage. The walls and floor shook as the unseen thing made its way into the Fiesta Room and stopped just outside the locked door.

The door itself seemed to come alive as the entity inhaled and exhaled its breath against it, causing the wooden partition to bend in and out. As Carl stood motionless, locked in a explosion of fear, three panels on his left suddenly sprung open from the wall, revealing hidden passageways behind their plush, tan padding. Confusion mounted as he quickly surveyed the dark recesses before him. Did they lead to safety, or to certain death, he asked himself as the hall door began shaking violently and the dead bolt slammed open with the hammering force of a bolt-action rifle. There was no time to lose! Carl knew the demonic creature was about to come through the door after him, so he crawled into the middle compartment and hid himself inside it.

The very moment he entered the waiting orifice, all three panels slammed shut, concealing their secret existence behind them and leaving Carl swallowed up in the darkness of the lonely chamber. He hurriedly reached into his shirt pocket and pulled out his penlight, surveying the pitch black of the small area. He realized there was no way out except the way he came in.

Carl put his ear to the door. He could not hear any sounds and hoped this meant whatever was chasing him had decided to give up and go away. He put the penlight back in his pocket and pushed his hands against the panel, trying to ease it open just a crack, so he could take a peek to make sure.

He pressed gently against the door, but it did not budge. He pushed harder, but it still would not move. He retrieved his penlight and searched the door jam for a latch of some kind, but could not see one. Panic, once again, began to well up inside him as he rammed his right shoulder against the stubborn board. Failing to get any response, Carl spun around and kicked both feet repeatedly against the door, but to no avail. He was trapped.

"They tricked me! They wanted me to come in here!" he stammered. "Don't lose your cool, Carl. You can get out of this."

He pressed the palms of his hands against his mouth, digging his fingernails into the sweaty flesh under his eyes while staring at the wall helplessly. What's next, he wondered quietly.

Chapter Nineteen

Bobby had no difficulty remembering what happened when he took Janet to the hospital. This is the way he remembers it.

* * * * *

Bobby was at Bethesda Hospital in Cincinnati, awaiting word about his wife and baby's condition. He had a strong, unbending faith that everything would be okay; at least, that is what he kept telling himself.

He was sitting in one of those stiff waiting-room chairs when a middle-aged, heavyset nurse came through the stainless steel doors and walked directly to him. She would surely have some good news, he thought at first, but she was smiling one of those "it's going to be fine" smiles that they must teach doctors and nurses to wear when they are not sure of a patient's condition. Bobby recognized that look right away.

"What is it?" he asked.

"Oh, it's going to be okay!" the brown-eyed nurse replied. "I just came out to tell you your wife is resting now, and the labor has stopped. Why don't you go on home, and we'll call you if there's any change. You look like you could use some sleep. There's no sense in you staying here all night."

Bobby was reluctant to leave his wife, but he was tired, and the nurse assured him they would call if anything happened. It was three thirty-three in the morning when he left the hospital. As he drove toward Kentucky, something came over him, and he felt compelled to go by the nightclub on his way home. There was no explanation for this sudden desire; it was just something he had to do. As he drove closer to the Ohio River, he seemed to sink deeper and deeper into a state of unawareness. His mind was on his wife and child, and yet, on nothing at all. Rubbing his right hand against his sleepy eyes, he drove across the Central Bridge from Ohio into Kentucky.

Driving south on York Street in Newport, he pushed his turn signal on and came to a stop at Eleventh and York then waited for the red light to turn green. Closing his eyes for a brief moment, Bobby sat motionless, his tired body trembling from lack of sleep. He sat in silence until he heard the clink-clack of the traffic light as it changed to green. He opened his eyes and gave a tired yawn, then started to turn the car west on Eleventh Street, heading for the nightclub.

As he turned the corner, a large black Chow dog appeared in front of the car, blocking his way. He honked the horn several times, but the mongrel would not budge.

"Get out of the way, you lousy mutt!" he yelled out the window.

The dog stood its ground, growling and barking, moving back and forth in front of the car, as if it was determined not to let Bobby pass.

"Forget it! I don't need to go to the nightclub anyway," Bobby complained loudly. "I'm going home."

Bobby breathed an exasperated sigh, then wheeled the car around and headed in the opposite direction. "I need to get home in case the hospital calls, anyway," he told himself. His thoughts drifted in and out as he drove toward home. As he passed from Newport into Southgate, traveling south on U.S. 27, he saw flashing lights appear in his rear view mirror. It was a police car, coming up fast, behind him.

"What's next?" he groaned in irritation as he pulled his car to the right side of the road. He got out of the automobile and walked toward the Southgate police officer, expecting a lecture and a ticket.

The thin, dark-haired officer greeted Bobby with a cheerful tone of voice, advising him that he was exceeding the posted speed limit. Bobby explained the situation to the man, and was very surprised when he was told to go on, but to slow down and be careful. He thanked the officer, climbed back in his car and drove for home.

Chapter Twenty

Carl had no difficulty remembering the details of what happened to him as the hellish night continued. This is exactly the way he remembers it.

* * * * *

Carl fought like a crazed maniac, trying to free himself from the hidden chamber inside the wall. He kicked, slammed, beat, pushed and shoved, bruising every bone and muscle in his body. Suddenly realizing something was moving in the darkness behind him, he froze.

"Oh No!" he groaned with a quick breath, realizing that whatever or whoever was in this hidden chamber with him was expelling its breath on his neck, causing the hair at the base of his scalp to stand at rigid attention.

Raging anxiety, like that of a man watching the Grim Reaper appear for his very soul, raced up and down his spine as Carl quickly turned in the darkness to face his fate, beaming his penlight in front of him.

Before Carl's eyes stood a half-dead looking dwarf with decaying, rotting, brown and green teeth. The tiny man was balding, with sunken eyes that glowed a morbid, red. He began laughing at Carl, his voice shrieking through the stale air. The sound of a heartbeat began growing inside the room, becoming so intense that Carl felt his eardrums would burst. The floor and walls suddenly began shaking and vibrating from the compelling pulse that was filling the small chamber and the room filled with a sickening stench.

Carl moved away from the dwarf, sliding his back against the concealed doorway through which he had entered, and, to his surprise, the hidden door instantly swung open, causing him to plummet backwards from the chamber and roll out into the hall.

Carl sprung to his feet, with his fists clenched at his sides, and glared into the black hole, waiting for the dwarf to come after him, but to his amazement, the man was gone, vanished in thin air, just like all the other horrible entities that he had fallen victim to in the past. Carl raised his right foot and slammed it into the padded door, forcing it back into the recessed of the hall.

He thanked God the little man was gone. He didn't like dwarfs anyway. Once, when he was nine years old, he got in a fight with another kid who stomped his butt. He later learned that the tough boy was a sixteen-year-old dwarf. Until then, he had no idea little people like this really existed.

Carl cautiously opened the hall door and stepped into the Fiesta Room, and as he did, clawing and screeching sounds came from the ceiling above his head. Then sounds like that of someone raking their fingernails across the blackboard came from behind the liquor room door. He moved into the barroom and headed toward the stage, ready for his next encounter with the evil spirits from "Hell's Gate!"

Occasionally looking back over his shoulder, Carl made his way behind the stage and cautiously inched his way down the creaking stairs that led to the basement. Just as he reached the landing, he heard heavy footsteps coming down the stairs behind him. He turned and stood motionless, listening, waiting, his eyes staring up the stairwell, but no one appeared. Even though he did not see anyone, it was as if someone was standing on the stairs only a few feet away. Someone pleased with the terror that they had instilled upon him. He wondered how long it would be before the entity would try to finish him off. After what seemed an eternity, he shrugged his shoulders and moved through the main basement heading for the China Room, his eyes ever watchful as he went.

As he reached the China Room, the wooden door swung open striking him in the face and knocking him to the ground. Jumping to his feet, he saw a pot-bellied, bald-headed man who appeared to be fifty or so standing in the doorway.

The man held a meat cleaver in one hand and a large butcher knife in the other. He was clad in a bloody butcher's smock, and he stood there silently, staring at Carl with cold, gray, beady eyes. His pugnacious countenance told Carl he was dealing with more than some guy who liked to play with knives. Without saying a word, the man seemed to be silently daring Carl to come forward, but, when he failed to respond, the devil-in-human form raised the meat cleaver above his head and lunged toward the terrified handyman.

Carl tried to run, but his feet would not move. He closed his eyes and waited for the razor-sharp blade to embed itself in his skull and spill his brains onto the concrete floor. He knew he was about to die, but for some peculiar reason, he almost welcomed it.

"You're not real!" Carl shrieked as he raised his hand up in front of his own face and made the sign of the cross. "Be gone in the name of Jesus!"

As Carl's words soared into oblivion, some invisible, piercing force passed through his body like a cold dagger, and he instantly opened his eyes only to find himself staring into an empty room. The menacing apparition had disappeared.

"Dear, God," he whispered aloud in a pleading tone, "please give me the strength to do this!"

Carl took a deep breath then moved through the doorway into the China Room, but spun around quickly when laughter rang out from behind him. He gasped for breath when he saw six men, dressed in black, hooded robes, standing there, staring back at him while holding onto a baby calf, repeatedly chanting, "Hail Satan!"

The same man who had confronted him only seconds before, stepped out of the group with a large knife in his hand, and spoke to Carl with a gravely voice: "Join us and you can reap the blessing of almighty Satan!"

Carl did not need an introduction. He somehow knew the man was Johana's father. Five of the men gripped the calf tightly as the man who had threatened him turned around and cut the animal's throat with the large knife. The men rubbed their hand in the gushing blood and licked it from their grubby fingers as Carl became convulsive from watching this grisly act.

"Go to Hell!" Carl screamed, then slammed the China Room door shut, leaning his back against it, trying to regain his composure as the men continued chanting outside the room.

While leaning harder against the door, sounds like that of a platoon of soldiers marching came from the floor above his head, followed by a symphony of groans that radiated from the stairway that led nowhere. Then a scream came from somewhere upstairs, followed by a single gunshot that was followed by yet another terrifying event. The jukebox in the ballroom came on and began playing "Anniversary Waltz," the sounds of the song echoing throughout the entire structure.

As Carl stood there in awe, an eerie squeak came from his left. He turned toward the sound to see the heavy steel door swing open and slam against the wall with such magnitude that it broke away from the rusty hinges and fell to the floor with a thunderous echo. Peering into the brick cubicle, he shuddered at the sight of Alonzo and his friend, suspended in mid-air by hangman's nooses. He wanted to turn and run, but he could not take his eyes off the corpses. He seemed hypnotized as he stood there gazing at the sight before him. The sunken black eyes of Alonzo, hanging on the left slowly opened and his right hand came forward.

"Oh, God!" Carl gasped aloud when he realized the dangling corpse was holding the head of Pearl Bryan.

"Hey, don't lose your head!" the corpse laughed to the other one, as he, too, opened his devilish eyes and joined in with the hellish merrymaking.

"I won't," the other apparition chuckled, "but the bitch did!"

Lost in a world of terror and disbelief, Carl pulled the vase and bottle of Holy Water from his pockets with trembling hands. He poured the water into the vase and ran over to the hole in the China Room floor. He emptied the powder from the small envelope into the liquid, stirring it quickly with his finger, then jumped down through the gaping wound in the floor.

As he disappeared under the flooring and maneuvered himself toward the well on his hands and knees, Carl heard the slamming of a door followed by the sound of scurrying footsteps on the floor above him, then came the sound of feet smacking against the dirt. Someone had jumped into the crawl space with him. There was no time to lose. He quickly held the vase over the opening of the well when all at once a staggering thought shot through his mind. He had been instructed by the Gypsy woman to pour the Holy Water into the vase *while he was over the well*! He hadn't done as he was told!

"Oh, God! I forgot! Help me, Lord! Please let this work!" he cried out in a panic.

Proceeding with the ceremony, he recited the Lord's Prayer as he began pouring the mixture into the well opening. Suddenly, the vise-like grip of a massive hand on his foot began pulling him away, causing him to drop the vase at the edge of the hole.

"I rebuke you, Satan, and seal you in Hell for all eternity!" Carl screamed.

He yelled the words over and over, digging his hands into the ground in an attempt to stop the entity from dragging him away from his task. As he fought back, hideous laughter rang out through the entire basement, and a strong wind that came from nowhere filled the crawl space as a horrible breath-taking stench enveloped the chamber.

Out of desperation, he screamed one last time, "I rebuke you, Satan, and seal you in Hell for all eternity!"

All at once, what sounded like a roar of a train vibrated the floor above Carl's head. He found himself suddenly slipping in and out of awareness. Still being pulled from the well, now by dozens of unseen hands, he felt his body begin to tremble, his heart began pounding and everything started going black. The laughter and wind grew stronger and the floor above him shook violently as if it would surely collapse on top of him.

"I lost! I lost!" Carl whimpered with what seemed his last dying breath as the ground slid by underneath him. After all, he had not followed the exact instructions to rid this place of evil presence.

Suddenly, some giant force grabbed up Carl's body and lifted it into the air spinning the man in a circle at a blinding speed, everything becoming a blur.

"Holy God! Help Me" he cried out as the unseen thing from Hell let loose of its grip, sending Carl flying through the darkness, his head striking the foundation wall under the China Room floor with such force that he began slipping in and out of consciousness. As he fought to stay alert he saw a large ball of fire suddenly shoot up out of the well, and it instantly reminded him of the mushroom like explosion of a nuclear bomb. From within the flames, he saw the image of the goat-man demon, and it made the hair on the back of his neck stand out like a frightened dog as his heart jack hammered inside his chest.

A twisted smirk formed on the Devil's lips and with loathsome indignation the thing scowled, "Bow to me and become my disciple or I'll feed your soul to the flames of Hell!"

Spying a baseball size rock within his reach, Carl grabbed it in his trembling hand and defiantly threw it toward the demon, but the granite missile missed its mark. Instead, it ricocheted off the ground and hit the top of the vase sitting beside the well causing it to fall into the well. I'm going to die, Carl thought as he stared at the howling demon and suddenly everything turned black and silent, his body going limp and numb as he passed into a total state of unconsciousness.

Chapter Twenty-one

A warm, gentle smile formed on Carl's face as he talked about what happened next. It was apparent that he enjoyed recalling this part of the story. This is the way he says it happened.
* * * * *

The musty taste of dirt and mold lingered on Carl's tongue as he slowly opened his eyes. The China Room floor was hard and gritty, but it felt cool and soothing to his battle-weary body, and he suddenly realized that, yes, he was alive even though every fiber of his being ached with fatigue.

He strained his tired eyes to focus in the dim light of the basement and could barely make out the figure of someone standing nearby, but for some reason, he felt no animosity toward this new presence.

The sweet, soft scent of roses lingered in the air, and Carl felt a new sensation of peacefulness and warmth caressing his spirit. He gazed up at the young woman, before him. She was a beauty with long, light brown, flowing hair and mysterious, intriguing eyes. Her petite figure gracefully supported a stunning, white, floor length, lace-covered, Victorian gown.

A moan escaped Carl's lips as he placed his palms flat against the floor and pushed his exhausted frame into an upright position, crossing his ankles in front of him and sitting like an Indian in front of a campfire.

He looked up at the girl and grinned sheepishly, and, when she returned his smile, for some reason unknown to Carl, it made him blush. He could feel the heat in his cheeks as they glowed a rosy pink, and for a brief moment, he felt a oneness with the girl before him.
"Johana," he said as he gazed into those dark, haunting eyes, but she did not answer. She just stared down at him, and suddenly he noticed a small tear form on her cheek and glide down her face, a little puff of dust rising up as it landed on the floor at her feet.

"Don't cry!" Carl pleaded as he started to climb to his feet. "Everything's okay!"

Suddenly he realized that even though he was looking directly at the woman, he could also see the old shelves that lined the China Room wall behind her.

The smile faded from her face, and her eyes bore into amazed handyman's as if searching his soul. She stretched her hand out, and Carl, more from reflex than fear, flinched backwards, but regained his composure and leaned forward.

As her hand touched his forehead, a cold, but yet warm, feeling of satisfying comfort embraced the warrior who, just a short while earlier, had battled the demons of Hell and won. Carl again stared into her eyes, and the smile returned to her face.

"You did it, Carl! You sealed the well, but you must find Pearl's head."

"How?"

"You'll know the answer in time!" Johana told him. "Janet and Shaunda are okay. You sealed the well before they got to them."

"Who's Shaunda?"

"You already know the answer, Carl. You have been given a psychic gift, so learn to use it."

Before her words could fade away, Johana gently withdrew her hand from Carl's forehead, and, still smiling, she turned and moved through the threshold that led out of the China Room. Scrambling to his feet, he ran to the door and searched the darkness in every direction, but the ghostly woman was nowhere in sight.

"You'll be back! I know you will," he whispered to the air, and suddenly, in his own mind, he was aware of something splendid and wonderful.

"Shaunda?" The name was not familiar to Carl, but it kept flashing him his mind's eye, and for a moment he wondered what it meant. Then suddenly he realized that it was a baby, but not just any baby. It was the name of Bobby and Janet's newborn baby girl. At that time Carl had no idea that the baby was born only weighing one pound and fifteen ounces from being born so premature. Contemplating this new turn of events for a moment, Carl finally put his arms into the air, shook his head in amazement, and wearily climbed the stairwell back into the main ballroom.

"Thank you, Lord," he said as he strode past the bar and down the mirrored hallway.

Walking outside, he turned and locked the big, brass double doors and headed for home, the scent of roses lingering in the early morning air as he went. As far as Carl was concerned, this entire matter was closed. The evil was contained. Satan and his followers were bound in Hell where they belonged. Everyone was safe now.

He had only one more task ahead of him, and that was to find Pearl's head. He figured that his ghostly friends would lead him to the decapitated orb in time so he could see that the woman's skull was buried with her body.

PART - TWO
(THE POSSESSION)

Chapter Twenty-two

The months passed quietly and almost a year had passed without any demonic show of force. Bobby opened the nightclub for business and Carl moved into the upstairs office after converting it into an efficiency apartment. Janet even got over most of her fear of the place.

Although Carl thought he had sealed the evil in the well and put an end to the demonic activity inside the nightclub, he was soon to learn that it was far from being over. The following is how Carl remembers the activity resuming:

* * * * *

It was three-forty-five in the morning. Thunder boomed as lightning cracked the sky apart. Raindrops pelted the glass panes of the three square windows as Carl Lawson tossed and turned under the tan comforter. He tried to ignore the raging storm, but the volley of thunder continued rocking the building. It was as if the structure was sitting directly in the middle of a war zone. Then he heard it: the scratching inside the walls, the loud banging of the downstairs doors, horrendous footsteps climbing the stairs, heading for his apartment. The door at the top of the landing began bending in and out, breathing on its own, as if it had come to life.

Carl threw back the comforter and jumped to his feet just as the wooden door exploded open. Some force wrapped its unseen arms around him, throwing him to the floor, face up. Fiendish laughter filled the confines of the room, followed by moans and groans that rose up from the first floor. A single gunshot rang out from somewhere in the main ballroom and the jukebox came to life playing "The Anniversary Waltz."

Invisible fingers wrapped around his throat, choking him. Carl could not move. It was getting hard to breathe. Just as everything started going black, a series of lightning bolts flashed across the sky, illuminating the inside of the apartment.

He saw it, now...It was the same demonic thing he had encountered months earlier. The fiery eyes blazed with hatred and its sulfurous breath was assaulting Carl's nostrils.

* * *

"Jesus" Carl shrieked as he jerked upright in the bed and realized that he had just had a horrible nightmare. The demon choking him, and the hideous laughter, was nothing but a bad dream, but it had seemed so real. Too real!

Carl slid his feet over the side of the bed and stared quietly out the window as the rain beat against the glass. He watched the lightning rip through the sky and listened to the thunder that had made his dream more terrifying.

The hunger to go downstairs and check the filled-in well gnawed at his heart. He tried to convince himself that everything was okay. Sitting alone in the room, however, he could not help thinking about what he and Janet had endured only months ago. The terrifying memories came rushing back in his mind, and, no matter how hard he tried to dismiss the hellish nightmare that had seized him, the worse it got. One thought after another whipped in and out of this mind so quickly that he wanted to scream.

"The hell with it," he groaned with a rough, sleepy voice. He frowned, then stood up, rubbing his knuckles into his eyes. He made up his mind to go down to the basement and make certain the well was still sealed.

He flipped on the brass lamp that sat on the wooden nightstand, and then slowly surveyed the room. His bed sat against the west wall directly under a small window that looked out over the roof toward the Licking River. On the north wall, next to the closet door, sat a four-drawer oak chest where Carl kept most of his clothes. On the south wall was an oak bar with two black stools in front of it. Behind the bar, fastened to the west wall was a stainless steel sink with two wood-grain cabinets over it. The east wall was bare, except for the three windows that looked down on the road. They were windows that had seen, and sometimes reflected, the secrets of this giant, old building.

Carl crossed the room, wearing only a pair of white jockey shorts and grabbed his faded jeans off of the chest. He slipped into the pants, then opened the top drawer of the chest and pulled out a black T-shirt, putting it on as he moved to the doorway that led downstairs to the main floor.

He twisted the brass knob, and then stepped out onto the top landing where he stood motionless, staring down the stairs. He sighed and tried to convince himself that it was just a bad dream...nothing to worry about, but still he had to be certain.

Swallowing the growing fear of what he might encounter, he descended the stairway. He opened the wooden door to his right, stepping into the game room. It had originally been known as the Fiesta Room until Bobby opened the bar for business. There were now two green felt regulation pool tables in the twenty-by-fifteen-foot paneled room, and various video arcade games lined most of the walls.

The room was dark. All the lights throughout the first floor were switched off. Carl squinted hard, trying to adjust his eyes to the pitch black of the building. He walked across the black tiled floor, stepping through one of the double archways that led into the main barroom. He passed the end of the long, black padded bar on his right, then walked into the main ballroom where he felt his way along the wall until he found the circuit breakers.

He methodically flipped on all the switches until every area on the first level came to life, the bright lights illuminating the interior of the building. As the electricity surged through the wiring, like blood flowing through veins, the video arcade games in the game room began ringing and clamoring, the sounds of their carnival-like melodious tones echoing throughout the building.

Carl shuddered at the thought of going down to the basement. His eyes prowled the huge, oak-paneled ballroom then stared past the table-filled chamber at the two archways that sat on either side of the stage. Once again, he gritted his teeth and tried to convince himself there was nothing to worry about.

The young man moved through the sea of tables and crossed the hardwood dance floor until he reached the stage. He jumped onto the fifty-five-foot-wide wooden platform, and then moved back stage through the arched doorway on his left. The back stage area was cluttered with drum cases, guitar cases and other musical equipment. He walked over to the west wall and opened the wooden door that led down to the basement. As he gazed down the old stairwell, he was elated to see that, when he had flipped on the circuit breakers, the lights had come on downstairs, too.

"I oughta just go back to bed," Carl grumbled as he shook his head. He was disgusted with himself for wanting to check the well. It was just a bad dream. He was sure of it!

He groaned slightly, and then walked down the stairs, the old wooden planks squeaking under his feet as if announcing his approach. At the bottom of the steps he turned right through the doorway to the main basement area heading for the China Room. The main basement was a long open chamber with large wooden beams stretching up from the ground to the rafters, giving the main floor extra support. To his left was a row of small dressing rooms last used when the place was a gambling casino in the 1930's and 1940's.

Carl strolled forward, whistling some country tune as he went. He reached the China Room where he filled the doorway examining the room in all directions. Nothing seemed different. Everything was quiet, but it was almost too quiet. He stared at the opening in the middle of the floor that led to the sealed well and was relieved to see that everything was okay. Satisfied now that it was just a bad dream, he turned around to leave the room. Suddenly the lights began flickering off then on throughout the basement as if some unseen hand was flipping the switch repeatedly.

From out of nowhere, a twirling, bawling, freezing wind congealed under the floor near the well. It shot up through the opening, piercing his body like icicles, then rocketed through the doorway of the China Room and roared through the main basement area like a tornado, swirling up dust and debris from the floor as it went.

Carl, now frozen in shock, felt the fear coming back as he quickly realized that the undeniable horror he had lived through before had returned. Outside, the thunder bellowed and groaned as if it was a symphony announcing the conductor's arrival and then the lights died.

Total darkness...

"God, Noooo!!!" He shrieked as a giant ball of fire shot up out of the hole in the floor, and he saw the creature standing inside the flames. It was the same monster he had envisioned in his dream, the same malevolent son-of-a-bitch that he had sealed inside of the well only a few months ago. It was Satan himself standing there before him grinning a heinous smirk.

"Noooo!" He screamed frantically again. "I beat you! I sealed you in Hell!"

The monstrosity raised its left arm and pointed an elongated finger at the horror stricken man. "Get out! Now!" The creature growled, its multi-toned voice dark and liquid. The floor and walls vibrated as the creature spoke.

Carl wanted to run, to get as far away from there as possible, but his feet would not move. He was as stiff as stone, unable to budge an inch. He tried to force his eyes away from the beast, but they were locked inside their sockets, staring blindly at the dancing, roaring flames that surrounded the Prince of Darkness.

As he stood motionless an invisible force closed in all around him, and he felt certain that he was about to die. Unseen fingers wrapped around his throat and neck then jerked him up into the air, his feet dangling about four feet above the floor.

He began gagging, kicking his feet wildly. He flailed his arms, but could not break free of this invisible creature's grip. Then hundreds...no...thousands of disembodied voices began chanting throughout the room. "Kill him! Sacrifice him! Kill him!" They called out in unison to the unholy creature inside of the flames.

For some unexplainable reason, the entity violently slung Carl to the floor, his body smashing to the ground with a dull thud. The impact knocked the wind out of the petrified man. He found it almost impossible to move, but he was so filled with fear that he somehow struggled to his feet. His eyes shot to the doorway leading back to the main basement. There was only empty space between him and the threshold.

Gasping for air, Carl bolted for the door, racing for his life. It had happened! Someone or something had unsealed the well and released the evil force from its prison. But who, he asked himself.

That was not important right now. He had to escape this place before he was killed. He knew Satan would take revenge on him and he had to get out of here if he wanted to remain among the living.

He raced through the basement as the walls began cracking and tearing. The wooden beams that supported the rafters began swaying and a river of blood began pouring from the ceiling and flowing down the walls on all sides. The basement quickly filled with the sounds of hideous laughter, and every door began slamming violently back and forth against its frame.

Just as he was about to reach the doorway leading back upstairs, he came to an abrupt halt and stood motionless once again. He could not believe what he was seeing. Sitting in the middle of the open chamber was the yellow Fiat convertible with its top down. The engine was racing wide open and the headlights shone directly at him.

"There's no way!" He cried in agony. "There's no damn way!"

This was hard for him to swallow. The car had been stripped of parts even before Bobby had purchased the property. Bobby had allowed it to remain in the basement in case someone showed up wanting what was left of it. The carburetor and gas tank had been removed. It was impossible for the car to run. But, there it was...just like in some horror movie, ready to run him down.

He knew he only had one chance. He had to reach the stairway before the driverless car ran him over. He sprang forward, racing for the doorway on his left as the auto lurched toward him, the tires squealing and sending a trail of smoke into the air.

His heart jack hammered and every muscle in his body tensed as his feet pounded the floor in an attempt to escape death. The car was coming closer, picking up speed as it went. As the Fiat reached him, Carl leaped through the air over top of the left fender and fell into the safety of the stairwell. He jumped to his feet and took the stairs three at a time, fleeing from this Hell as fast as he could possibly go.

As he raced up the stairs, he saw the wooden door at the top of the landing slam shut. He reached the doorway and twisted the knob, but it would not budge. He cursed under his breath as he shoved his left shoulder into the wooden partition, trying desperately to force it open.

Hellish laughter rose up from the basement and filled the stairwell. He tried to ignore it. He continued slamming his body against the door with all his might when suddenly it flew open causing him to spill out into the backstage area.

Carl leaped to his feet and stared intently down the steps, but all he saw was an empty basement.

Satisfied that nothing was in the stairwell, he turned and raced out of the room, quickly sprinting for the front door. He was getting the hell out of the building before anything else happened. After racing through the main barroom, he ran down the long mirrored hallway and was elated when he pushed through the front entrance door and found himself standing outside of the building...ALIVE!

Without hesitation, he turned to his right and headed to the blue 1978 Cutlass that sat all alone in the gravel parking lot. He bolted through the pouring rain and climbed inside his car, shoving the key into the ignition, then pulled the gear lever into the drive position and sped out of the parking lot.

Carl drove south on Route 9, heading for St. John's Catholic Church. The relentless wind shrilled through the valley and the rain streaked the car windows like tears while the windshield wipers raked across the glass in unison. Carl turned the auto left on John's Hill Road and sped up the highway, the headlights piercing the eerie darkness like a pair of flaming arrows racing for a hidden target shrouded by the rain.

"Son-of-a-bitch, I passed the church." He groaned, realizing that his preoccupation with his narrow escape had caused his mind to wander. He slammed on the brakes, locking all four wheels and causing them to screech. He looked up the road, and then in his rearview mirror to make sure no other cars were in his path. Seeing it was clear, he wheeled the car around and quickly drove back to the church where he brought the car to a fishtailing halt in front of the gray-stone building.

Carl stared at the large, double oak doors of the structure, then sighed deeply as he stepped out of the auto into the rain. He closed the door gently then ran up the concrete steps, gripping the brass knob and stepping inside of the church.

He looked around the foyer and fixed his eyes on the white porcelain stand in the corner. It contained what he was looking for. "I'll be a no good mother.......!" Carl started, and then remembered he was standing inside God's Home. "I forgot a bottle for the Holy Water."

He quickly looked around the foyer, staring at the white walls and white tile floor, but he didn't see anything that could hold the Holy Water.

Disgusted with himself, Carl moved back through the front door and bolted back to his car through the onslaught of rain. He pulled out his car keys and opened the trunk where he spied an empty 16-ounce soda bottle that still had the lid screwed on it.

"This'll do!" he said with a smile as he grabbed the bottle and slammed the trunk. He turned and ran back into the church, heading for the container of Holy Water and in a matter of seconds the bottle was filled. "Time to go!" Carl whispered as he walked out of the church and climbed into his car. He was ready to return to the nightclub and exorcise the demons back to Hell. It had worked once...and he prayed it would work again.

Halfway back to he nightclub he felt the car trying to veer off to the right of the road as if something had taken control of it. He gripped the steering wheel with both hands and kept the Oldsmobile in its lane of traffic, squinting his eyes hard through the fog and rain staring at the yellow line that divided the highway.

Carl tried to relax and swallow the fear that was rising up in his throat. He wanted to turn the car around and drive as far as possible from the bar, but he was not going to be run off by some demon from Hell. He began feeling cold, but he told himself it was because he was wet. A sick, nauseating feeling kept growing inside him as he drew closer to the nightclub, but still he stayed on course. He wasn't going to give up.

Staring into the night, at the blacktop pavement, he thought of the horror that might be awaiting his arrival when suddenly he saw something inside the beam of light piercing the fog. The sight was horrifying. He jammed his right foot on the brake pedal, but the car accelerated. Just as the auto was about to slam into the beast he had seen in the basement earlier that night, the headlights went out and now there was only blackness.

He slammed the brakes with both feet, over and over, but the car continued picking up speed. He looked down at the dash lights to check the speedometer, but they were out too!

The rain grew worse, rat-a-tat tatting on the roof of the car like a thousand tiny snare drums, when suddenly, all of the car's lights sprang back to life and the Oldsmobile began slowing just as the headlights shone on the front entrance of the nightclub.

Carl pressed on the brakes again and this time they worked. He wheeled the faded blue vehicle into the parking lot, turned off the ignition and sat motionless staring at the building without making a sound. He was exhausted, but he knew he had to go into the basement and exorcise the Devil and his army of demons back to Hell just like he had done months prior!

"Oh, my God, I am heartily sorry for having offended thee", Carl whispered, saying the Catholic's Act of Contrition as he prepared to enter the building. "And I detest all of my sins because of thy just punishments. But most of all, because they offend thee my Lord, who art good and deserving of all my love. I firmly resolve with the help of thy grace to sin no more and to avoid the near occasion of sin...AMEN!"

As his words faded away into nothingness; the dense fog and rain drifted away from the nightclub as if God told it to do so. Everything outside went still and calm, but that was outside. Carl knew that something inside of the building was breathing, growling, chanting magical spells, and waiting for the very moment that he stepped back into the club!

Chapter Twenty-three

This chapter is the result of many hours of questioning with Carl. For several days and nights, we methodically reviewed what happened next. He had a great deal of difficulty in conveying this information because of what he had endured. To the best of Carl's recollection, this is the way he says it occurred.

* * * * *

Carl knew he was being watched, but he was not sure if it was something inside the building spying on him, or if it was the structure itself watching and waiting for him to come inside. He was wide-awake now. He rubbed his eyes with the palms of his hands, and then gripped the soda bottle that was filled to the lid with Holy Water. He climbed out of the car, made his way across the gravel parking lot, opened the front door of the nightclub, and stepped into the long mirrored hallway. He stared straight ahead at the double swinging doors that led into the main ballroom and waited for something to happen, but nothing did. "Maybe they're gone," he tried to delude himself. "Maybe it really was just a bad dream."

Almost convincing himself that everything was okay, he ambled up the hall looking at his reflection in the mirrors as he went. He pushed through one of the swinging doors and stepped into the main barroom, looking in all directions for some evil presence to appear before him, but to his surprise, except for the old floorboards creaking and complaining, as they always did, the only sound in the room was that of his heart beating.

He moved past the open bar to his left and made his way up onto the stage. He started across the platform, heading for the back room area when something behind him caught his attention. He wheeled around on the balls of his feet, searching the main ballroom and dance floor with his eyes. There was no one there. But if that was the case, what made the thumping sound that caused him to stop and turn around? He strained his eyes harder, squinting through the semi-darkness of the room, and just when he was beginning to think he was all alone...he saw it! His face distorted into a look of agony, and he felt a wave of darkness wash over him as he stared at the creature.

There he was again, the same repulsive beast that he had seen in the basement, the same malignant entity that he saw standing inside the fog only moments ago.

As the demon stood at the edge of the dance floor in front of the first row of tables, smoke billowed up all around it, swirling and dancing, rising up and disappearing into the darkness.

Carl stood there in awe staring at the beast as it raised a bony, elongated finger and pointed it at him. Its yellow stained fangs hung down from its upper jaw as a pool of slobber drooled out of its mouth.

Carl found himself unable to move. His eyes locked on the demon's red, glowing orbs, and he knew he was being hypnotized, but there was nothing he could do to help himself. He could feel his will being drained away and replaced with something else-- something evil.

The room became instantly cold. A freezing wind congealed and twirled through the room like a huge spinning top, knocking over tables and chairs.

This can't be happening, his brain shrieked. This isn't real! But, he knew it was. He tried desperately to run, to move his feet, if only an inch, but something he could not fight was holding him at attention, taking control of his body. He felt himself changing, his skin splitting open, his muscles rippling up and down his arms and legs in giant waves and an overwhelming pressure inside his head.

The demon moved closer to the stage, and, as it did, Carl saw his own reflection in the monster's blazing eyes. He saw what looked like icicles forming on his face, hanging from his eyelids, and then his own eyes began to change color. The freezing wind was now enveloping him, and he suddenly became aware of the fact that some presence had entered his body. His eyes now glowed red and he felt his thoughts changing. He heard the voices inside his head, hundreds of them, chanting "Hail Satan!" He knew he was being possessed by a demon, becoming one of them, now. It had already taken possession of his body and it would not be long before it would have his mind and soul.

As his thoughts became more confused and he felt as if he would black out, he noticed something strange. He was staring down into the demon's eyes and he suddenly realized that he was floating some five or six feet in the air above the stage.

If things were not bad enough, the unplugged jukebox suddenly came on and began playing "The Anniversary Waltz." The ballroom became filled with hundreds of demons in human form. They were laughing and mocking Carl, enticing him to join them.

"Hail Satan! Lord of the flies, I am yours!" They chanted over and over, louder and louder. He found himself chanting the same words in unison with the legion of demons.

Still staring into the demon's eyes, looking at his own reflection, he saw that his facial expressions were slowly changing from fear to an eerie contentment. An evil smile crossed his lips, and, as he began slowly descending to the stage floor, the bottle of Holy Water began to bubble up and became hot, searing the veins in his hand and arm.

"Get rid of that goat piss!" The ancient one sneered as he pointed his bony finger at his new disciple, then at the outside door that suddenly flew open.

Carl jumped from the stage and quickly ran to the door, throwing the bottle of Holy Water across the railroad tracks and into the woods just as the lid exploded off the top of the container. As the door slammed shut, he stepped back and broke into a maniacal laugh. He now was one of them. It was time to entertain his guests. After all, he lived here in the upstairs apartment and that made him the host. It would not be polite not to show his new master and friends a good time.

Chapter Twenty-four

During the course of doing interviews and researching the resulting leads, I was led to an ever-expanding number of people who had experienced bizarre happenings inside, or as a result of having been inside the nightclub. Placing the stories in chronological order, this chapter is the first in a series that developed from interviewing these people.

Abigail Wathen lived in Cincinnati, Ohio. She was raised a Christian and believes in God and the Devil. Since childhood, she has had numerous dreams that have come true. She cannot explain the phenomenon, but feels she has some kind of unusual gift. Her two brothers and three sisters used to tease her about her dreams, but, after she had predicted several things that came to pass, her family started to believe her.

This is the first part of Abigail's story.

* * * * *

It was eleven thirty Friday night and the nightclub was in full swing. The crowd was larger than usual. People waited in line just to get inside. Men lined the open bar on both sides wearing their Stetson cowboy hats, Levis and large rodeo belt buckles. The game room was packed to capacity with some people playing pool and others just watching.

The dance floor was jam packed with couples dancing to one of Bobby's slow, tear-jerking, country songs. The ballroom was buzzing with the laughter and chatter of men and women sitting at the sea of wooden tables that were covered with red tablecloths. The waitresses scurried through the crowd trying desperately to wait every customer.

Abigail Wathen, a five-foot-six-inch, blonde-haired beauty, sat at the end of the bar near the dance floor, brushing back the long strands of hair from her face. She knew her own special power to please. Men clustered around her, waiting for their turn to take the woman out on the dance floor and hold her in their arms.

As she sat there smiling, sipping on a Long Island Ice Tea, she heard a growling sound to her left. She spun around on the bar stool to see Carl Lawson sitting next to her.

"Hi," he said with a smirk. "I like your outfit."

Abigail was wearing a long, white, floor length, lacy gown. She was obsessed with the dress styles of the 1930's and had accumulated quite a large wardrobe of dresses, hats, and other women's clothing from that era. She considered herself a modern day southern belle.

"Why, thank you!" she said with a flirtatious smile, her big blue eyes staring into his.

"You remind me of one of the ghosts in here," he said quite bluntly. "If I didn't know better, I'd swear you were her."

Her smile vanished from her face and she stared at him with a suspicious look. "Ghosts, huh!" she remarked with a smirk. "Do you see them a lot?"

"Sure do, all the time. I work here. In fact, I live in the apartment upstairs. You wanna dance?"

"Aah, no...I don't think so." She almost laughed. "Your ghost friends might not like that. Besides, I don't dance with kooks!"

"Are you making fun of me?" He sneered, his eyes now revealing anger, his voice changing to a raspy tone as he spoke. It was becoming apparent to Abigail that the man seemed to be taking on a different personality. She figured he had simply had too much to drink.

"No!" Abigail replied. "But I'll tell you one thing...you better go see a doctor, pal!"

"Is that right?" he scoffed. "If you're making fun of me...you'll be the one seeing a doctor. I'll put a spell on your ass and then we'll see who the kook is!"

"Why don't you take a hike?" Her words almost biting at the man beside her. "You're nuts!"

"I'll show you nuts!" Carl said, furiously, his words lifting in a shout that almost stopped everything dead. "Ya wanna see nuts? Watch this!"

He raised his hands over his head and whispered a series of mumbo jumbo words while still staring at the woman. His eyes bore into hers like invisible daggers and she could have sworn they almost turned red.

"When you come back here again, you'll apologize to me and my friends." He said with the breathy voice of an alcoholic.

"You're full of crap," Abigail said, tension making her voice tight. "I'll never apologize to you...you're a damn crack pot!"

"Is that right?" He taunted her. "You'll—"

"Drop dead!" Abigail interrupted him. "I'm getting away from you. You're as crazy as a bed bug!"

Before he could reply, she climbed off the stool and gulped down the rest of her drink, heading for the front door. She was going to find another bar. "Ghosts!" She laughed as she disappeared into the crowd.

"You'll be back!" Carl whispered, gritting his teeth. "You'll be back to apologize."

She walked outside to the parking lot and climbed into her gold Chevy Nova, then looked back at the building. It almost seemed like it was watching her. She could not quite put her finger on it, but she felt an uneasiness gnawing at her now. Dismissing the thought, she finally convinced herself that she was simply allowing her imagination to get the best of her because of the conversation she had just had with that whacko.

She did not believe a word Carl said, but she knew he was right. She would be back, but not to apologize to him. She loved country music and had collected hundreds of old records by country singers. That was not the only reason she would return here. She wanted a steady boyfriend and this place was a meat market. The men outnumbered the women three to one.

Shaking her head in disgust, she could not believe she had let Carl upset her enough to make her leave. It wasn't even midnight. "What the hell," she laughed. "I'll come back early tomorrow night."

She started her car and turned left out of the parking log, heading north on Route 9, toward home.

Chapter Twenty-five

Many people were hired by the Mackey's to perform various jobs at the nightclub. Robert Ranshaw was a carpenter. He grew up with three sisters in Covington, Kentucky, a community not far from Wilder. He was living alone, happy in his life-style as a divorced man. A burly man, six feet tall, he had never believed in such things as ghosts. This is his story.

* * * * *

It was the next day, and the Saturday afternoon sun scorched the black-shingled roof of the nightclub. Carl was in his apartment sleeping off the wild, drunken party he had thrown for his friends after the bar had closed for business the night before.

Robert Ranshaw had been hired by Bobby to do some remodeling. He was busily stacking a pile of new two-by-fours in the main corridor of the basement when he heard someone call his name. He turned around and stared down the long passageway, flashing his hazel eyes left and right, but he did not see anyone. He stared at the row of dressing room doors on his left, but still saw no one.

"Who's there," he called out, his voice deep and husky as he tucked his black T-shirt into his jeans.

No response.

"Carl, is that you?" He looked past the gray walls and dressing rooms toward the exit door, but it was closed.

"Just my imagination," he laughed as he turned around to finish stacking the lumber.

"Hey, Bob!" A soft, wispy voice called out from behind him. He turned around again, but still was unable to see a person calling his name. He knew it wasn't Carl. He heard it clearly that time. It was definitely a woman's voice.

"Knock it off," he barked.

No response.

He started to call out again, but froze in his tracks when a piercing, frigid wind shot through his body like a surge of electricity. It was as if some evil force had just passed through his body, making its presence known.

It became apparent that he was not alone in the basement, but it was not a human being down there with him. As he stood there motionless, he felt someone tap him on the right shoulder, and he shrieked as he spun around only to see an empty room again.

"What in the hell's going on?" he groaned.

Before his words faded, a soft scent of roses filled the air around him, and then came the footsteps. Not just one pair of footsteps, but hundreds of them marching across the ballroom floor above him, like a battalion of soldiers, every step in unison.

"Dear God," he sighed, "what's happening?"

Ranshaw raced for the stairs, taking them two at a time until he reached the back stage area. He moved out of the room and stood in the arched doorway of the stage. The marching sounds instantly stopped. There was no one to be found. Just another empty room, ...just like downstairs.

"I'm gettin' the hell outta here!" Trying to hide his fear he walked across the stage and jumped down on the hardwood dance floor. He quickly moved through the ballroom and headed for the front door. Suddenly, the jukebox began playing "The Anniversary Waltz."

That did it! He fled through the building, racing for the exit door as though his life depended on it. Suddenly, Robert Ranshaw, the skeptic, realized that he now believed in ghosts.

Chapter Twenty-six

This is the continuation of Abigail Wathen's story. What happened next was far beyond her wildest dreams. This is the way she said it happened.

* * * * *

Abigail drove her two-door Nova down Pete Rose Way in Cincinnati, heading for Bobby Mackey's nightclub. It was five past seven on Saturday night and she was looking forward to another night of drinking, flirting and just having a good time. She was wearing a knee-length black dress, and matching hat, and black patent-leather boots. She knew, with this outfit, she would stand out over all of the other women in the club.

She was driving past the row of tall city buildings on her left, looking out the window to her right at the Ohio River. Abruptly, the car tried to veer off to the left. Abigail held the steering wheel with both hands, attempting desperately to control the auto that suddenly had a mind of its own. The car began swerving recklessly to the right and then to the left toward oncoming traffic.

It was becoming harder to keep control of the Nova. Her back and neck muscles tensed as she squeezed tighter on the wheel with a death grip. She leaned back hard against the tan bench seat and slammed both feet on the brake pedal. Instead of slowing, the car accelerated ... 40 ... 50 ... 60 ... 70, and then she smelled it: the soft scent of roses filled the interior of the vehicle.

"God help me!" she screamed as the Nova veered left then right. The front fenders and hood of the auto began shaking and vibrating as if they were going to explode. The front windshield began bending in and out as if the glass was actually breathing. The radio turned itself on, and the volume shot all the way up, the rock & roll song drowning out her frantic screams for help. The windshield wipers came on and began scraping against the dry glass and the accelerator slammed harder to the floor, the speedometer needle passing eighty.

I'm going to die, she thought as tears welled up in her eyes.

Raspy laughter from the back seat filled the interior of the car and suddenly a horrifying thought seized Abigail's brain. Carl Lawson had cursed her! He really had put some kind of spell on her, and now she was going to pay for mocking him. Pay with her life!

"Dear God!" she cried, "Please let me live. I'll never make fun of Carl again," but her prayers were not going to be answered so easily. She was not going to get away with mocking him and the evil spirits without paying a price. The car headed for a path of suicidal destruction.

The steering wheel spun violently to the right, and the Chevy slammed head on into a concrete wall with overwhelming force. Abigail's body was flung forward like a rag doll, her face smashing into the windshield. She fell back into the seat as the front end of the auto came to rest against the wall, smashed in like soup can. Steam poured out of the radiator, as she lay sprawled out on the front seat covered in blood. Her chin was split open to the jawbone and she found herself going into shock.

Several motorists, who had seen the wreck, came to her aid. In a matter of minutes, the Cincinnati Police and Paramedics arrived.

Abigail, slipping in and out of awareness, tried to tell the police officers that some invisible demon took control of the car and caused the crash, but the officers were not buying her story. She was taken to University Hospital where she received four stitches in her chin. She was asked by one of the police officers to submit to a blood alcohol test because he thought she was either on drugs or had too much to drink. After all, he had heard every story imaginable, but "A demon causing an accident" ---No way!

Abigail submitted to the blood test and the results revealed no signs of alcohol or drugs in her body.

Abigail lay on the hospital bed waiting for her sister to come get her. Her thoughts were on Carl Lawson, and only on him. In her mind, she knew that somehow he had caused the wreck. All she wanted to do was go to the nightclub to see the mysterious stranger before something else happened to her. Carl was right! She was going to tell him she was sorry for making fun of him and his ghostly friends.

Chapter Twenty-seven

Even though it had been a long time since any signs of a demonic force had showed itself, Janet still felt uneasy inside the place. Carl usually stayed upstairs in his apartment until the bar opened for business. Mary Torres, nicknamed "Cookie," was the first of the waitresses to arrive for work this Saturday evening.

Cookie was single and lived in an apartment in Newport, Kentucky, about two miles from the nightclub. She has four sisters and one brother. She attended Our Lady of Providence High School. Since graduation she had spent most of her time working as a cashier during the day and a waitress at night.

The following is the result of several joint, and individual, interviews with Janet Mackey, Carl Lawson and Mary Torres. This is the way they all agreed it happened.

* * * * *

Janet arrived at the nightclub around ten minutes after seven. She wanted to get there before the help began arriving around seven-thirty. She did not relish the idea of being alone in the building, even for a few minutes, but she knew Carl would be upstairs in the apartment if she needed him, and he had repeatedly assured her that the evil was gone.

She hated everything about the building, but she knew she would never convince Bobby to sell the property. Business was excellent and he still did not believe any of the stories about the ghosts.

From the moment she stepped inside the nightclub, she felt a sense of aloneness, but yet she felt as if she was being watched. She tried to dismiss the thought as she walked through the mirrored hallway and entered the main barroom, but she had not felt this way since before Carl sealed the well. This was not just her own jumpiness. This was the same sense of foreboding she had experienced before.

She moved through the room, spying Carl sitting at the end of the bar. She walked up to him just as he lit a cigarette and inhaled deeply. She pulled up a stool and sat down next to him, laying her purse on top of the bar with a dull clunk.

"Hi, Carl. What are you doing down here so early?"

"Just checking things out before everyone starts arriving," he answered slowly as he exhaled the tobacco smoke.

"Carl," Janet said, switching to a serious tone. "We need to talk."

"About what?"

"Ever since you did that exorcism or what ever you did over the well, I've felt pretty safe in here, but, when I walked in this place tonight, I felt that same feeling that I had when I was attacked, before," Janet exclaimed. "I've got a bad feeling about everything. I think our friends are back. Have you had anything happen to you in here?"

"Why do you ask that?" he asked with a touch of irritation.

"I don't know. And I don't know why, but I can feel something watching us. I'm afraid it's starting again. I—"

"That's bull!" He blurted out with a rough, stern voice. "It's over. I don't want to talk about it again!"

His tone startled her. She was taken aback with his attitude. He had never snapped at her before. Then suddenly, the thought hit her like a rock. It was not the building that scared her at this very moment. It was Carl who sent a shiver up her spine. There was something different about him. For some shapeless reason she could not quite figure out, he was different. Nothing inside the building had changed. Everything was exactly as it had been for the last few months. Janet felt a new terror washing over here, something evil, something powerful, radiating from Carl.

Before she could respond to Carl's outburst the handyman clenched his fists, wheeled around, climbed off the bar stool and walked away from her, stomping his feet as he went.

Janet sat there, motionless, watching the man storm from the bar and disappear into the game room, heading for the upstairs apartment. For some strange reason their conversation had caused Carl to become enraged. He was not going to discuss the possibility that the evil spirits had returned. But why? The question tormented Janet.

Carl was hiding something from her, but what? She wondered as she forced herself to get going. The waitresses would be arriving soon and she had to get everything in order before the nightclub opened for business at eight o' clock.

Janet busied herself turning on all the lights, and then checking all the bottles of liquor behind the bar to make sure she had an ample supply of booze for the large crowd of customers that would soon be plowing through the front doors.

Janet had managed the entire operation as much as possible. She always arrived early and assigned each employee their duties before the club opened. Bobby always showed up around ten thirty and gave three 45-minute shows before the bar closed at two thirty in the morning. Everything had gone okay until tonight. This can't be happening again, she thought as she checked the inventory behind the bar.

Janet kept flashing back to the first day that she had entered this building. She felt the presence of evil then, something watching her every move, but try as she may, she was never able to convince Bobby that the nightclub was haunted.

She tried to force herself to forget about the demonic attacks that she had endured, but the thoughts stuck with her and would not go away. The prior months of being terrorized by some demonic thing were still burned deep into her mind.

She tried to tell herself to forget about it, but she could not shake the memories.

Something was wrong...worse than before. She grabbed a bar towel and began wiping down the black counter top just as Mary Torres pushed through the swinging double doors of the mirrored hallway. The woman was wearing a black jumpsuit and black patent-leather shoes.

Janet looked up and felt a sigh of relief when she saw a friendly face. "Hi Cookie!" Janet said with a jubilant tone. She was glad someone had arrived. She would be okay now. She was not alone in the bar anymore.

"How's it going?" Cookie asked as she walked over to the middle of the bar and sat down on the stool facing Janet, who was still behind the bar.

"Okay...now!" Janet laughed.

"Now?" the woman said. "What's that supposed to mean?"

"Nothing." Janet giggled. "Just a personal joke."
Cookie was a waitress at the nightclub, but she did not know about the ghosts and spirits that had been there. Bobby had given explicit instructions to both Carl and Janet not to discuss the matter with the help nor the customers. Carl had told him of his ordeal in the basement and how he had done an exorcism, sealing the evil spirits back in Hell, and, as far as Bobby was concerned, the matter was closed. He still did not believe any of Carl and Janet's story, but if they wanted to believe the spirits were sealed in Hell, that was fine with him, just as long as it was not mentioned again.

Janet and Cookie began discussing where the waitresses would work that night. The rows of tables had been divided up into sections with each waitress being given a designated area to work each evening. Janet changed the station assignments almost daily so the women got equal chances at obtaining the highest tips. The big spenders were usually near the front of the ballroom by the dance floor and stage.

Cookie was assigned that particular area tonight, so, while Janet continued wiping the bar, the woman ambled over to the front row of tables to make sure the red tablecloths were on straight and that each and every table had a glass ashtray on it.

Cookie was Puerto Rican and had a soft, dark complexion. She had short, dark brown hair and deep brown eyes. A lot of the male patrons referred to her as "the little Latin Princess." She had a medium build and stood five-foot-three. She was a jubilant woman, full of life. She always had a happy smile on her face and the customers loved her.

As Cookie busied herself, a sudden cold chill pierced her body. It was like a wall of ice passing through her, causing her hairs on the back of her neck and arms to bristle and stand out at attention. She stopped and looked around the room to see what had caused her to experience this strange feeling. It was about 80 degrees inside the building. The air conditioner was on the blink, and there was no reason for such a chill. After carefully surveying the room with her eyes, Cookie shrugged off the eerie feeling and continued her chores, but, just as she started to push a chair closer to the table, she felt something breathing on the back of her neck, causing the hair on her nape to ripple. She whirled around to see who was behind her and found herself being overcome by a gut-twisting fear when she found no one there.

Just as everything seemed to return to normal and she tried to dismiss the unexplainable events that had just occurred, the jukebox came on by itself, playing "The Anniversary Waltz."

Cookie spun around and stared at the glass machine, then searched the empty stage with her eyes. Microphone stands were spread out around the platform and the white drum set and symbols sat in the middle, towards the rear of the stage, but there was no one there. She scanned the rest of the room only to find herself alone.

Cookie slowly moved past the jukebox and crossed into the bull room. She searched the area for any sign of people inside the room, but to no avail. What in the world's happening, she wondered. Either someone's playing a sick joke on me or I'm losing my mind!

She headed toward the barroom to tell Janet what had happened, but when she reached the bar she saw that Janet was not there. Cookie crossed the black tile floor then walked through the arched doorway into the game room in search of her boss.

As she stepped into the room, she heard something coming from inside the liquor storage room, which was located in the far right hand corner of the chamber. She crossed over the floor past the two pool tables and reached out for the doorknob, when suddenly, some invisible force slammed against her chest pushing her backwards. The woman froze in horror and disbelief. Her eyes widened and her heart began beating like a bass drum. She stood perfectly still, staring at the wood door in front of her.

"Janet!" she tried to call out, but the words stuck in her throat.

The entity slammed her again, this time pushing her back about three feet. Cookie had no doubt now. Some evil thing was inside the building with her. It pushed her again. This time she stumbled backwards, swinging her arms behind her in case she fell. The frigid chill pierced her again and she immediately realized she had to get out of the building...now! She wheeled around and started for the barroom, and, as she did, she saw Janet coming through the doorway holding a large cardboard box.

Janet recognized the look on Cookie's face. "What's wrong?"

Cookie turned back around and looked through the room, but saw nothing. She turned back toward Janet with a horrified expression. "Somebody pushed me!" the girl choked out the words almost crying. "Not somebody," she stammered, "a spirit...something evil."

"My God!" Janet almost screamed the words as she, too, searched the room with her eyes. "Come on, Cookie. Let's get out of here!"

Janet cautiously turned and waked back to the bar with Cookie right behind her. She laid the box of napkins on the middle of the bar and looked around the room. After what seemed an eternity of silence, Janet turned toward Cookie.

"Don't be afraid!" She said, trying to be reassuring. "It's okay."

"What in the heck's going on?" Cookie's voice was quivering. "There's ghosts in here...isn't there?"

Her words hit Janet like a freight train. The entity had revealed itself to Cookie. There was no doubt in Janet's mind now that the evil had returned. A Bible passage she learned while attending Sunday school flashed through her mind.

The Scripture referred to a man being possessed, not a building, but could it be the same? If it could, then that meant whatever was here before brought back seven more unclean spirits with it. The thought was horrifying! Why was Carl acting so strange? Janet suddenly wondered, could the evil force have taken control of him? Could he be possessed?

"Janet! What's going on?" Cookie's urgency caused Janet to snap back to the present.

The question hung in the air between them for several tense seconds, then Janet found the courage to tell Cookie of her own past experiences while inside the nightclub.

After finishing her bizarre story, she pleaded with Cookie not to quit working for her and Bobby. Cookie was more of a friend than an employee, and right now Janet needed all of the friends she could get.

"I won't quit," Cookie promised. "But I'll never come in here by myself, or be left alone inside here again."

"That's fine," Janet agreed. "I don't blame you a bit."

"What do we do now? I mean...how do you get rid of the spirits if they've returned?"

"I don't know. I'll have to talk to Carl about it, but he's upset about something right now, so I'll speak to him later tonight."

Just as Janet's words faded away, some of the other waitresses began arriving. Janet greeted the ladies and began assigning them their duties for the night. Cookie stayed near the group, constantly looking over her shoulder and expecting anything to happen at any moment.

Janet wondered if maybe she was wrong about Carl. It might not be that some evil force was controlling him. It was possible that he knew the entity had returned, and just the thought of it had upset him so much that he could not discuss it. Maybe he had been attacked by the diabolical force and did not want to tell her for fear of upsetting her.

Whatever it was, Janet had to get the bar open for business. Then after everything got in full swing, she was going upstairs to Carl's apartment and confront him. He knew something and she was determined to find out what.

Chapter Twenty-eight

Now that most of the help had arrived, Janet felt sure everything would be okay for the rest of the evening. She and Cookie had agreed not to mention what had happened, except to Bobby or Carl. But—the evening had just begun. This is Margaret Collinsworth's story.

The five-foot-two Margaret was from a fairly large family, with two brothers and four sisters. She graduated from Holmes High School in Covington, Kentucky, and had been a waitress for several different establishments since then. She was accustomed to being around a lot of people and the furthest thing from her mind was some disembodied spirit harassing her. Margaret did not believe in ghosts.

* * * * *

The nightclub was about to open for business. Cookie followed Janet into the ladies' restroom to secretly discuss what had happened before the other employees began arriving. Margaret Collinsworth, a blonde-haired, green-eyed, bombshell, went into the bull room to check her station, making sure all of the tables were arranged properly.

The bull room was formerly called the Casino Room. It had once been filled with every kind of gambling apparatus, but now a brown, leather mechanical bull sat tall and proud in the middle of the room surrounded by tables on three sides.

Margaret had been assigned the task of waiting tables in the bull room tonight. The tips were not as good in here, but she enjoyed the rowdy cowboys lining up and waiting their turn to climb on "El-Toro," the bucking mechanical bull. The guys were always trying to strike up a conversation with her because of her sexy build. This particular night she was wearing tight, white shorts and a matching halter-top. She would drive the cowboys crazy. Since everything seemed to be in order, she headed back to the main ballroom to chitchat with Janet and Cookie, but as she reached the stage area she saw a large black dog run across the dance floor and leap up onto the stage. Her eyes followed the animal as it ran through the arched doorway on the left and disappeared back behind the stage.

"How in the heck did that mutt get in here?" She snickered. "I better shoo it outside."

She swayed past the jukebox and climbed the three brown, carpeted steps and walked back stage, but when she looked for the canine. The dog was gone, vanished in this air.

"Where'd it go?" she whispered, confused.

She looked straight ahead at the back stage door that led down to the basement. It was closed. She knew there was no way the dog could have gone through there. "Maybe the stupid thing ran out through the other door." She turned to walk out front.

"Maaaarrrrgaretttt!" Someone whispered her name like a cloud floating through the air.

The woman turned around and stopped cold when she realized no one was in the room with her. She called out apprehensively.

"Who's there?!"

No response.

"Okay. Real funny!" she said with a bite. "I don't have time for your silly games." She turned back around and headed for the stage, but just as she stepped through
the doorway she heard it again.
"Maaaarrrrgaretttt!"

"Knock it off," she sighed deeply. "You can come out now!"

Silence.

"Who in the hell's back there?" She was getting angry. She marched back into the room and walked the distance of the floor to the other arched doorway. She looked everywhere she could think of to try and find someone hiding backstage, but it became apparent to her that no human was calling her name. The thought sent a shiver up her spine, and, for the first time since she started working here, she did not like this building anymore.

What had just happened was not normal. Margaret was certain that she had just been singled out by some unseen entity, and she didn't like it at all! She wondered if the dog she had seen only moments prior had anything to do with all of this. She became more frightened as her thoughts ran away with her. She quickly left the room to find some of the other employees. Just as she stepped out onto the stage, the jukebox turned on and began playing "The Anniversary Waltz." She spun around to see who had dropped their money in the slot, but, once again, there was no one there. Margaret turned around and looked for any sign of the other employees, but no one was in the room.

Janet and Cookie were still in the ladies' room whispering about the ghosts when they heard the eerie melody filling the inside of the nightclub.

"I hate that damn song!" Janet said, disgusted. "Let's go see who played it. God, I hope it wasn't one of the ghosts!"

Cookie and Janet walked out of the restroom and saw Margaret walking at a fast pace toward them.

"Everything okay?" Janet asked hesitantly. Margaret was wearing a look of sheer terror on her face.

"I'm not sure," Margaret stammered as she looked at Janet, then Cookie. "I think this place is haunted."

Margaret's words sent terror gushing through Janet and Cookie. Janet did not want Margaret to quit so she quickly went into action.

"That's just Carl pulling one of his sick jokes," Janet lied. "There's no ghost here. Come on. Let's get ready. It's time to open the doors."

"But, Janet," Margaret pressed on as the "Anniversary Waltz" continued playing.

"I saw a big black dog run behind the stage, and, when I went to look for it, the damn thing wasn't there. Then somebody called my name, and I looked to see who it was, and I couldn't find one single person. Then that stupid jukebox came on by itself."

"It's Carl," Janet insisted, trying hard not to show the fear that was overtaking her. "He's acting weird. He's getting some kind of kick outta trying to scare us. He did it to me and Cookie earlier."

Janet turned toward Cookie. "Tell her, Cookie. Tell her I'm right."

Cookie looked at Janet, then at Margaret. No sense in letting the cat out of the bag, she thought. After all, Janet had promised she would talk to Carl and figure out how to get rid of the ghosts.
"Yeah! That's right," Cookie said slowly. "Carl tried to scare me, too. I saw him sneaking off right after he played that dumb song."

Just as cookie finished speaking, the jukebox clicked off and everything went calm inside the building. As the women stood there looking at each other, the rest of the employees came out of the game room where they had congregated to take a smoke break before the doors opened for business. I was seven-fifty-five in the evening.

"Let's get busy!" Janet said, loudly. "It's time to get to work."

The employees moved to their assigned positions as Janet and Cookie headed for the front doors to open them. There was a long line of patrons waiting to get inside.

"Thanks," Janet said to Cookie as she unlocked the front doors. "Margaret would've quit for sure if you hadn't helped me. I promise I'll get something done about this as soon as possible."

"The sooner the better!" Cookie replied.

Janet pushed open the doors and the crowd started pouring in. Cookie headed for her station, scared stiff. Janet headed for the bar to start serving drinks. Bobby Mackey's was open for business.

Chapter Twenty-nine

While conducting the interviews, I was told of a man who had worked for Bobby briefly as a sound engineer. I contacted him and asked that he tell me what he had experienced while inside the nightclub. At first, like most of the other people involved, he was reluctant to talk. After learning that many other people were coming forward telling of their own experiences, he relented.

Danny Hanavan is an only child and a graduate of Ross High School. He had completed training at Cincinnati Tech, Columbia School for Sound Engineering. He is five feet tall, with short brown hair and brown eyes. He works full time as a pipe fitter and welder. This is his story.

* * * * *

The bar was in full swing. People shouldered their way through the crowd. It was an ordinary night of laughing, dancing and singing. Bobby Mackey stood center stage in his black sport shirt and blue jeans, singing his heart out to some honky tonk, country tune. He scanned the crowded dance floor and smiled at the people who were swinging and swaying to the music.

Bobby had become an overnight success in Cincinnati and Northern Kentucky. The business was doing better than he had ever expected. He had recorded several songs in Nashville, commuting to the country music capital at least twice a month. His determination had paid off. Two of his songs had made it to the country music national charts and he was busy making his first music video. It looked as if his dreams of being a country-recording star would surely come true.

As the singing continued, Danny Hanavan sat in the back of he ballroom at the large, black soundboard. He was busy adjusting slide controls, keeping each instrument at the desired level so everything stayed perfectly balanced.

Danny was doing Bobby a favor by filling in on the soundboard this evening. He was a Christian and really did not like the barroom scene, but he enjoyed controlling the sound equipment for different bands. His wife rarely accompanied him to the bars, especially here. The first time she had set foot in Bobby Mackey's Music World, she felt something strange about the place. She told him that the building seemed strange, as if the place harbored some ancient secret, filled with memories of cruelty and death. He had not given her statement much thought at the time.

As he sat at the soundboard, he noticed that the meters on the panel began going crazy. The needles were bouncing left and right inside their glass enclosures. He looked down at the knobs and gasped when he saw two of the slide controls on his left moving up and down on their own, as if something unseen was standing beside him moving them. Danny had never believed in ghosts, but he knew something was dreadfully wrong.

"What the heck?" he growled as he reached over and grabbed both controls, moving them back to their original positions. Nothing like this had ever happened to him before. This was too strange and he felt something evil in the air. His wife's warning came crashing back into his mind.

"I'm losing my daggone mind," he muttered. He shrugged off the feelings and continued monitoring the equipment, but was suddenly confronted with a wave of terror when he looked up at Bobby and the band members on stage. He saw a pale, human form congeal out of the air and move across the stage toward Bobby. He sat frozen in his seat watching the entity move through the country singer as if he had become transparent. He found himself looking through Bobby, at John Hoffman, the drummer, and just the thought of it made him want to scream.

The sight was terrifying...almost too much to bear. The fear hit him like a hammer, causing him to break out in a cold sweat. He felt his skin crawling and realized he was not just imagining this apparition.

"My God," he whispered, "this is really happening!"

He watched the white, cloud-like thing move through Bobby and continue on to the right, toward Ernie Vaughn, the silver-haired bass guitar player. Danny could not believe his eyes.

The disembodied spirit penetrated Ernie exactly as it had just done to Bobby. The five-foot-nine Ernie was standing in the arched doorway at the end of the stage, near the jukebox, moving left and right, sliding his fingers up and down his white bass guitar. The apparition pierced through the man's white sport shirt and jeans, and then his flesh, without him even feeling it.

Danny blinked his eyes, and then quickly looked in all directions at the crowd to see if anyone else had noticed the entity. It was obvious that he was the only one who had seen the phenomenon that had just taken place.

'I've got to tell somebody', he thought, 'but whom'? If no one else had seen what had just happened, and he opened his mouth, he knew everyone would make fun of him, and call him a crackpot. He decided to sit back and watch and wait. If anyone else came forward saying that they, too, saw this strange occurrence, then he would talk.

As he tried to regain his composure and keep his thoughts on his job, he felt something icy cold go through his body. It hit him in the chest then came out through his back, and before he could move a muscle he felt something breathing on the nape of his neck.

Danny wheeled around in the chair only to find no one there. He surveyed the back of the ballroom and saw a group of people sitting at a table on the far west wall. He looked away for a split second, and then glanced back at the wall, and when he did, he found the table full of people gone, vanished from sight. With that, Danny wanted to get up and run and get away from this madness, but he knew if he did, Bobby would never forgive him for abandoning him right in the middle of the show.

He tried to swallow his fear. All he wanted was to hold onto his sanity and make it through the night. He hoped someone else would come forward and tell Bobby they, too, saw the ghost on the stage. All he could do for now was watch and wait...and pray!

Chapter Thirty

This chapter required interviews with Janet and Carl to piece together the next sequence of events. One customer had his own bizarre experience this same evening while inside the nightclub. Combining the pieces, this is the way they said it happened.

* * * * *

Everything was moving along quite well. The waitresses were busy going from table to table and the bartenders were filling the orders as fast as they came in. Bobby and the band were banging out a country tune and Janet found this the opportune time to head upstairs and talk to Carl about the demonic harassment that had taken place earlier tonight.

She moved out from behind the bar and made her way to the stairs that led to Carl's apartment. Reaching the door at the top of the staircase, she knocked softly three times.

"Who is it?" Carl's voice echoed out from inside the room.

"It's me, Carl. Can I come in?"

"Yeah."

She twisted the knob and walked in. From the moment she entered the apartment, she felt something strange, something dark and mysterious, almost life threatening. She looked around the room and saw Carl sitting in an old wooden rocking chair, rocking back and forth with his back to her.

"Carl," Janet said apprehensively. "We have to talk."
"Bout what?" he asked sarcastically, his back still to her. "What do you wanna talk about?"

"They're back, Carl! The demons showed themselves to Cookie and Margaret."

"I just wish people would leave me alone!" Carl snarled. He slapped his hand against the arms of the rocker, stood to his feet and turned around facing Janet with an angry look disfiguring his face. "Are they hurting anyone?" he asked bitterly.

She was again taken aback by his attitude. She felt certain it was not Carl she was talking to, but some spirit inside his body, controlling his thoughts and words. Carl's voice was different. It was deep and raspy, and he stared at her with a murderous look.

From that very moment, Janet knew she would not be able to count on Carl to help her rid this place of the evil force. He had become one of them. But, if she tried to convince Bobby of that, he would have a tizzy. She had to find someone to help her. But who?

"Never mind, Carl," she said as he continued staring at her, his eyes now like invisible knives. "It's just my imagination. I guess I'm being silly. Too many old memories, you know, from what we went through before. I've got to get back downstairs. I'll talk to you later."

With urgency in her walk, she turned and left the room. Carl stood perfectly still, watching her as she disappeared through the doorway.

Once back at the bar Janet began serving drinks again. Her trembling hands were making it difficult to do her job. It was she, however, who was determined to win this time. It was she who would swallow her fear and find a way to defeat this evil. She was going to find a psychic, a priest, or some trained exorcist to come here and help her rid this place of evil, with or without Bobby or Carl's help.

"Drink!" A deep male voice called out over the crowd, "I wanna drink!" The man's words caused Janet to wheel around just in time to see a mountain of a man sit down at the bar and smile at her with a mischievous grin.

"What can I get you?"

"I wanna rum and Coke, but don't give me no cheap booze. I want the best...Bacardi, one-fifty-one...if you please."

"No Problem," she smiled and headed to get a glass to mix the drink. In only seconds, Janet brought the man his rum and Coke and sat it gently down on the bar. She collected his money, but as she started to head for the register to deposit the cash, the man stopped her.

"Aren't you Janet Mackey, Bobby's wife?"

"Yes. Do I know you?"

"Nah. I've only been here a couple of times before, to see a buddy of mine. I'm waiting for him to show up, but he ain't here yet. My name's Ralph...Ralph Bartholomew. Everyone calls me 'Hollywood.'"

Ralph looked like a lumberjack. He had short dark brown hair, parted on the left side, and a full beard that needed trimming. His cold gray eyes were hypnotic and Janet found them almost frightening after what she had already gone through tonight. She wondered if he was a ghost, so she reached across the bar and gently patted him on the top of his right hand, just to see. She was relieved when she felt real flesh and bones.

"Nice to meet you, anyway," she said with a smile, then headed for the cash register to deposit the man's money. Ralph took one sip of his drink then stood up and headed for the men's restroom. He pushed his way through the crowd when suddenly he stopped cold.

He found himself gazing at a large mirror that hung on the south wall of the ballroom. He saw the images of people behind him, walking towards the dance floor as Bobby began singing a love song. In the middle of all the people, he saw the image of a headless woman in a white gown moving through the room, as if she was heading for the bar.

He stared deeper into the glass and watched as the headless girl floated right through the bar where his drink was sitting. He wheeled around on the balls of his feet and searched the room for the apparition, but she was gone, vanished into thin air.

"Damn!" he growled as he tucked his white shirt into his brown dress pants. "I'm going nuts!"

The man knew it was not the rum. He had just arrived here and ordered his first drink for the night, and he had only taken one sip of that.

"The hell with it!" Ralph shrugged off what had just happened and headed on. He walked down the paneled hallway leading into the men's room and thought it strange that he did not have to wait in line for his turn to reach the urinals. There was not one single person in the restroom.

"Guess that damn ghost scared everyone off!" he laughed as he reached the long, white porcelain urinal and started to unzip his pants. Out of the corner of his eye, he saw something moving toward him. He spun around and saw a big black dog standing beside him. The Chow was watching every move the man made, as if inspecting him.
"How the hell did you get in here?" Ralph sneered at the dog.

"He's mine," a deep voice called out from the hallway. "Don't worry. He doesn't bite."

Ralph found himself staring at the large boned, brown-haired man with a cigar hanging out of his mouth. The man was wearing black slacks, and a white long-sleeved shirt and a green vest.

"Come to Buck," the man said as he knelt down in the doorway. Ralph looked at the dog, then back at the stranger. Something did not set right with him, so he decided he did not need to urinate anymore. He cautiously walked away from the dog and past the man, then strode up the hall and out of the room.

Outside, Ralph still felt it. He did not know why, but he had to wait for the man and the dog to come out. As he stood there waiting, he watched five or six other men walk in and out of the restroom, and finally he asked a short, bald-headed man in a white shirt and jeans if he had seen a dog and a big man in there.

"Nope, I didn't," the guy replied, then walked on.

Ralph could not believe it! Since there was only one way in or out of the restroom, the man and dog had to still be in there. He waited until another guy, in a red and black-checkered shirt, headed down the hall into the men's room, and he followed close behind.

Once he reached the inside of the restroom, Ralph found himself engulfed in a state of fear and confusion. First, he had seen a headless woman, and now the man and dog had disappeared as if they had never existed.

That was it. He had seen enough. Ralph walked back out of the restroom, and then hurried for the front door. He wanted out of this place before anything else happened. He sure could have used the drink that he left on the bar, but he was not staying in here for another second.

The burly man pushed through the front doors without saying a word to anyone. All he wanted to do was get as far away from Bobby Mackey's Music World as possible!

Janet noticed that the man did not return for his drink. She picked up his glass and poured the contents into the sink. It puzzled her that someone would pay good money for a shot of Bacardi, take one sip of it, and then just leave. Maybe he was a ghost, she thought. She had no idea why Ralph Bartholomew had left so suddenly.

The rest of the night went smoothly. Janet assured Cookie once again, that she would get something done, but she made the girl promise not to mention this to anyone until she found a solution.

Several hours later, at closing time, Carl stood at the window of his apartment and watched Bobby, Janet and the employees drive from the building.

"Something's wrong with me," he muttered aloud. "I feel like something's inside me." Carl was his old self for now. The spirit that had possessed him was lying dormant, waiting for the right time to use his body again. Carl did not remember Janet coming upstairs tonight. He did not really even recall the evening that the entity had entered his body, but he knew something was wrong. He turned from the window and walked across the room, then lay down on the bed staring up at the ceiling. He had no idea that his body was being used and controlled by some diabolical force, the entity entering and leaving him at will.

Chapter Thirty-one

Bobby and Janet had a lot of heated discussions over the possibility that some demonic force inhabited their nightclub. Janet needed to tell him that their employees were beginning to complain. His disbelief made this difficult

* * * * *

The afternoon sun bathed the area with a dazzling light as marvelous swan-like clouds passed over the Mackey's house in Highland Heights, Kentucky.

Janet and Bobby lived in a three-bedroom, yellow buffed-brick, ranch-style home with their two daughters, Anita and Shaunda. Bobby sat at the round oak table in his blue jeans and black sport shirt drinking a diet Pepsi and tying to tie up some loose odds and ends before he packed up and headed south. He was booked for five days in Nashville to shoot film footage for a music video of his latest hit, "Hero Daddy."

Janet knew he had a lot on his mind, and he certainly would not want to hear what she had to say, but she figured she might as well get it over with. She walked into the kitchen, pulled up one of the wooden armchairs and said down across from Bobby. She took a deep breath and looked around the peach-colored room, trying to figure out an easy way to bring up the subject of the ghosts.

She studied the dark-stained cabinets, Coppertone stove and matching, magnet-covered refrigerator as if they could provide her with answers.

"Bobby," Janet finally said hesitantly, her eyes already revealing the dread that was welled up inside her.

"What is it?" he asked as he laid the letter he was reading down on the table.

"We need to talk," she said with a sigh. "We've got a problem at the nightclub."

"What kind of problem?" now giving Janet his full attention.

The woman tapped her fingers on the table for a few seconds, staring silently at her husband before speaking.

"Well? What's up?"

"You're not gonna like what I've got to say, Bobby! Do you remember when I kept telling you there were ghosts at the nightclub and ---"

"Not that again!" Bobby growled as he sat erect in his chair staring at his wife.

"Don't even start that stuff. If you and Carl want to believe that he sealed the Devil in the well in the basement, that's fine with me, but I don't want to hear about it, again!"

"Well, you're GONNA hear about it!" Janet declared, her voice rising and falling as she spoke. "That is, if you want to keep any help!"

"What's that supposed to mean?"

"It's not just me and Carl, now. The spirits are back and they bothered Cookie and Margaret last night and –"

"Oh, that's great!" Bobby interrupted his wife. "You and Carl promised me you wouldn't tell anyone about your stupid ghosts friends!"

"We didn't!" Janet defended herself. "Nobody had to tell anyone anything.

Whatever's in there is bothering the help now, and as much as you want to ignore it, you're going to have to get involved. There's no telling how many others the ghost might have frightened and we just don't know about it. If you don't help me do something, we won't have any help to run the nightclub."

"Who says some ghost bothered them?" Bobby asked disgusted, his face showing irritation and frustration.

"I told you – Cookie and Margaret, but that isn't the only problem. Carl is acting strange! I tried to talk to him about this tonight and he nearly bit my head off. It's like he's one of them."

"That's not it!" Bobby argued. "When you were in the hospital giving birth to Shaunda, I told Carl I didn't want him talking about ghosts to you anymore. He promised he wouldn't. He was just keeping his word to me."

"He was drunk, Bobby! When I went upstairs to talk to him, I could tell he was three sheets to the wind. I know he drinks, but not like that. I could smell the booze coming out of him ten feet away. I'm telling you something's wrong with Carl. I think he's possessed."

"That's a bunch of nonsense! Pure nonsense!"

"You're wrong!" Janet snapped back. "I know what I'm talking about. There's something wrong with him."

"I'll tell you what," Bobby said, shaking his head in distaste, "you handle it. Call a priest if you want to and have him come and do some mumbo jumbo exorcism on Carl and the building. Just don't get me involved in none of this. And don't be talking about this to no one else, or we won't have to worry about not having any help. We won't have any customers."

Mocking Bobby, Janet shook her own head in disgust. "I wish whatever's in the club would show itself to you. Then you'd believe me! I've got a felling this isn't going to be like the last time the demons appeared in there. It's going to be a lot worse."

"Just handle it, Janet," Bobby scoffed. "I've got enough to worry about, so you'll have to take care of the ghosts and demons at the club. As far as Carl is concerned, I've noticed he's been drinking a lot lately. I'm going to insist that he joins A.A. or I'm going to have to find somebody to take his place."

Before Janet could respond, Bobby stood up, shook his head and walked toward the living room to use the phone. "Ghosts!" he groaned as he left the kitchen.

Janet found herself alone and confused. She could not count on Bobby to help her and she felt certain she couldn't get any help from Carl. She didn't know what to do, but she had to figure out something before things got out of hand.

She sighed deeply, then stood up and disappeared into the bedroom to take a nap. She wanted to be alone for a while to sort out her thoughts.

Chapter Thirty-two

Bobby Mackey had hired Roger Heath to do some general maintenance and repair work at the nightclub. Carl was to help Roger in this endeavor.

Roger, age thirty-seven, moved from North Carolina to Northern Kentucky in 1973, when assigned to recruiting duty in Cincinnati by the U.S. Army. After six and a half years of service, he decided to leave the military for a less regimented civilian life. He and his wife Linda returned to North Carolina. While in North Carolina, Roger "got religion" and started attending school at Mount Olive College. After two years, he became an ordained minister in the Central Conference of the North Carolina Association of Original Free Will Baptists and began pasturing a small church in the community of Indian Springs, not far from Mount Olive.

While at Indian Springs, Roger continued classes at the college as well as working at the school's maintenance department to sustain himself and his wife. It was there that he learned he had a God-given talent for woodworking, and constructed many fine pieces of office furniture for the college, which put him in a favorable light with the college president. Although older than most of the students, his 3.6 grade point average, friendly personality, willingness to help, and ability to communicate with people, made him popular among the students, the staff, and professors at the college.

It was during his tenure at Indian Springs Free Will Baptist Church that things began to change for Roger. Not so much physical change, but an emotional and spiritual change. He was not losing his religion as some might have thought. In fact, he became more and more perceptive to what he believed to be the true meaning of God's teachings in the Bible, but somehow these revelations did not jive with those of the church, and, after a little more than a year, the church leadership quietly suggested that he either change his position on certain issues or resign his pastor ship. After much prayer, thought, and discussion, Roger and Linda decided to "pack it up" and move back to Northern Kentucky. Almost immediately, Roger renewed his friendship with an old acquaintance, Bobby Mackey.

The following is the result of several interviews with Roger and Carl. That is what they say happened next.

* * * * *

Carl awoke from a fitful sleep as the pounding on the front door of the nightclub echoed up the stairway and hammered away at his ears. Slowly rising from his bed in a clumsy, half-asleep daze, he stood to his feet and pulled back the heavy blue drape that covered the window of the upstairs apartment, the morning sunlight momentarily blinding him. Shielding his eyes with his empty hand, he immediately recognized the gray-haired, heavy-set man clad in blue jeans and a white shirt standing below. He grinned sheepishly as he yelled through the glass, "Just a minute!" He had forgotten Roger was coming today to take down the old, unused light fixtures in the bull room.

Releasing the curtain, Carl turned and spied a pair of black jogging shorts carelessly thrown on the floor next to the wooden rocker. Had it not been for the white striping on the side of the shorts, he probably would have never seen them.

Fumbling, he picked up the shorts, put his feet through the legs, and pulled them up to his waist. The snap of the elastic waistband smacking against his flesh caused him to wince. He plopped down in the rocker and stretched out his arms to reach the black and white sneakers that were on the floor in front of him. He briefly contemplated his bare feet and lazily slid them into the tattered canvas shoes, not bothering to tie them.

Carl strained his sleep-weary muscles to push himself up from the rocker and stumbled through the door to the landing at the top of the stairs. Flipping on the light, he muttered a curse and cautiously descended the steps.

"Good morning!" Roger smiled as Carl swung open the wooden door between them. "What's happening, buddy?"

"Not much," Carl remarked as he squinted at the longhaired brown-eyed man before him. "C'mon in. I'm going to go back upstairs for a minute. You know where all the lights are, don't you?"

"Yeah. I'll see you in a little bit." Roger slid past Carl and headed into the bowels of the old building to turn on the lights.

As Carl trekked back upstairs, Roger groped around in the darkness until he found the door to the power room. Feeling along the wall, he located the switch then flooded the room with bright, almost blinding illumination. After waiting a few seconds for his eyes to readjust themselves, he walked over to the electrical panel and flipped on the circuit breaker for the bull room lights. Leaving the power room, he went into the old cashier's office where he knew Carl stored the twelve-foot aluminum ladder he would need to remove the old fluorescent fixtures.

As Roger entered the office, he stared at the huge cylinder-shaped safe that dominated the room. It was a massive piece of masterful workmanship. He had seen it only briefly a couple of times before, and it fascinated him.

Even though he knew that no one would mind if he examined the safe, Roger cautiously peered over his shoulder before he grasped the handle of the unlocked door and swung it open. The thickness of the safe almost stunned him when he compared the inside chamber to the outside dimensions of the behemoth hulk, he saw the safe's walls were at least six inches of solid case-hardened steel!

The inside chamber was lined with satin-finished stainless steel, and the outside was painted a light greenish-gray, lettered on each side "Specially built for E.A. Brady." I don't know who this Brady guy was, Roger thought, but he sure didn't want anybody gettin' to his money.

Shutting the door back to the position in which he found it, Roger realized something else about the huge vault...no one could have possibly fit it through the office door. The office had to have been built around it.

Roger heard Carl walking down the creaking stairs and quickly grabbed the aluminum ladder and wrestled it through the office door just as Carl entered the bull room.

"Well, ready to earn your pay?" Roger playfully asked as the two men set up the ladder and gazed at the two rows of antiquated fluorescent fixtures overhead.

"As ready as I'm gonna get," Carl contemplated the job ahead of them.

Time passed quickly as the two men worked at the simple, but tedious task. Carl spent most of the time in the attic holding the bolts so they would not turn, while Roger, below him in the bull room, loosened the nuts that anchored the fixtures. The heavy-set Roger looked at his watch and was surprised to see that it was already past two o'clock in the afternoon.

"Hey, Carl!" Roger yelled up through the ceiling. "You wanna come down and get some lunch?"

"Sounds good to me!" Carl's exasperated voice answered as it filtered down through the ceiling tiles above.

Roger heard the sound of scuffing feet, and, within seconds Carl's dirty, sweaty-soaked body brushed past him as the be-ragged man rushed to the back door and began inhaling huge gulps of fresh clean air.

"Jeez, little buddy! You look like ten miles of bad road!" Roger remarked somewhat amused by the sight before him.

"Have you looked in a mirror lately?" An impish grin crossed Carl's face. "You look like you fell face first into a pile of coal!"

It was obvious that Roger had not given any thought at all to the dirt and dust that had collected for years on the fixtures and had fallen onto his own sweaty face. He examined his reflection in the glass of one of the arcade games.

"Well, bro, I gez weez bedda put deez heah lights away a' fo' weez cut de watermelon, huh?" Roger quipped.

"Right on, mah man!" Carl answered. "Gimme five!"

The two men laughed loudly as their palms smacked together, and then turned to begin putting away the fixtures they had already taken down. Roger began stacking the various parts near the doorway as Carl hauled them down the stairs into a storage room in the basement.

The afternoon sun was hot and both men were perspiring profusely, so much, in fact, that Carl had removed his shirt and was now wearing nothing but the black jogging shorts and sneakers. He was panting heavily and had returned for the last load.

"Hey, Carl! Who've you got down there with you?"
"What're you talking about?" Carl stooped to pick up the last of the fixtures.

"Stand up and turn around here," Roger insisted as he lit a cigarette and strode over to his friend. "Let me see!"

"See what?" Carl asked as Roger grabbed him by the shoulder and turned his back toward the light of the doorway.

"Just go to the ladies' room and look for yourself in that full-length mirror!" Roger demanded, his wide eyes accentuating his bewildered expression.

Carl took off in a full gallop toward the women's restroom not knowing what he was going to find, but he knew Roger well enough to know that something was wrong, and it worried him.

"Son-of-a-bitch!" Roger heard Carl scream from behind the closed door. "What the hell?" He exploded through the door and sort of aimlessly walked back to the bull room.

Roger was on the landing of the stairwell now peering down at the opened door to the storage area where Carl had been stacking the old fixtures. He had expected someone to appear from inside, but so far, nothing.

"Roger!" Carl called out to get the stocky man's attention. "How could this be?"

Roger walked back inside and around behind Carl. As he studied the two small, dirty hand prints still on Carl's back, he wondered if his friend was up to another one of his practical jokes and decided to play around with the idea. He knew that Carl, even the fun-loving mischief-maker that he was, could never keep a straight face for very long no matter how well planned and thought out the joke was.

"So, who's your girlfriend?" Roger asked, still staring at the hand prints on Carl's back.

"I swear I don't know, Roger! There's nobody here but me and you!" Carl insisted, intentionally standing still so that his friend could look at his back. "I don't know how they got there!"

Roger and Carl both almost jumped out of their skins as the jukebox came on and the lyrics of "The Anniversary Waltz" filled the huge chambers of the nightclub.

"What the hell's going on?" Roger exclaimed as Carl turned to face him. "First, you've got a woman's hand prints on your back as if she was hugging you, and now the frigging jukebox comes on! This ain't funny, Carl!"

"I don't know," Carl meekly whispered as tears began to well up in his eyes.

Roger looked at Carl's expression and immediately assessed that if this was a practical joke, it was not of Carl's doing. But, who did this? And why? He also somehow knew that when his buddy said he did not know what was going on, he was holding back something.

As the last notes of "The Anniversary Waltz" faded away, Roger noticed Carl's body was trembling, and, although he had managed to restrain his tears, Carl's eyes were still glassy with moisture.

Roger was not hungry anymore, but maybe if he could get Carl to eat something, he might calm down and they could talk about what had just happened.

"Why don't we get cleaned up and go get something to eat?" he asked then turned toward the restroom to go wash up.

"Okay, I'm going upstairs. I'll be back down in a few minutes."

"All right, buddy," Roger answered as Carl disappeared into the hallway and up the stairs.

Leaving the bull room, Roger looked to his right and froze in his tracks. The jukebox was dark. None of its lights were on.

"That's impossible," he blurted out as he examined the power cord. It was plugged in. He then climbed up onto the stage and reached inside the doorway, feeling for the switch that sent power to the receptacle below. His fingers finally finding the switch, he flipped it up, and the jukebox lights immediately flickered and came on in a display of brilliant colors. My God in heaven, he though as he turned off the switch and the machine went dark once again. This is ridiculous!

Roger quickly got down off the stage and headed for the restroom to clean up. He was not a man who was easily frightened by either man or beast, but this was something that was beyond comprehension, even for an ex-clergyman.

After washing up, Roger went back into the bull room and shut and barred the doors, then tuned off all of the lights. He then went into the barroom and sat at the bar waiting for Carl to come back downstairs. It was eerie inside the massive, darkened chamber, and a strange uneasiness washed over him. It was not fear. It was some abnormal deviation that he could not quite put his finger on.

As he sat at the bar, staring through the portal that led into the game room, his thoughts were interrupted by the soft touch of someone running their fingers through his shoulder length hair on the back of his neck. He quickly turned to see who this amorous playmate might be, but discovered that he was alone. Must have been the wind, he thought, and instantly realized that all of the doors were closed and nothing else inside the building had moved, not even the cobweb that hung down from the ceiling less than two feet away. He could hear Carl walking around in the upstairs apartment. It couldn't have been him.

"Jesus! What's going on?" Roger turned on the bar stool back toward the bar. Looking forward, he realized that he could see his own reflection in the mirror on the opposite wall if he would move over one stool to his left. Once he repositioned himself, he waited and watched, never taking his eyes off the mirror.

After several seconds, Roger felt the light touch on his neck again, but saw nothing in the mirror. His muscles tensing, he quickly sprang around and grabbed at the air, but came up empty handed. "This is nuts," he practically screamed just as Carl came down the stairs and walked into the barroom.

"What's nuts," Carl asked with a knowing look.

"Someone was...ah, nothing. Forget it," Roger answered, the anxiety clearly revealed in his voice. "Let's get outta here and get something to eat!"

The two men left the nightclub and went to eat at a popular fast food restaurant in south Newport for hamburgers. Once they had settled down to their meal, roger tried to press Carl for answers about the goings-on at the club, but he would only jokingly talk about ghouls and goblins. He was hedging on the questions, and Roger couldn't figure out why. Was Carl afraid of being reprimanded by Bobby or Janet? Maybe he thought Roger
would laugh at him. Or was he afraid of something at the nightclub?

"Come on, Carl," Roger pleaded. "You know we're friends and anything you tell me stays between me and you. If I'm going to work there, don't you think I have a right to know what's going on? After all, man, my sanity's at stake here, too!"

"Okay," Carl finally gave in. "I'll tell you, but not here. There are too many people around. Wait till we get in the car."

The two men finished their meal and left the restaurant. On the drive back, Carl told Roger about the building's sordid past. He ended the tale with the information in Johana's diary. He was not about to tell Roger about the demons and the raging battle he had been forced to fight, and he was not going to tell his friend that the demons were back. He had not known that himself until today since only he was controlling his own thoughts now that the demons were allowing him to do so.

"It makes for one hell of a Halloween story, doesn't it?" Carl remarked as they pulled up in front of the building. "Don't worry, though. They're just tying to make you feel at home."

The two men laughed as they got out of the car and strode toward the front door. Carl had said "they" not "she," but Roger didn't want to let on to Carl that he had heard the discrepancy. He knew Carl was still holding something back, but he would either figure it out for himself or wait until Carl got ready to tell him the rest of the story. He knew it was no use in prodding the maintenance man any further.

"What's this?" Carl asked as he reached out and pulled a note off one of the glass panes of the front door. He unfolded the paper and read, "Carl, did you forget that you were to come to the house and cut the grass today? Janet."

With a concerned look, Carl handed Roger the keys to the nightclub. "Here," he said looking at his watch. "I've got to go to Bobby and Janet's. I promised them I'd cut their grass this morning and I forgot all about it. I'll be back by six, maybe earlier. Lock the front door and don't let anybody in except me. Anybody else who needs to get in already has a key."

"Yeah, but I can't take down those lights by myself." Roger stated.

"I know, but you can do that work up on the stage that Bobby wanted done, can't you?"

"Sure. I guess I'll see you around six then."

As Roger locked the door behind him, Carl got into his car and drove toward Highland Heights. Reaching the end of the mirrored hallway, Roger pulled the mini flashlight from its holster on his belt and shined it in his path. There was no need to turn on any lights other than those on the stage since he would be working in that area.

Bobby had told Roger that he wanted the stage, including the speaker columns at each end, dusted, cleaned and organized. It was a monumental task that would take three or four hours for one man to do, but Bobby had been adamant about it, and what Bobby wanted, Bobby got! The new sound engineer, Tom Weber, had informed him that dirt and dust had very adverse effects on the quality of the sound produced by the tons of expensive equipment Bobby had purchased. For some reason unknown to Bobby, Danny Hanavan refused to work the soundboard anymore, so Bobby had found Tom Weber to fill in temporarily.

Roger had been busy for about an hour completely oblivious to anything except the job he was doing. He was facing toward the back of the stage, dusting off the drums when he heard a faint female voice call out his name from somewhere behind him.

"Yeah!" he answered as he turned to find the room completely empty. He suddenly realized that all of the ballroom lights were on.

"Who's there?"

No one responded.

"Cut the comedy!" He climbed down from the stage and walked toward the back of the room. "This ain't funny!"

His eyes scanned the area, but he saw no one. He walked out into the hallway to the front doors. They were locked.

"I don't believe this," he muttered as he walked back through the swinging doors into the barroom, but saw nothing.

Rushing to the power room, he turned on the breakers, flooding the entire building in a sea of light. Going from room to room, the methodically searched every nook and cranny, trying to find the prankster, but to no avail.

"This is impossible," he said as he headed back for the stage. He knew that he had not turned on the ballroom lights, and he knew that there was no other living human being in the building except him.

Roger sat on the edge of the stage trying to make some sense of what had just happened when his thoughts were suddenly interrupted by a loud crash from behind the stage.

"Son-of-a-bitch," the ex-preacher screamed as he jumped to his feet and ran through the door at the right of the stage, scrambling around the power amplifiers and crashing through the backstage door. To his surprise, everything was in place and no one was in the room.

"Roger," a soft voice whispered, as he stood there, motionless, contemplating this latest event. The voice came from somewhere out front in the ballroom. Racing back out to the stage, he arrived just in time to see a dark shadow move along the wall by the old kitchen and disappear.

"Hey! You!" he yelled to the now empty room. Jumping from the stage, he ran toward the kitchen. "Hey! Come back here!" he screamed as he reached the door that led inside the kitchen. Flinging the door open, he was greeted by an empty room.

He searched the room, but no one was to be found.   "This is insane!" he exclaimed as he walked out of the room, sweat pouring from his face. "I ain't believing this! This is enough to make a preacher cuss."

Suddenly, a loud rap came at the front door, and Roger hurried down the hallway to see if anyone was really there this time. He was relieved to see Carl's face through the glass panels. Fumbling for the key, he nervously unlocked the door and let Carl inside.

"What's wrong?" Carl asked as he noticed the anxious look on Roger's face.

"Carl, you ain't going to believe this, but I swear it's true!" Roger exclaimed, telling his friend what had happened.

After Roger finished his story, Carl awkwardly smiled and reassured Roger that Johana was just having one of her mischievous days. There was nothing to worry about. She would never bring any harm on him.

Somewhat suspicious but willing to accept Carl's explanation, for now at least, Roger looked at his watch and gave a sigh of relief. It was now five-thirty, and that sounded like going home time to him.

Asking Carl to let him out, Roger headed through the door to his car. It was time for a hot meal, a warm bath, and an evening of quiet reflection. It had been a long time since the ex-minister had spent an entire evening praying, but tonight he planned on doing just that.

Chapter Thirty-three

During the course of my investigation and lengthy interviews, I learned that it was not just employees and customers who had strange experiences at the nightclub. The demonic forces had even played havoc with some of the local police officers when they found reason to be on the property. This chapter deals with what some of those officers experienced.

* * * * *

Wilder patrol Officer Larry Hornsby looked at the silver Timex on his left wrist. It was four-forty-five in the morning. The full moon stood high over the roof of Bobby Mackey's Music World as the patrol car's headlights fixed on the building. He was driving north on Route 9, checking the business district to make sure all of the stores and other establishments were secure.

The black-haired, brown-eyed Hornsby was a graduate of Eastern State University where he studied Law Enforcement and received a diploma for successfully completing the Police Academy. He had also received diplomas at Northern Kentucky University for various other police-related courses over the years. Hornsby had been with the Wilder Police Department for over ten years. There wasn't much that ever surprised him.

As he was driving past the nightclub he looked toward the entrance doors. Something caught his attention. Shadows of what appeared to be two people were moving up the mirrored hallway. He wheeled the auto around in the middle of the street and climbed out of the white patrol car. With his black flashlight in hand, he walked over and peered through the glass panes of the front doors, but was unable to see anyone inside. He checked the doors. They were locked. Hornsby got back into his car and drove around the building to check the back doors. He turned off the headlights and the engine, and then lifted his six-foot stocky frame from the vehicle, tucking his white uniform shirt into the blue pants, as he stood erect. He stared up the concrete steps that led to the back entrance.

Hornsby straightened the black gun belt around his waist, then switched on his flashlight and climbed the steps, his black patent-leather police shoes squeaking as he made his way up to the door.

He gently pushed on the door, and, to his surprise, it swung open wide, allowing the cop to look inside of the main ballroom. Hornsby called in to the dispatcher on his portable radio and requested another officer to meet him at the back of the building. He didn't know if someone had just simply forgotten to lock the door from the inside, or if he had stumbled onto a burglary while it was still in progress. Maybe someone escaped out this door, he thought. That would explain the two shadows he saw moving in the front hallway.

It didn't take long before another officer pulled into the back of the nightclub with his headlights out. The blonde-haired, blue-eyed man walked to the stairs and met Hornsby at the top of the landing where the officers discussed the possibility of a break-in. Hornsby told the other cop that Carl lived in the upstairs apartment and advised him not to shoot at anyone unless it became necessary. He didn't want to take a chance on Carl being injured accidentally.

The men entered the building, being careful not to make any noise. Hornsby walked through the dimly lit ballroom toward the old kitchen while the other officer made his way to the game room. Just as Hornsby reached the kitchen door, he heard two voices. It was a man and a woman arguing. Hornsby motioned to the other cop, who was coming around the end of the bar toward him.

"Do you hear those voices?" Hornsby whispered.

The cop nodded his head, indicating he, too, heard them.

"Let's go," Hornsby said softly.

The voices were coming from behind the stage and music began playing from the same area. The men looked at each other with a puzzled look, and then continued on until they reached the stage. Officer Hornsby drew his .357 Magnum out of its holster and pointed it at the arched doorway on the right of the stage. The other policeman covered the left doorway.

"Who's there?" Hornsby called out loudly. As he did, the music stopped and the man and woman instantly quit arguing. There was only silence. A heart wrenching deafening silence.

"Police Officer!" He shouted louder. Come out and show yourselves!"

No response.

The officers waited for several long seconds, but no one appeared.

"Come on," Hornsby said to the other cop.

The two men climbed up onto the stage and directed their flashlights through both of the arched doorways. With their guns pointed in front of them, the officers stepped through opposite portals, moving back stage. It didn't take long for the men to meet in the middle of the room. They were unable to find anyone in the area. They looked up at the trap door leading to the attic. It was pad-locked.

"Nobody went up there," Hornsby whispered with a puzzled look.

The officers looked over at the door leading down to the basement. The slide bolt was still in place.

"Damn," Hornsby whispered. "No one could've gone down there, either!"

The men looked at each other as if they had both lost their minds.

"You did hear the voices and music didn't you?" Hornsby had to ask again.

"Yes, but there's no one here!"

Nothing like this had ever happened to either of them before. They had indeed heard the voices and the music, but it became apparent that it was not from some living human being.

"Do you believe in ghosts?" the other officer asked Hornsby with a serious look on his face.

"Not until now. Let's check the rest of the building and get the hell out of here."

They walked out onto the stage and methodically checked each room for an intruder. They made their way upstairs and checked Carl's apartment, but he wasn't there.

Hornsby shook his head in disbelief as both men walked back downstairs making their way, once again, into the main ballroom.

As they reached the middle of the bar, the back door they had entered through earlier slammed shut by itself with a loud bang.

"Son-of-a-bitch!" Hornsby shrieked. "Come on!"

Both men scurried across the room and, in mere seconds pushed open the door. They figured they would see some burglar racing down the stairs, tying to escape before they found him, but to both men's surprise, no one was anywhere in sight.

"There's no way someone could've got away that quick without us seeing them!" Hornsby complained loudly. "I ain't telling anyone about this. They'll think I'm nuts! If I was you, I'd keep my mouth shut, too."

"Don't worry about that," his partner replied. "They'd kick us off the force."

"I'm not saying this as a fact," Hornsby sighed, "but I think we just had a run in with a ghost! Let's call the owners and have them come down here and lock this place up so we can get out of here."

"Sounds good to me," the cop almost laughed.

They walked back to the bar, and Hornsby picked up the tan telephone that sat next to the cash register. He looked at the emergency night phone number that was listed on the side of the register and quickly dialed Bobby Mackey's home.

Janet, still half asleep, answered the phone on the fifth ring. Officer Hornsby told her he had found the back door open and that he and another officer searched the interior of the building, but everything seemed to be okay. He wasn't about to tell her what he had just experienced. He didn't even want to admit it to himself. After a brief conversation, Janet asked him just to close the door behind him and she would come down later and lock it.

Hornsby had no way of knowing that Janet was lying. She wasn't going near the building tonight. As far as she was concerned it was one of the demons trying to lure her back there. She didn't care if some burglar carried everything out of the building. In fact, she hoped they would. It would have tickled her pink to close the business. She didn't care if she ever saw that place again.

Hornsby hung up the phone and told the other cop what Janet had said. They walked back to the door and stepped out onto the concrete landing. Hornsby closed the door and then gently pushed on it to see how easily it would open, but to both men's surprise, the door was locked.

"No way!" Hornsby growled, and then shoved on the door with both hands. It still didn't open. Hornsby looked at the other man and without saying a work they descended the steps, got in their patrol cars and drove away.

"I know I just had a run-in with a ghost!" Hornsby grumbled as he drove south on Route 9.

Completing his tour of duty on the night shift, Officer Hornsby sat at the desk inside of the Wilder police station waiting for Officer Steve Seiter to relieve him.

The brown-haired, green-eyed Seiter pushed through the office door at six-fifty that morning.

"Bout time you got here!" Hornsby said jokingly as the five-foot-nine Seiter walked over to the desk, yawning robustly. The twenty-four-year-old Officer Seiter was a stocky man. He was married with four children and lived in a one-story white clapboard house directly in front of the white wood frame police station.

"You're lucky I came in at all," Seiter grinned. "I didn't get much sleep last night."

"I need to talk to you about something," Hornsby stated as Seiter sat down in a metal chair next to the desk.

"What's that?"

"Do you believe in ghosts?"

"I believe in demons," Seiter responded. "Why do you ask that?"

Hornsby sighed, and then began telling Officer Seiter of his experiences inside of Bobby Mackey's nightclub. Once Hornsby had completed his story, Seiter shook his head and grinned sheepishly. Besides going through the Police Academy and a homicide training school, Officer Seiter had just recently completed in-service training on satanic worship. He was taught what to look for and how to deal with such matters. Seiter had been raised a Catholic, but had converted to Baptist.

"I wondered how long it would be before you had something happen to you at that place." Seiter stated quite bluntly. "You're not the only one that has experienced strange things down there. That building, as far as I'm concerned, is very evil."

"Have you had anything happen to you?"

"Sure have. I responded to a burglar alarm down there one night, at around four-thirty in the morning. Officer Harrison and I saw the back door of the building unlocked. We walked up the back steps, and just as we reached the door it slammed shut. There was some old song playing on the jukebox, and the lights were on inside the place. I tried to open the door, but it was locked."
"What did you do?"

"Well, we went around to the front of the building and checked the front door. It was unlocked so we went inside to look for a burglar. The funny thing was, I had checked the front doors before I went around to the back of the building and they were locked, then.

"We heard someone walking through the building so we started searching everywhere," Seiter continued with his story. "We went behind the stage and Officer Harrison climbed up a ladder that led into the attic. He was making sure no one was hiding up there. Just as he reached the top rung, he stopped cold and yelled down, ordering me to quit pulling his leg. He looked down and saw me standing at the bottom of the ladder and almost croaked when he realized that I hadn't touched him."

"This is too strange for me." Hornsby shook his head in wonder and almost wished he hadn't asked Seiter about the nightclub.

"I'm just getting started!" Seiter said solemnly. "Anyway, we checked out the attic and no one was there, so we went back into the main ballroom. Then we heard a toilet flush in the men's room. Just as we turned around toward the restroom, a real strong, icy wind blew past both of us. Scared the you-know-what out of me!

"I guess so!" Hornsby commented.

"So, anyway," Seiter went on, "we went to the restroom and looked in there, but nobody was around. We knew then that the damn place was haunted, so we decided to get the heck out of there. We went to the font door to leave, but we couldn't get out. The damn thing was locked with a key. We tried to open the windows, but they wouldn't budge. It was like they were nailed shut. We were trapped inside of the place."

"What in the world did you do?" Hornsby asked.

"We had to call Bobby Mackey to come down and let us out. I'm telling you: That place is evil!"

"What did Bobby say when he got there? I mean about you being locked in the place with no way out."

"He just laughed and said the doors and windows stick from the inside and sometimes it's hard to get out of the building. I didn't push the issue. I'll tell you this, though. He made us wait to leave until he locked the place up. I think he knows more than he's willing to talk about."

Seiter continued telling Officer Hornsby of other bizarre things that had happened to him at the nightclub on different occasions. He had responded to a traffic accident one night, right in front of Bobby Mackey's nightclub. While he was on the scene, trying to help the injured people, a young girl with long brown hair, wearing a long white gown came out of the bar carrying some red tablecloths. She gave him the tablecloths to cover up a man and woman who had died by then from their injuries. After he completed making the accident report, and the life squad took the people away, he went to the bar to thank the girl for her help, but no one was there. It was locked up, tighter than a drum.

"I called Bobby Mackey the next day to ask him to thank the girl for her help," Seiter said, "and Bobby told me there was no way that the girl came out of the bar. He said he didn't even have anyone fitting that description working for him. I knew then that I'd seen a ghost."

"I've heard enough!" Hornsby said, shaking his head. "I'm going home."

Hornsby walked out from behind his desk and left the building as Seiter stood there watching him leave. Both of the officers knew that Bobby Mackey's nightclub was haunted, but they weren't going to say anything to any of the other cops. They would wait until the next police officer came forward telling them of his experiences, and then, and only then, would Hornsby and Seiter share their bizarre stories.

Chapter Thirty-four

Sandy Tomanelli had been hired by Bobby to make some signs and paint some pictures to hang on the walls of the nightclub. A graduate of Western Hills High School and the Art Academy of Cincinnati, this talented lady could paint or draw anything.

A five-foot-four, brown-eyed woman with short brown hair, she lived with her mother and brother in Cincinnati in an apartment complex approximately twenty miles from the nightspot. She had never been afraid of ghosts or unseen forces of any kind, but, after working inside the nightclub alone one afternoon, she changed her mind. This is what she said happened.

* * * * *

It was late Thursday afternoon. Blue arms of rain reached down toward the earth as a turbulent thunderstorm marched through the sky from the west, heading toward the nightclub. The fierce, steady wind shrilled through the valley, slashing and shoving against everything in its path. Sandy sat on the edge of the stage looking through her gray toolbox that was filled with various paints and brushes. While selecting the brushes she needed, the jukebox suddenly lit up and began playing "The Anniversary Waltz."

"Good God!" she shrieked. The startled woman jumped down from the stage and walked over to the jukebox. She stared down at the machine and quietly wondered how the stupid thing could have come on by itself. She reached around the back of the old Wurlitzer and unplugged it, the music instantly stopped and everything in the room became quiet again.

"Sheesh!" Sandy shook her head and walked back to the stage to get her paints. As she reached the center of the platform, she stopped cold and quickly wheeled around looking in all directions. She couldn't believe it! Her box of paints and brushes had disappeared, but there was no one in the room that could have taken them. Carl had let her in the building earlier, locking her inside, then left to go visit his dad. As far as Sandy knew, there was no one else inside the building.

The woman searched the ballroom with her eyes and slowly moved through the row of tables toward the bar when she saw her toolbox. It was sitting in the middle of the bar with the lid closed.

"Okay," she called out, trying to force a laugh at the same time. "I don't know who's playing these stupid games, but it isn't funny."

No response.

She hoped it was Carl trying to pull some dumb prank on her, but she knew he had left the building, and, to her knowledge, he had not returned.

Sandy grabbed her toolbox and walked to the large mirror on the wall in the rear of the ballroom. She opened the box and pulled out a brush and a small bottle of red paint. She was going to draw some figures on the mirror.

She unscrewed the lid, setting it down on top of a stack of empty beer cases next to her. She dipped her brush into the bottle then gently dabbed the paint onto the lower right hand corner of the glass, but, when she did, the paint stuck to the brush. Not one drop adhered to the glass.

"That's crazy," she whispered as she placed the palm of her hand to the mirror to see if it might be sticky from cigarette smoke.

"Ouch!" she screamed as she quickly withdrew her hand from the glass, the searing pain shot through her flesh. "That hurt!"

The glass was hot, like a steam iron. It burnt her palm, and, as she stood there inspecting her injury, a sudden cold chill pierced her body as if something had just passed through her, something evil, frightening. She knew she was being watched, but not by human eyes.

'I've got to get out of here!' Sandy's brain shrieked. "Now!"

She grabbed the lid for the bottle, screwed it on, and dropped it into the toolbox. She flung the brush into the container with the paint still dripping from it, and closed the lid as quickly as she could. Sandy grabbed the box and scurried for the front door, but just as she walked down the mirrored hallway, she saw Carl unlocking the front door and stepping inside the building. His black pants and white T-shirt were completely soaked from the pouring rain. Carl saw the look on her face, and knew by her expression that she was terrified beyond belief.

"What's wrong?" He asked as Sandy quickly moved past him and pushed through the door stepping outside.

Carl wheeled around and followed her out to the parking lot. "Sandy!" he called out as she continued walking away, pushing through the vicious wind and rain. She turned around just as Carl reached her. "What's the matter?" He asked again.

"Carl," her voice quivering, "there's something wrong in there. I think the place is haunted!"

"Listen," he said softly, "this place is just big and spooky when you're in here alone. I think I see and hear a lot of things, but it's just my imagination. Come on back inside."

"No," she snapped at him as she shook her head, the raindrops dripping down her face. "I'll come back later when there's more people in there. I put my hand on the mirror back in the ballroom, and it burned my skin." She held up the palm of her hand and showed the burn mark to Carl. "And then something went through me. It was cold...real cold. I think it was a ghost! I've got to go. I need to go home, I don't feel well."

Carl knew he wasn't going to convince her to go back inside. Sandy was visibly shaken and nothing he could say or do right now would change her mind.

"Okay," he said with a gentle smile, "I'll see you later."

Sandy turned and headed for her car. Carl walked back inside of the building heading for the basement to check the well.

After entering the structure and locking the front door from the inside, he made his way through the ballroom and walked down the backstage stairs to the basement. He strode through the lonely corridor then entered the China Room, but, as he did and before he could even try to protect himself, the unseen entity slammed into him, quickly possessing his mind and body. The evil swept over him like a tidal wave, consuming him. He cried out in anguish, doubling over and clapping both hands to his waist as if he were in excruciating pain. He twisted and turned violently, then suddenly collapsed to the floor where he lost all consciousness.

Chapter Thirty-five

After interviewing many customers and employees of the nightclub, this author took it upon himself to talk to the band members. It was learned that they, too, had experienced strange things while inside this establishment.

Ernie Lainhart grew up in Boone County, Kentucky, with his four brothers and two sisters. He is a dark-haired man with piercing green eyes and a well-trimmed beard. Even though he plays music in a honky tonk nightclub, Ernie is a devout Christian. He graduated from Holy Cross High School in Northern Kentucky, and part of his education was an extensive series of classes on religion. He denies the existence of ghosts, but, due to the biblical background, he feels certain that demons walk the earth looking for a body to call "home."

Tom Weber is on the tall side of six-foot, with a full head of long, curly brown hair and silver-rimmed glasses. He has bright hazel eyes and can always find something to smile about. He graduated from Ottawa High School in Grand Rapids, Michigan, where he was born and raised. He has one brother and one sister, and is married to a loving woman. He loved music more than anything else and was one of the best sound engineers in the business. He felt as if he had it all, but, like so many other musicians and sound engineers, he found himself living out of a suitcase, going from one town to another most of the time.

Ernie Vaughn stands five-foot-nine, with a stocky build. His full head of wavy hair is silver-gray. He and his wife live in a comfortable home in Forest Park, Ohio, a suburb of Cincinnati, about twenty-five miles from the nightclub. He is a very warm and caring person and is highly respected by all of his friends or acquaintances.

Tim Lusby stands six-foot-tall, with a one-hundred-eighty pound body that is solid as a rock. He has full head of dark brown hair and a clean-shaven face. He was living with his mother and father in Fort Mitchell, Kentucky, a small city almost twelve miles from the nightclub. He was an only child who grew up a devout Baptist, and, like Lainhart, he found it ironic that he played music in a country nightclub. He was a graduate of Dixie Heights High School, a parochial school, where he avidly studied religion. Their stories follow.

* * * * *

Later that evening, around six, lead guitar player Ernie Lainhart slipped his key into the front door of the nightclub and entered the establishment. Bobby had given Ernie an extra key to the building as he used the nightclub to give guitar lessons to a few selected students.

Ernie was good looking, very loyal and trustworthy. He was the type of person that one would instantly take a liking to. He had a special gift when it came to singing and playing guitar. It only took one time for him to hear a song, and he could play that tune without making any mistakes.

He liked country and rock and roll music, but he especially loved the blues. The customers at Bobby Mackey's, and everyone who had heard the man play the guitar, constantly told him he was the absolute best. Ernie, however, was the shy sort. He only considered himself good.

He left the door unlocked so his students could come inside. He walked into the main barroom wearing a red sport shirt, designer jeans, and his three hundred dollar, gray snakeskin boots.

He ambled past the bar and made his way to the stage where he picked up Bobby's acoustic guitar from its stand. He walked over to a nearby table next to the dance floor, sat down in one of the wooden chairs and began tuning the Ovation guitar, getting ready for his first student to arrive.

As he twisted the keys on each string, a radio came on from behind the bar, blaring out some tune.

Carl must've brought his clock radio down here, Ernie thought as he lay the guitar on the table. He stood and headed for the bar to turn the thing off, but just as he reached the bar the music suddenly stopped.

I better find that radio and unplug it anyway, he thought. He didn't want it coming back on while he was in the middle of giving a lesson. He felt a loyalty to his students and wanted to give them every minute that they had paid for. The lessons were only thirty minutes long and that didn't give him a lot of time to go through the sessions, making sure his students practiced what he had taught them the week before.

He searched the top of the bar, looking for the radio, but could not find it. He crawled over the counter at the end of the bar and looked everywhere for it, but there was no radio to be found.

"Now, wait a minute," he said aloud to the stale, empty air, "I'm not crazy. I heard a damn radio playing, full blast!" Frustrated, he moved out from behind the bar just as his first student, Mike Gruber, came walking through the front doors, carrying his black guitar case in his right hand.

Mike was wearing faded, Wrangler jeans and a western style, blue long-sleeved shirt. He had a black Stetson cocked back on top of his short brown hair. He had deep brown eyes and weighed about one-hundred-fifty-five pounds, and stood five-foot seven-inches tall.

"Hey, Ernie!" Mike said with a big grin on his face. "I'm here."

"Yeah, you and who else?" He remarked aloud, his thoughts escaping his lips. He quickly said a silent prayer as Mike gave him a puzzled look.

"Waddaya mean? Who's here?"

"Never mind," Ernie patted the young cowboy on the left shoulder. "Let's get busy on your lesson."

The men walked side-by-side back to the ballroom and sat down at the table where Ernie had laid the guitar. Ernie picked up the instrument, breathed a deep sigh, scanned the ballroom with his eyes, and then began going over some guitar chords that he had taught Mike the week prior.

Nothing else out of the ordinary occurred while Ernie gave the lessons, but still, deep down in his gut, the guitar instructor knew he had just had a run-in with some disembodied, demonic force. If that wasn't bad enough, he had to stay here tonight as the band members had all agreed to meet later that evening to practice some new country songs. The club was closed on Thursday nights, and the men used this free time practicing and learning new tunes that were on the country charts.

The guys in the band began arriving around nine o' clock. Ernie was sure glad to see them. The men tuned their instruments, and then knuckled down to some serious practice. After about an hour of hard work, they decided to take a break and headed for the bar. Since all of the booze was kept under lock and key, they each grabbed a clean glass off of the silver tray near the popcorn machine and headed for the soft drink dispenser. After they finished downing their drinks, the men walked over to the soundboard where Tom Weber sat at the controls all alone. Since Danny Hanavan gave up his job at the nightclub, Tom had agreed to help Bobby out by manning the sound board for a couple of weeks until Bobby could find a suitable replacement.

As the men sat around the sound board laughing and telling jokes, Ernie Lainhart decided to find out if anyone else in the band had ever experienced anything strange inside the nightclub.

He looked over at Ernie Vaughn, the silver-haired bass guitar player.

"Ernie, do you believe in ghosts?" He simply blurted out the question, causing everyone to come to a dead silence.

Tim Lusby, the dark complexioned steel guitar player, broke out in a low snicker after the question sunk in.

"No! I mean it," Lainhart insisted. "You guys know me well enough to know that I wouldn't joke about something like this. When I was in here alone tonight, a radio started playing over by the middle of the bar, and, when I went to turn it off, the music suddenly stopped. I looked everywhere ...on both sides of the bar, but there wasn't any radio."

"Maybe you better try getting more rest at night," Lusby laughed again as a grin passed over his face. "Especially if you're starting to hear things that aren't there!"
"No, I'm serious," Lainhart pressed on. "I swear I'm telling the truth."

Lainhart had directed the question to Ernie Vaughn because of the man's stability, and besides, Vaughn had been here at the nightclub longer than anyone else in the band.

After Lusby finished laughing, Vaughn answered Lainhart's question with one of his own. "Do you think this place is haunted? Carl tried to tell me that a while back."

"I don't know," Lainhart shook his head, "but you know me well enough to know that I'm not making this up."

Tom Weber sat at the soundboard staring at Lainhart for a couple of seconds, and then gave a big grin.

"I've had something happen to me," he said.

"What?" Lainhart asked with a quick breath. "What happened to you?"

Weber looked at Lainhart then at Lusby and Ernie.

"This is going to sound crazy, but I stopped by here earlier today to check out the sound levels on the microphones, and, while I was doing a microphone check, groaning and moaning sounds came through the monitor on the sound board. I instantly looked up at the stage to see who was playing games with me, but there wasn't anyone around. Then I heard someone whispering through one of the mikes while I was staring right at the stage. There wasn't anyone there. In fact, there wasn't anyone in the building except me. Bobby gave me an extra key to let myself in so I could test the equipment. Carl's car was gone, so I know he wasn't here. You guys don't know me that well yet, but I'll tell you this ...there's something strange about this old building."

Tom's statement sent a chill up Lainhart's spine, and it caused Lusby's grin to quickly disappear.

Lusby sat there staring at the other men with a serious look. After hearing Tom Weber's story, and knowing Lainhart as he did, the hazel-eyed Lusby figured there had to be something to all of this. He and Lainhart had become personal friends and spent a lot of time running around together.

"Wait a minute," Lusby fired the words at Lainhart. "Remember last Friday night when we took a break and walked off the stage? We all came back here and sat around the soundboard. Do you remember what happened?"

"I sure do!" Lainhart grinned, nodding his head at the same time.

"What?" Weber asked with wide-eyed anticipation.

"We were all congregated back here, and, all of a sudden, we heard someone strum the strings on one of the guitars, and, when we looked up front, there was no one on the stage. That's about the same thing you had happen to you, Tom."

"Almost," Weber replied, "but I heard voices come through the monitor. It was someone whispering something to me, and then I heard the moans and groans. It was real strange. That's all I can tell you."

"Maybe the place is haunted," Lusby replied as he gazed around the room.

"Maybe we oughta spend the night in here and see if we can stir up the ghosts. Maybe they'll show themselves to us."

"Not me!" Vaughn laughed. "First of all – I don't believe in ghosts! But if there is one in here, I suggest we leave it alone. I can't wait to tell Bobby about this. He'll say you're all nuts!"

"If we're done for the night, I'm ready to get out of here," Lainhart exclaimed. "It's been a long day."

"Sounds good to me," Lusby replied.

The men strolled up to the stage and packed up their guitars while Tom Weber flipped off the switches of the soundboard.

Everyone left the building except Ernie Vaughn. He decided to change the strings on his guitar before heading home. Just like Bobby, he wasn't buying any ghost stories about the nightclub, but, being the kind of man that he was, he waited until everyone was gone before making fun of them.

"Ghosts!" He laughed aloud as he sat on the edge of the stage and began taking off the top string of his instrument. "OOOOOOOO." He burst out in laughter, his mocking sounds echoing off the walls all around him. "Hey, Carl! I don't know how you did it, but you scared those guys!" Ernie called out with merriment in his breath.

Just as his words faded into the walls, the P.A. system sitting on the stage to his right began hissing and popping, and before he could lay down his guitar, the entire black cabinet began smoking. Ernie scurried over and quickly unplugged the P.A., but it was too late. The power supply of the electronic device had shorted out, melting the wires, transistors and everything else inside the unit.

"How in the heck did that happen," he wondered aloud to no one in particular.
He shook his head, walked over to the edge of the stage and picked up his guitar to complete his task, but when he did, he suddenly felt something icy cold blowing on the back of his neck.

"What the heck!" He shrieked as he quickly wheeled around, holding the guitar by the neck and raising it over his head as a weapon. He scanned the room only to find that he was the only living being inside the huge chamber.

He was sure some one had just blown on the back of his neck, but whom? The conversation that he had with Ernie Lainhart and Tom Weber, about the ghosts being inside the nightclub, suddenly slithered its way back into his mind, and now he wondered if there might be something to Lainhart's story after all.

"I've had enough of this," he grumbled to himself. "I'm getting out of here before I let my imagination run away with me."

The man quickly placed his guitar in its tan case, and then snapped the locks shut. He headed for the front door with the guitar in his left hand, his right fist hanging to his side clenched tightly, just in case. After stepping outside the building, Ernie locked the front door and headed across the parking lot to his car. He climbed inside, started the engine and drove north on Route 9. "Nothing to worry about," he told himself as he headed home.

Chapter Thirty-six

Some of the people who told of their experiences while inside the nightclub stated that they did believe in the supernatural and always wanted the chance to see a ghost.

Joe Lucas graduated from Milford High School about twenty miles west of the nightclub, on the outskirts of Cincinnati. He had wavy, shoulder length brown hair and blue eyes. The five-foot-nine, medium-framed Joe was in his early thirties. He grew up a Baptist, and, even though he knew better, he had been known to play with the Ouija Board from time to time. The possibility of a spirit world intrigued him.

This is what happened when his wish came true.

* * * * *

The bar was about to open for business. It was Friday night, and a hard, blowing wind, as frigid and viscous as syrup was blowing debris all around the exterior of the nightclub. The air slashed and shoved against the large crowd of patrons who were waiting for the front doors to open so they could get inside.

Carl Lawson stood at the window in a black jogging suit, looking down at the crowd. His ears were tuned to catch the whispers on the wind. It had been cloudy all day, but the rain had failed to fall. Dirt blew into the people's eyes, their hair, and between their teeth as they shifted their weight from one foot to the other, fighting off the unusual, icy complaint of the wind.

The backdrop of the overhead light shining in his apartment highlighted Carl's figure. He looked at his reflection in the windowpane and noticed that his eyes had a veiled, liquid look to them. His face showed signs of fatigue and worry.

Downstairs, in the bull room, Joe Lucas was busy checking the bolts on "El-Toro," the bucking mechanical bull. Bobby insisted that the bucking apparatus be checked every night before the bar opened. He didn't want anyone getting hurt due to a loose nut or a mechanical defect.

It was part of Carl's job to operate the bull, but earlier that night he told Janet he didn't feel well and was going upstairs to his apartment to rest for awhile.

Joe volunteered to run the machine. Janet had no choice but to accept his offer. He was wearing black cowboy boots with silver pointed toes, a red Wrangler rodeo shirt and jeans. As he inspected the bolts underneath the bull, he saw that a nut had worked itself loose so he headed for the old kitchen that was located at the back of the ballroom, to get a wrench to tighten the nut. Bobby kept a pretty good selection of tools inside the big gray toolbox in the closed off kitchen for just this reason. It seemed that something always needed tightening or repairing.

Joe opened the door and without turning on the light, stepped inside the room, but, as he did, he saw something out of the corner of his eye, soaring through the air at him. He ducked just in the nick of time. A metal brace that had been lying on a nearby table came flying through the air directly at his head. The object slammed into the east wall with a loud thud, and then fell to the floor.

Joe hurriedly looked around the room without saying a word, and saw that he was the only one inside the cubicle. He knew there was no way in or out of the old kitchen, except through the doorway that he had just passed through.

"Who in the hell threw that at me?" he asked as his eyes continued searching the dimly lit shadows of the old kitchen. Joe stood his ground, looking in all directions, but as he did, he felt something breathing on the back of his neck. Without hesitation, he spun around and drew back his right hand, the fist clenched tightly, ready to strike whoever was behind him.

"Bull shit!" He groaned when he realized that there was no one in the room with him. "If you're a ghost, you can kiss my ass! I ain't afraid of you! Why don't you show yourself?"

His challenge was met head on! As he stood motionless, looking toward the far wall, something slammed against his chest, forcing him back toward the door. He swung wildly at the air, but didn't connect with anything solid.

"Damn," he whispered with a low, shaky voice. "It really is a ghost!"

Before he could turn to leave the room, something pierced his body from behind and came out his chest. The man did not move a muscle. He was obviously overcome with fear, but yet, he wanted to see this thing that had just penetrated his body. He knew it was a ghost, a spirit from the other side that had just pierced him, causing his skin to raise up with hundreds of tiny goose bumps from the frigid feeling the entity left behind as it passed through his being.

Then, right before his very eyes, he watched a dark patternless shape, like some sort of greasy, swirling fog, float through the room in front of him, and as it did, it began taking on form. At first, it was small, dense, dark, drawing in and extracting the normal darkness that surrounded it, becoming blacker, larger and taking on a human-like form. Now he could recognize that it was a spirit moving in front of him, a woman clad in a silk dress. He could not distinguish the color of the gown because he hadn't bothered to turn on the light when he entered the room. There was only enough illumination for him to see the faint from of the ghostly woman. As the apparition moved toward the far wall, a new wave of sheer terror washed over him when he suddenly realized the ghost had no head.

"Dear God," he tried to force the words out of his mouth. He turned and started to run out of the room, but something in side him made him stop. He looked over his shoulder and to his amazement, he watched the headless spirit float down through the floor in the middle of the room and disappear. He took a deep breath, trying desperately to digest what had just happened, and, as he stood there, he heard a soft voice calling out to him from underneath the floor.

"It's here," the mournful female voice trailed away. "Find it. Please!"

"Find it yourself," Joe said as he rushed over to the toolbox, jerked open the lid, grabbed a wrench and got the hell out of the room.

Once outside of the kitchen, Joe pushed the door shut and headed for the bull room. The curious man, who liked to play with Ouija Boards, had finally got his wish! He saw a ghost, a headless ghost, but he wasn't going to say anything to anyone about what he had just experienced. He knew quite well that if he said anything at all, he'd never live it down. The apparition could find someone else to help her locate whatever she was looking for. He would never go anywhere in this place by himself again! NEVER!

Chapter Thirty-seven

This chapter is about an employee who was completely unaware of the strange things happening at the nightclub and still was not aware of what she had experienced until this story leaked out and people began sharing their stories with each other. After talking with Janet and the employee involved this is the way the author interpreted this chain of events to have happened.

* * * * *

Lisa Stadtmiller, a brown-eyed, five-foot, five-inch woman in her late twenties, was busy checking behind the bar, getting everything ready for the herd of good ol'boys and girls who would be crashing through the front doors any minute now. Lisa had short brown hair and wore glasses. She had a medium build and was wearing white sneakers, jeans and a burgundy, "Bobby Mackey" souvenir T-shirt. She was a young lady with mercurial quickness, wit, directness and intelligence about her. She was totally likeable.

Since the ice machine was on the blink, Lisa was doing Janet's duties until she returned. Janet had left the nightclub to get some bags of ice for the mixed drinks and cokes they would be serving.

Since Lisa had everything ready, she grabbed the straw broom and dustpan, quickly sweeping the floor behind the bar. Completing the task, she started to walk back to the north end of the double-sided bar, when something lying on the floor caught her attention.

"How'd that get there?" She asked. She quickly scanned both sides of the bar area to see if someone had sat down and pushed the green piece of paper over the counter top onto the black-slate floor. No one was near the bar on either side.

"That's crazy!" She spoke aloud to herself. "I just swept this entire area and that paper wasn't there."

She leaned the broom and dustpan against the bar, walked over to the discarded piece of paper, bent down and picked it up. She stood erect and found herself in a state of total confusion. She was holding a canceled check issued to G.M.A.C. in the amount of $18.29. The check was dated October 18, 1929, and the signature was still legible. It was signed, "J. Jewell."

Lisa had worked for Bobby and Janet since opening day and had helped Janet scrub the stainless steel beer and wine coolers that were located under the counter top of the bar. She knew that check hadn't been there before, but she shrugged off any thoughts about it and placed it in the cash register for Janet to worry about.

Some time later Janet returned to the bar, struggling with six bags of ice that she could barely carry. She sat them down on the floor, then, one by one, lifted them over the counter top to Lisa. While Janet made her way around the end of the bar, Lisa opened the bags of ice and poured them into one of the coolers.

"Hey, Janet. I found a canceled check on the floor and I put it in the cash register for you to look at."

"One of ours?"

"Ah, no," Lisa said with a confused look. "I swept up while you were gone and when I finished, I saw the darn thing laying in the middle of the floor. It wasn't there when I swept and I have no idea how it got there. Go look at it."

Janet walked to the end of the bar, opened the register pulled out the check and inspected it. She felt a wave of terror wash over her.

"This is from 1929," she said to Lisa. "How in the world could this have gotten here. You and I cleaned every inch of this place the day we opened for business, and we've done it a thousand times since."

"I don't know."

My God! Janet's brain shrieked when she saw the signature on the draft. "J. Jewell," she read silently as she wondered if this could be a canceled check that Johana had written years ago.

"Weird, huh?" Lisa said, interrupting Janet's thoughts.

"It sure is," she said in a low whisper as she put the check back into the register, then pushed the drawer closed. "I'll take this home and let Bobby look at it. He likes going through all of the old papers here for some strange reason." Janet shook her head, then looked back at Lisa. "Let's get busy we've got a couple of minutes left before that crowd starts pouring in here."

"Okay," Lisa responded as she began stacking the clear drinking glasses on silver trays, and then placed them on top of each other at both ends of the bar. The women kept plenty of eight-ounce glasses ready at all times. It was common for them to serve five to six hundred mixed drinks during the course of a normal night.

Chapter Thirty-eight

While conducting the various interviews I learned of a friend of the Mackey's who had worked for them on an "as needed" basis.

Sandy Murray is five-foot-five, with short-blonde hair, and big blue eyes. Sandy has two grown daughters, Debbie and Melissa, and lives with her husband in Florence, about fifteen miles from the nightclub. Her full-time job was as a saleswoman at a jewelry store in Florence. She stated that she had always known some unseen force dwelled inside the nightclub, but she kept her feelings to herself until she came face to face with an apparition. This is what she said happened.

* * * * *

Margaret had called in sick, so Sandy had volunteered to help out at the bar for the evening. She had been a friend with Janet and Bobby even before the Mackeys had purchased the club. She and her husband, Marty, often frequented the country nightclubs where Bobby was performing prior to the opening of his place.

Janet had asked Sandy to wait the tables in the front ballroom, directly in front of the dance floor. As she walked between the rows of tables, checking her station before the nightclub opened for business, she heard someone whisper her name. The soft voice came from the stage. She turned to her right and found herself staring at the form of a woman wearing a long white gown. The apparition had long brown hair and was standing in the arched doorway at the right of the platform.

"Follow me," the disembodied spirit pleaded. "Please!"

Sandy stared at the woman, and, as she did, the specter turned and disappeared into the back room. Sandy felt something drawing her, almost hypnotizing her thoughts, and without realizing it, she made her way up onto the stage and had walked into the dimly lit back stage area.

She reached the doorway leading down to the basement and looked everywhere for the ghostly woman, but she was nowhere to be found. As she stood motionless, staring at the door, something icy cold pierced her back and exited through her chest. Even though she didn't see anything, she knew a spirit had passed through her body and then through the door in front of her. It was trying to lure her down to the basement.

"Follow me," the whisper assaulted her ears again, only this time, coming from the closed stairwell.

Sandy reached for the slide bolt to unlock the door, when suddenly someone tapped her on the shoulder. She turned around only to find no one there. She realized where she was and something inside her told her to run, to get out of the room and do it now.

Sandy moved through the arched doorway, quickly walking back to the ballroom to find Janet. She wanted to tell her what had just happened, but as she made it to her assigned area, the crowd came rushing in.

I'll tell her later, Sandy thought as the tables before her quickly filled with rowdy cowboys, demanding to be served.

Sandy nervously took an order from four men, all of whom were wearing black dusters and Stetson hats. She headed for the bar to get the beer and shots of Jack Daniels they had requested, when something caught her attention again. She found herself staring through the crowd at the large mirror on the back wall. What she saw frightened her out of her wits.

It was a headless woman in a long, white gown, moving through the row of tables toward her. Sandy could see the apparition in the mirror, coming closer and closer. She wheeled around to her right; flashing her eyes through the people filled the room. The headless woman was nowhere to be found. As Sandy stood there, staring through the room, she suddenly smelled the soft scent of roses in the air all around her.

"That's it!" She groaned, not caring if anyone heard her remark. "I command you, in the name of Jesus Christ, to leave me alone!" Just as quickly as Sandy's words faded away into the roar of the crowd, the rose aroma evaporated into nothingness, and everything returned to normal.

Sandy wanted to leave the building, but she knew Janet and Bobby were short-handed tonight, so she decided to stick it out until closing time. The woman shrugged her shoulders, and then got busy serving drinks to the customers. She made up her mind to get Janet alone after all of the customers went home. She was going to give the Mackeys some startling news: they owned a haunted nightclub!

Chapter Thirty-nine

When Carl told some people that the nightclub was haunted, they laughed and poked fun at him. Some of them even challenged the spirits. This is what happened to one of those patrons.

* * * * *

The night continued on without any more apparitions revealing themselves to Sandy, but somewhere in the bull room, something evil was lingering in the air, waiting for the right moment to show itself.

Carl decided he wasn't sick anymore, so he told Joe Lucas that he was feeling better and that he would operate the mechanical bull the rest of the night.

Joe moved out from behind the wooden booth, and Carl quickly sat down behind the oak podium, placing his right hand on the control lever. The lever moved up and down and was numbered from one to ten, adjusting the action depending on how long and fast a patron could ride the bucking apparatus.

Carl shouted, "Who's next?" with a loud, almost daring tone, to the long line of people waiting to ride "El-Toro."

"I am," a deep voice answered.

Mike Gruber, the same man who had come to the nightclub the prior night for guitar lessons, stepped up and plopped two one-dollar bills down in front of Carl.

"Let's see if that sucker is as good as everyone says it is!" Mike grinned as he stood there staring at Carl. Mike was wearing a black Stetson, a red shirt and denim-washed jeans.

"I wouldn't say that!" Carl defiantly met his challenge head on, as he glared back into Mike's eyes.

"Why not?"

"Because this place is haunted, and if you challenge the ghosts in here, you'll be sorry."

"Is that right?" The cowboy laughed. "Well, you tell your ghost friends to come on. First of all, I don't believe in ghosts, and whatever you're drinking or smoking, you better leave it alone!"

Carl grinned an evil smirk, and then gripped the control lever with both hands. "Don't say I didn't warn you," he said jokingly, but meant every word of it.

Mike turned and walked over to the black mat that covered three layers of foam rubber on all sides of the mechanical bull. He mounted "El-Toro" on the left side, and then cocked his hat back with his right index finger.

"Ready when you are!" he announced loudly.

He leaned back, gripped the tan leather handle of the bull with his left hand, and then raised his right arm over his head, just like the real rodeo riders do.

Carl looked at the crowd, then at Mike. He pushed the control lever up to one and the bull began slowly turning around in a circle. He pushed the lever to four and "El-Toro" began to buck and twist like an out of control tornado.

Carl maneuvered the controls back and forth, trying to throw Mike off of the mechanical bull, but to no avail. The modern-day cowboy held on as if he were glued to the saddle. After the prescribed amount of time for each ride, Carl began to slow down the bull until it stopped.
"Tell your ghost friends, better luck next time!" Mike mockingly blurted out as he sat on top of the machine and straightened his hat.

Carl stepped out from behind the controls to go to the restroom as Mike continued to sit proudly on top of the bull, grinning at the girls to his right. As Carl rounded the counter, the bull suddenly jerked and began to turn once more.

"Hey!" Mike screamed as the bull suddenly came to life, twisting, turning, bucking, and picking up tremendous speed as if it had been thrown into fast forward.

"What in the hell are you doing?" Mike yelled at Carl in a near panic as he gripped the handle of "El-Toro" and held on for dear life.

"Son-of-a-bitch!" Carl shrieked as he quickly turned and almost threw himself back behind the controls, only to find that everything was turned off.

"Turn it off!" Mike screamed, but there was nothing Carl could do. There was nothing on to switch off!

"It ain't on!" Carl yelled back with urgency. "Jump! Jump now!"

"The hell it ain't, you ding-bat!" Mike screamed as he flailed around like a rag doll, trying desperately to hold on.

The bull had already reached its pre-top speed, but continued to gain momentum, bucking, turning and twisting faster and faster.

"Jump, you damn idiot!" Carl bellowed over the increasing clamor of the out-of-control machine, but it was too late. Mike couldn't hold on another second. His body sailed toward the control panel, the black Stetson falling to the floor as he flew through the air some three feet from "El-Toro."

Miraculously, Mike landed on his feet, facing Carl. He wheeled back around and gave a quick look toward the bull and was stupefied to see the machine at a dead stop. The man reached down and picked up his hat, putting it back on his head, then turned to face Carl.

"That was a stupid joke," Mike snarled. "I could've been killed, you moron! I oughta whip your ass!"

"I told you not to make fun of the ghosts in here. You're lucky you weren't killed. I tried to warn you.

Mike was angry. He wanted to hit somebody, anybody, but he had watched Carl walk out from behind the counter before the bull went crazy, so he knew the man wasn't guilty of trying to harm him. He knew there was more to this than met the eye, but he wasn't going to admit it. He gave Carl a blistering look and shoved his way through the crowd of onlookers, heading for the bar to get a drink. For the first time in his life, he was frightened. Of what, he wasn't sure. He was certain, however, that no living being had touched those controls, and that thought sent a shiver up his spine. He decided right then and there, that he would never make fun of Carl and his ghostly friends again. No matter what!

Chapter Forty

Many of the employees at the nightclub had a difficult time telling of their experiences inside the club for fear of ridicule. Once it was made clear, though, that this book would be the result of many statements, and since there is the perception of safety in numbers, many of the people involved finally gave in and conveyed their stories.

This Chapter took several months to compile, as it required numerous interviews with the Mackeys, their employees, band members and even customers. After rehashing this sequence multiple times with each person involved, this is the way I interpret this to have happened.

* * * * *

Vickie Metcalf, a five-foot-five, medium-framed woman with short blonde hair, sat in the middle of the bar, her blue eyes gazing across the counter into the ballroom. The thirtyish-looking woman was feeling the effects of too many Long Island Iced Teas, especially since she hadn't eaten anything all day.

She plopped her elbows down on the top of the bar and laid her head on the counter top with her hands gripping the back of her neck. She and Janet had been friends for quite some time, and, when Janet saw that she had too much to drink, she became concerned.

"Are you okay?" Janet stood behind the bar, directly in front of Vickie.

"I need to lie down," she said, raising her head and smiling at Janet. "This isn't like me to get this way. I don't feel drunk. I kinda' feel sick."

"Why don't you go in the office and rest for awhile. I'll come in and check on you in a little bit."

"Okay."

"Do you need me to help you get there?"

"No. I can make it." Vickie stood up from the stool and walked away, heading for the office just inside the bull room. The Mackeys had converted the old cashier's office into an office for their own use.

She stepped inside the dimly lit room and squinted her eyes for a brief moment, looking around the ten by twelve foot cubicle. She walked over to the black leather couch, plopped down and laid on her left side, closing her eyes and releasing a deep sigh at the same time. In only minutes she fell into a sound sleep, completely tuning out the loud music and rowdy customers just outside the office door.

* * *

The bright overhead lights came to life as Bobby sang "Turn Out the Lights, The Party's Over." It was closing time. The customers filed out of the building, one after another until only the employees remained inside the bar. The band members packed up their equipment and walked over to the bar on the ballroom side, where Janet and the waitresses sat around talking before everyone headed home. Bobby and Carl locked all of the exterior doors and emptied the coins out of the arcade games and pool tables.

Sandy Murray took a deep breath, then looked at Janet with a 'should I or shouldn't I?' look. She was trying to muster up enough courage to tell Janet what she had experienced earlier. She had preferred to tell Janet about the incidents alone, but she figured, if she brought it up in front of other people, maybe someone else would come forward. Somebody had to see something, she assured herself. I couldn't have been the only one who has seen a ghost in here!

"I need to talk to you," Sandy interrupted Janet as she sat at the bar conversing with a couple of the waitresses. "I need to tell you something, but before I do I want to ask you a question."

"What's that?" Janet asked looking confused as she spun around on the stool to face Sandy.

"Do you think I'm crazy?"

"Why, Lord no! Why would you even ask me that?"

"Do you believe in ghosts?" Sandy's eyes bored into Janet's.

Her question took everyone by surprise, especially Janet. Margaret looked at Cookie. Cookie looked back. Everyone found themselves holding their breath as Sandy continued.

"Janet, I saw a headless woman in here tonight. I saw her image in the mirror right back there!" She said, raising her right hand and pointing toward the large mirror on the far wall. "That isn't all," she went on. "Before that, I heard someone call my name, and, when I turned around, I saw a woman go behind the stage. I went back there to see who it was, but the woman was gone. Then something icy cold went through me. I went through the door leading down into the basement and then I heard the same voice. It asked me to follow it. I got scared and came back out here. I waited to tell you about this until now, because I wanted to see if anyone else saw or heard anything. I'm telling you this place is haunted."

"Don't tell me Carl did that!" Margaret blurted out, her words assaulting Janet's ears before Sandy's statement could fade away. "This place is haunted!"

Janet couldn't hide the fact that some entity had become active inside the nightclub anymore. All of them began sharing their encounters with each other, and it was a welcomed relief to each of them to learn that they were not the only ones to experience something here. Whether any of them wanted to acknowledge the fact that ghosts really did exist, it didn't matter anymore. They had all experienced something, but had kept their mouths shut for fear of ridicule, but, since the word was out, they wanted something done about it...NOW!

Janet promised the group that she had already taken steps to rid the place of the entity. She hoped they didn't ask her what she had done, because so far, she had not done anything at all. This is the perfect time to get Bobby to believe me, she thought just as Carl and Bobby approached the cluster of people.

"Bobby!" Janet said with an I-told-you-so tone of voice, even before she broke the news to him.

"What is it?" Bobby asked grinning as he sat the blue gym bag full of quarters on the bar.

"All of the help says they've seen a ghost or heard something strange while they were inside here."

His expression instantly turned to a frown. "Bologna!" he blurted out as he shook his head back and forth in disgust. "I want to know who's starting all of this nonsense!"

"It's the truth!" Most of the waitresses and band members began speaking out, repeating the words one after another as Carl stood behind Bobby with an UH-OH look plastered all over his face. He knew he'd get the blame for this. It was Bobby's only way out!

Bobby made the mistake of asking everyone what he or she had seen or heard. He got more than he bargained for. He stood in the middle of the ballroom listening to Ernie Vaughn, Margaret Collinsworth, Cookie, Ernie Lainhart, Tom Weber and Sandy Murray tell of their encounters, some seen and some unseen, while they were inside the nightclub. He would have popped a cork had the other people who had experienced something been there to convey their stories.

After listening to some of the most bizarre things he had ever heard in his entire life, Bobby got dealt another blow from Mike Gruber, who was still there, hanging around with the band members. Mike told him what he had experienced with the bull and Bobby quickly turned around to face Carl.

"What do you know about this?" He asked with fire in his eyes.

"Hey!" Carl defended himself. "It wasn't my fault. You heard Mike tell you the darn thing was turned off when I walked away."

"Did you threaten Mike with your ghost pals?"

"All I said was, he shouldn't make fun of the ghosts or they'd get him." Carl responded like a scolded child, dropping his head as he finished speaking.

"Well, don't be threatening anyone with you little invisible friends again!" Bobby said with a bite, but before he could finish reprimanding Carl, Debbie Murray, Sandy's nineteen-year-old daughter, hit him with another ghostly tale. Debbie had her boyfriend drop her off at the club earlier that evening so she and her mother could go out for breakfast at a local restaurant not far from there. Debbie had shoulder length brown hair and sparkling green eyes.

"Bobby," she started. "I had something happen to me tonight, about a half an hour ago, but I didn't say anything to anyone."

"Why not?" Debbie's mother asked bluntly. "Why didn't you come and tell me?"

"Because I was afraid you'd think I was drinking or taking drugs, Mom!"

"Well, go ahead and tell us what you saw," Sandy told her daughter.

"It started as soon as I walked in the front door tonight. I smelled roses, real strong, and then while I was standing near the mirror in the back of the room I felt something ice cold go through me. I haven't been able to get warm since. Oh, one other thing! Just before the band quit playing, I thought I saw what looked like two dark figures in black hoods move through the back of the room near the kitchen. What I saw and felt doesn't compare to what some of you others have, but I know what happened."

Bobby shook his head again, still in disbelief. He had heard enough about the ghosts and goblins walking around inside the nightclub. He looked at Janet sitting on the bar stool, a cocky look etched all over her face.

"The scariest thing that ever happened to me in here was when I met my ex-wife!" John Hoffman, the six-foot, sandy-haired drummer blurted out with a big grin.

"There ain't no such thing as ghosts!" the dark-haired, Diane Turner, stated to Janet. Diane and her gray-haired husband Arnold were friends of the Mackeys and came to the nightclub almost every night. Arnold quickly agreed with his wife, which strengthened Bobby's position concerning the haunting at the nightclub.

"I'll tell every one of you something," Bobby said, almost laughing. "I'm going to have Janet find a psychic to come down here right away and check the place out. If any of you see or hear anything else, do me a favor and tell Janet, because until I see a ghost, I'm just not going to believe any of this."

Before anyone could say another word, Bobby headed for the front door with the moneybag in his hand. Better take the money home with him tonight, he laughed to himself, he didn't want the ghost breaking into the safe and stealing the cash!

Once again Janet did her best to assure everyone she would have something done right away. Bobby turned out the lights and walked down the hallway giving everyone the hint that it was time to go home.

Janet and the others walked out of the building and bid each other good night. Carl locked the front door behind everyone, and then walked to his car. He was heading for an all-night chili parlor in Newport to get something to eat.

Because everyone had come forward to tell their experiences while inside the building, Janet completely forgot about Vickie being asleep in the office, and, since Bobby decided to take the money home instead of putting it in the safe like he usually did, the unsuspecting lady was left all alone inside the nightclub.

Bobby Mackey drove toward home, listening to Janet go on and on about the ghosts inside their nightclub.

"Bobby, you can't ignore this any longer," she insisted. "Did you see the look on everyone's faces?"

"As far as I'm concerned, you can call a psychic, a priest, or whoever you want." Bobby answered her abruptly. "In fact, I want you to get someone down there right away and have them check the place out so I don't have to listen to anymore of this mumbo-jumbo about ghosts."

"It's not mumbo-jumbo!" Janet met fire with fire!

"First, it was you and Carl being bothered by demons and ghosts, and now it's the help and patrons! I don't know what to make of any of this, but nothing you or anyone else can say or do will make me believe in ghosts!"

"Oh, yeah! You'll believe in them if one shows itself to you down there!"

"Then why in the hell don't they do it?" Bobby challenged. "I'll tell you why! Because this is some sort of childish prank that Carl is pulling on everyone, and you all are falling for it! I don't know how he's doing it, but I know he's responsible for this, and if it doesn't stop, Mr. Lawson is going to find himself out of a job!"

What if I do get a psychic to go down there and they say it is haunted," Janet wanted to know, "What then?"

"Call 'Ghost Busters'!" Bobby remarked between clenched teeth as he thought, chewed and frowned on her question.

"Real Funny!"

"I'll tell you what," Bobby offered, "if some reputable psychic says the place really is haunted, I'll make a phone call to a friend of mine. Do you remember me talking about Larry Kidwell?"

"Yes," Janet replied in a somewhat less combative tone. "He's the man who has a big advertising agency over in Florence, isn't he?"

"That's right; he's the man that sets me up to do all of the television commercials for different companies in Cincinnati."

"Why him? I mean, what can he do to help us?"

"It's kind of ironic," Bobby continued, "but when I filmed that last commercial a few weeks ago, for a video store, the owner, Larry and I got talking, and somehow this minister friend of Larry's got brought into the conversation. He goes around the world doing faith healing and casting out demons from people. I remembered the conversation because I thought of you and Carl at the time."

"Who's the minister?"

"I don't have the foggiest idea."

"Did you tell Larry what happened to me and Carl?"

"Heck, no!" Bobby laughed. "I wasn't about to mention any of that. Do you think I'm nuts?"

"Well, if you tell Larry about what's happening, will he help us?" Janet felt a slight glimmer of hope. "Maybe I should talk to him."

"You get a psychic to go there first," Bobby stated, but find somebody with credentials. I don't want no fly-by-night, involved in this. If you get someone who knows what they're talking about, and they say there is some bad spirit at the club, I'll get in touch with Larry and see if he can help you."

"What do you mean, me?" Janet raised her voice again. "You mean us, don't you?"

"I'm not getting involved in any of this malarkey, Janet," Bobby said, disgusted. "Look! I said I'd call Larry and tell him what you and the others are saying, but, after that, it's up to you and him to decide what to do, if he'll even get involved. I'm not going to jeopardize my singing career by telling people that I have a haunted nightclub. That would sound like some sick publicity stunt. I'm too close to a recording contract to let something like this mess it up!"

"I guess you're right," Janet gave in, "but you will call Larry and see if his minister friend will help, won't you?"

"I said I would, after your fortune teller checks it out," Bobby replied as he wheeled the car into the driveway of their home.

"That's all I ask," Janet said with a slight smile.

"Good!" Bobby switched off the ignition and looked over at his wife with a warm smile. "Now, let's get inside and go to bed. I'm exhausted."

The couple climbed out of the auto and disappeared into their home, ready to get some sleep. Bobby was in total wonderment, thinking about the ghostly tales that were now circulating around the nightclub. Janet was just relieved that her husband had finally promised to help her, even if he still refused to acknowledge the fact that something evil dwelled there.

Chapter Forty-one

It was said that most of the ghostly sightings occurred when the nightclub was closed for business and some unsuspecting person was all alone inside the massive structure.

* * * * *

About an hour after everyone had gone, Vickie Metcalf gave a slight groan and awoke inside the office. She stretched her arms over her head, and then yawned deeply as she sat up in the middle of the couch.

"Sheesh! It sure is quiet." She whispered the words as she gently rubbed her fingers against her sleep encrusted eyelids. "I wonder what time it is?"

She wearily climbed to her feet and walked slowly to the door, pushing it open and stepping out into the bull room. All the lights were off, making it difficult for her to see. Once in the darkened chamber, it didn't take the woman very long to figure out that everyone had gone home, leaving her behind.

"I don't believe this," she complained loudly, her voice echoing off the walls in the room. "Janet forgot about me being here."

She squinted her eyes, trying to adjust them to the pitch black of the room, and began taking slow, careful steps down the hallway that led into the game room. She was trying to be cautious not to trip over anything as she inched herself forward. Just as she reached the game room she heard someone whispering and instantly stopped, holding her breath, trying to hear what was being said, but the sounds ceased.

Vickie waited for several long seconds. She heard nothing but the sound of her own heart beating, and the eerie popping and cracking of the floor and walls from the settling of the giant, quiet building.

"Who's here?" she called out as she stepped into the main barroom.

Silence.

She stood there in the darkness, motionless, waiting to hear the sound of a friendly voice, but instead, she was greeted by the sudden sound of the jukebox coming to life and playing some old, quaint song. It was "The Anniversary Waltz."

"Those idiots are sitting up there by the stage, listening to music," she said, laughing under her breath as she walked past the bar, heading for the stage and the jukebox.

Just as the woman rounded the north end of the bar and stepped into the main ballroom, the music stopped, the melody quickly fading away, as if suctioned into the walls. Everything became still and calm. Too calm! Vickie felt something ice cold hit her chest and pass through her, coming out her back.

The room was hot! There was no reasonable explanation for her to feel something that cold. She became aware of another presence in the room. A sweet smell of roses wafted through the room like a feather blowing in the wind, but then came the stench! A foul smelling odor that would make the strongest of stomachs begin to churn.

She suddenly realized that it wasn't the Long Island Ice Teas that had made her woozy earlier. She hadn't felt sick until she stepped foot in this place. It was the same force that was standing in the shadows with her, the same entity that had caused her sudden illness tonight.

Now frightened beyond belief, she flashed her eyes toward the stage, but saw no one. The foul odor closed in on her like a giant hand, wrapping itself around her body and squeezing at her senses. She held her hand over her mouth and gagged repeatedly. It was hard to breathe and she felt she would surely suffocate before she could escape this mad house. She wanted to turn and run, to flee as fast as her feet would carry her, but a premonition told her to stay put. She felt a presence standing in the darkness, right behind her, breathing its foul breath against the nape of her neck. She was stuck in a nightmare that couldn't be escaped by simply waking up.

As she stood there, almost in shock, she heard someone tapping their fingers on top of the bar. Somehow she found the courage to turn around to face her doom. The blood rose in her body like a jet as she slowly turned around, praying silently to herself, and looking through the darkness of the ballroom toward the bar. Her heart was pounding like a bass drum and large beads of sweat formed on her forehead. She slowly, methodically, scanned the rows of tables with her eyes, but couldn't see anyone until she fixed her sight toward the wall clock hanging over the middle of the bar. Sitting directly under the dimly lit clock, was the silhouette of a dark haired man with a hangman's noose draped around his neck. Vickie couldn't make out the stranger's face, but she knew by the low snicker that she was in danger.

"Who are you?" She forced the words out between trembling lips.

The man laughed louder, but gave no reply.

"Who are you!" Vickie screamed at him this time.

No response.

She couldn't take it anymore. Scared or not, she was going to find out who he was and why he wouldn't answer her. She saw an empty beer bottle sitting on the table in front of her and quickly reached down and picked it up, taking her eyes off this menacing person for one split second.

"No way!" The words escaped the woman's lips in a terrified whisper. "He's gone!"

She had only looked away for an instant. The man didn't have enough time to hide. He had not made a sound. There was absolutely no way that he could have hidden from her in such a short span of time and she knew it. Once again, the woman felt the sense of aloneness as a new wave of terror pounded against her.

Realizing that she had just encountered a ghost, Vickie gasped for air, and although she couldn't see him, she knew he was still in the room with her.

There was a brief dome of silence hanging over the room as she surveyed the darkness with her eyes and then she heard the voice again, the same whisper that she had heard just before she walked into the game room.

"Vickieeeeee," the bodiless voice called out in a choked whisper.

The wooden floors began creaking and groaning louder, and the wall clock began ticking like a thunderous heartbeat. The brutality of what was taking place sent the horrified woman over the edge. She shrieked and bolted through the room, knocking over tables and chairs, and fleeing for her very life. She raced past the open bar on her left and rounded the corner of the doorway, pushing through the double swinging doors and fleeing down the mirrored hallway. Just as she reached the front entrance the right door swung open, wide, as if someone had opened the door for her, allowing her to escape from this house of evil.

Vickie exploded across the threshold, turned to her left and ran toward the lower parking lot that sits at the north end of the building. She kept her eyes straight ahead. She didn't want to look back. She was terrified at the thought of seeing that manifestation of evil again. She didn't know if he was following her, and she wasn't going to look over her shoulder to find out. All she wanted to do was reach her car and get the hell out of this place before it was too late.

Chapter Forty-two

Even though he still didn't believe, Bobby had finally given in and told Janet to contact a psychic to see if, indeed, the place might be haunted.

Patricia Mischell, a red-haired, green-eyed beauty in her early forties, is known worldwide for her psychic abilities. She became famous by helping different Police departments solve cases throughout the United States. She earned a reputation as an outstanding author, teacher, lecturer, counselor and parapsychologist. She is the founder of the Positive Living Center and H.O.P.E. Ministries where she teaches classes such as self-development, positive thinking, and meditation and "Mind Power" techniques. She had been involved in outreach programs in Peru, Costa Rica, Finland, Washington D.C. and California. She has traveled to Egypt, Greece, Israel and Jordan, using her psychic abilities to help people wherever she was needed. She had appeared on numerous television programs and was the subject of many newspaper and magazine articles. She and her husband lived in Fairfield, Ohio, about twenty-five miles from Bobby's nightclub.

The following is how they said it happened.

* * * * *

It was almost noon. Janet answered the phone on the third ring, sitting down on the couch as she picked up the receiver.

"Hello," she said cheerfully.

"Janet!" The caller almost screamed through the line. "This is Vickie and I've got to tell you something very important!"

Oh, my God, Janet's brain kicked in. She forgot and left her in the building last night!

Janet could tell by the urgency in Vickie's voice that something dreadful had happened. Her smile quickly turned into a frown as Vickie gave her a blow-by-blow description as to what had happened inside the club the night before. Janet allowed her to tell her entire story before she gave any reply.

"What are you going to do about it?" Vickie wanted to know. "I'm not making this up!"

"Don't worry," Janet assured her. "First of all, I want you to know that I believe you. I've heard similar stories from a bunch of different people in the last couple of days. I was just getting ready to call some psychics to see if any of them can help me. Surely, one of them will have a solution."

"They'd better, or I'll never step foot in that place again!"

"Don't worry about it," Janet tried to calm her down. "Why don't you try and get some rest and I'll get busy trying to find someone to take care of this."

"Okay," Vickie said with a sigh. "Call me as soon as you know anything."

"I will," Janet affirmed. "I promise I'll get everything taken care of."

Janet bid Vickie good-bye, and hung up the phone. She reached over and pulled out the phone book from the brass rack next to the sofa. She plopped the book on her lap and thumbed through the yellow pages until she found the listing for clairvoyants.

"God, please let someone believe me," she whispered as she took a deep breath, then let it out.

Janet picked up the receiver and dialed a phone number of one of the psychics. She got a busy signal. She pushed the disconnect button and tried another number. This time, she got through.

Although hesitant, Janet explained the entire situation to the woman and was elated when the lady on the other end of the line agreed to help her. When Janet realized whom she had contacted, she felt confident that, if anyone could help her, it was Patricia Mischell.

The psychic told Janet to have Carl meet her at the nightclub later that afternoon. She said she wanted to walk through the building and see if she could get any vibrations from any spirits inside the place.

Janet asked the woman if she should meet her there and was relieved when the psychic told her to stay put until she had toured the building.
After giving the woman explicit directions on how to find the nightclub, Janet hung up the phone and leaned back against the cushions of the couch.

"Thank God!" she whispered joyously.

Patricia Mischell had assured Janet that she could help her in one way or another, and the promise made her feel confident that this entire ordeal might soon be over. All she could do for now was wait until the psychic called her back.

Bobby came walking into the living room wearing a navy blue jogging suit. He walked over and sat down next to Janet.

"What's up?" he asked as he reached forward and grabbed the remote control off the glass coffee table in front of him.

"I found a psychic," she replied, just as Bobby aimed the remote at the black Magnavox console TV and clicked it on.

"You did, huh?" He almost laughed as he pressed the channel button and flipped through the stations until he found a country music program.

"I sure did, and she's going to the nightclub this afternoon to check it out."

"What's this going to cost us?"

"I don't know," she answered with a puzzled look. "She didn't say anything about charging me. I wonder how much she will want? She's going to call back later on and tell me what she found out. I guess she'll tell me then."

"Well, before she goes doing some mumbo-jumbo, voodoo spell, or whatever those people do, you'd better find out how much she charges," he insisted. "I'd hate to get a bill for a thousand dollars for her running off some ghost that probably isn't there anyway!"

She gave him a quick, angry glance, but she held her tongue. "I just want something done!" She picked up the phone again.

"Who are you calling now?" Bobby asked as she pressed the buttons on the phone.

"Carl. I've got to tell him to make sure he leaves the front door unlocked so Patricia Mischell can get inside. She wants to talk to him too!"

Janet waited patiently until Carl answered on the tenth ring. She told him about the psychic and was relieved when Carl seemed to be his old self. After a brief conversation, she hung up and looked over at her husband, who was watching a country video.

"Carl said he will watch for her. He seems like he's in a good mood about something."

"Probably is! He's got all of you people believing in ghosts!"

Janet shook her head, got up and headed into the kitchen to cook lunch. Bobby grinned and rolled his eyes at his wife as she left the room. Spooks! It was all he could do to keep from bursting out in laughter.

Bobby had completed his latest album BRIGHT LIGHTS, and the lead song, "Hero Daddy" had reached the Gospel music charts and was doing quite well. He was preparing to leave for Nashville again, as he was looking for some new songs to record. He was working on a possible recording contract with a major country music label and it was imperative that he found the right upbeat song that they were looking for. He didn't have time to worry about the "ghosts" that were scaring Janet and the other people, and he only hoped that this psychic, whoever she was, would not come back and announce that the nightclub was indeed haunted.

* * *

Janet picked up the phone on the first ring. She was sitting on the couch next to Bobby watching the seven o'clock world news. It was the call she had been waiting for all afternoon. Patricia Mischell identified herself and gave her the dreadful news. After about a ten-minute conversation, she thanked the woman and hung up the phone. She looked over at Bobby, her features carrying a startling load of information. She bit her bottom lip, and then took a deep sigh as she sat there staring silently at her husband.

"Well?" Bobby asked, after hearing the one-sided conversation. "What did she say?"

Janet looked at Bobby for a brief moment without answering him. He had smug expression. He knew by Janet's look that he really did not want to hear what the psychic had to say, but he figured he might as well get it over with.

"Come on, tell me what she said."

"You're not gonna like it!" She spoke slowly, feeling her way.

"Probably not, but lay it on me anyway!" His voice brimmed with distaste.

"Okay," she replied with wide-eyed anticipation. "The psychic told me she met Carl and he took her through the entire building. She said when she went into the basement to go into the China room, a bat attacked her, but they finally shooed it off. She told me that when she went into the old kitchen, she got instantly nauseated and dizzy and she felt death...a lot of death. She said she could see a woman's head floating in water somewhere under the floor and..."

"Oh, bull," Bobby snarled. "That's a bunch of bunk! What else did she say?"

Janet shrugged her shoulders and rolled her eyes, then continued. "She said you were a singer at the nightclub in another era. Your name was Robert Randall, and some girl's jealous father murdered you in the place. Her name was Johana."

"This is ridiculous!" Bobby remarked.

"It is not!" Janet snapped. "She knew about Johana, didn't she!"

"Carl could've told her about the little ghostly friends. I'm sure he told the woman her name."

"No, he didn't! She told me she had a long talk with Carl, but she instructed him not to give her any names of the spirits because she wanted to tune into them herself! That isn't all! She also said that the ghosts are using Carl's body at will and that they can be very dangerous if they're provoked."

"That's it!" Bobby groaned loudly as he stood up, waving his arms over his head. "I don't want to hear any more of this insanity!"

"Hold on, Mister! You better keep your word to me. You promised you'd call your friend, Larry, and get him to call that minister."

"I didn't think it would get this far," Bobby replied, almost in a shout. "Larry will think we're all crazy! What am I going to tell him? 'Oh, Larry, my nightclub is haunted and Carl Lawson, our handyman, is possessed!' He'd laugh me out of town!"

"I don't care," Janet insisted. "You gave me your word and you better not go back on it. Give me Larry's number. I'll call him."

"Oh, no you won't!" Bobby was having trouble controlling his anger. "I'll call him myself, in the morning. I'll keep my promise, but he's going to laugh his head off when he hears this. Let's go to bed. I'm tired and I want to get plenty of rest so I can try to explain this to Larry tomorrow. I'll have to have a clear head when I try to convince him that you people really believe this nonsense!"

Janet nodded her head and smiled at Bobby. She turned off the lamp and television, and then followed her husband into the bedroom to try to get some sleep. She was elated that Bobby was going to help her, even if he didn't believe any of the stories he had heard from her and the other people.

Chapter Forty-three

Being a man of his word, Bobby contacted a friend of his to call in a minister to come and check out the nightclub.

Larry Kidwell had been in radio and television advertising for quite some time. His advertising company, Kidwell and associates were located in a high-rise office building in Fort Mitchell, about nine miles from Bobby's nightclub.

Larry and his wife had recently gone into real estate as a sideline and were acquiring one piece of rental property after another. With the man's busy schedule, he really didn't have time to get involved with some sort of ghost hunt, but just the thought of it intrigued him beyond words.

After talking with Bobby and Larry, this is the way I interpreted this to have happened.

* * * * *

Larry Kidwell, a six-foot, burly sort of man, hung up the black phone and shook his head in disbelief as he sat behind the wooden, executive-size desk in his office. He had just had a lengthy conversation with Bobby Mackey concerning the strange goings on at the nightclub. The sandy-haired Kidwell knew Bobby well enough to know the country singer wouldn't joke about something like this.

"Boy! Wait till I tell Glenn about this!" Larry said aloud to himself as he leaned back in his black leather, high back chair thinking about the conversation that he had just had.

Larry was a lot like Bobby. He had to see it to believe it. Even though Bobby had told him he thought everyone was letting their imaginations run away with them, Larry still felt there had to be something strange going on at the nightclub. Bobby had omitted no details, keeping him glued to the phone for almost an hour, telling him everything.

Curiosity killed the cat, Larry thought, but what the hell. He gave his word to Bobby that he'd call his Pentecostal preacher friend, Glenn Cole, and see what the man had to say about the possible haunting at the country bar.

Larry leaned over the desk and picked up the phone, calling Pastor Cole at his church, Havilah Temple in Cincinnati.

The minister answered on the fourth ring. Larry identified himself, and then proceeded with the story. He was completely taken aback when the pastor told him the nightclub was probably haunted and possibly inhabited by demons. The minister explained that spirits and demons don't possess buildings, but they do exist in structures where people live, or come and go, so they can possess those humans whom they choose. The man of God went a step further, telling Larry that the handyman was probably the person that the unseen entities were using.

The pastor told Larry he would be more than happy to go to the nightclub and inspect it, but, most of all, he felt an urgent need to meet Carl. He told him the man was probably in danger and didn't even know it. He said an exorcism might be necessary.

Larry volunteered to set up a meeting at the bar, but insisted that he be allowed to bring a camera with him. Being involved in television and radio, Larry wanted to capture a spirit on film if one existed there. The minister agreed to Larry's request and told him he would be available to meet at the nightclub on Thursday, July 25, at around eight in the evening.

He was filled with excitement now! He couldn't believe he was actually going to meet Glenn Cole at the nightclub and maybe take on some unseen spirit.

The thought of it was frightening, but the possibility of filming a real, live exorcism, and maybe seeing a ghost or demon, was totally beyond his wildest dreams. This was one endeavor Kidwell wanted to be part of!

Larry picked up the phone and dialed Bobby's home. He asked him to contact Carl and insist that the handyman meet him and Reverend Cole at the club the following Thursday at eight o'clock.

Since Bobby had changed band practice from Thursday to Wednesday evenings, he agreed to Larry's request and promised that Carl would be there, waiting for them.

Chapter Forty-four

The ghosts were not happy with the decision to correct the situation at the club. Their first warning has been written exactly as it happened.

* * * * *

It was Saturday night, July 20. It was nearly midnight and the bar was jam-packed. Bobby stood center stage belting out a love song. Carl sat in the middle of the bar, on the ballroom side, thinking about the brief conversation that he and Bobby had only minutes ago.

Bobby had told him of his promise to Larry Kidwell and had insisted that Carl meet with the preacher and Larry at the bar that following Thursday evening.

Carl knew something was dreadfully wrong. Even though he did not remember anything that had happened when the spirits had control of him, he still felt certain that some diabolical thing was taking authority over him, using his body at will, and the thought was terrifying.

Thinking of meeting Larry Kidwell, and some Holy Roller preacher bothered him, but, down deep, he welcomed it. He hoped, maybe, just maybe, the minister could help him figure out what had come over him. Besides, he was too frightened to do anything to help himself.

As he sat at the bar in the midst of the customers, he suddenly caught a whiff of smoke. He turned around on his stool looking through the crowded ballroom; when someone abruptly called out, "Fire! Fire!"

As the room quickly filled with smoke Bobby stopped singing and motioned with his hand for the band to quit playing. "Everyone please leave the building...now!" He ordered, speaking loudly through the microphone.

Surprisingly, the patrons quickly walked out of the structure in an orderly fashion. No one ran or panicked. Bobby found it hard to believe that the people didn't push and shove each other while heading outside.

Carl, in the meantime, ran to the old kitchen area. When he opened the door, he saw the fire. The flames were dancing and licking at the west wall of the room. He bolted into the ballroom and grabbed a fire extinguisher off the wall. Several other employees saw what he had done and followed suit, grabbing the other extinguishers that were placed throughout the ballroom.

Carl pushed open an emergency, exit door and looked down the concrete steps at the outside wall. Flames engulfed a four-foot section of the partition, the smoke billowing up and disappearing into the night sky.

He raced down the stairs, taking them two at a time, with three other men right behind him. They emptied the extinguishers into the flames, and, in a matter of minutes, the exterior fire was out. He ran back upstairs and found another extinguisher, spraying it into the smoldering hole inside the kitchen wall, making sure that the flames had died inside the building.

As he emptied the extinguisher into the wall, the Wilder Fire Department arrived and took control of the situation. Since the fire was still smoldering, the firemen chopped several holes into the partition, then placed a fire hose into it, completely soaking the wood until they were certain that everything was safe.

Bobby couldn't believe the crowd had stood outside waiting for the fire department to allow them back in. In less than forty minutes, the fire chief gave his permission for Bobby to re-open the bar. The people swarmed back inside the nightclub as Bobby and the band returned to the stage. It was business as usual.

"You're the most loyal fans a man could ever ask for!" Bobby said sincerely to the crowd. "Let's get back to the music."

Grinning, Bobby and the band began playing "They Call Me the Fireman," and everyone, but Carl, got a big kick out of his choice of songs. Everything returned to normal. The people lined the bar on all sides ordering drinks. The dance floor was full, and everyone went back to having a good time. Carl walked to the kitchen and opened the door, staring into the darkened room, wondering what had started the fire. The fresh smell of burned wood sill lingered in the air. He had overheard the fire chief tell Bobby that he couldn't understand what had caused the sudden outburst of flames. There was no wiring inside the wall where the fire ignited and there was absolutely no evidence of arson.

Could this have been a warning, Carl asked himself. Could some demon have started the fire in an attempt to destroy the building before Pastor Cole arrived here next Thursday? Either way, he wasn't sure. He only knew he wouldn't be able to sleep inside the building until he knew the answer. He decided right then and there to sleep in his car until Thursday night. He wasn't going to take any chances on being killed inside the building.

The rest of the night went by without any further incidents. At closing time, Bobby sang "Turn Out the Lights," and the crowd filed out of the building. Once the patrons had gone, he thanked Carl and the other employees for acting so quickly and putting out the fire. He asked Carl to keep a close eye on the nightclub tonight and to call him at home if anything else happened. Carl nodded as Bobby, Janet, and the other employees left the building.

Once every one was gone, Carl walked into the old kitchen and stood all-alone inside the pitch-black of the room.

"Please don't harm this building, or me," he pleaded softly. 'If you started the fire because of that minister coming here, don't worry about it. I won't let him run you off. Johana...Buck, if you can hear me, don't worry! Everything's gonna be okay."

As Carl's words faded away into nothingness, loud, heavy breathing sounds filled the room, as if the walls had come alive. It was as if they were giving a sigh of relief, signaling to Carl that they had heard his words and approved.

Listening to the labored sounds echoing all around him, Carl turned and walked out of the room, heading for his car. He was going to sit in the auto all night and watch the building. He was too terrified to stay inside the structure. He wished Bobby hadn't made arrangements for the minister to come.

Chapter Forty-five

Carl's first meeting with the minister has been written exactly the way it happened.

Reverend Glenn Cole stands six-foot-three and has short brown hair that he combed back on his head. The brown-eyed man had the meticulous grooming of a TV lawyer. He had been a Pentecostal preacher for eighteen years. He and his wife, Diane, lived in Covington, Kentucky about two miles from Larry Kidwell's office. He had traveled around the world several times with another evangelist, preaching God's word of deliverance to anyone who would listen, but after years of traveling and being away from his family, he started his own church, Havilah Temple, in Norwood, Ohio, a suburb of Cincinnati. The church was about fifteen miles from Bobby Mackey's nightclub.

* * * * *

Larry Kidwell stood outside the front doors of the nightclub, watching the traffic zipping up and down Route 9. He was wearing a white long sleeve shirt and blue jeans. He checked his watch and wondered where the Reverend could be. As he looked up the highway again, he was relieved to see the minister's silver 1974 Lincoln Continental pulling into the upper parking lot.

The clergyman parked the car and walked toward Larry smiling, carrying a brown Bible in his left hand.

"How's it going?" the preacher asked as he gazed past Kidwell, staring intently at the building they were about to enter.

"Real good...I think!" Larry answered with a slight chuckle. "But maybe I better not say that until we see what happens in there."
"Have you met Carl yet?"

"Ah, yes I did. He seems real nice. Kind of quiet, but not weird at all. I think Bobby's right. Some of the help here is probably just letting their imaginations run away with them."

"Maybe. Maybe not!" The pastor replied quite matter-of-factly as he pushed his right index finger against the bridge of his wire-rimmed glasses, straightening them on his face.

Reverend Cole was clad in a blue suit, a white long sleeve sport shirt, and a red tie.

"Are we about ready to get started?" the minister asked.

"I guess so," Larry arched his eyebrows. "Ready as we'll ever be! Come on, I'll introduce you to Carl. By the way, I brought along three cameramen and a news reporter just in case anything happens. They'll stay out of the way, though."

"No problem," the Reverend smiled. "Let's get the show on the road."

The minister followed Larry up the mirrored hallway and into the main barroom, where they spied Carl sitting at the south end of the bar near the swinging doors. Larry made the introductions between the two men, and then left them alone so they could get to know each other. Kidwell headed for the old kitchen area to see if the cameramen were about finished setting up the equipment.

Carl looked at the minister with a warm, yet apprehensive smile. He was dressed in his usual white sneakers, blue jeans and a black, short-sleeve sport shirt. "Larry told me he explained everything to you," Carl blurted out. "Have you ever heard of such a thing?"

"Yes, on both counts," Glenn smiled as he answered him. "Larry told me about the haunting here and of the possibility that you might be possessed. I don't know a lot of the details, but that doesn't matter. I'm here to help you, Carl."

"I'm afraid if you try and run the spirits off, they'll hurt me," Carl exclaimed with a slight tremor. "This could be pretty dangerous."

"Let me worry about that. The Lord, thy God will protect us!"

"Have you ever done anything like this before?" Carl had to ask. "I mean, have you ever done an exorcism before?"

"Many times! I've been in the ministry for eighteen years, and I've come close to seeing it all."

Just as the minister finished speaking, Larry returned to the bar and announced that everything was ready. Carl and the minister followed Kidwell into the old kitchen area where three cameramen and a local news reporter stood against the west wall of the room.

The room had been stripped of the sink, stove and other cooking paraphernalia. The wooden walls were bare. For the past several months, the old kitchen had been used primarily as a storage area. The north wall was cluttered with tables and chairs that were stacked on top of each other. The south wall, at one time had been lined with large windows, but now, the outside had been boarded up so that no one could see through the glass. In the middle of the wooden floor sat a square wooden table with four chairs placed around it. The scene reminded Carl of the death chamber at some prison. He felt like he was the inmate, about to be electrocuted, and the news reporter and cameramen were there to cover the story.

Pastor Cole sat on the south side of the table facing Carl. The news reporter sat next to the minister with a pen and ledger pad in his hand. He was ready to take notes of what was about to happen.

Reverend Cole looked at Carl with a warm smile, and then began by praying aloud for the Lord's help. Completing the prayer, he looked across the table into Carl's eyes and saw the fear radiating from them.

"If there is a spirit in Carl Lawson," Reverend Cole began in a cool, calm voice as he continued looking at Carl sitting across the table, "I ask that it speak and identify itself tonight, RIGHT NOW! I'm not afraid of that spirit!"

Carl's hands were palms down on the tabletop, pushing hard against the surface. He began nodding his head up and down, and began mumbling something under his breath in a low, different tone of voice.

The minister asked the spirit speaking through Carl, what it had said.

There was a long pause.

"Carl says he wants to be delivered and you spirits have to leave so he can fill his temple with another spirit," the pastor pressed on.

Another moment of silence.

"I can't speak," Carl's voice finally uttered the words, barely able to choke them out.

"Why?"

"Don't know," Carl stammered.

"You can't, or you won't?" Glenn quizzed the spirit.

"Don't want to," the entity answered in a low growl.

"Why?"

"I don't want to hurt anybody."

The spirit spoke in a raspy tone, talking through Carl as if it owned his body.

"The word of God says deliverance is Carl's!" Glenn argued to the entity that now possessed the young man. "You spirits listen to this!" Glenn demanded as he opened his Bible that lay on the table in front of him. "If there is a spirit in Carl Lawson, I want you to listen to me. If you have died in the past, you need to listen to this!"

The preacher quickly thumbed through the pages of the text, and then began speaking in a loud tone.

"In Ecclesiastics, Chapter One, the Scripture says Solomon asked God for wisdom. He wanted answers for all things in life. Now listen to this!"

Reverend Cole took a deep breath as he looked at Carl, then continued reading from the Bible.

"What profit have a man of his labor, that taketh under the sun? One generation passeth away and another cometh.' The Bible is talking about the cycle." Glenn continued boldly.

"The sun also riseth and the sun goes down to the place where it arose. The wind goeth to the south and turneth around in the north and the wind returns again according to its circuits.'"

The minister stopped and looked into Carl's glassy eyes. "There's the cycle again!" He expounded his knowledge of the Holy Bible.

"'All the rivers run into the sea, yet the sea is not full unto the place to whence the rivers come, thither they return again!'"

Reverend Cole was getting into it now! He gripped both sides of the opened book, squeezing the text with white-knuckle tenacity as his eyes bore into the printed words on the text.

"THERE'S THAT CYCLE AGAIN!" he proclaimed loudly. "Now the spirits that have been bothering you, Carl...It's my opinion that they don't know they have died and it's time for them to leave and go on into the realm of the spirits for that recycling of that spirit."

It became apparent now that Pastor Cole and his own beliefs concerning biblical text, and he knew what he was doing. Most ministries denied the existence of spirits and only believed that demons walked the earth, but not this man of the cloth.

"I speak to all of you spirits!" he exclaimed with authority. "And I tell you there's a future for you if you'll go on into the spirit world. Carl! You must resist these spirits!"

Carl's eyes were now focused on the man of God sitting across the table. "They'll get me when I'm alone in here!"

Glenn knew it wasn't Carl talking, but some entity who was trying to play on his sympathy.

"If you accept Jesus Christ as you Savior, you won't be alone," the minister argued. "Carl, accept Jesus as your Savior! God says 'You'll never be alone if you believe in me! I won't forsake you!' You have to come to know Christ as your personal Savior so you can learn to resist the spirits that try to overtake you and your body!"

There was a deafening silence. Neither Carl nor the spirits could speak.

"What are your thoughts right now, Carl?" Glenn demanded, still aware it wasn't Carl that he was speaking to, or if it was, the man wasn't letting go of the spirits for some reason.

"I can't understand what you're saying," Carl barely got the words out. "Part of me won't let me hear what you're saying. I can't explain it to you. They don't want to harm anyone. They want to be left alone."

"That's a lie!" the sandy-haired reporter blurted out without thinking. "They're hurting you, Carl!"

"They want to take over! They're lying to you," the minister interrupted. "They're telling you they don't want to harm anyone, but they want to harm you, Carl, and that's a violation to your right of freedom and victory to God! Do you feel like these spirits are trying to do something now?"

Carl swallowed hard. The entity inside him answered the minister. "I feel like something's trying to tell me to tell you that they'll leave me alone if you don't try to make them leave this building. They want to stay here. It's where they belong!"

"They belong in the spirit world," Glenn insisted to the spirit, still playing dumb, acting like he was talking to Carl. "If they scare people and use them like they're doing with you, then they're doing something they're not supposed to do. Therefore, it's time for them to leave."

The spirit didn't answer.
"Carl, you have to fight them. Let me read something else out of the Bible," the preacher took a deep breath, and then continued. "James, Chapter Four, seventh verse... 'Submit yourself therefore to God, wherefore he saithe resist the Devil and he will flee from you.' The next verse gives us the key to make it work! 'Draw nigh to God

and cleanse your hands you sinners, and purify your hearts, you double-minded.'"

The minister was becoming absorbed into the Word of God, and he felt the power of the Holy Ghost washing over him.

"St. John, Chapter ten, verse seven......" he declared in a fire and brimstone voice as he quickly thumbed through the pages of his Bible until he found what he was looking for. "'I am the door of the sheep. All that ever came before me are thieves and robbers; but the sheep cannot hear them. I am the door! By me, if any man enters in, he shall be saved and find pasture. The thief cometh not, but to steal, kill and destroy. I am, so that they might have life and more abundantly. I am the good shepherd. The good shepherd giveth life for the sheep.' Jesus gave his life for you, Carl. He died that you might have life. You must make a commitment unto him. I'm going to lead you in prayer and when we call upon the name of Jesus the spirits have to leave because I'm here as a son of God to take authority over them... Just like Jesus did when he walked the earth."

Glenn reached across the table and grasped the top of Carl's wrists. He began praying aloud over the man, and, when he did, Carl's body began shaking violently and he tried to pull away from the minister's grip, but Glenn held tight, commanding the spirits to leave Carl's body and the building.

"Satan! I denounce you, I denounce your ways!" Glenn shouted "I denounce everything you stand for and in the name of Jesus, I command the spirits, right now, in the name of Jesus Christ, to leave Carl alone!

"Father God, in the name of Jesus, I take authority and domination over the spirits and command them in the name of Jesus Christ of Nazareth to loose their hold on Carl. In the name of Jesus Christ of Nazareth, I speak to you spirits and I command you to LEAVE! I command you to loose your hold on Carl!"

As the minister's words began to fade into the air, Carl's body began jerking and he again tried to pull free from Pastor Cole's grip, but the minister held on tightly, refusing to let go. Carl began quivering and shaking violently, his entire being squirming and jerking like a fish out of water, but as Reverend Cole continued commanding the spirits of leave, Carl went limp and dropped his head down into his arms, that were still spread out across the table in front of him.

"Look at me!" Glenn Cole demanded of Carl as he still gripped the man's wrists.

Carl groaned slightly, then answered him as a slight smile formed on his face. "I feel different," he said with a weary sigh. "Something in me has changed."

"It's over," Glenn stated softly as he let go of Carl's wrists. "But the spirits will return and try to take over your body again."

"I won't let them! They're gone, and they're staying gone!"

"Good!" Glenn smiled as he stood from the table. "I want you to try and get a good night's sleep. I'm sure you're exhausted. Would you mind if I stay in touch with you from time to time?"

"No. Not at all." Carl answered, as he too, stood up and moved away from the table.

Larry Kidwell watched as the reporter walked out of the room obviously disappointed. Larry stood silent, watching the cameraman as they quickly packed up their equipment. It was very apparent that everyone was disappointed. Even Larry was let down with the way things had happened. They had come here tonight expecting to see something right out of some terrifying horror movie, but it wasn't like that at all. Larry figured what the hell! It was worth a shot, anyway. If he could have obtained some good film footage of items flying through the air and someone being levitated, he might've made some big money with the footage.

Carl walked out of the room and opened the back door leading to the concrete steps. He sat down at the top of the landing and lit a cigarette. He wanted to be left alone.

Larry walked over to Pastor Cole and shook his head in disappointment as the reporter and the cameramen left the building. "I guess we can get out of here," Larry grumbled. "I sure expected more than this."

Glenn smiled at the man and patted him on the shoulder. "Let's go outside and talk, but, first, let's tell Carl we're leaving."

"Okay," Larry was puzzled. "I'll follow you."

The men walked out of the old kitchen area and found Carl sitting on the top step of the concrete stairs where he sat silently, staring up at the clear sky, the moon and stars shining brightly overhead.

"You okay?" Glenn asked. "We're getting ready to leave."

"I'm fine," Carl replied, not even looking at the men. "I just need some time alone to think."

"I understand," Glenn said consolingly. "I'll call you or stop by sometime, if that's okay."

"Sure," Carl whispered.

Glenn turned and walked through the ballroom, heading for the front doors with Larry right behind him. Once they stepped out of the building, and saw that the reporter and cameramen had already gone, Glenn turned around and looked Larry in the eyes. The minister had a serious look on his face.

"It isn't over," he declared. "Carl, or a spirit, was lying to me. The spirits aren't gone! Carl was either protecting them because he's terribly afraid, or he doesn't want them to leave."

"You're kidding!" Larry said, his voice high and reedy. "Why did you quit, then?"

"Larry, this isn't like some picture show made in Hollywood. What we're dealing with here are numerous spirits or demons and this type of matter has to be handled with kid gloves. First, of all, the spirits aren't going to show themselves to a crowd of people. If I can cast them out, and I use the phrase cautiously, then they don't want a lot of witnesses. That would be an excellent testimony of the power of God! The devil doesn't want people to see God's authority over him. That's why they got Carl to lie to me, and that's why they're still here!"

"What do we do now?" Larry looked at the front doors of the nightclub.

"We come back and try again!" Glenn stated matter-of-factly. "And we keep coming back until we finish it, but next time, we come alone! I didn't fool them one bit. They know we're going to return. To get rid of these spirits or demons, I'm going to have to pray and fast! It's the only way!

"When do you want to come back?" Larry asked.

"I'm not sure. I'll pray about it! God will let me know when it's time to return. I want to warn you, though: It could get pretty tough next time!"

The preacher's words sent a chill racing up and down Kidwell's spine. Larry had known Glenn for a long time, and he knew by the minister's tone that he was dead serious.

"Let's go," Glenn said. "We've done all we can do for tonight."

Larry nodded. The men walked to opposite parking lots and climbed into their cars heading home, Larry half frightened of the idea of returning here again and Pastor Cole praying to the Lord of wisdom as to how to handle the situation when he came back to this house of evil.

Carl locked the back door, then made his way through the building to the front entrance. He slipped his key into the deadbolt, securing the door, then headed for his apartment.

"I told you I wouldn't let them run you off!" he said aloud as he disappeared into the game room, making his way upstairs.

Chapter Forty-six

This chapter covers the second meeting between Carl and Pastor Cole and has been written exactly as it happened.

* * * * *

A week passed by without any interference from the spirit world. Everything at the nightclub seemed perfectly normal, and Carl couldn't help but wonder if the minister had, somehow, run off the entities that had inhabited the place. He hadn't experienced any loss of time, as before, but most of all, he felt at peace. Something that he hadn't felt for a long time!

About eight o'clock, on that Thursday evening, Reverend Cole and Larry Kidwell drove north on Route 9, heading for Bobby Mackey's nightclub. They were going to pay Carl a surprise visit.

The minister had called earlier that day, and asked to meet Larry at his office at around seven that evening. While the two men drove toward the bar Larry told Glenn that he had informed Bobby that his nightclub was indeed, haunted. Glenn asked Larry what Bobby had to say about the matter and wasn't a bit surprised when Larry told him that Bobby didn't believe a word of it.

Reaching the nightclub, Larry parked his gray and white Chevy Van in the south parking lot. The men stepped from the vehicle and walked over to the front doors, and as they did, Carl came walking out of the building, greeting them with a warm smile.

He invited the men inside and led them into the main barroom, where they sat around talking about everything, but what they were really there for.
After about fifteen minutes of ordinary chitchat, Pastor Cole suddenly changed the topic of conversation. "Are the spirits still here, Carl?" Pastor Cole blurted out the question.

"Yes!" A deep, raspy, multi-toned voice answered the question from somewhere deep inside Carl's body. "We're still here!"

The minister knew instantly that it wasn't Carl who had answered him. He saw the instant rage and anger that suddenly appeared on the man's face when he asked about the spirits. He knew he was now talking to some entity, and that Carl had no idea as to what was taking place. Carl turned away from the minister and walked from the bar to the far wall, placing his forehead against the game room wall, mumbling obscenities under his breath.

"You know you have to leave!" Pastor Cole exclaimed to the spirit as he walked over to Carl.

Larry quickly turned on the video camera that he had brought along, just in case something happened, but he was taken aback when it wouldn't work. He had checked it thoroughly before meeting Glenn tonight. It worked fine then. He became aware of the fact that some force wasn't going to allow him to film anything in here tonight. Especially the confrontation between the spirits and Pastor Cole. Just the thought of it scared the hell out of Larry.

"We've been here long before you came around!" The entity growled out the words to the minister as Carl's body instantly spun around and faced the holy man. "We've never harmed anyone, so why do you want us to leave? Is Carl Lawson worth all of the lives you're going to cost if you try and make us leave?"

"Carl's a human being," the minister replied. "He deserves a life!"

Pastor Cole knew from the wretched expression on Carl's face that he had scared the spirits this time. He felt the fear radiating from the man's body, but a voice inside Glenn's mind told him not to push it tonight. He decided to ease out of this confrontation and let the spirits have some time to chew on the thought that he'd be back. The minister also knew that, when he did return, all hell would break loose! It wouldn't be so easy next time.

"I'm going to leave, now," he told the spirit. "But I'm coming back to see Carl again!"

With those words, the entity hid itself inside Carl's body and allowed the man to take control of his senses again. As Carl became conscious as to where he was, he looked at Glenn with a sick and worried look.

"Glenn!" he blurted out in a frantic and pleading tone, his eyes showing tremendous concern. "There's something coming in and out of me, and I want it to leave me alone. I want a life of peace! I'm not their property!"

Carl paused and took a deep breath. He gripped his stomach with both hands as if he were going to vomit.

"In order for me to make them leave you alone," the minister replied, "they have to leave the building, Carl. Spirits and demons don't possess buildings. They inhabit people! We're going to leave for tonight, but we'll be back. I want you to get plenty of rest and pray constantly, until we return. Ask God for deliverance. Don't eat much. You have to fast in order to run these devils out of you!"

"Okay," Carl agreed as he looked around the room with frightened eyes, still clutching his stomach.

"I'll call you before we return," the minister told Carl, knowing the spirits were listening, too. He knew exactly when he intended to return to this place, but he wasn't telling anyone, not even Larry. Glenn figured he'd give the spirits some time to worry about the upcoming confrontation.

He'd simply call Larry, and meet him at this office, when the time was at hand. When they returned to the nightclub again, it would be time to wage a Holy War against the dark forces of evil that walked this building and possessed Carl Lawson's body at will!

Reverend Cole and Larry Kidwell bid Carl good night and left the nightclub. Carl was more confused now than ever. He was at his wit's end. He hoped like hell that he had not infuriated the spirits when he told Glenn that he wanted them to leave him alone.

As Carl stood inside the barroom, all-alone, he suddenly became aware of the fact that the crotch of his pants was soaking wet.

"My, God!" he stammered as he undid his belt and pulled his pants down below his knees. "It's blood!" he shrieked. His white jockey shorts were completely soaked in blood, and it was still oozing out of this body through his rectum. Carl jerked up his pants, ran over to the light switches and quickly turned them on. He raced into the ladies' restroom and positioned his back near the mirrors that lined the walls inside the pink cubicle. He dropped his pants to his ankles and bent over, looking over his shoulder.

"Noooo," he groaned in a long, slow whisper as his eyes fixed on the large, red, pus-filled sores that were clinging in and around his rectum.

It was not just ordinary hemorrhoids. These were tremendous in size, growing and spreading like poison ivy, and hurting like hell! They had appeared from out of nowhere, and Carl knew that this was punishment for seeking help.

"I'm sorry!" he screamed to the top of his lungs as he jerked up his pants and raced for his upstairs apartment. "Give me another chance! I won't let them come back, again!"

Carl fled upstairs, crying out in pain, and promising, over and over, that he would not let the minister return if the entity would release him from this curse. He made his way into his bathroom and quickly filled the tub with scalding water, ripping off his clothes, and blistering his skin when he threw himself into the hot liquid. He prayed that the scalding water would stop the swelling and bleeding before it was too late.

Chapter Forty-seven

This is a transcription of the exorcism that took place inside the nightclub. Documented on videotape, this rite took over six hours. What I have presented here are the highlights of that exorcism, and the events immediately preceding and following the ritual.

* * * * *

Another week passed without any demonic disturbances. The employees had begun to let go of their fears and suspicions, at least that is what they tried to tell each other. Carl, on the other hand, stayed upstairs in his apartment most of the time. His hemorrhoids had lessened in size, but they still continued bleeding and hurting unbearably. He had gone to the doctor and was given suppositories and told to soak in hot water several times a day. Even though he had done exactly what the doctor had told him to, he was unable to get much relief. He found himself becoming more nauseated each day, and it was all he could do to force himself to eat anything.

There was no doubt this sudden illness was some curse from Hell, for allowing Pastor Cole to try and exorcise the spirits from the nightclub. He had made up his mind that when the minister called him again, wanting to return, he would simply make up some lame excuse, and keep putting him off, until the preacher got the hint and gave up on this endeavor.

It was Thursday afternoon and he was lying in the tub, soaking, staring up at the single fly that was crawling on the ceiling. It was obvious from his haggard looks that this cursed affliction was getting the best of him. He could not get warm, no matter what he did, and his eyes were wells of pain and despair.

As he lay in the hot steamy water, a foul stench slowly found its way into the bathroom, engulfing the small, white tiled room, causing him to become aware of some presence in the room with him. He didn't have to see it. He knew it was there, and he quickly felt an overwhelming fear gripping him again. He slowly, cautiously raised his head up, just a little, and stared at the white wooden bathroom door. It was closed tight.

As he shifted his eyes left and right, looking at the door, and then at the walls, the wooden door suddenly sprung open, slamming against the outside wall with a thunderous bang. Carl gripped the sides of the tub and held his breath, waiting for his impending doom, but to his surprise, nothing happened for several long seconds. Then the raspy voice assaulted his ears. "I told you to tell that preacher to piss off!"

"Who's there?" Carl barely managed to get the words out.

The door slammed shut and the foul odor seized the bathroom causing him to vomit in his bath water. After up heaving the little bit of food that he had consumed earlier, he came to a crouching position inside the tub, and just as he started to stand to his feet, the entity plowed him in the stomach, then in the side of the jaw, knocking him back down into the soapy liquid. Carl lay face up in the tub, momentarily stunned from the attack. He tried to get himself together, but before he could try to defend himself, the entity violently, forcefully, grabbed him by the hair and shoved his head under the surface of the water, holding him there, trying to drown him.

He opened his eyes and looked through the liquid as best he could, and now he could see his attacker. It was the same man who had assaulted him before. It was Alonzo!

Carl held his breath, kicked, twisted, and thrashed his arms and legs, trying to break free of the man's grip before he drowned.

"Tell that preacher to piss off!" The raspy words soared through the water and into his ears like a torpedo.

"God, help me!" Carl's brain shrieked in terror as he began swallowing large gulps of water. The entity shoved his head to the bottom of the white, porcelain tub and spoke again.

"Bow to Satan or die now," he demanded as the bath water quickly turned into bright red blood.

"I bow!" Carl screamed out, now swallowing several gulps of red plasma and choking on it. He closed his eyes, waiting to die.

As suddenly as it had begun, the attack ended. The entity let loose of Carl and suctioned itself back into the air as if it was never really there. Once the spirit let loose of Carl, his eyes sprang open and the horrified man jerked up out of the water, choking, spitting and coughing violently, gripping the tub on both sides, and crying like a baby as tiny drops of blood rolled down his face and fell from his chin, splashing into the tub.

Regaining his breath after what seemed an eternity, Carl climbed out of the tub and grabbed a towel from the rack, quickly wiping the blood from his body the best he could. He was at the edge of insanity and he had to get out of the building before he lost it completely. Besides, he wanted out of here before that bastard came back and finished the job!

He raced into the living room and quickly slipped into a pair of blue jeans, a black short-sleeved shirt and gym shoes. He ran from the apartment, down the stairs, and through the bar as fast as he could. He exploded through the swinging doors, and raced down the mirrored hallway, heading for safety. As he reached the entrance, he froze dead in his tracks at the sight before him.

Oh, noooo, Carl's brain screamed as he stared through the glass panes of the front doors. On the other side of the entranceway, standing just outside the door, stood Pastor Glenn Cole and Larry Kidwell.

They were supposed to call first, Carl's mind cried frantically over and over.

"Open up, Carl," the minister demanded. "It's time!"

Carl sighed and knew now why he was suddenly attacked moments ago. The demons wanted him to get out of here before the preacher showed up. They knew he was coming.

Carl reluctantly pulled out his key and slipped it into the hole, unlocking the door, allowing Larry and Glenn to come inside.

"Is something wrong?" Glenn asked when he saw the terrified look on Carl's face.

"No," he quickly lied. He was not about to say anything to the men as to what had just happened. He was terrified beyond belief, afraid for his own life, and was not going to take any more chances on getting the spirits angry with him again.

"Carl," Glenn said softly. "It's time to end this matter once and for all. I'm here to send the spirits away. You won't have to be troubled anymore.

"Can't we put this off until another night?" He pleaded with the minister, trying to get out of the exorcism. "I'm really tired and I was..."

"No! The spirits knew I was coming here tonight to take them on. There's no running away now. We're here to finish this. Tonight!"

Carl looked at Larry, then back at Glenn Cole. He was trapped. There was no getting out of this confrontation.

"Okay," he finally agreed, but I hope you know what you're doing. I've got a feeling that they're going to put up one helluva fight."

"Don't worry," the minister assured him. "It's going to be okay."

"I left that table in the kitchen from the last time you were here," he said. "We can go back in there, if you want."

"That'll be fine," Glenn answered with a sympathetic smile.

Carl led the way, with Larry and the pastor in tow. Larry had a video camera in each hand. Carl flipped on the lights and the men walked into the room. Glenn and Carl sat at the table talking about everything but the spirits, while Larry set up his cameras and put them in the record mode.

He announced that the cameras were rolling, and that he was going to sit out in the main ballroom so the two could be alone. He left the room and sat down at a nearby table, just outside the kitchen.

"I guess we're ready," Glenn announced as he looked at his wristwatch. It was eight-fifty-five P.M. on August 8.

"Are you okay?" Glenn asked Carl. "You seem pretty nervous, or something."

"I'm sort of nervous," Carl answered timidly. "I'm at a point where I know there's a lot of evil going on in here. Even some of the customers worry me now."

"Well, like I told you before, Carl, I want to help you," Glenn said, like a father talking to his son. "I don't want you to go through life like you have been. Peace is what you need. There's more to life than going through it like you've been doing. We don't know what the future holds, but there is a place that you can get into and you can live in it."

Glenn paused for a moment and stared into Carl's eyes. He recognized the fear radiating from them, but it wasn't Carl that was afraid now. It was one of the spirits.

"You see," the minister continued, "the Bible says that Jesus came to give us a new life, and Jesus Christ of Nazareth will be the place where Carl Lawson needs to get to. I want you to remember that!"

"It's starting again!" Carl blurted out as he looked desperately into Glenn's eyes.

"They're going to leave, Carl. They're gong to let you have a life of peace, but you have to understand something; not only do the evil spirits have to leave, but so do the good spirits!"

"But what about Johanna and Buck?" Carl asked, showing obvious disappointment. "They don't bother anybody!"

"Maybe they don't, Carl, but they are trapped in a world where they don't belong and they are suffering because of it. They have to leave, too, so that they can find peace and happiness."

"But, they're my friends! They're the only ones I have to keep me company during the week. Without them, I'll be all alone."

"Carl, you don't understand. If they're your friends, wouldn't you want them to be happy?"

"They are happy! They like it here!"

"That's only because they don't know any other place to be! They're lost in this world. It's time for them to move on to the next world where they'll find greater happiness. It's best for them and it's best for you! They need to leave, and so does the evil that's in this place!"

"But, they'll come back...the evil ones!" Carl argued, his voice suddenly child-like as he began aimlessly mumbling beneath his breath about the people who frequented the nightclub years ago.

"Carl!" Glenn shouted to get the young man's attention. He immediately recognized what was happening. "You have power over these things!"

"No, he doesn't!" A harsh voice, from deep within Carl rebuked the minister. The voice was unlike Carl's. It was a guttural sound, dark and liquefied, threatening.

"And just who are you?" Glenn calmly asked the spirit that had suddenly taken possession of Carl's body.

"Sam!" the sneering ghost answered as Carl's eyes gazed up and down at the Preacher, apparently appraising him as an adversary.

"Sam who? What's your last name?"

"Tucker," the voice snarled. "Sam Tucker. Why do you want us to leave? We've been here for years. There's no way to make us leave. We're not bothering anyone!"

Before the clergyman could respond to Sam's declaration, another voice suddenly erupted from Carl's lips.

"Charlie!" the voice shrieked.

"Charlie, who?" Glenn asked, still calm and authoritative.

"Charlie Lester!"

"How old are you, Charlie?"

"I don't know," the entity replied slowly, seemingly confused by the minister's question.

"It's time for you to leave, Charlie. It's time for you to go on to the realm of the spirit."

"Carl needs me!" Charlie replied.

"No he doesn't! You have to leave!"

"I'm not leaving!" the spirit shouted once again. "If I leave, then we all have to leave!"

"Then all of you leave!" Glenn commanded as his body began to tense and anger started to creep into his voice.

"Well, dammit! You leave!" the wraith shrieked, its words a volley of verbal missiles intent on destroying the minister's psyche. "There are more of us than there are of you!"

"I don't care," Glenn scoffed. "I've got something greater in me than what you are! You're leaving! Do you understand that?"

"I ain't going no where!" the spirit challenged Glenn with murderous tones.

"Yes, you are!"

"Man of God, I prayed to God in my lifetime, and he never gave me nothing, but trouble!"

"That's because you didn't yield to him!"

"I don't yield to NOBODY!"

"You're gonna yield to God!" Glenn's voice became loud and overbearing.

"The hell, I am!" The entity mocked Glenn and everything the pastor stood for. "We're coming back!"

"No, you're not!"

"The hell, we ain't!" the spirit shouted, becoming more aggressive with each exchange. "And when we do, there'll be seven more with us!"

"I don't care!" Glenn countered, his mind recalling Biblical teachings of the seven-fold return of demons. "I've got seven holy spirits with me!"

"Ah, bull shit! If you try and take Carl from us..."

"I'm not taking Carl anywhere," the clergyman interrupted. "I'm sending you and your friends into the realm of the spirit where you belong!"

"I don't belong there! We ain't had enough war. There's a lot of work for us to do, yet!"

"You're leaving! Do you hear me?"

"No! I don't hear you!" the spirit laughed as an evil smirk etched Carl's face.

"Yes, you are!"

"The hell I am," the entity snarled. "My Lord's on his way!"

"Well, tell him to come on!" The clergyman challenged the entity, its word revealing to Glenn that he was not talking to a spirit, but to a demon instead. "I've got something greater than him, and something in me is greater than you. Do you understand that?"

Without answering, the demon inside of Carl caused the handyman to suddenly turn his head away from the minister's stare.

"Oh, no, you don't! Look at me! It's time for you to leave!"

"Ever since Carl was a little kid," the demon began, "All he wanted to do was go to church and pray, but I got him riding around here on his bicycle! Carl's so stupid! He didn't even know what happened to him!"

"I know he didn't, but I do! I'm telling you, it's time for you to leave! Look what I've got right here, and you know what it is!" Glenn said as he bent over and picked up his Bible and held it up in from of Carl's face.

"Stick that stupid book up your ass," the demon screamed defiantly as it winced at the sight of Glenn's Bible.

"This book compels you to bow to God."

The demon sneered with disgust.

"You know I have the power to make you leave because this Bible, God's word, gives me the power to make you leave!"

The minister paused, and took a deep breath. He stared intently into Carl's eyes. He felt something dark and evil watching him, but still he continued, "In the name of Jesus of Nazareth, I command you to leave. I command Charlie and the other spirits, in the name of Jesus of Nazareth, to leave Carl alone. I command all of you to leave right now, in the name of Jesus, and you know it works. You have to go now!"

The clergyman placed his Bible back on the floor and through Carl's eyes, recognized that the spirits were beginning to weaken.

"By the authority of God's word," Glenn continued, "I command you to leave!"

Carl's body began to jerk and quiver, and the spirit caused him to try to push himself away from the table, but the man of God quickly reached over and grabbed both of Carl's wrists. Carl pulled and tugged violently, trying desperately to break free from Glenn Cole's grip, but to no avail.

"We'll be good!" the spirit promised in a pleading, child-like voice when it realized it wasn't going to get away from the preacher.

"You're leaving Carl! And you're leaving now!"

Carl's body continued jerking and shaking back and forth, but the minister held on, and then Carl's demeanor changed again. He stopped moving and stared at the minister's hands wrapped around his wrists. He looked Pastor Cole in the eyes with an evil smirk.

"Do you know who you're talking to?" A new voice asked. It was apparent that another entity had now taken control of Carl. "You don't scare me Holy Man!"

"You don't scare me, either," Glenn responded with a cool, firm voice.

"I will, though!" The entity shouted to the top of Carl's lungs.

"No, you won't!" Glenn yelled back. "You're leaving, too!"

The minister tightened his grip on Carl's wrists and began praying aloud for the Lord, Jesus Christ, to loose Carl Lawson from these spirits, and as he did, Carl's body stiffened. His eyes rolled back in his head, and he sat erect in the chair until suddenly the man flew backward into the air, breaking free from Glenn Cole's grasp.

Carl's body slammed into the floor, about five feet from the table. He lay face up, his eyes fixed in a cold gaze.

"Yea!" The minister yelled as he stood and walked over to Carl. "Leave him in the name of Jesus!" The minister yelled again.

"SCREW YOU!" another spirit suddenly screamed out the words. "SCREW EVERYBODY! Carl's mine! We don't need him, but we need his body!"

"Well, you're not going to have it, anymore," the minister exclaimed calmly with a defiant tone. "I'm going to bind you and the other spirits in the name of Jesus, tonight!"

"How the hell are you gonna bind me?" the entity yelled out as a chorus of multi-toned voices chanted inside of Carl.

"Because God is inside of me!"

"What in the hell do you think you've got to bind me with? My Lord's on his way. He's coming right now!"

"Bring him on!" Pastor Cole dared the entity as the room began filling with an intense, sickening smell.

"He's coming down strong and I'll tell you what! There ain't a damn 'Holy Man' ever gonna come in here and try to run us off again, cause there's thousands of us here.
We've been here for years."

"I don't care! You're leaving! Do you understand that!"

"I don't have to go nowhere! This body is mine!"

An empty wheelbarrow sat beside him. He grabbed the handles and violently flipped it over, slamming it down, then jumped on it on all fours and started to growl viciously like a wild animal. His facial expressions began contorting and the light bulb in the room began to flicker. The loud banging of doors began ringing out from down in the basement and clamorous pounding came from the attic. Carl's pulse began dropping, but his heart raced to full speed. His breathing became labored and his body convulsed with waves of wrenching shudders.

A single ray of bright light appeared between the minister and Carl as if it was some sort of supernatural barrier put there to keep the clergyman away from the spirits.

"Depart, you spirits, and go to the world where you belong!" Pastor Cole screamed as he quickly bent down and wrestled Carl to the floor. He held his right hand on top of Carl's head and began praying aloud, his voice now rising up and down in a series of shouts.

The pounding became worse, then growling and gasping sounds escaped from Carl's body, and even the walls in the room began shaking violently.

"It's time for you all to leave!" the minister shouted the command. "In the name of Jesus Christ of Nazareth, and on the authority of God's word, I command each and every demon and spirit to leave, and I command Carl Lawson to take control of his own body."

The fire and brimstone preacher was filled with it now! The power of the Holy Ghost was surging through his entire body in waves of electric energy. He was winning the battle. God's power was there, inside the man of the cloth, radiating from his face. A golden haze seemed to circle the minister and as he stared into Carl's eyes, he watched the man's pupils turn colors and dilate over and over. The demons and spirits were leaving, one after another. A foul smell, a stench that could have only come from Hell, escaped out of Carl's mouth, and his tongue wagged back and forth until another voice began speaking.

"They're all gone, but me!" the spirit said in a low, threatening tone.

"Who are you?"

"You're talking to Alonzo!" the spirit replied with wry amusement. "If you want that bitch, Pearl's head, dig under this floor. They hung me and my friend for the crime. Did you know that? And that ain't all! It was me that threw that pregnant woman down the stairs in here. I died for killing one pregnant woman and her baby so what's one more!"

The Reverend didn't know what the spirit was talking about. He figured it was trying to change the subject to stop the minister from casting it out of Carl's body.

In response, Pastor Cole tightened his hold on Carl with tremendous force, and again began praying aloud. The spirit groaned, croaked and cried out for the minister to stop, but there was no holding him back.

The power of God was beaming from the cleric, and he was determined to put an end to this once and for all.

The pastor shouted out one prayer after another, commanding the spirits to flee from Carl Lawson and the nightclub. The words flowed from the preacher like a river. Carl's body weakened, then suddenly went limp as one long gasp escaped his lips and he dropped into the minister's arms like a mere rag doll. For several long seconds, the room was silent.

"Open your eyes, Carl," the clergyman finally commanded. "Take control of your body. It's over. They're gone!"

Carl's body shook slightly, then he slowly opened his eyes and rose up, sitting next to Glenn.

"Are you okay?" the preacher asked. "I guess so," Carl was confused and looked lost. "What happened?"

"It's over, Carl. You're free, but I have to warn you of something. When a spirit, or spirits, are cast out, they search the world over, looking for a new home, but, if they can't find one, they return to their old house, and, if that house isn't clean and filled with another spirit, they'll return with seven more, and that person is much worse off than before. It's very important that you start going to church. You have to fill yourself with the Lord Jesus, and most of all, you can never entertain these spirits again. If you ever feel their presence, you have to pray for the Lord to wash and cleanse you. You have to resist them! Do you understand that?"

"Yes," Carl said, breathing a deep sigh and looking around the room.

"Jesus," a voice whispered out. "Is it over?"

Both, Carl and Pastor Cole turned and looked at the door. It was Larry who had asked the question. He had a look of sheer terror and disbelief on his face. "If I hadn't seen and heard some of what just happened, I'd never have believed it!" Kidwell said, shaking his head in awe.

"It's over," the minister stated with a smile. "I warned you it wasn't going to be like some Hollywood movie. What you just saw was the real thing, the power of God over the forces of evil."

Glenn helped Carl to his feet and led the weary man over to the table. They sat down, this time beside each other. The minister led Carl in prayer while Larry quickly gathered up his video equipment, still in awe at what he had just witnessed.

Completing the sinner's prayer, the minister told Carl to go up to his apartment and get some rest. He handed him one of his church business cards and told him to call him anytime if he needed to. He shook Carl's hand, and then patted him on the shoulder.

"It's really over," he said again with a warm smile. "We're going to leave, now, but once again, you must remember never to invite these spirits back. You must never allow yourself to entertain them again! Not even the friendly ones. If you invite one, you invite them all to return! Always keep that thought in the back of your mind!"

Carl thanked both Pastor Cole and Larry Kidwell. He told them he felt a great burden had been lifted off of him. It was as if he was a new man. He wasn't frightened anymore. He walked them to the front of the building, but before bidding them good-bye, he grabbed Pastor Cole and hugged him tightly, a single tear sliding down the left side of his face, and falling down to the floor. The minister hugged him back and told him to seek out God. Carl nodded. The minister and Kidwell walked to their car and headed back to Larry's office. Carl locked the front door and walked back into the main barroom when a sudden thought seized his brain.

"The well! What if it isn't sealed?"

He broke into a dead run, racing through the building as fast as he could. He ran down the back stage stairs and raced through the basement until he came to the China Room.

He hurried over to the hole in the floor and gasped for breath when he saw that the well was sealed again. It was really over. The evil was gone, and suddenly he became aware of something else...so were his hemorrhoids. His body had healed itself when the minister cast out the spirits. He could get on with his life now, and not have to worry about ghosts and demons anymore.

With a grin on his face, he headed upstairs for his apartment to get some rest, but first he was going to call Janet to tell her the good news.

Stopping at the bar, he grasped the receiver in his left hand and dialed with his right. He couldn't help but feel a little sadness over the loss of Buck and Johana, knowing that they, too, had gone on to the realm of the spirit world.

"Damn!" he whispered, not remembering Reverend Cole's warning, and not realizing what he was saying, "I wish they'd come back!"

"Hello?" Janet said to a faint 'click' and a low hum on the open phone line.

"Is anyone there?" Carl asked then hung up the phone when he too, heard nothing but an open line. Sighing deeply Carl told himself his body needed rest. He would call the Mackeys later. He headed upstairs to try and get some sleep and hope that this madness was finally over this time.

Author's Note

I am sure you have found some of this story hard to believe. When I first considered writing this tale of terror, I felt the same way. It simply sounded too incredible; far too unbelievable to accept as reality. Then pieces started falling together that made even a skeptic like me take a second look. I knew that I was on to something really big.

The story presented itself to me by fluke. Bobby Mackey was at my place of business filming a television commercial. A friend of mine asked me how my stories were coming along, and I took that as my cue to show off! I pulled my latest manuscript from my desk and read a few passages aloud.

Bobby expressed surprise at my being a writer, and, with a grin, stated that people had been trying to convince him for years that his nightclub was haunted. He said his wife, employees, and even customers had sworn that they had been victimized by some demonic entity while inside the club but he had kept it quiet for fear of bad publicity.

After some pleading on my part, Bobby gave me permission to snoop around and see what I could learn about these tall tales. Upon arriving at the nightclub, I first approached Carl Lawson. I asked him to tell me what he knew about the haunting. His answer was short and to the point: "I don't know what you're talking about." He flatly refused to tell me anything at all. After some reassurance and coaxing by Bobby, Carl reluctantly gave in and told me of some of the things that he had experienced. I found his tale too bizarre to believe.

Wanting to learn the facts, I investigated Carl's statement. I researched old newspapers and local history books. I searched page after page for clues that would help me substantiate or refute his story. I spent the next two weeks studying the history of the site that the nightclub sits on. What I found stunned me.

Armed with the information I had gathered, I went back to Carl. During our earlier meeting, Carl had purposely omitted certain details that he felt would bring him ridicule, but, after seeing the documentation I had, he opened up and began telling me everything he could remember. After interviewing Carl, I talked to Janet Mackey. What she told me was very frightening. After Janet, I began talking to the employees and then customers. I found myself lost in a horrifying fairy tale come true. There were just too many people experiencing these strange things while inside the nightclub. After completing the interviews and investigation, I took a long hard look at the evidence that would prove that Bobby Mackey's nightclub was haunted.

The facts are as follows:

Carl told me of a ghost named Buck who was always accompanied by a large black dog. The safe, in what was the old cashier's room, is inscribed on each side with the words "BUILT SPECIALLY FOR E. A. BRADY." E.A. Brady was the former owner of this nightclub. The records stated that Brady owned the massive building when it was a thriving gambling casino known as The Primrose. Because of the success of his business, he was given an ultimatum by the mob---sell out to them, or die! Brady was arrested in connection with the gangland-style, non-fatal shooting of Albert "Red" Masterson on August 5, 1946. He was acquitted September 24, 1946. Ultimately forced out by these gangsters, rumors say that he swore the place would never again thrive as a gambling casino.

Several times during the early 1950's the new owners of Brady's old club were arrested on gambling charges. In 1955, Campbell County Police broke into the building with sledgehammers and confiscated the gambling equipment.

Brady's nickname was "Buck." His death on September 17, 1965 was attributed to suicide. One would have to wonder if that was true?

Carl spoke of a headless ghost named Pearl and her murderers who were identified as Scott Jackson and Alonzo Walling.

KENTUCKY POST articles reported that indeed, two men, Alonzo Walling and Scott Jackson, were hanged March 21, 1897, for murdering and decapitating a young woman, Pearl Bryan. The crime occurred less than two miles from the site where the nightclub now stands. The woman's head was never found. The men were offered a life sentence in lieu of death if they would produce Pearl Bryan's head, but both of them refused and let themselves be hanged behind the courthouse in Newport, Kentucky. It was the last public hanging in Campbell County.

People said Jackson and Walling were afraid of suffering Satan's wrath if they exposed his sacrificial grounds and that this is why they refused to tell the whereabouts of Pearl's head. Up to the moment of his death, Alonzo Walling denied participating in the murder of the pregnant Pearl Bryan. On the gallows he threatened to come back and haunt the area. One reporter covering the hanging commented in his March 20, 1897, KENTUCKY POST article, that an "evil eye" had fallen on many of the people who were connected with the Pearl Bryan Murder Case. The local theory is that the head was disposed of in the slaughterhouse that once stood on the site that is now home to Bobby Mackey's Music World.

The restroom Carl had been trapped in by the bats had been torn down and relocated near the front entrance. Installation of a new air conditioning system in the club required cutting out some of the flooring to install ductwork. To the technician's surprise, a piece of the wood he had cut out was completely burned! The area he was cutting through had been the floor of what once was the original restroom where Carl had been trapped.

I, too, personally witnessed some of the paranormal activity. I was present when the psychic, Patricia Mischell, toured the building. Until that day, I did not believe in psychic abilities. I was present at all three of the exorcism meetings, and I transcribed the included sequences from the videotape. The successful exorcism in Chapter 47 took place on August 8, 1991, thirteen years after Bobby Mackey's Music World opened for business. Still today, Bobby refuses to acknowledge that his nightclub is or was haunted, but his resolve is weakening. Maybe he doesn't want to admit it for fear people would quit frequenting his establishment. Bobby, and some professional songwriters in Nashville, wrote a song for the woman who committed suicide inside the building years ago. They named it "The Ballad of Johana." Bobby sings this tune almost every weekend, and, while he sings the song, it seems that no one wants to dance. Even Bobby will admit that while he sings the haunting melody there seems to be an uneasy calm about the place.

This book was based on the interviews and sworn statements of each person named in the text. I have in my possession copies of every sworn affidavit supporting this story.

The exorcism, as stated earlier, was documented and recorded on film. Since the exorcism of Carl Lawson by Reverend Glenn Cole, it appeared that, for the time being, the terror was over, but Reverend Cole stated that it is very possible for spirits and demons to return to their former haunts. After the exorcism Carl Lawson could not remember most of the details of his ghostly encounters. Reverend Cole said this happens quite frequently when one is freed of their demons. They seem to lose their memory of what happened.

Bobby Mackey still denies the existence of ghosts, but, for some reason, after viewing the film footage of the exorcism, and after going to work at the nightclub alone one night, he suddenly made plans --- that same night -- to tear down the structure and build another nightclub on an adjacent piece of property.

Maybe Bobby was simply tired of the ghost talk or did he have an encounter with some ghostly inhabitant that he refuses to talk about? Shortly after hiring a construction company to construct a new nightclub those plans were halted when an unexplainable sixty-foot deep fissure opened up across the property that he was to build on. The sudden crack in the earth stretched completely across the property causing the Corp of Engineers to deem the land unsafe to build on. Bobby had no choice but to stay where he is still today.

Current evidence demonstrates that the demons have indeed returned. Bar stools move on their own accord; the water faucets in the ladies room turn on by themselves along with toilets flushing at will. Doors swing open with no one there and to top it all, one patron, who made fun of everyone confirming the ghostly attacks, was found unconscious in the men's room. When paramedics, called to the nightclub, revived him he identified the ghost of Alonzo Walling as attacking him in the men's room. This particular man confronted Bobby about the ghostly attack and when Bobby scoffed him the man sued Bobby in Campbell County, Ky. Court demanding Bobby hire someone to run off the unclean spirits that walk the halls of this place. The Judge ruled that Bobby Mackey has no control over ghosts and dismissed the case. Shortly after the trial Bobby Mackey, on the advice of his attorney, had a sign placed at the front door of the establishment. The sign remains there today. The sign reads,

"WARNING THIS ESTABLISHMENT IS SAID TO BE HAUNTED.
MANAGEMENT ASSUMES NO LIABILITY.
ENTER AT YOUR OWN RISK."

Bibliography

Messick, Hank, *Syndicate Wife*. New York: MacMillian Co., 1968

Messick, Hank, and Nellis, Joseph L., *Private Lives of Public Enemies*. Wyden Publishing House, 1973.

Reis, Jim, *Pieces of the Past*, Covington, KY 41011. Kentucky Post, 1988

Newspaper Articles:

Newport Auto Gunman Wounds "Red" Masterson; "Buck Brady" Arrested After Search by Police, The Cincinnati Enquirer, Kentucky Edition, August 6, 1946, Page 1.

Buck Brady, 1920's Bootlegger, Is Dead. The Cincinnati Enquirer, Kentucky Edition, September 22, 1965, Page 2.

HEAD CUTT OFF! The Kentucky Post, Covington, Saturday, February 1, 1896, Page 1.
WEAVING A WEB The Kentucky Post, Covington, Saturday, February 1, 1896, Page 1.
WANTED A HEAD The Kentucky Post, Covington, Friday, February 7, 1896, Page 1.

CONFESSION Jackson and Walling Preparing a Final Statement of the Murder. The Kentucky Post, Covington, Thursday, March 18, 1897, Page 1.

TWO CONFESSIONS Which Jackson and Walling Sent to the Governor. The Kentucky Post, Covington, Friday, March 19, 1897, Page 1.

TWO LIVES FOR ONE. Murder of Pearl Bryan Expiated by the Death of Jackson and Walling on the Gallows. The Kentucky Post, Covington, Saturday, March 20, 1897, Page 1.

SCENES AT THE SCAFFOLD The Kentucky Post, Covington, Saturday, March 20, 1897, Page 2.

EVIL EYE. The Kentucky Post, Covington, Saturday, March 20, 1897, Page 3.

Cohen, Anne B., *Poor Pearl, Poor Girl! The Murdered Girl Stereotype in Ballad and Newspaper* Austin, TX 78712: University of Texas Press

Summary of Hell's Gate.

THE MURDER OF
PEARL BRYAN
History & Hauntings of Bobby Mackey's Music World
Wilder, Kentucky

Wilder, Kentucky is a small town that is located just south of Cincinnati, Ohio. For many years, the town has been subject to visits from curiosity-seekers, tourists, paranormal investigators and media reporters. They come here in search of a place called Bobby Mackey's Music World, a night club and tavern that may be one of the most haunted, and most sinister, locations in America!

The building where the nightclub is now located has a long and bloody history in the area, from its origins as a slaughterhouse to its tangible link to one of the greatest ghost stories of southern Indiana. It was constructed back in the 1850's and was one of the largest packing houses in the region for many years. Only a well that was dug in the basement, where blood and refuse from the animals was drained, remains from the original building. The slaughterhouse closed down in the early 1890's, but legend has it that the building was far from abandoned. According to the lore, the basement of the packing house became a ritual site for occultists. The well was used to hide the remains of small animals that were butchered during their ceremonies.

The Bryan Home in Greencastle, Indiana

Apparently, a small satanic group made up of local residents gathered at the empty building, managing to practice their rituals in secret. However, they were exposed in 1896 during one of the most spectacular murder trials ever held in northeast Kentucky. It was so large that tickets were sold to the hearing and more than 5,000 people stood outside the Newport, Kentucky courthouse for information about what was taking place inside. The trial, and the murder that spawned it, has become an integral part of Bobby Mackey's haunted history.

Pearl Bryan, the daughter of a wealthy farmer, was an attractive, young woman who lived in Greencastle, Indiana in 1896. She was the youngest of 12 children from a prominent family and by the age of 22, was one of the most popular girls in the area. She had graduated from Greencastle High School in 1892 and had more than her share of suitors. Unknown to her friends and the polite members of Greencastle society, Pearl was pregnant. Her cousin and close friend, William Wood, had recently introduced her to Scott Jackson, who was then attending the Ohio College of Dental Surgery in Cincinnati. He and Wood, who was then attending medical school at DePauw University, became close friends but unbeknownst to Wood, Jackson was an alleged member of the occult group that met the former slaughterhouse in Wilder. Jackson's family was as well-to-do as the Bryan's and so he was immediately accepted as a suitor for Pearl. He soon seduced her however and she became pregnant. Pearl turned to Wood, who in turn, informed Jackson of the problem. He made arrangements to remedy the situation with an abortion in Cincinnati.

Pearl left her parent's home on February 1, 1896 and told them that she was going to Indianapolis. Instead, she made plans to meet with Jackson and his roommate, Alonzo Walling, in Cincinnati. It would be the last time that her parents would ever see her alive. She was at that time five months pregnant.

Jackson's medical skills were apparently much more inept than he had led his friend William Wood to believe. He first tried to induce an abortion using chemicals, apparently cocaine. This substance was later discovered in Pearl's system during an autopsy. After that, he tried to use dental tools, but botched that as well. After an hour or so, Jackson and Walling has a frightened, injured and bleeding young woman on their hands and that's when the story takes an ever darker turn.

The three of them left Cincinnati and traveled across the
Ohio River and into Kentucky. Jackson took them to a
secluded spot near Fort Thomas and here, he and
Walling murdered Pearl Bryan. Using dental
instruments, they severed her head from her body. It was
a "clean cut", according to the testimony of the doctor
who later examined the body. He also determined that
Pearl had been alive at the time because of the presence
of blood on the underside of some leaves at the murder
scene.

Pearl's body was found about two hundred feet off the
Alexandria Turnpike and less than two miles from the
abandoned slaughterhouse. As her head was nowhere to be
found, Pearl was identified by her shoes. They bore the
imprint of Louis and Hays, a Greencastle shoe company
that was able to confirm that they had been sold to Pearl
Bryan. During the trial that followed, Walling testified that
it had been Jackson's idea to cut Pearl up and distribute her
body in the Cincinnati sewers. Only the head was taken, for
which Jackson apparently had other uses. Pearl's luxurious
blond hair was later found in a valise in Jackson's room.

Alonzo Walling   Scott Jackson

Pearl's head was never found and legend has it that it
was used during a satanic ritual at the slaughterhouse. It
was then dumped into the well of blood and was lost.
Jackson and Walling were brought to trial in 1897 and
were quickly found guilty and sentenced to death.
William Wood was later arrested and charged as an
accomplice. Charges against him were dropped when he
agreed to testify against the other two men. According to
reports, Jackson and Walling were both offered life
sentences instead of execution if they would reveal the
location of Pearl's head. Both men refused. They went to
the gallows behind the courthouse in Newport on March
21, 1897. It was the last public hanging in Campbell
County.

The gallows where Jackson & Walling were Hanged

The stories spread that Jackson and Walling were afraid of suffering "Satan's wrath" if they revealed the location of Pearl's head. The slaughterhouse was then a closely guarded secret and other occultists would have been exposed if the two men had talked. One reporter commented later that Walling, as the noose was being slipped over his head, threatened to come back and haunt the area after his death. The writer also stated a few days later, in an article in the *Kentucky Post* newspaper that an "evil eye" had fallen on many of the people connected to the Pearl Bryan case. Legend has it that many of the police officials and attorneys involved in the case later met with bad luck and tragic ends.

After the trial ended, the slaughterhouse fell silent and remained empty for many years. It was eventually torn down and a roadhouse was constructed on the site. During the 1920's, the place became known as a speakeasy and as a popular gambling joint. Local lore has it that during this period, a number of murders took place in the building. None of them were ever solved because the bodies were normally dumped elsewhere to keep attention away from the illegal gambling and liquor operation.

The Nightclub Years

After Prohibition ended in 1933, the building was purchased by E.A. Brady, better known to friends and enemies alike as "Buck". Brady turned the building in a thriving tavern and casino called the Primrose. He enjoyed success for a number of years but eventually the operation came to the attention of syndicate mobsters in Cincinnati. They moved in on Brady, looking for a piece of the action. Brady refused offers for new "partners" and outright bids to buy him out of the Primrose. Soon, the tavern was being vandalized and customers were being threatened and beaten up in the parking lot. The violence escalated until Brady became involved in a shooting in August 1946. He was charged and then released in the attempted murder of small-time hood Albert "Red" Masterson. This was the last straw for Buck and he sold out to the gangsters. It was said that when he left, he swore the place would never thrive again as a casino. Brady committed suicide in September 1965.

After Brady sold out, the building re-opened as another nightclub called the Latin Quarter. Several times during the early 1950's, the new owners of the bar were arrested on gambling charges.. In 1955, Campbell County deputies broke into the building with sledge hammers and confiscated slot machines and gambling tables. Apparently, Brady's promises had come to pass.

It was also during this period that the legends of the building gained another vengeful ghost. According to the stories, the owner of the club's daughter, Johanna, fell in love with one of the singers who was performing here and became pregnant. Her father was furious. Thanks to his criminal connections, he had the singer killed. Johanna became so distraught that she attempted to poison her father and then succeeded in taking her own life. Her body was later discovered in the now infamous basement... and according to the autopsy report, she was five months pregnant at the time.

Bad luck continued to plague the owners of the tavern. In the 1970's, it became known as the Hard Rock Cafe, but it was closed down by authorities in 1978 because of some fatal shootings on the premises.

Bobby Mackey's Music World

Finally, the building was turned into the popular bar and dance club that it is today. Bobby and Janet Mackey purchased the building in the spring of 1978 with the intention of turning it into a country bar. Mackey was a well-known as a singer in northern Kentucky and had recorded several albums. He actually scrapped his plans to record in Nashville in order to renovate the old tavern. Once the bar was opened up, it immediately began to attract a crowd.

Bobby Mackey's Music World

Despite a number of years success with the place though, the good times have never been able to erase the "taint" caused by the history of murder and death. The hauntings at Bobby Mackey's Music World remain stained with blood.

Carl Lawson was the first employee hired by Bobby Mackey. He was a loner who worked as a caretaker and handyman at the tavern. He lived alone in an apartment in the upstairs of the building and spent a lot of time in the sprawling building after hours. When he began reporting that he was seeing and hearing bizarre things in the club, people around town first assumed that he was simply crazy. Later on though, when others started to see and hear the same things, Lawson didn't seem so strange after all.

"I'd double check at the end of the night and make sure that everything was turned off. Then I'd come back down hours later and the bar lights would be on. The front doors would be unlocked, when I knew that I'd locked them. The jukebox would be playing the 'Anniversary Waltz' even though I'd unplugged it and the power was turned off," Lawson told author Doug Hensley, who has written extensively about the haunted tavern.

Soon, the strange events went from strange to downright frightening! The first ghost that Lawson spotted in the place was that of a dark, very angry men that he saw behind the bar. Even though others were present at the time of the sighting, they saw nothing. A short time later, Lawson began to experience visions of a spirit who called herself "Johanna". She would often speak to Lawson and he was able to answer her and carry on conversations. The rumors quickly started that Lawson was "talking to himself". Lawson claimed that Johanna was a tangible presence though, often leaving the scent of roses in her wake.

Odd sounds and noises often accompanied the sightings and Lawson soon realized that the spirits seemed to be the strongest in the basement, near an old-sealed up well that had been left from the days when there was a slaughterhouse at the location. The lore of the area, Carl knew, stated that the well had once been used for satanic rituals. Some of the local folks referred to it as "Hell's Gate". Although he wasn't a particularly religious man, Lawson decided to sprinkle some holy water on the old well one night, thinking that it might bring some relief from the spirits. Instead, it seemed to provoke them and the activity in the building began to escalate.

Soon, other employees and patrons of the place began to have their own weird experiences. They began to tell of objects that moved around on their own, lights that turned on an off, disembodied voices and laughter and more. Bobby Mackey was not happy about the ghostly rumors that were starting to spread around town. "Carl starting telling stories and I told him to keep quiet about it. I didn't want it getting around, because I had everything I own stuck in this place. I had to make a success of it," he said. He was not one to believe in ghosts or the supernatural and he didn't want his customers believing in it either. But when Janet Mackey revealed that she too had encountered the resident spirits, Mackey was no longer sure what to think!

Janet told him that she too had experienced the strange activity. She had seen the ghosts, had felt the overwhelming presences and had even smelled Johanna's signature rose scent. She also had a very frightening encounter in the basement. While she was there, she was suddenly overcome by the scent of roses and felt something unseen swirl around her. "Something grabbed me by the waist," Janet later recalled. "It picked me up and threw me back down. I got away from it, and when I got to the top of the stairs there was pressure behind me, pushing me down the steps. I looked back up and a voice was screaming 'Get Out! Get Out!'"

At the time of this terrifying encounter, Janet was, like Johanna and Pearl Bryan before her, five months pregnant. A coincidence?

Once Janet admitted that she had seen the ghosts in the building, other people began to come forward. Roger Heath, who often worked odd jobs in the club remembered a summer morning when he and Carl Lawson were working alone in the building. Heath was removing some light fixtures from the dance floor and Lawson was carrying them down to the basement. Just before lunch, Lawson came up the stairs and Heath noticed that he had small handprints on the back of his shirt. It looked just like a woman had been hugging him!

Erin Fey, a hostess at the club, also confessed to encountering Johanna. She had laughed one day at Lawson when he was talking to the ghost. She stopped laughing when she also got a strong whiff of the rose perfume.

Once the stories starting making the rounds, they caught the attention of a writer named Doug Hensley. He decided to investigate the stories and started hanging around the club, striking up conversations with the regular customers. No one was anxious at first to talk about ghosts. "When I first talked to these people, almost every one of them refused to be interviewed," Hensley said. After he talked to Janet Mackey though, many other people came forward. Soon, Hensley had thirty sworn affidavits from people who experienced supernatural events at the club.

He continued to collect stories and sightings, intrigued by the various spirits who had been seen, including a headless ghost who was dressed in turn-of-the-century clothing. Strangely, independent witnesses provided matching descriptions of the phantom, never knowing that she had been seen by others. That was when Hensley turned to historic records to shed some light on the building's past. He was stunned to discover that events of the past were closely connected to the hauntings of the present. In old newspaper accounts, he found the story of Pearl Bryan and photos of Buck Brady that matched the description of an often seen ghost. None of the witnesses to the present-day paranormal activity were even vaguely aware of who these people had been or what connections they had to the building!

Hensley has since compiled his stories into a book and has been a part of many of the investigations at the club, including a 1994 exorcism of the place that failed miserably. The activity continues to occur and several individuals have even been physically assaulted by spirits. One customer even tried to sue Bobby Mackey in 1994, claiming that he was attacked in the restroom by a ghost wearing a cowboy hat! The case was later dismissed.

Bobby Mackey's Music World remains perhaps one of the strangest haunted sites in the Midwest and one that has proven to be a major attraction for ghost hunters and enthusiasts alike. Few go away disappointed from a tavern where "spirits served" has another meaning altogether!

Visit Bobby Mackey's Nightclub online @ www.Bobbymackey.com

Read Douglas Hensley's other books @ www.lulu.com/DougHensley

MAIN BAR IN BALLROOM

MAIN BALL ROOM

DRESSING ROOMS

CHINA ROOM

STAIRS THAT LEAD NOWHERE

ROOM WHERE CARL SAW THE
TWO MEN HANGING

27?

HANGING OF SCOTT JACKSON AND ALONZO WALLING

Bibliography

Messick, Hank, *Syndicate Wife*. New York: MacMillian Co., 1968

Messick, Hank, and Nellis, Joseph L., *Private Lives of Public Enemies*. Wyden Publishing House, 1973.

Reis, Jim, *Pieces of the Past*, Covington, KY 41011. Kentucky Post, 1988

Newspaper Articles:

Newport Auto Gunman Wounds "Red" Masterson; "Buck Brady" Arrested After Search by Police, The Cincinnati Enquirer, Kentucky Edition, August 6, 1946, Page 1.

Buck Brady, 1920's Bootlegger, Is Dead. The Cincinnati Enquirer, Kentucky Edition, September 22, 1965, Page 2.

HEAD CUTT OFF! The Kentucky Post, Covington, Saturday, February 1, 1896, Page 1.

WEAVING A WEB The Kentucky Post, Covington, Saturday, February 1, 1896, Page 1.

WANTED A HEAD The Kentucky Post, Covington, Friday, February 7, 1896, Page 1.

CONFESSION Jackson and Walling Preparing a Final Statement of the Murder. The Kentucky Post, Covington, Thursday, March 18, 1897, Page 1.

TWO CONFESSIONS Which Jackson and Walling Sent to the Governor. The Kentucky Post, Covington, Friday, March 19, 1897, Page 1.

TWO LIVES FOR ONE. Murder of Pearl Bryan Expiated by the Death of Jackson and Walling on the Gallows. The Kentucky Post, Covington, Saturday, March 20, 1897, Page 1.

SCENES AT THE SCAFFOLD The Kentucky Post, Covington, Saturday, March 20, 1897, Page 2.

EVIL EYE. The Kentucky Post, Covington, Saturday, March 20, 1897, Page 3.

Cohen, Anne B., *Poor Pearl, Poor Girl! The Murdered Girl Stereotype in Ballad and Newspaper* Austin, TX 78712: University of Texas Press

APPENDIX

TO THE READER: The following is the actual sworn affidavits signed by some of the witnesses involved in this bizarre story of Bobby Mackey's Nightclub. The author has in his possession the actual signed statements. These affidavits have been added so that you the reader can read the actual stories told by the witnesses.

****

I Bobby Mackey do hereby give this statement to Douglas Hensley of my own free will and I do hereby allow Douglas Hensley, his agents, any book publisher or movie producer that Mr. Hensley contracts with, to use my story in conjunction with Douglas Hensley's book titled 'Hells Gate'.

My wife, Janet Mackey, has told me that she has been attacked by an unseen entity while inside our nightclub. Numerous employees and customers stated that they have had strange dealings with some unseen force while inside of my nightclub. I personally, have never seen any ghosts inside my nightclub.

SIGNED: Bobby Mackey   WITNESS_Douglas Hensley   DATE_6-18-89

****

I Janet Mackey have read the entire manuscript, 'Hells Gate'. This story has been written exactly as I have told it. I attest that the facts and details in this story actually happened. I have given my permission to Douglas Hensley, to use my correct name, and to write this story as I have told it. I have given my permission to Douglas Hensley to write this story without any promises of financial reward, or any other promises. He has written this story from my experiences that occurred inside of Bobby Mackey's Music World. I waive any legal rights, claims, or actions against Douglas Hensley, that I may have, resulting from my legal name being used in this story. I waive any and all legal action or claims against any publisher or Film Producer, who may wish to use this manuscript, for publication, of either a movie or a book. I understand, by signing this form that I have allowed my name and story to be told by Douglas Hensley, and any of his publishers or agents. I have experienced an unseen force that threw me down the stairs. I have watched a ladder that appeared to walk toward me and fall directly at me. It was as though some force tried to harm me. I have seen what appeared to be blood, pour from an old sink faucet. This substance was black in color, but appeared to be blood. I've heard voices that have ordered me form the building. I was pregnant when I was thrown

down the stairs. All of the above was typed for me, exactly as I have told it. This is all true. There is, in my opinion, a force that dwells inside of this building. It's been said, sometimes, it seems, that some force has entered my body. People have said to me, I am a different person at this nightclub, than when I am way from this place.
DATE: 6-18-89 Janet Mackey   Sandy Tomanelli (Witness)

****

I _Carl A Lawson have read the entire manuscript, 'Hells Gate'. This story has been written exactly as I have told it. I attest that the facts and details in this story actually happened. I have given my permission to Douglas Hensley, to use my correct name, and to write this story as I have told it. I have given my permission to Douglas Hensley to write this story without any promises of financial reward, or any other promises. He has written this story from my experiences that occurred inside of Bobby Mackey's Music World. I waive any legal rights, claims, or actions against Douglas Hensley that I may have, resulting from my legal name being used in this story. I waive any and all legal action or claims against any publisher or film producer, who may wish to use this manuscript, for publications, of either a movie or book. I understand, by signing this from that I have allowed my name and story to be told by Douglas Hensley, and any of his publishers or agents. I have had this typed for me and this is my statement. I have told Douglas Hensley of the experiences that I have encountered inside of Bobby Mackey's Music World. He has written this book exactly as I have told him. The details in this book, did happen. I have seen this spirit, called Johanna. I have seen other spirits in here. I cannot explain my ability to see this unseen force, but it is true. I still see these spirits, and I experience strange things from time to time. I have felt an unseen force make love to me. I have had this force leave hand prints on my back. I am the only person who has ever stayed in Bobby Mackey's Music World. I smell rose perfume every time something bad is about to occur. I smelled it one time just before a woman died on the dance floor. I smelled it when a man was shot.
DATE: _6-18-89
Carl A Lawson   Douglas Hensley (Witness) Jack Gaitskill
(Witness)

****

I, ABIGAIL WATHEN have read the entire manuscript, "Hell's Gate". This story has been exactly as I have told it. I attest that the facts and details in this story actually occurred. I have given my permission to Douglas Hensley, to use my correct name, and to write this story as I have told it. I have given my permission to Douglas Hensley to write this story without any promises of financial reward, or any other promises. He has written this story from the experiences that occurred inside of Bobby Mackey's Music World. I waive any legal rights, claims, or actions against Douglas Hensley that I may have, resulting from my legal name being used in this story. I waive any and all legal claims against any publisher or film producer, who may wish to use this manuscript, for publication of, either a movie or a book. I understand that, by signing this form, I have allowed my name and story to be told my Douglas Hensley, and any of his publishers or agents. I was in Bobby Mackey's Music World some time after the nightclub had opened form business. I heard Carl Lawson walking around and talking to a ghost. He called her Johanna. I laughed and made fun of Carl and his ghost friend. He warned me not to do this, or something bad would happen to me. I continued mocking him and his ghost. I smelled a funny fragrance of perfume. I smelled like a rose or lavender type perfume. I felt a cold chill pass right through my body. I left as it was closing time, not thinking anything about this. I assumed that Carl was just drunk. The next night, I was driving my car in Cincinnati, Ohio enroute back to Bobby Mackey's Music World. All at once, I smelled that same rose perfume. Some invisible force grabbed the car steering wheel. I had no control over my car, whatsoever. My car crashed into a wall, completely demolishing my car, and cutting my chin wide open. I was taken to the hospital for my injuries. There is a police report on file, concerning this incident. The funny thing is, the street that I wrecked on, is now called, Pete <u>Rose</u> way. I have not made fun of Carl or any ghost inside of Bobby Mackey's Music World, since that day. I have felt a cold chill pass through my body on several different occasions. This was typed for me and this story is true.

DATE: _6-26-89
Abigail Wathen   Doug Hensley (Witness) Jack Gaitskill
(Witness)

****

I, _Robert S Ranshaw have read the entire manuscript, "Hell's Gate". I attest that this story has been written exactly as I have told it. The facts and details in this story actually happened. I have given Douglas Hensley permission to use my correct name, and to write this story as I have told it.
I have given my permission to Douglas Hensley to write this story without any promises of financial reward, or any other promises. He has written this story from the experiences that occurred inside of Bobby Mackey's Music World. I waive any legal fees, rights, claims, or actions against Douglas Hensley, that I may have, resulting from my legal name being used in this story. I waive any and all legal claims that I may have, against the publisher, or film producer, who may wish to use my name in this manuscript, for publication of, either a movie, or a book. I understand that by signing this form, I have allowed my name and story to be told by Douglas Hensley, and any of his publishers or agents. I have been in Bobby Mackey's Music World when an unseen force has tapped me on the shoulder. I turned around to find an empty room. This occurred while I was alone, working in the building. I was in the basement working one day, alone, when I heard loud footsteps in the main bar room. I sounded as though some one was running or marching. I raced upstairs to find the building vacant. I checked all of the doors and windows and the building was secure. I had it locked while I worked in there. This occurred when the business was closed. I have felt a cold type breeze pass right by me while I was alone in the building. I smelled a rose or lavender fragrance or perfume each time this occurred. I have witnessed the jukebox turn itself on and play songs, especially, Anniversary Waltz. Once while I was taking a break, I was sitting at the bar all alone, when a drinking glass, that was at the end of the bar, turned over by itself, and rolled past me to the other end of the bar. I've heard gasping and scratching sounds come from the far wall, next to the railroad tracks. All of these things occurred inside of Bobby Mackey's Music World. This statement has been typed exactly as I have told it. Everything that I have stated is true. I have never said anything to anyone, for fear of being made fun of. I have came forward and told my true story, after I learned, other people were telling of their unexplained experience's inside of this building. I have heard Carl talk to the ghost.
DATE: _6-27-89

Robert S Ranshaw   Doug Hensley (Witness) Jack Gaitskill
(Witness)

****

I Mary (Cookie) Torres have read the entire manuscript, "Hell's Gate". This story has been written exactly as I have told it. I attest that the facts and details in this story actually happened. I have given my permission to Douglas Hensley, to use my correct name, and to write this story as I have told it. I have given my permission to Douglas Hensley to write this story without any promises of financial reward, or any other promises. He has written this story from my experiences that occurred inside of Bobby Mackey's Music World. I waive any legal rights, claims, or action against Douglas Hensley, that I may have, resulting from my legal mane being used in this story. I waive any and all legal action or claims against any publisher or film producer, who may wish to use this manuscript, for publication, of either a movie or a book. I understand, by signing this form that I have allowed my name and story to be told by Douglas Hensley, and any of his publishers or agents. I, Mary Torres, attest that I have experienced a cold chill pass through my body on numerous occasions while inside of the building now know, as Bobby Mackey's Music World. I have heard the jukebox turn itself on several different occasions, playing, Anniversary Waltz. I have experienced an unseen force, push against my body in an attempt to stop me from entering different parts of Bobby Mackey's Music World. I can't explain this but, I have felt someone actually breathing on the back of my neck, only to turn and find no one there. I was present when a man was shot to death inside of this building. The gun was never found. I think some entity hid the gun. I also attest that I am afraid of a small room that is used for storage. This statement is true
DATE: _6-19-89
Mary Torres   Doug Hensley (Witness) Jack Gaitskill   (Witness)

****

I Danny Hanavan have read the entire manuscript, "Hell's Gate". This story has been written exactly as I have told it. I attest that the facts and details in this story actually occurred. I have given my permission to Douglas Hensley, to use my correct name, and to write this story as I have told it.
I have given my permission to Douglas Hensley to write this story without any promises of financial reward, or any other promises. He has written this story from the experiences that occurred inside of Bobby Mackey's Music World. I waive any legal rights, claims, or actions against any publisher or film producer, who may wish to use this manuscript, for publications of, either a movie or book. I understand that, by signing this form I have allowed my name and story to be told by Douglas Hensley, and any of his publishers or agents. I was working on some old plumbing inside of a wall, in Bobby Mackey's Music World, when I looked into the darkness, of the overhead rafters, seeing two blue eyes staring at me. I could not see a person, only the two blue eyes. Once, when I was inside of this building, I was with Carl Lawson working in the building with him. He had his shirt off, walking away from me for a moment. When he returned, he had a small hand print on his back. Neither he nor I can explain this. I have placed my tools beside me, only to find them moved. There was no one near me at the time. I have experienced a coldness appear over my head and shoulders, when it was 96 degrees outside. The air conditioner was not working at that time, causing it to be extremely warm inside of this place. There should not have been any such cold air near me. I felt a cold

breath on my neck and shoulders when this occurred. The knobs on my sound
board have been moved when no one was near it. Once, I was watching Bobby
Mackey and Ernie Vaughn, as they were singing on stage, when a pale form
appeared, almost allowing me to see through both of them. I have seen people
sitting at a table only to blink and find them gone. My wife is extremely afraid of
this place. She prays each time she enters this place. I'm afraid of the large mirror
that hangs on the wall, in the rear of the main bar room. I've seen ghosts or what
appeared to be ghost at this mirror, only to find them gone, when I look away for a
second. This statement is true and has been typed for me, exactly as it has
happened.
DATE: _July_8_89   Danny Hanavan
Jack Gaitskill (Witness) Doug Hensley (Witness)

****

I Margaret Collingsworth have read the entire manuscript, "Hell's Gate". This
story has been written exactly as I have told it. I attest that the facts and details in
this story actually occurred. I have given my permission to Douglas Hensley, to use
my correct name, and to write this story as I have told it. I have given my
permission to Douglas Hensley to write this story without any promises of financial
reward, or any other promises. He has written this story from the experiences that
occurred inside of Bobby Mackey's Music World. I waive any legal rights, claims,
or actions against Douglas Hensley, that I may have, resulting form my legal name
being used in this story. I waive any and all legal claims against any publisher or
film producer, who may wish to use this manuscript, for publications of, either a
movie or a book. I understand that, by signing this form, I have allowed my name
and story to be told by Douglas Hensley, and any of his publishers or agents. I have
seen a large black dog appear in here, only to see it not be there when I close my
eyes or look away for a second. I've heard the jukebox turn on and play,
Anniversary Waltz, when no one was near it. I've heard my name called from the
back of the stage, when no one was there. These things have happened to me on
different occasions, while I was inside of Bobby Mackey's Music World. This is a
true statement. This has been typed for me, exactly as it occurred.
DATE: _8-8-89
Margaret Collingsworth

Doug Hensley (Witness)
Jack Gaitskill (Witness)

****

I Ralph E Barthaolomew have read the entire manuscript, "Hell's Gate".
This story has been written exactly as I have told it. I attest that the facts and
details in this story actually occurred. I have given my permission to Douglas
Hensley, to use my correct name, and to write this story as I have told it. I have
given my permission to Douglas Hensley to write this story without any promises of
financial reward, or any other promises. He has written this story from the
experiences that occurred inside of Bobby Mackey's Music World. I waive any legal
rights, claims, or actions against Douglas Hensley, that I may have, resulting from
my legal name being used in this story. I waive any and all legal claims against any
publisher or film producer, who may wish to use this manuscript, for publication of,
either a movie or a book. I understand that, by signing this form, I have allowed my
name and story to be told by Douglas Hensley, and any of his publishers or agents. I

have given this statement to Douglas Hensley exactly as it happened to me. I have no affiliation with Douglas Hensley or Bobby Mackey. I was a customer in Bobby Mackey's nightclub one night when I started walking to the restroom. There is a large mirror that hangs on the wall in the back of the nightclub. I was looking into that mirror as I walked toward the men's room. I could see the people behind me waling to the dance floor while the band was starting to play a slow song. As I looked in the mirror, still walking, I saw what appeared to be a headless women walk through the crowd as if she was walking toward the bar. I turned around to find whatever I saw gone. I went into the restroom to find it empty, except for a large black dog, that looked like a Doberman and some other large dog mixed. I stopped dead in my tracks when a voice came from behind me. It was a man's voice. I turned around, as the voice said, "Don't be afraid. It's my dog. I turned around to see a large man with a handle bar mustache smiling at me. I got out of there looking back to see the dog and the man gone. There is only one door leading in and out of that restroom. There was no way for them to get out of there, unless they were ghosts. I didn't say anything to anyone. I walked straight to my car and got out of there. I haven't said anything to anyone, until I learned of the other people coming forward, telling what happened to them. This is true and exactly as I have worded it. I have never worked for Mr. Mackey or Hensley. I was just a customer who had the chance to see some sort of ghost. I had got there and had just got my first drink, that I left on the bar half full, when this occurred.
DATE: _8-30-89
Ralph E Bartholomew
Doug_Hensley (Witness)
Jack Gaitskill (Witness)

****

I Roger C. Heath have read the entire manuscript, "Hell's Gate". This story has been written exactly as I have told it. I attest that the facts and details in this story actually happened. I have given my permission to Douglas Hensley, to use my correct name, and to write this story as I have told it.
I have given my permission to Douglas Hensley to write this story without any promises of financial reward, or any other promises. He has written this story from my experiences that occurred inside of Bobby Mackey's Music World. I waive any legal rights, claims, or actions against Douglas Hensley, that I may have, resulting from my legal name being used in this story. I waive any and all legal action or claims against any publisher or film producer, who may wish to use this manuscript, for publication, of either a movie or a book. I understand, by signing this form that I have allowed my name and story to be told by Douglas Hensley, and any of his publishers or agents. I have been inside Bobby Mackey's Music World and have experienced the following things, I have felt an entity breathe on the back of my neck, or rub the hair on the back of my neck. I have seen the jukebox come on and play Anniversary Waltz, with no one near the jukebox. I was alone with Carl Lawson, inside of Bobby Mackey's Music World, on a certain day, Carl walked to the basement to put some things away. He was only wearing shorts. When he returned, there was two dirty handprints on his back. They were smaller than Carl's hands. It appeared that some one had hugged him. Carl could not explain this. The building was empty, other than Carl and myself. I have felt a cold breeze pass right through my body, as though some unseen force had passed right through me.
DATE: 6-30-89

Roger C. Heath
Doug Hensley (Witness)
Jack N Gaitskill (Witness)

****

I, Larry Hornsby do hereby give this statement to Douglas Hensley concerning my experiences while inside of Bobby Mackey's nightclub in Wilder, Kentucky. I give this statement to Mr. Hensley without any promise of financial reward and I understand that by signing this form that I'm giving my permission to allow my story to be used by any book publisher, movie production company or anyone else that Mr. Hensley enter into a contract with. I am a retired police officer and while I was employed by the local city government where Bobby Mackey's nightclub stands I have encountered several strange things while doing routine checks on and inside of the building. Once while I was on duty I found a back door open and had another police officer meet me in the rear of the building where the door was ajar. I pushed on the door lightly and the door came open all the way and the other officer and I went inside to secure the building. I went one way through the building and the other officer went the other searching the interior. I was walking up to the stage where the band plays and I heard music and voices. I was a woman and a man talking and it sounded like they were arguing. I motioned for the other officer with his flashlight to meet me by the stage and I asked him if he heard music and a man and woman talking and he said yes. We searched the stage area and the back room and couldn't find anyone. When we came off of the stage I smelled a sweet smell like roses. We searched the rest of the building, but still couldn't find anyone. There was no wind, not even a slight breeze that could have caused this to happen. It was a clear night. As we walked toward the door and pushed on it came open and we checked outside but no one was there that could have slammed the door. No one would have had enough time to have run away without us seeing them after the door closed. We called Janet Mackey and told her the door was found open and she asked us if anyone was in the building or anything was disturbed. I told her no one was there and everything was okay. She had us lock the door when we left after we checked and made sure Carl Lawson wasn't upstairs in his apartment. Another time I found the front door open. As I drove by the building I saw shadows, two of them, in front of the doors and when I pulled in to see who was in the hallway no one was there. Once again I went inside and searched the building but no one was there. Once I was inside of the building with Carl Lawson and we heard a toilet seat slam down in the men's restroom and when we went in there to see who slammed it so hard no one was there. We also heard foot steps as if at least two people were walking around in the old kitchen and when we checked out the room no one was there, I've never believed in ghosts or spirits until now!
Larry Hornsby
DATE_10-12-91
WITNESS_Doug Hensley
WITNESS_Roger C Heath

I, Steve Seiter, do hereby give this statement to Douglas Hensley concerning the hauntings at Bobby Mackey's nightclub. I am allowing my story/statement, to be used in the book titled, "Hell's Gate", and I am allowing any movie producer/book publisher to use my story without any promise of any financial reward. I responded to a burglar alarm drop at Bobby Mackey's nightclub at approximately 4:30 in the a.m. and I checked the front doors only to find them locked. I drove around the back of the building and saw a back door ajar at the top of the stairway. I called for another officer to back me up and as we walked up to concrete steps the door slammed shut in our face. I tried to open the door but it was locked. The other officer and I drove back to the front of the bar and then I checked the front doors again and they were unlocked. When we had walked up to the back door the lights were on in the building and the jukebox was playing some old, slow song. We walked into the front entrance to check for a possible burglary and as we did I remembered that the lights were of fin the front hallway, but they were on now. The floors were creaking as if some one was walking through the building. We checked each and every room and behind the bar. The other officer started climbing the ladder behind the stage with me below him. We were going to check the attic for a burglar. As we climbed the ladder the other officer kept telling me to quit pulling on his leg. I told him I hadn't touched him. He was near the top of the ladder and I was still near the bottom. We checked the attic and left after we found it to be empty. We walked into the main bar area and while the other officer checked the ballroom I heard the toilet in the men's room flush. As both of us turned toward the restroom something icy cold blew past us with a strong force. We checked the restroom, but no one was there. We rechecked the entire building and then found that we were locked inside of the building. We had to call Bobby Mackey's home and have him come to the nightclub with a key so we could get out of the building. Once when I went to an actual break-in at the bar I found a large bag filled with money lying on the extreme end of the bar. The cash was wrapped in bundles and when I awoke Carl Lawson upstairs in his apartment the told me that there should be no money lying around. Since we left the money where it was Carl, myself and the other officers went back to the bar and found the money missing. We called Bobby Mackey at home and he advised us he had deposited the money in the safe and there was no way that any cash could be lying around. Once when I was at an auto accident in front of Bobby Mackey's nightclub where two people died a woman with long light hair, wearing a light colored, ling evening gown, came out of Bobby's bar and gave me some red tablecloths to wrap up the injured people with. After the life squad people took the injured parties to the hospital I went to the front entrance of the bar to thank the woman for her help, but the bar was locked and to my surprise no one was there. I went to the hospital to check on the injured and to finish filling my report since two of the people died. A man and woman had died to the accident. The woman was still wrapped in the table cloth and it was soaked in blood. In fact, some of the other victims were still covered in the blood soaked tablecloths. Later, I talked to Bobby Mackey and told him of the young, pretty woman who had brought me the tablecloths form inside the bar, and when I thanked him for her help, he advised me that there was no way someone came out of the bar and gave him any tablecloths. In fact he said no one worked for him that fit that description. I have been at the bar when people, for no apparent reason, go insane. It's like they are possessed and controlled by some unseen force.

Steven J Seiter   Date: 1-04-92 WITNESS: Doug Hensley

WITNESS: Roger C Heath

****

I Sandra C. Tonanelli have read the entire manuscript, "Hell's Gate". This story has been written exactly as I have told it. I attest that the facts and details in this story actually occurred. I have given my permission to Douglas Hensley, to use my correct name, and to write this story as I have told it.

I have given my permission to Douglas Hensley to write this story without any promises of financial reward, or any other promises. He has written this story from the experiences that occurred inside of Bobby Mackey's Music World. I waive any legal rights, claims, or actions against Douglas Hensley, that I may have, resulting from my legal name being used in this story. I waive any and all legal claims against any publisher or film producer, who may wish to use this manuscript, for publication of, either a movie or a book.

I understand that, by signing this form, I have allowed my name and story to be told by Douglas Hensley, and any of his publishers or agents.

I have experienced different things occur inside of Bobby Mackey's Music World. I have placed things next to me, only to turn around to find that item moved to another location inside of this place. I have witnessed the juke box turn itself on and play songs. I have felt a cold chill pass right by me as though some force was passing by me. This statement is true and I have told this to Douglas Hensley, exactly as it has happened. Once when I was decorating the nightclub for Halloween, I was painting a witch on a large mirror that hangs on the back wall, and the mirror became very hot. It was as if something was telling me not to draw on this mirror. There were three spots that became so hot that it almost burned my hand to touch it.

DATE: 6-28-89

Sandra C Tomanelli   Diana L Holt (Witness) Lisa A Stadtmiller (Witness)

****

I Ernie Lainhart do hereby give this statement to Douglas Hensley concerning my experience while inside of Bobby Mackey's nightclub. I do give my consent for Douglas Hensley, his agents or any book publisher or movie producer to use this statement in conjunction with Mr. Hensley's book titled "Hell's Gate". I understand by signing this statement that I am allowing it to be used without any promises of financial reward. I was inside the nightclub on a week night preparing to give guitar lessons to some of my students. I use the nightclub to give guitar lessons when the business is closed. While I was in the building, waiting for my first student to arrive, I picked up a guitar from the stage and began walking back to a nearby table in the ballroom to sit down when I heard a radio come on and began playing music. It was coming from the middle of the bar and when I walked over to the bar to turn off the radio, there was no such radio there. At first I really thought that someone was playing a trick on me, but when I looked for the radio and couldn't find one I realized that wasn't the case. I'm no whacko and I thought the ghost stories being told around the bar were funny, but I have no explanation for this at all! In fact, if there is some reasonable explanation for this, I'd like for someone to ell me what it is.

Ernie Lainhart   Date 7-5-91 Witness: Doug Hensley

I Thomas P Weber do hereby give this statement to Douglas Hensley concerning
my experiences while inside Bobby Mackey's nightclub in Wilder, Kentucky. I give
this statement to Mr. Hensley without any promise of financial reward and I
understand by signing this form that I am giving my permission to allow my story to
be used by any book publisher, movie production company or any one else that Mr.
Hensley enters into a contract with. I work for a company that does live sound and
I was inside of the main ballroom checking the sound system. There was no one
near the stage while I was working. I was doing a microphone check and while I
was checking the sound levels of one particular system a voice whispered through
the microphone and came through the monitor. It sounded as if it was a groaning
and moaning sound coming from someone, but no one was near the microphones
and I can't explain how this happened. This statement is true and has been typed
exactly as I have stated it.
Thomas P Weber Date 6-2-91 Witness: Doug Hensley

I Ernie Vaughn have read the entire manuscript, "Hell's Gate". This story has been
written exactly as I have told it. I attest that the facts and details in this story
actually occurred. I have given my permission to Douglas Hensley, to use my
correct name, and to write this story as I have told it.
I have given my permission to Douglas Hensley to write this story without any
promises of financial reward, or any other promises. He has written this story from
the experiences that occurred inside of Bobby Mackey's Music World. I waive any
legal rights, claims, or actions against Douglas Hensley, that I may have, resulting
from my legal name being used in this story. I waive any and all legal claims against
any publisher or film producer, who may wish to use this manuscript, for
publication of, either a movie or a book.
I understand that, by signing this form, I have allowed my name and story to be told
by Douglas Hensley, and any of his publishers or agents.
I have experienced a cold wind touch my shoulder and neck, when no one was near
me. It was like someone blowing their cold breath on the back of my neck. I have
turned around when this occurred, only to find no one there. One time when Carl
Lawson told me of a spirit appearing here, I joked about it, and the sound system
went wild, shorting out the P.A. system. This occurred inside of Bobby Mackey's
Music World. This statement was typed, exactly as I have stated it, and this is a
truthful account of my experience inside of Bobby Mackey's Music World.
DATE: 7-2-89
Ernie Vaughn Doug Hensley Witness) Jack Gaitskill (Witness)

I Tim Lusby do hereby give this statement to Douglas Hensley concerning my
experiences while inside of Bobby Mackey's nightclub. I do give my consent for
Douglas Hensley, his agents or any book publisher or movie producer to use this
statement in conjunction with Mr. Hensley's book titled "Hell's Gate". I
understand by signing this statement that I am allowing it to be used without any
promise of financial reward. I was inside of the nightclub and the band had just
taken a break when some of the band members and I walked back to the sound
board in the rear of the main ballroom. While we were standing there talking I
heard a guitar being strummed come through the P. A. system. The other band

members heard it too. We all looked up on stage to see who had picked up a guitar, but when we looked at the stage no one was there. This sounded like someone had walked past one of the guitars and strummed their fingers across the strings. The sound man said this could have possibly been caused by some sort of feedback, but I can't say either way. I can prove this happened by the other band members who heard it. I'm not saying a ghost did this because I'd have to see a ghost to believe it. I'm merely stating I heard these sounds and this happened. I have no explanation for this.

Tim Lusby
DATE: 7-5-91
WITNESS: _Doug Hensley

****

I, Joseph Lucas do hereby give my permission to Douglas Hensley, his agents, or any book publisher or movie company to use my statement in conjunction with Douglas Hensley's books titled "Hell's Gate", Part One and Two. I understand that by signing this agreement that Douglas Hensley may use my name or statement without any promise of any financial reward.

I was in Bobby Mackey's nightclub during the day helping Roger heath do some light remodeling inside the building when a large, basketball arcade machine came on playing music. When I walked into the room the machine came on playing the song and it isn't suppose to do this unless someone puts money in the coin slot. No one was near the game when it did this. Once when I went into the old kitchen to get some W-D-40 a metal brace flew off of a table by itself and I felt something icy cold go right through my body. I've felt something breathe on the back of my neck and when I turned around there was no one there. I've heard the juke box come on by itself and go back off. I've been near the stage and heard someone call my name and when I looked for someone there was never no one there. I've also felt someone tap me on the shoulder when I was alone in one of the rooms inside the nightclub and I would turn around only to find no one there again. I've also seen the shadow of a woman with long hair back by the old kitchen and when I start toward her to see who it is she fades away into the wall. I couldn't tell what she as wearing because like I said all I could see was her image by the wall before she disappeared. I've given this statement to Douglas Hensley exactly as he has typed it and this is a true statement. I've even felt someone brush their hand across my face and again, no one was there. I've felt someone leaning over me and I've felt long hair brush against my back when I was stooped over working on equipment inside the bar. I have also seen a headless girl walk through the ballroom in the crowd. I saw her image in a mirror in the back of the room.

Joseph C Lucas
DATE: 8-31-91
WITNESS: Doug Hensley

****

I, Lisa A Stadtmiller do hereby give the following statement to Douglas Hensley concerning his book titled "Hell's Gate". I further give my permission to Douglas Hensley, his agents, any book publisher, or movie producer that Doug Hensley contracts with, to use my story in conjunction with Douglas Hensley's book titled "Hell's Gate." I have not been made any promises of a financial reward by giving this statement.

I, _Lisa A Stadtmiller_ found a check lying on the floor behind the bar after I cleaned the floor. I don't have any idea how the check got there. The check was written go G.M.A.C. by a J. Jewell for a car payment. It was dated Oct. 18 1929 for $18.29.
Lisa A Stadtmiller
WITNESS: Janet Mackey   DATE: Nov 13, 1992
WITNESS: Mary "Cookie" Torres

****

I, Sandra J Murray do hereby give this statement to Douglas Hensley and I have given him permission to use this statement in his book titled "Hell's Gate". I understand by signing this form that I am allowing Mr. Hensley to use this statement in his book and he may use this statement in conjunction with any movie producer or book publisher without any further consent. I understand that I am giving this statement without any promises of any financial reward and I waive all claims against Mr. Hensley or his agents or any book publisher or Movie Company that he signs a contract with concerning the sale of this book. Many times over the past several years I have heard someone call my name from behind the stage in Bobby Mackey's nightclub. When I go to investigate I find that no one is there. Sometimes this happens so much that I find myself walking toward the stage without realizing it. It's like I'm pulled into some sort of hypnotic trance. Whatever it is calling my name, it's trying to lure me to the basement for some crazy reason. I've never been in the basement of the building because I'm afraid of it. I feel that there is some strong, evil force trying to get me to come down there for some reason. I have been inside the building when something cold has passed through my body. It was like an icy wind that pierced its way through me. I've had feelings that someone was standing next to me or right behind me and when I turned around no one was there. I've even felt someone touch me and I turned around only to find no one there. I've seen a lady with long brown, light colored hair, walk through the building and disappear. She seems to be troubled and it appears that she's looking for someone. It seems to make me sad when I see her from time to time and I can't stop thinking about her. I've also seen the reflection of a headless woman walking though the ballroom when I look into the large mirror that hangs on the wall. I smell the scent of roses from time to time and it reminds me of a funeral home. This statement is true and I have had it typed for me exactly as I have stated.
Sandra J Murray
DATE: June 15th 1991
WITNESS: Doug Hensley

****

I Michael Gruber do hereby give my permission to Douglas Hensley to use my statement in his book without any promises of financial reward, and I waive any legal rights, claims, or actions against Douglas Hensley, his agents, or any publisher or movie producer who wishes to use my statement in conjunction with this book. I understand that by signing this form that I have allowed my name and story to be used in this book. This statement has been typed exactly as I have told it and this statement is true. I was in Bobby Mackey's nightclub at approximately three fifteen in the morning helping Bobby and Janet lock up and secure the bar area after the nightclub had closed for normal business. I was standing at the end of the bar getting ready to leave and while I was talking to Bobby Mackey, Carl Lawson, and

Danny Hanavan, we all heard the double swinging doors open and close and when we turned and looked at the doors leading out into the hallway, they were swinging open and closed by themselves. It was as if something invisible had entered the bar and was moving the doors back and forth.

When I left the nightclub I got in my car to leave and noticed a strong odor of roses inside my car. It was cold outside and while driving home I tried repeatedly to get my heater to work but it would only blow cold air. The next day my heater worked fine, blowing hot air. I have noticed that people change when they come inside the bar. It's as if something takes control of their personalities and emotions. I have talked to several people who say that this building draws them back to it constantly and I am one of those people. I have felt something cold pass right through me when I'm inside the old office. I have also witnessed the front entrance door shock numerous people and I was the first person that I know of to be shocked by it. It was as if some electrical force was in the door. There are no wires touching any part of this doorway. I've heard sounds come from inside the wall like someone walking up stairs and found out later that there was a secret passageway behind the wall with a set of steps, but no one else was in the building except me and Roger Heath and there should have been no such sounds. I was making fun of Carl and his ghost friend when I got on the mechanical bull and when I started to ride the bull, it went up to full speed and I yelled for Carl Lawson to slow it down, but he couldn't. It was like some force took control of the bull and Carl couldn't do anything about it. He turned it off, but the bull continued at full speed and threw me head over heels into the air, I don't know how but I landed on my feet.

Mike Gruber
DATE: 3-2-91
WITNESS: Doug Hensley

****

I Vickie Lynn Metcalfe, do hereby give this statement to Douglas Hensley concerning my experiences while inside of Bobby Mackey's Nightclub. I do give my consent for Douglas Hensley, his agents or any book publisher or movie producer to use this statement in conjunction with Mr. Hensley's book titled "Hell's Gate". I understand by signing this statement that I am allowing it to be used without any promise of financial reward. I was in the office area at Bobby Mackey's nightclub and when I came out of the office I saw a dark haired man standing near a wall clock that was lit up over top of the middle of the open bar. When I approached the man he disappeared as if he was a ghost. I've heard my name called while I was inside the bar and when I turned around I found no one there. I have smelled rose perfume and I've heard the juke box come on by itself and play 'The Anniversary Waltz'. I have had this statement typed for me exactly as it has happened. This statement is true.

Vickie Lynn Metcalfe
DATE: 6/25/91
WITNESS: Douglas Hensley

****

I, Debora J. Murray, do hereby give this statement to Douglas Hensley and I give my full consent for him to use this in his book titled "Hell's Gate". I give Mr. Hensley permission to use this statement and also to allow any movie producer or book publisher to use this statement with my full consent. I have not been promised any financial reward for this statement and I have had this typed exactly as I have stated. There has been many times that when I walk through the front doors of Bobby Mackey's nightclub, I smell a strong odor of roses and there was none anywhere near the area that I smelled them. I have been standing at the bar and all at once I'd feel something ice cold go through my body like a spirit going right through me. Once when this happened the cold felling wouldn't leave my body. It was as if the spirit wanted to stay in me and it frightened me. No matter how hard I tried to shake the feeling, it wouldn't go away. I've got some bad feelings inside the building sometimes and it make me feel that some spirit is almost asking for help or is trying to tell me something.

Debora J. Murray
DATE: June 15, 1991
Doug Hensley (WITNESS)

****

I/We, Richard Broering, and Donna Clifton, give our permission to Douglas Hensley to use our statement in his book, "Hell's Gate". We understand that by signing this form that we waive any legal action against Douglas Hensley, Bobby Mackey, their agents, or any movie or book company that would wish to publish or use any or all of the story. We have given this statement at our own free will without any promise of any kind. We understand that by signing this form we have allowed our statement to be used in the book, "Hell's Gate". I, Richard Broering, and Donna Clifton have been inside Bobby Mackey's nightclub when the place was closed for normal business. We were working inside the building and have heard the jukebox come on and play songs. The songs were old songs probably from back in the 1930 or 1940 era. We go spooked, but continued our work. We didn't say anything to anyone because we were afraid of being made fun of.

Richard L Broering
Donna M Clifton
WITNESS: Douglas Hensley   DATE: 7-11-90

****

I Johnny France, do hereby give this statement to Douglas Hensley concerning my experiences while inside of Bobby Mackey's nightclub. I do give my consent for Douglas Hensley, his agents or any book publisher or movie producer to use this statement in conjunction with Mr. Hensley's book titled "Hell's Gate". I understand by signing this statement at I am allowing it to be used without any promise of financial reward. I was inside of Bobby Mackey's nightclub doing some minor cosmetic repairs and general maintenance when I heard a noise coming from the ballroom and when I turned around to investigate the noise I saw an entire row of chairs fall over, one after another as if they were dominos. They fell over as if something invisible was in the room walking between the rows of chairs and knocking them over. I can't explain this, but it happened exactly as I have stated. I kept this story to myself until I learned of other people coming forward and telling of their experiences while inside this place. I didn't say anything to anyone for fear of being made fun of, but now that so many other people have told about their dealings in this place, I've decided to tell what happened to me.

Johnny Fitzgerald France
DATE: 6-29-91
WITNESS: Doug Hensley

****

I, Patricia D. Kennedy, do hereby give this statement to Douglas Hensley concerning my experiences while inside of Bobby Mackey's nightclub. I do give my consent for Douglas Hensley, his agents or any book publisher or movie producer to use this statement in conjunction with Mr. Hensley's book titled "Hell's Gate". I understand by signing this statement that I am allowing it to be used without any promise of financial reward.

I have only been to Bobby Mackey's nightclub once in my life and that was as a customer in the summer of 1980. My friend Karen Byrd accompanied me. After having one drink, I was persuaded (against my better judgment) to ride the mechanical bull. People that know me are surprised to learn that I even rod the bull in the first place. I stood in a long line for quite some time before it was my turn to ride. When I got on the bull I asked the operator to set it on three. He was that three was too fast for me and stopped the bull. I asked him to slow it down to one. He reset it on one. Everything was fine for a few minutes and then the bull went crazy and accelerated to a high rate of speed. I was thrown forward on the bull and injured. Somehow they managed to stop the bull immediately. A waitress brought me a towel and ice. She told me that the bull was on ten. My lip was busted open and I had extensive facial abrasions. No one could explain what had happened. I was treated and released at Mercy Hospital in Fairfield, Ohio. I have a Polaroid picture that was taken of me at the nightclub right before the accident happened. I do not look like myself in the picture. My face has taken on different features. Even though I just found out several days ago about the nightclub being haunted. I have always felt that there was some mysterious force involved. The situation frightens me. This statement is true and has been typed exactly as I have stated.

Patricia D.Kennedy
DATE: 7-13-91
WITNESS: Doug Hensley

****

I, William McCollum, have read the entire manuscript, "Hell's Gate". This story ahs been written exactly as I have told it. I attest that the facts and details in this story actually occurred. I have given my permission to Douglas Hensley, to use my correct name, and to write this story as I have told it.

I have given my permission to Douglas Hensley to write this story without any promises of financial reward, or any other promises. He has written this story from the experiences that occurred inside of Bobby Mackey's Music World. I waive any legal rights, claims, or actions against Douglas Hensley, that I may have, resulting from my legal name being used in this story. I waive any and all legal claims against any publisher or film producer, who may wish to use this manuscript, for publication of, either a movie or a book.

I understand that by signing this form, I have allowed my name and story to be told by Douglas Hensley, and any of his publishers or agents.

I have not read the manuscript, but I was contracted to Bobby Mackey to install a central air conditioning unit inside of his nightclub. While running duct pipes, I had to saw through five layers of floor near the stage and bar room. I found one layer of flooring completely burned and charred in one area. I asked how this could happen and no one could explain it. I found out from Carl Lawson that this area was where the old men's restroom had been located. There was no reasonable explanation for one layer of flooring being burned and the other were in tact. There was no evidence of a past fire near anything else. I was glad to get the job done and

get out of there. This has been typed for me exactly as I have stated. I give my permission to Douglas Hensley to use my story in his book entitled "Hell's Gate".
DATE: 10/03/89
William C McCollum
Doug Hensley (Witness)
Roger Heath (Witness)

****

I, R, do hereby give this statement to Douglas Hensley concerning my experiences while inside of Bobby Mackey's nightclub. I do give my consent for Douglas Hensley, his agents or any book publisher or movie producer to use this statement in conjunction with Mr. Hensley's book titled "Hell's Gate". I understand by signing this statement that I am allowing it to be used without any promise of financial reward. I am giving this statement to Douglas Hensley of my own free will, but I am not signing my real name for fear of ridicule. If need be, I will identify myself to anyone necessary concerning this statement, but I do not wish my real name used in the book titled 'Hell's Gate' part one or part two. I was in Bobby Mackey's nightclub and went into the old kitchen around 2:30 a.m. and I saw one of my dead relatives twirling inside of a window that looks like a mirror. As I watched on her dress was torn form her body and as she twirled around inside the glass her flesh began being torn off of her body in shreds. I became sick and instantly hot and ran out of the room. I ran to the ladies restroom and almost vomited. The reason that I went into the old kitchen was to try and exorcise the spirits out of the building. There is a lot more to this that I've stated on this paper but I will tell the rest of the story to someone concerning this book at the appropriate time.
Signed: "R"
Date 10/03/1989
Witness: Doug Hensley
Witness: Lisa Stadtmiller

NOTE TO READER: THIS PERSON'S IDENTITY HAS BEEN CONCEALED FOR FEAR OF RIDICULE. THIS IS BY AGREEMENT BY THE PERSON GIVENG THIS STATEMENT AND DOUGLAS HENSLEY. THE PERSON INVOLED WILL DISCUSS THIS STATEMENT WITH PERSON/S IF NECESSARY AND IT WILL BE UP TO HER TO IDENTIFY HERSELF TO THAT PERSON AFTER I ADVISE HER THAT SHE IS NEEDED FOR AN INTERVIEW.

****

I, Wayne Smith, do hereby give this statement to Douglas Hensley concerning my experience while inside of Bobby Mackey's nightclub. I do give my consent for Douglas Hensley, his agents or any book publisher or movie producer to use this statement in conjunction with Mr. Hensley's book titled "Hell's Gate". I understand by signing this statement that I am allowing it to be used without any promise of financial reward. I was inside of Bobby Mackey's Nightclub making fun of the supposed ghost that everyone talks about. I was there as an observer with Doug Hensley, and a psychic, Patricia Mishell was brought into the building by Hard Copy to try to communicate with the spirits. While I was laughing about this something icy cold passed through my arm and shoulder several times. It was about eighty degrees inside the building and there is no explanation for this. While the psychic was inside a kitchen room, Doug Hensley, Carl Lawson and I heard voices coming from another part of the building as if there were a group of people talking. When Doug and I went to investigate, the talking stopped and there was no one inside the room at all. I manage a grave yard and am not afraid of the dead and I am a skeptic. I have no explanation as to what I experienced, but this statement is true and correct.

Wayne S Smith   Date: June 28, 1991 Laura J. Wathen (Witness)

NOTE: To see documentaries about this book visit www.youtube.com or Google Videos and type in Bobby Mackey. Watch The Unexplained, Part One and Two , Ghostly Adventures from the Travel Channel, GATEWAY TO HELL and many more videos concerning Bobby Mackey's haunted nightclub.

Buy more of Douglas Hensley's books at any online bookstore or visit his website@ www.lulu.com/doughensley

To read Douglas Hensley, father's book, "Chilling Tales Of The Paranormal" visit: www.lulu.com/denverhensley or type in DENVER HENSLEY at any online bookstore.

www.ingramcontent.com/pod-product-compliance
Lightning Source LLC
Chambersburg PA
CBHW032143020726
47496CB00003B/688